WIDE
ASLEEP

Other Titles by Nick Nolan

Strings Attached
Double Bound
Black as Snow

WIDE ASLEEP

Tales from Ballena Beach
Book 3

Nick Nolan

The characters and events portrayed in this book are fictitious. Any similarity to real persons, living or dead, is coincidental and not intended by the author.

Published by Lake Union Publishing, Seattle

www.apub.com

ISBN-13: 9781477817971
ISBN-10: 1477817972

Cover design by The Book Designers

Library of Congress Control Number: 2013916753

Printed in the United States of America

A LETTER TO YOU FROM THE AUTHOR

Dear Reader,

Have you ever analyzed a fairy tale?

I hadn't either, until I began writing them.

And I found that although they vary widely, some common threads weave their way through them all: Fairy tales feature a hapless heroine or hero, an evil person or a leader of minions, magic or supernatural forces, and a cast of supporting characters who help—or hinder—the main character's transformation into a better and braver person. Then as the story wraps, we usually detect a moral to the story—which this author thinks we need more of in today's world.

In order to mitigate confusion about the series sequence, *Wide Asleep* is book #3 in Tales from Ballena Beach, following Book #1: *Strings Attached*, based upon *Pinocchio* and Book #2: *Double Bound*, which referenced *Jack and the Beanstalk*. Book #4: *Black as Snow*, which traces *Snow White*, features characters from Ballena Beach but doesn't contain much storyline about Arthur and Jeremy, the stars of books #1 and #2.

If you didn't already suspect it from the title, *Wide Asleep* shadows elements of *Sleeping Beauty*, but in this case the deadly spinning wheel is a metaphor for time that eventually pricks *all* our fingers.

Just like in other fairy tales, in each book of this series the reader will find a somewhat bewildered protagonist, an evil puppet master, and common people who pitch in to help the hero(ine) get the job done.

But that's where the similarities end.

Tales from Ballena Beach has been written for adults who, as Frank Mundo from the *New York Journal of Books* wrote when reviewing *Black as Snow*, ". . . aren't afraid of open discussions of sex, religion, and politics . . ."

In other words, these novels were *not* written for kids.

My stories' characters are gay, straight, bisexual, and indefinable.

They have sexual relations.

They use foul language.

They sometimes hurt each other or fall victim to terrible acts of violence.

They might have political views that disagree with yours (and mine).

And they get what's coming to them—for better or worse. *Usually.*

In other words, these "fairy tales" are a lot like real life—especially where the moral of the story is concerned.

So why this note to you, dear reader?

I'm hoping my writing will encourage you to suspend your disbelief when the characters you are about to meet encounter paranormal (fairy tale?) events such as premonitions, "resurrection" from the dead, and conversations with apparitions or visitations from the three Fates . . . or even when someone falls into bed with someone you weren't expecting them to.

But most of all, I want to thank you for taking a chance on my work.

I hope you enjoy the story.

Nick Nolan
January 2014

For Jaime:
Thank you for being my warrior and muse.

PROLOGUE

Antinous stood up in the boat and then dove into the river to join his companion.

The blissful wetness closed in over his head as he sliced into the current; then, just as quickly as he'd descended, he began rushing upward.

His head broke the surface. "It's beautiful!" he shouted, shaking his curls. "When will the herb begin taking effect?"

"Soon."

Only moments later, Antinous detected numbness prickling his toes and feet and creeping up his calves toward his knees. "I feel it!" he called out, treading water with wide sweeps of his arms while scanning the sandy riverbank. "Yet I see no Osiris yet, no Isis." He turned to Lucius. "When did the priestess promise we would see the gods?"

"Very soon." Twin onyx eyes scrutinized him. "Very, very soon."

"Is the herb also affecting your legs?"

"It is not," Lucius answered coolly, his bronzed arms swirling the water with ease.

Antinous began struggling to stay afloat. "Why is it affecting me this way?"

"Because I only pretended to take the herb."

"Why?" Antinous now sensed only dead weight below his knees, and his fingertips had grown cold—and then, just that quickly, he ceased feeling his fingers at all, as if they had turned to marble. He looked around for their barque but saw it had drifted away, its unused anchor listing the craft slightly to one side. The riverbank now seemed as far away as the few clouds pressing the sky. "I feel great weakness, Lucius. Help me!"

"Do not fight the will of the Fates, whom you should see at any moment."

"The . . . *Fates?* You said we should see Isis and Osiris, not the Fates; Atropos only appears when one is dying!"

"You should not fear death, Antinous. You will awaken with the gods, and your beloved will receive the gift of your sacrifice. A life for a life. Your remaining thread tied to Hadrian's."

"No—"

"—Yes."

Antinous's breaths now came in ragged spasms. "You are—doing this because you know of—Hadrian's plan for me . . . but the letter has—been sent to Rome." The numbness had now traveled from his arms to his shoulders, and his breaths were increasingly labored, as if leather belts were cinching tighter around his torso. "My . . . beloved, this . . . will—kill him!"

"Henceforth it shall be written," Lucius said, "Antinous died so the emperor might live longer. This is what you must want for him: to be rid of his maladies—although someday he will join you, and for him you must wait in the underworld. Together you will be like Alexander and Hephaestion or Castor and Pollux, bright constellations crossing the heavens; all of Rome will pray to you for protection and make sacrifices in your names."

Antinous sank suddenly below the surface of the water, but the other young man quickly swam to him and hefted him up so his head broke the surface.

Antinous gasped, coughing water.

"I—must—hear it—from your lips," Lucius panted, trying his best to keep them both afloat, "so I may—truthfully tell the emperor you said this: *I sacrifice myself—so the emperor might live a—longer life.* These are the only—words that will carry him through—his mourning: *I sacrifice myself so the emperor—might live a longer life.* Tell this to me!"

Now realizing he had no choice and his strength was gone, Antinous whispered, "I sacrifice myself . . . so the emperor . . . might live a longer life."

"May I kiss you, my brother, immortal Antinous, beloved of the Emperor Hadrian, savior of Rome? I want the gods to know your lips touched mine last, so we might also be joined for eternity."

With tears in his eyes Lucius pressed his lips to the lax mouth.

Antinous felt the tenderness of his assassin's kiss, at once recalling last evening's carnal pleasures—the frenzied drums and haunting music, the flickering firelight, the sinuous, sweat-lacquered bodies, the ecstasy of their simultaneous release.

Instinctively, Antinous drew his arms around Lucius's neck.

Stronger arms broke his grip and pushed him down. *Hard.*

Water garbled his protests.

Antinous forced open his eyes and saw before him the exquisite nakedness of his murderer flailing slowly and dreamlike amidst the shafts of sunlight spearing the emerald water.

He struggled against the hands.

Ten breaths were bursting in his throat.

Those hands were like iron.

His body erupted in one final spasm as his lungs surrendered.

The sacred Nile flooded him.

:::::::::

Peace.

CHAPTER

one

From the beige leather club chair in the corner where he was reading last month's *Road & Track*, Arthur heard the scratch of Jess's key in the door.

His stomach twisted into itself. *Is this it?*

The lock's tumblers rattled into place and the door swung open, allowing a frigid gust into the room.

Arthur looked up at Jess as Jess looked down at Arthur.

In one hard glance, Arthur knew. He placed the magazine atop the coffee table. "When do you start?"

"On the first." He shut the door and tossed his briefcase onto the sofa.

"Congratulations." Arthur performed a quick mental calculation: *A little less than two weeks.* "Did they make you the deal you wanted? Are they paying your moving expenses?"

"Pretty much." Jess nodded. "Yeah."

"I'm happy for you. If this is what you want, I'm happy for you."

"Hold on—I gotta pee." Jess slid his keys and cell phone onto the kitchen counter and strode into the bathroom.

Arthur waited, his mind idling as he surveyed the room, figuring what he might want to keep and what he'd be glad to relinquish: *New sofa? Old dining chairs? My coffeemaker? His television?*

Don't care.

Then his eyes settled upon happy, smiling Bingham—panting obliviously at his feet, as if today's events were business as usual. He reached down and petted the furry black head; then the dog flipped onto his back, and Arthur reached down to massage his belly and chest with its snow-white blaze, his four paws kicking the air.

If he takes you with him, I'm stealing you back.

Arthur heard the toilet flush and the faucet turn on and off.

Jess reappeared, leaning against the doorjamb that separated the hallway from the living room. "Artie, you know I never went looking for this—"

Arthur held up his hand and smiled. "Jess, don't. It's what's best, and we both know it. OK?"

"OK then."

"No harm, no foul, as they say. Let's just get through this the best way we can. No blame, no more hurt feelings."

"I just feel bad because of your—"

"Don't give it another thought," Arthur stated coolly.

Silence filled the room.

"So what're you gonna do?" Jess finally asked. "Are you gonna stay here after I'm . . . by yourself?"

"Thanks to your crappy FICO score, the condo's mortgage is in my name, so I really don't have a choice."

"I thought you said no blame?" Jess said, his voice rising, but then took a breath. "Look, I'll pay my share through the end of May like we discussed; that'll give you enough time to sell the place if you want to. What more do you want?"

"I want the last four years back, is what I want—to somehow

magically rewind my life to the point where we were about to move in together, but instead I'd like for you to be honest with me and let me know that when things got rough you'd bail, and you didn't have it within yourself to stick it out. That when—" He stopped himself after watching Bingham stand and then slink away to hide under the lamp table.

Jess stood up straight in the doorway. "That's not fair, Arthur. When you needed me to take you to the hospital and to drive you to your appointments I was there for you, wasn't I?"

"Yes, you did that for me. And I thank you for it."

The two of them looked at each other for a long moment, and then Jess shook his head. "I'm out of here tomorrow," he said. "I called my friend Karen, and the moving company she works for is showing up at seven in the morning, so I'd better start packing."

"Tomorrow morning?" Arthur asked, surprised at how stung he felt.

"I figured the sooner I'm out of here the better it'd be for both of us, and it looks like I'm right."

"What about Bingham's vet appointment Friday? He's gonna need antibiotics for that skin infection." Arthur reached down and patted the front of his chair, and Bingham hurried out of hiding to him, leaning against his legs while Arthur scratched under his collar. Arthur looked up at Jess. "You're not taking him to Seattle, are you?"

"The apartment I found online doesn't allow pets." Jess glanced away, but then returned Arthur's stare. "You probably intended to keep him anyway; after Spot died, he kinda became more your dog than mine."

Arthur sighed. "Thank you."

"It's OK."

They stared at each other, a collage of thoughts and memories flashing between them.

"I loved you," Arthur finally told him.

Jess looked dully back at him. "I loved you, too. And I know you *think* you loved me."

Arthur laughed. "So now you're a mind reader?"

"Look, Artie. It's *over*. I tried. We *both* tried to the best of our ability—whatever that was. And there was a time when we loved each other and it kinda worked. But that time's gone, OK?" He leaned against the doorway again. "Hey, something tells me we're not the first queers in the world to break up."

Arthur gave Jess a short, solemn nod. "So . . . do you think it'll be any different with Larry?"

Jess's mouth set in a hard line. "He goes by Lawrence."

"With *Lawrence*, then?"

Jess shrugged. "I don't know, but I need to find out—just like you need to finally find out if it'll work with you and your beloved Jeremy."

Arthur raised a hand in protest. "Look, I—"

"You're free now, Artie," Jess shot back, eyes glazed. "Do—or don't do—whatever the fuck you want. I'm sorry, but I'm through with caring so much about what happens to you anymore. You—dragged me into this, and now you're facing something I can't handle. OK? I just can't handle it! Especially when it's not me you want with you at the end."

That dropped Arthur against the back of his chair. "I think that's the cruelest thing anyone's ever said to me," Arthur replied, folding his arms over his chest. He squinted across at him, now knowing that what was finally transpiring would be for the best. "The sooner you're out of here the better."

"It's the truth and you know it—we *both* know it."

"Just get out of here, so I can try to forget what just came out of your mouth. Happy anniversary, by the way."

"Yeah, I didn't get you anything either," Jess said, and then marched into the bedroom to begin gathering his belongings. "Tomorrow morning this'll all be over."

"It's already over." Arthur swallowed hard, then moved to the sofa and patted the cushion beside him. "Come on up here, Bingham boy."

The black dog looked up at him and jumped onto the sofa, padded two complete circles atop the cushions, and then flumped down next to Arthur. Arthur slid his hands inside Bingham's luxurious fur, pulled him to his chest, and kissed his head. "Why am I such a failure at relationships?" he whispered into Bingham's ears.

Bingham only panted happily back at him.

"Well . . . at least we've got each other."

CHAPTER

two

At just before seven that morning, after washing up in the guest bath and wriggling into his most comfortable Levi's, his red sweatshirt, and his tan corduroy jacket, Arthur heard the doorbell and then boisterous female voices in the living room.

Movers.

Arthur knew he needed to be out of the house while Jess directed the team of cargo-shorts-wearing women; he didn't even care if his now "ex-partner" took more than his share of their belongings.

Where should I go?

That new coffeehouse down on the corner of Santa Monica and Robertson?

Nah—I don't want to run into anyone who asks me "What's new."

How about the beach?

In spite of his nervous stomach, Arthur gulped his pills with tap water, snatched Bingham's leash from the pantry—which set the dog spinning in circles—grabbed his wallet and cell phone and keys, snapped the leash onto Bingham's collar, and then, without making eye contact with Jess or the ladies, he exited the condo and headed downstairs to the building's underground parking.

I'd better call in.

He pressed the number for his office manager and predictably got his voice mail. "Greg, it's Arthur . . . I've got a lot going on today and won't be in. Short-story-shorter is Jess is moving out and I've got to clear my head, but I'm fine—don't worry. And please call the attorney and see if there's been any progress on that moronic paparazzi case. Call me on my cell for anything; I know you've got a heavy day so I'm here if you need me. Hi to John."

He ended the call as he and Bingham reached his black Jeep Wrangler, and in moments they were threading their way west through the early morning traffic on Santa Monica Boulevard.

When he came to fog-obscured Pacific Coast Highway, he headed north, passing the sandstone edifices of Santa Monica's palisades, which transitioned into Malibu's ragtag apartments and sleek residences. Finally, he arrived in Ballena Beach, his childhood home.

Arthur waited for the almost endless herd of oncoming south-bound cars to pass before making a quick U-turn into a parking spot next to a bank of boulders, and rolling to a stop, with Bingham now standing up on the seat, pink tongue lolling.

Moments later the dog was leading him toward the foaming brown waves.

Strolling along the sand, Arthur began categorizing his regrets while considering what the single life would look like: dinners alone; a partially filled coffeemaker; shopping for half his usual groceries; toothpaste and deodorant lasting twice as long. And he'd be making all decisions regarding Bingham and finances and weekend activities.

Not a problem.

But how would it feel coming home to that quiet condo each night, knowing Once Upon a Time there had been a couple of hot guys in their late thirties shopping at IKEA for furniture that somehow didn't look too cheap, which they would replace as soon as they could afford better. Bedroom furniture that had, depressingly, outlived their future—a future that Arthur had consciously or unconsciously sabotaged?

He glanced up at a nearby cliff, its lumpy blankets of ice plant crowned with dagger-like agaves. *Even if I'm alone for the rest of my life it'll be easier than being in a relationship beyond its expiration date . . . and if my health fails again, I'll only have Bingham to worry about.*

The fog clamped chilling hands onto his face and the back of his neck, so Arthur reached down and unhooked Bingham's leash and began jogging.

Bingham in turn galloped off toward the water's edge, but then shifted his trajectory to greet a woman walking her dog some distance away.

Arthur watched as the dogs met and began circling each other, then splashed the tide and shook the water from their coats.

"Sorry about that!" Arthur shouted, trotting toward them.

"No problem!" rang the familiar voice. "They've already made friends!"

God no.

Arthur slowed his approach, whistled for Bingham, and fought the urge to turn and run.

But it was too late.

"Arthur?" Katharine called out, waving. "Arthur? Is that you?"

Any day but today. Arthur dipped his head and waved back.

"I can't believe it!" She began trudging toward him. "What are you doing here?"

"I was raised in Ballena Beach," he said when he didn't need to shout. "Remember?"

"Of course I remember," Katharine replied. "And when did you get this creature?"

"I've had him a few years." *I can't believe she's playing friends.* "How about you?"

"This is Skipper. She belongs to Jeremy. He's away, so now she's mine—at least for the time being."

Away where? Arthur bent down and petted her as Bingham shot him a grin, his amber eyes glowing like topazes out from his black fur. "Hi Skipper. You're a beauty." He looked up at Katharine. *She looks older. I should be nice.* "How are you?"

"Well enough. You?"

"I'm fine." He hesitated. "So he's away? Business or pleasure?"

"If only either were the case. Thankfully, Tyler, Inc. is still limping along, despite Jeremy's absence and this unstable economy. How are you keeping yourself busy these days?"

"Started a security company a few years ago in West Hollywood. Bodyguards for celebrities, that sort of thing—just hired my fourteenth employee."

Katharine smiled. "I'm so pleased you *finally* found your niche."

"Actually, I've had a few good niches." Arthur said, feathers briefly ruffled. Then he took a breath. *Let it go.*

They stood together, watching the dogs.

"How is he?" Arthur asked, itching to acknowledge the elephant swaying between them. "It's been years since we've spoken."

"He's been . . . well, I should tell you I don't see him nearly . . . he doesn't come around much. It's a long story."

The elephant stomped, trumpeting silently . . .

"Well, I should probably—"

"Would you like to come up for some coffee? You'll never believe this, but just this morning I was wondering how I might reach you and, well, here you are."

Arthur gazed at a shadowy gang of cormorants loitering atop a rock, while recalling their last conversation. "You know, I'd better—"

Katharine held up her hand. "I owe you an apology."

"It's a little late for that."

"Arthur . . ." Katharine reached down and patted Skipper's head, "I was wrong about you and your relationship with Jeremy. I've had years to consider what happened, and during this time I've come to regret—*deeply* regret—what I said to you. I intervened where I should have not. And because of my meddling, my nephew has cut off almost all communication with me and is, quite frankly, in a downward spiral. Is there any way I could convince you to come up to the house so we might talk about what's transpired? And if you'd rather not, I completely understand."

Arthur checked his watch and reminded himself he had nowhere to be—and he could *really* use some coffee. *And I sure as hell don't want to be anywhere near my condo right now . . .*

His eyes followed Bingham and Skipper as they ran off into the waves once again. "I've got a few minutes."

Katharine beamed. "Wonderful!"

Arthur held out his hand. "After you."

"I'll have to catch that dog first. Skipper!" she called. "Skipper, come!"

Honey-colored Skipper stopped in her tracks, turned to look at her mistress, and then began loping toward Katharine with Bingham following, nipping at her elegant, feathered tail.

Moments later Arthur, Katharine, and two tail-wagging dogs were making their way toward the stairs leading up from the beach to the Tyler compound.

CHAPTER

three

I'm afraid the dogs are absolutely covered in wet sand," Katharine said, leading Arthur toward the gazebo by the cliff's edge. "And with this weather it'll be some time before they dry off. Would you mind if we took some coffee out here instead of in the house? I've had an outdoor heater installed recently."

"I've always loved that little gazebo," Arthur replied, noticing how the sun had begun burning through the fog, illuminating the cliffs below them in a hue red as the mansion's expansive clay-tiled roof. "Who's working for you now?"

"Someone capable, thank goodness," Katharine replied with a smirk.

One of the French doors opened and out trotted a compact, athletic figure with bronzed skin and black hair. "Arthur!" the young man yelled.

"Carlo?" Arthur jumped up to meet him.

They met and hugged each other.

"So you're the new butler?"

"*Personal assistant,*" Carlo corrected. "After you fled she tortured three different victims until they stormed out, so out of desperation she called me. That was two years ago, and I think it's working out pretty well."

"*Very* well," Katharine added. "Would you mind bringing us some coffee and iced water? Arthur, have you had breakfast?"

"No—and I could use something to eat."

"What would you like?" Carlo asked, dark eyes shining. "It's so great to see you!"

"You, too," Arthur replied. "Just some toast or a bagel would be great. Extra points if you can dig up some cream cheese."

"And some grapes and grapefruit," Katharine told him. "Oh, and some of that delightful chardonnay that's already open in the fridge." She turned to Arthur. "Two glasses?"

"Just coffee for me now."

"Comin' up," Carlo said before turning and trotting back toward the house.

Arthur turned to Katharine. "Chardonnay?" He made an obvious glance at his watch.

"It's the dowager's Bloody Mary. I've got nowhere to be and nothing pressing, and I've been up since four a.m., so it's lunchtime for me. I . . . can't say I've been getting much sleep these days."

Flashing upon what was happening in his condo, Arthur knew he had some sleepless nights of his own coming his way. *Don't think about it.* "What did you want to tell me about him—about Jeremy?"

"Before I launch into that debacle, please tell me more about yourself; I haven't heard about your mother or what brought you—a successful business owner—out to the beach by yourself on this wintry Tuesday morning."

Arthur glanced out at the velvety gray sea. "My mother's fine. Healthy enough, and completely devoted to oil painting and her grandkids. As to what brought me out here today, I . . . needed to clear my head and to get out of the way of the movers. My partner and I just split up after four years."

Katharine settled back into her chair, adjusting the sunglasses she wore in spite of the gloom. "I'm sorry you're undergoing a separation; I remember doing everything possible to avoid seeking one from my late husband." She smiled sympathetically. "And as we all know, I made the mistake of waiting too long. Was this a mutual decision?"

Arthur crossed his arms over his chest. "More or less."

"It's none of my—"

Arthur held up his hand. "It's all right, it's . . . just something I'm still trying to comprehend. Jess only told me last night that he got a job in Seattle and was moving out this morning."

"That's terribly sudden!"

Arthur shrugged. "It's just how it is. So what's going on with Jeremy?"

Katharine removed her sunglasses. "And this is where I'd like to elaborate on the apology I began on the beach."

"I'm listening."

"I am sorry, Arthur. More than you will ever know."

"Why? I mean . . . I think I know why, but I'd rather hear it from you." He reached down and began massaging the silken fur on Bingham's neck, and the dog fitted himself heavily against his leg.

Carlo appeared from the side of the house carrying an assortment of snacks, a half-empty bottle of wine and a single crystal glass, a coffee carafe, and a mug. Katharine and Arthur watched in silence as he neatly arranged the items on the table before them, poured Katharine her wine, and then Arthur his coffee.

"Don't stop talking on my account," Carlo said.

"We were—" Arthur began, tipping cream into his mug.

"Discussing Jeremy," Carlo cut in. "And I'm glad to see you two finally talking this out, because it's been forever coming and you've got a lot to work out. And . . . now I'm going back into the kitchen before I say something I'll regret." He turned on his heel and marched back into the house.

"You were saying?" Arthur raised the mug to his lips and sipped.

"I love that boy, but he's a bit outspoken."

"I think that's one of his more noble attributes. Please, go on."

Katharine leveled her gaze at Arthur. "I was beginning to tell you how sorry I am: sorry that I meddled where I should not have, and sorry that I listened to my head and my logic and my prejudices instead of listening to my . . . intuition. Sorry I was blind to what might have been wonderful for you both, and sorry that my blindness was contagious—and so very destructive."

Wondering where this was headed, Arthur remained silent, staring at her.

"I should not have demanded you leave him," Katharine continued. "I should not have threatened you. I should not have pried the two of you apart. I should have left destiny alone. And for those trespasses I am sorry."

"Why did you do it?"

Katharine sighed. "Women from my generation were taught to believe they would raise children, which I did not. Then, when Jeremy's father, Jonathan, came into my care, I raised Jonathan as if he were my own, as I did with Jeremy. I . . . had certain dreams that died with Jonathan, and then were resurrected with Jeremy."

"And those died a second time." Arthur put down his mug and leaned forward. "Jeremy's in trouble, isn't he?"

She sipped from her long-stemmed crystal glass, her eyes scanning the estate's primly clipped landscape: the deep green topiaries, the chartreuse box hedges, the pink and red rose blooms, and the flat emerald lawns with their razor-trimmed flagstone walkways. "You know we've never been able to stop that fountain from leaking"—she pointed—"and I remember how many times you tried to patch it, but the damn thing was cursed. And now we allow it to sit empty, and I'm just about ready to turn it into a giant flower pot or to take a sledgehammer to it myself."

"Katharine, what's going on?"

"He's been in rehab, but it didn't work," she said, her eyes locking his, "just like his mother. He's been arrested for drunk driving—only once, and thank God he didn't kill anyone—and he's been involved with a string of men, including one who's tricked him into a shady real estate deal involving a huge amount of Jeremy's trust money . . . some European playboy named Lazzaro, who's now presently missing somewhere in Europe."

Arthur looked down and sighed. "How long has all this been going on?"

"After you left he began showing this terribly self-destructive side. He's made one bad decision after another and he's long stopped listening to me . . . even he and Carlo are no longer close."

"Why didn't you call me?"

"I . . . I didn't know what to do, and I was too embarrassed to contact you. During rehab some issues came up that I tried to remedy with him—we had to participate together in therapy—but the reality is that Jeremy believes I ruined his life by chasing you away, and he's determined to never forgive me. But what scares me most is he doesn't seem to be able to forgive *himself* for listening to me—and to you."

"You mentioned he left Tyler, Inc. What happened?"

"I don't know where to begin." Katharine's eyes darted around. "He'd been drinking heavily for some time and it began affecting his work, and it ultimately affected his financial judgment. Then one day he called and said he'd just bought a property on the beach for half its market value. It seems this Lazzaro character owned an old waterfront mansion that had recently come into his possession. The man quitclaimed his property to Jeremy for some fast cash and then disappeared. Unfortunately—and perhaps because of his drinking—Jeremy didn't consult me or my attorneys, and although he now has claim to the mansion, the outstanding mortgage—which Lazzaro *somehow* neglected to tell Jeremy about—became payable in full, which happens with a quitclaim in circumstances of a complete change in ownership. In essence, the cash Jeremy paid for the property has vanished along with this man, and he is now deeply in debt."

"What does this have to do with his working for Tyler, Inc.?"

"When I found out about his bungled deal I refused to loan him another penny to pay off the mortgage. Until he does pay it off, he will not receive clear title to the property, and he now has a huge monthly payment, along with monstrous property taxes, with no income and little remaining of his trust. And I was forced to suspend Jeremy from any further Tyler, Inc. dealings until he gets his drinking resolved."

"In what capacity was he working for you?"

"Human Resources. Initially, he had his sights trained onto the director position, and he was progressing quickly. When finding a position for him in the company, I surmised that growing up with an alcoholic mother and then losing both his parents at a young age made him especially empathic and intuitive, and I was correct. He has a wonderful sixth sense when it comes to new hires, he was a stickler when it came to compliance issues, and our employees adored him. He was even transforming our image through social media, which delighted our stockholders after that Brazilian resort fiasco."

Arthur felt a flush of pride in Jeremy. "Well that sounds wonderful, frankly. Sounds like your company really needs him."

"And so we did. But what we didn't need was his coming to work hungover—*or worse*. So for the moment he is unemployed," Katharine continued, "and his property will most likely fall to foreclosure." She sighed. "I've tried to make him take responsibility for this financial debacle. I've absolutely refused to bail him out of this; after all, it was money from his own trust. But he's shown as much interest in correcting this mistake as he has in . . . bedding women."

Arthur watched a tiny lizard jump from the rose beds to skitter across the grass. "Where's he living now?"

"I have the address of the home, but I don't know if he actually resides there. Jeremy could be in China for all I know. And I won't even guess how much of his trust he has remaining, but the money is secondary to his personal well-being and safety. I don't—" she paused, her features pinched, "—I don't sleep anymore, Arthur, because I'm afraid the phone will ring with news of an arrest . . . an accident . . . *or worse*."

"What do you want me to do?"

She reached forward and grasped his hand. "Find him. Talk to him. Bring him home . . . and then make him yours again if it's in your heart. Is that too much for me to ask"—she laughed—"especially after I did everything to keep you two apart?"

"I don't know what to say."

"Say you'll at least try, because I have this terrible feeling something horrific will happen otherwise."

"When was the last time you spoke?"

"He came by about two weeks ago to pick up some belongings, but he had little to say to me in spite of how I dogged him."

"Can you give me the address you have?"

Katharine dug her iPhone from her pocket and began swiping its screen. "I always forget my damned reading glasses," she said, handing him the device.

Arthur, with some difficulty reading the information himself, managed to punch it into his own phone. "Got it . . . although it doesn't look familiar."

"He coaxed me into seeing the house one day, and I remember it being down a private road behind some rusting gates off the Pacific Coast Highway, so I'm afraid you might have trouble getting to it. He wanted me to assess its value and to say something encouraging, but when I saw its condition I was so disheartened that I couldn't even get out of my car." She threw back more of her wine. "I'd suggest e-mailing him or texting him, but he hasn't been answering anything from me—but then again, I am not *you*."

"I'll find a way to get down that road."

"Will you really go there and see him? When?"

He glanced at his watch. "Right now. But I can't promise anything; if I know Jeremy he's at least as angry with me as he was with you—I've never seen anyone who could hold a grudge like him."

"A classic Irishman, in more ways than one."

Arthur chuckled. "My grandfather was an O'Flaherty, so no explanation necessary."

"And Arthur, I fully accept that you can't promise me anything, and you owe me nothing. But just knowing you'll try has lifted my spirits."

"And here I thought it was the chardonnay."

Katharine laughed.

"What about Carlo?" Arthur asked. "You said they're not close anymore, so they must've had a falling out. Do you know what happened?"

Katharine scooted back her chair and leaned forward. "Let's go find him."

"Uhhh . . . if you don't mind, I'd rather speak to him alone. Guy stuff."

"Of course," Katharine replied, settling back. "You'll probably find him in the kitchen or in your old quarters."

Arthur stood and pushed his chair in, and Bingham looked up expectantly. "Will the dogs be OK out here?"

"I'll take them into the conservatory for water and snackies," Katharine said, patting Skipper on the head. "Sand or no sand, we need to keep those we love close by."

Arthur lifted his coffee mug. "I'll drink to that."

Katharine likewise lifted her glass. "That's all I drink to these days."

CHAPTER

four

He never got over you," Carlo told Arthur, wiping a scattering of bagel crumbs from the huge butcher block in the center of the kitchen. "Surprised?"

"No, because I never got over him." Arthur leaned back onto the marble countertop. "So what else happened? And don't spare me any details. It feels so weird to be here, by the way."

"I'll bet." Carlo craned his head to peer out the kitchen window. "Where is she?"

"Katharine said she understood us talking alone. Guy stuff, you know. Weenies and butts."

Carlo laughed. "She's probably lurking around here anyway." He wrinkled his nose. "I don't want her to hear any of this. My room?"

"Right behind you. You look great, by the way. Working out much?"

"Every day," Carlo replied. "And so do you—look great I mean; that salt-and-pepper daddy thing still works for you . . . even at your age." He flashed a playful smile. "How old are you now? Sixty? Seventy?"

"Forty-three," Arthur dryly replied. "You're still the same Carlo."

Arthur followed Carlo out through the kitchen and down the hallway to the cramped servant's quarters that had once been his own during the time he worked as the Tyler family's butler—or rather, when he was commissioned by the FBI to *pose* as the Tyler's butler while conducting an undercover investigation of Katharine's husband, Bill Mortson, who was ultimately exposed as an embezzler, drugs and arms trafficker, murderer, and all-around schmuck.

Carlo came to the room, twisted the doorknob, and swung open the door.

One glance inside brought back a torrent of memories: some great, some heart-wrenching, but none forgettable. "Oh my God," Arthur said. "It's exactly how I left it. Same bedspread, same desk, same cheap bookcase—"

"Same mattress where you and Jeremy fucked."

"*Made love*, you bitch," Arthur laughed. "And where you now lay awake at night pleasuring yourself, dreaming of that moment."

"Not anymore." Carlo shook his head. "Our Jeremy is one messed up boy."

"Tell me everything."

"You'd better sit down." Carlo pointed to the desk chair. "What did Katharine tell you?"

"He's living the life of a spoiled Hollywood actress: rehab and jail; running through the last of his money; a boyfriend who's bad news."

"That's only the beginning."

"How so?"

"Well," Carlo began, his gaze sweeping the room, "after that restful vacation to Brazil where you and *my boyfriend Jeremy* discovered your love for each other and I broke up with him—then he was kidnapped and almost died—things began to go downhill for him. He pretended, of course, that he understood your reasons for not wanting to 'hold him back' from his college years while being tied down to an old—sorry, *older*—man, but he kind of went off the deep end. Did Katharine tell you he was kicked out of USC for beating up a guy?"

"*Jeremy?*"

"He was at a party and everyone was boozing and some asshole started making comments about 'faggots' and one thing led to another. As you know, Master Tyler is a hungry bottom, but he can sure throw a punch. So the guy winds up in the hospital, and if you can believe it his family donated more to the university than Mrs. Katharine Tyler, so that was that; apparently new auditorium trumps Founder's Circle. But at least Katharine was able to shake off the family's lawsuit and get the criminal charges against Jeremy dismissed by threatening a self-defense countersuit with extenuating hate crime circumstances."

"How did Jeremy take getting kicked out?"

"Didn't faze him. More than anything he seemed relieved."

"I don't like where this is going."

Carlo chuckled. "Oh, it gets better."

Arthur sighed. "His drinking?"

"Let me put it this way," Carlo said. "He's the only guy I know who could get arrested for DUI *on his way* to champagne brunch . . . not to mention some new designer drug he's been experimenting with."

"*No.*"

"Yep." Carlo nodded. "In addition to that, apparently Jeremy discovered genuine *cock-tails* at USC. And he had lots of both. So once he was rid of the demands of school, he started screwing around. A lot. Especially now that we have those clever phone apps that tell you where the gay boys are lurking—as if he ever needed an app for that. I swear, you can actually *watch* guys—even straight guys—do double-takes when he walks by."

Arthur flashed upon his first memory of Jeremy at seventeen, so unsure and innocent and scared and disheveled. "I'm feeling sick to my stomach."

"I wish I didn't have to tell you." Carlo leaned back onto his bed pillows. "And I *do* tell you only because it seemed to me like he was trying to fill a void *you* left in him . . . or maybe it was a combination of his mother's death and his father's murder and you pushing him away *for his own good* that sent him over the edge."

"I was only doing what I thought was best."

"Oh come on," Carlo moaned. "Deep down you were afraid he'd find some charming, well-hung lacrosse player at USC, so you broke up with him before he could break your heart."

Arthur sat up ready to argue, but the look in Carlo's eyes told him he had a point. "Maybe it was a combination of that, and the fact that I didn't want to stifle him." He gazed out the windows at a cluster of seagulls scrambling the air. "I've never loved anyone as much as I loved that boy, and I've thought of him—ached for him—every day."

"That's because he's your soul mate, dummy, and you need to be together. Everyone saw that. Even Katharine sees it now. So why didn't you see it when you had the chance?"

Arthur looked up. "Of course I wish I'd done things differently with Jeremy—not to mention dragging Jess into a tepid relationship. Guess I got what I deserved. "

"Are you guys still together?"

"He's moving out today," Arthur grumbled.

"*So now's your chance!* Write a different ending to this grim fairy tale. And make it a happy ending this time. OK?"

"Is there anything more I should know? Tell me now while I'm already in shock."

"Oh yeah." Carlo took a breath. "Aside from Jeremy's sluttiness and drunkenness, he's gotten mixed up with this shady character—this shady *gorgeous* character. Looks like a Dolce&Gabbana model. And Jeremy was living with him until he disappeared, so I think it was kinda serious. The prick even got him involved in some bad real estate deal that Katharine won't discuss with me, so I'm not sure what happened."

"Katharine mentioned someone named Lazzaro."

"That's him. But something weird happened and no one's seen the dude in some time. And Jeremy doesn't like to talk about him, either. I'm afraid he's got the body all chopped up in the freezer . . . but better it be Lazzaro bubbling in the crockpot than Jeremy."

"Katharine gave me Jeremy's new address, so I'm going down there right after I leave. Have you been to the house?"

"Yeah, it's a creepy, big old mansion down a private road off PCH. I was there once and it was like . . . out of a Dracula movie. You'll see when you get there. Be careful."

"I'm always careful."

"And what about you?" Carlo asked. "What else have you been up to these past"—he counted on his fingers—"four years?"

"Started a business. Other than overcoming some health issues and trying to defibrillate a flat-lining relationship, that's pretty much all I've been up to."

"And which flat-lining relationship might you be referring to?" Carlo dryly asked. "Jess or Jeremy?"

"Point taken."

Carlo furrowed his eyebrows. "What health issues?"

"All in the past." Arthur smiled confidently. "No worries."

"But really—" Carlo hesitated, "—what happened with him? With Jess?"

Arthur pushed himself up from the bed. "He insisted that I never stopped loving Jeremy, and how could I argue?" He jingled his car keys. "Just wish I'd figured it out before Jess did."

::::::::

Inside the plant-filled conservatory, amidst pale pink orchids and chartreuse ferns and hot pink fuchsia blooms, Arthur found Bingham and Skipper resting on the floor next to Katharine, reclining as usual on her ancient wicker chaise.

"Did you find out what you needed to know?" she asked, her words noticeably slurred.

Arthur gave her a decisive nod. "I'm heading down to Jeremy's now. I'll give you a call afterward."

Katharine turned to gaze out beyond the windows. "Do I need to tell you again how much I appreciate your doing this?"

"We both made a mistake, Katharine. And we've learned." He clicked Bingham's leash onto his collar and led him to the door. "I'll call you."

"I'll be waiting."

::::::::::

Arthur slowed as the addresses along Pacific Coast Highway began approximating the numbers on his iPhone's screen, until he saw a cluster of rusted mailboxes that signaled an approaching private drive.

He wheeled the Jeep over to the side of the road and shut off the engine. Then after exiting and locking his car—with windows lowered for Bingham—Arthur began strolling down the rutted one-laner as it descended toward the assemblage of homes lining the beachfront. He spotted a few run-down cottages tilting off to the left and one dazzling concrete-and-glass structure shoring up the right-hand hillside, while the old mansion dead center looked just as Carlo had described: *out of a Dracula movie*.

Arthur verified the address on his phone with the numbers on the gate. *Yep*.

If not for the black Jaguar convertible parked sideways in the driveway Arthur would have thought the imposing chateau abandoned: a pair of high, rusted wrought iron gates stood chained and padlocked, the heavily draped windows showed no signs of life, and neither the bushes nor vines wallpapering the dingy walls had been trimmed in years. But the slate-tiled mansard roof looked reasonably sound, and the bronze dolphin fountain at the hub of the cobblestone driveway dribbled and splashed invitingly, its sprays refracting sunlight like liquid chandelier crystals.

With his heart pounding, he pressed the bell button on the side entrance gate.

Will I see him? Will I actually see Jeremy now?

Arthur waited, but nothing happened.

He pressed the button again. Longer.

Nothing.

After a third try at the bell and a few minutes shifting foot to foot, Arthur turned and began trudging back up the private drive.

Bingham's panting grin welcomed him at the Jeep as Arthur opened the door. But instead of climbing behind the wheel, Arthur grabbed a discarded envelope and a pen from the glove box.

Jeremy—
I know it's been a while but it sounds like we
should talk. Could you drop me a line please?
It's important that I speak with you.
My e-mail's still the same ablauefee@ballenabeach.com
—Arthur

Arthur folded the paper, dropped it inside the appropriate mailbox, got into his Jeep, and drove away.

A few minutes later Jeremy—half-empty beer bottle in hand—made his way up the road toward the highway, stopped at the mailbox, and then pulled out the note he'd watched, via the security cameras, Arthur fill out and deposit.

He read it, looked up, read it again, and was about to slip it into his pants pocket when a realization dawned on him.

He wadded up the paper and threw it out onto the highway.

Moments later—after draining his beer bottle in a skyward swig—Jeremy watched as a speeding black Lincoln Navigator vacuumed Arthur's note from the asphalt and launched it into oblivion.

CHAPTER

five

Jeremy slammed the chateau's heavy door behind him, trudged up the stairs, and crossed the hallway to check his e-mail and Facebook page in the spare bedroom he used as his office.

But after seeing nothing but junk e-mails and tedious Facebook postings from people he cared nothing for, he began descending into his familiar depression.

What the hell could've happened to Lazzaro?

It's been over a month now since he left for Europe.

He thought back to the afternoon he'd met Lazzaro, when he (after washing down his Subway Tuscan Chicken Melt with a buttery, apple-caramel chardonnay) and Skipper, the dog he'd impulsively adopted from a Facebook rescue site, had been meandering along the beach. Jeremy was hungover and fatigued yet restless, a result of the prior evening's romp at the Chateau Marmont with an attractive and distinguished Canadian couple in their forties. Sex with them had been electrifying, but as their encounter progressed and Jeremy saw how much physical passion and tenderness the men still expressed toward each other after seventeen years together, it made him ache.

They have what I wanted with Arthur.

He crouched down on the sand next to Skipper and scanned the flat, metallic sea, gently resting his hand on the teddy bear velvet of her head.

Then a heroic figure swaggered into view.

Wow.

The man was spectacularly built: wide shoulders, narrow hips, and long legs, and he looked to be just over six feet tall with olive skin juxtaposed with spiky blond hair. And as he drew closer Jeremy ticked off the perfection of his features: large dark eyes and full lips, strong jaw and sculpted cheekbones, muscular neck and arrogant nose.

Fuck me!

Skipper had scampered off to greet the Adonis, and Jeremy approached him with the insouciant courage that a bottle of chardonnay consumed mid-day provided. "I don't care if you're straight or gay or whatever," Jeremy off-handedly told him, "but I'd like to massage you and tease you and play with you until you can't remember your name."

They exchanged tentative, mischievous smiles and then Lazzaro replied, in that exotic baritone of his, "I had already forgotten my name the moment I saw your handsome face."

Fifteen minutes or so later, Jeremy found himself sharing a bed with the god in an expansive bedroom of the man's dilapidated seaside mansion—the same mansion Jeremy now called home.

After a whirlwind three-week courtship, during which time the men spoke by phone or e-mailed each other several times a day (Lazzaro refused the invitation to text, insisting it was too impersonal), Jeremy and Skipper left the guesthouse at the Tyler Compound and moved in.

And the men got along with surprising ease, as if they'd known each other for years: Both shared a passion for swimming and hard exercise, for fast European cars—Lazzaro drove a red Maserati convertible and Jeremy had his own black Jaguar XKR Cabriolet—and gay nightlife. Lazzaro treated Jeremy the way a continental playboy might treat his trophy girlfriend: Together they frequented the toniest restaurants and bars of Beverly Hills and West Hollywood, where an attentive Lazzaro made certain Jeremy was adorned extravagantly (Armani suits, John Lobb shoes, Hermes watches). But in spite of Lazzaro's excessive gifts and public fawning, he never bothered to reveal the vulnerable man underneath his aloof disguise—so much so that Jeremy began doubting his own sanity for being involved with him in the first place . . . that is, until the unforgettable night Lazzaro disclosed his past.

Lazzaro had introduced Jeremy to a new drug he'd been taking called *Sueño Gris* or Gray Dream, which he explained to be a synthetic hallucinogen that delivered both heightened awareness and empathogenic qualities. "In addition," Lazzaro continued, "this drug makes you fully awake and aware of your surroundings, yet at the same time that area of your brain that inspires your dreams can also be alert, so at times you might see sights and experience feelings you may have only dreamt of—like on a morning when the full moon is shining in a deep blue sky."

"You're . . . awake and asleep at the same time?"

"Something like that. And besides being perfectly safe, it will heighten our lovemaking; I've taken it many times under those circumstances." Lazzaro lowered his eyelids, smiling seductively. "I promise you will *not* be disappointed."

Jeremy drew back from him. "I don't know. Someone gave me a drug once that paralyzed me," he told Lazzaro, recalling his trip to Brazil and the horrifying events that unfolded there. "I've been afraid of anything stronger than pot since then."

"I have been using the *Sueño Gris* for some time now with no ill effects," Lazzaro assured him. "What if I take it first, and you can watch me and then decide?"

But because more than a few beers had been consumed in exchange for Jeremy's lunch, and the idea of some drug-fueled fucking sounded fun, he thought, *What the hell.* So Lazzaro squeezed a tear of the solution from an eyedropper into his own nostril before administering one into Jeremy's, and then they continued to swig their Heinekens until the drug began taking effect.

An hour or so later Jeremy felt himself giddy and euphoric.

He found himself hypnotized by the ocean's turquoise waves as they systematically rose up from flat water, crested, and then curled down onto themselves in an explosion of luminous white foam.

Ordinary colors began gaining the hues and translucency of stained glass windows.

A lyrical cantata Lazzaro had selected for the occasion transported Jeremy to inside the orchestra pit.

The sea breeze gusting through the open French doors carried the pickled reek of primordial creation.

Gravity seemed somehow . . . *stronger.*

And Lazzaro's physical beauty stultified Jeremy into a state of reverence and awe—he appeared a living Roman statue miraculously animated.

Jeremy felt peaceful . . . yet clear-headed, confident, and happy.

The happiest, in fact, that he'd felt since being separated from Arthur.

And boy oh boy was he horny.

The men shed their clothing and made love intensely . . . carefully at first and then feverishly, with their orgasms building simultaneously and accompanied by loud moans and shouting and declarations of adoration; then with the drug still cresting they showered together, soaping each other's back and shoulders and buttocks, and then pulled on their gym shorts and strolled outside to the deck overlooking the arcing band of sand hemming the vivid blue ocean.

Jeremy shielded his eyes from the sun as it baked the horizon—its white-hot glare bright as frozen lightning—and watched as a ghostly flotilla of Spanish galleons materialized on the bay. They drifted west at the speed of clouds, their sails—each emblazoned with a red Spanish cross—pregnant with wind.

"Do you see them?!" Jeremy pointed excitedly. "The ships! It's like the *Pirates of the Caribbean*! There must be thirty of them!"

Lazzaro placed a friendly arm around Jeremy's shoulder and pulled him close. "It is your gray dream, Jeremy. I see nothing but a beautiful man."

"But there they are! Heading west!"

Then Jeremy watched the ships slowly vaporize, as if they'd been conjured from fog. He turned to Lazzaro. "They're gone now."

"I am happy you saw them. Are you feeling all right?"

Jeremy checked himself and determined he was beginning to come down. "I'm fine."

"Then I would like to tell you something I have never told anyone. It is disturbing, but I feel the need to disclose this to you. Can I trust you?"

"Sure you can trust me."

"My father . . . he . . . *murdered* my mother."

"What?!"

"She was Russian," Lazzaro continued. "A beautiful orphan girl who loved to dance and grew up to become a ballerina with the Bolshoi until an injury killed her career. She had no family and no other professional skills, so she was forced to live on the streets, where she became a prostitute to survive.

"My father is from an ancient, aristocratic family. At this time he was married, with a wife and children at their main residence in Venice. He was traveling on business when he employed the services of my mother and then returned home.

"Nine months later I was born, and when I was old enough my

mother gathered enough money to take me to Venice, where she located my father. She only asked him for enough money to support me and to allow her to live an honorable life, but he insisted I could be any garbage man's son, so she threatened to expose him unless he agreed to pay her . . . and the next morning her body was found in the Grand Canal. She was shot in the head. And because she was only a prostitute, no one took the time to investigate her death."

"That's unbelievable!" Jeremy nearly shouted over the sudden thunderstorm of waves thrashing the shore. "I'm so sorry. Then how did your father find you?"

"His men followed her back to the room she rented for us. She was killed that night when she went out for bread, and after she did not return the men brought me to him, lying to me, saying they were taking me to my mother.

"My father introduced me to his family as a street urchin under guidance of the Church—my prostitute mother dead and in need of a home—so I was raised alongside his other children who are my half brothers and sisters . . . but only they are his legitimate heirs."

"What kind of relationship do you have with him now?"

"I hate him. He killed my mother."

"Funny you should say that," Jeremy muttered, amazed at how beautifully the sunlight illuminated the lapis lazuli of Lazzaro's eyes' irises.

"Why is this funny?"

"I know how you feel. And I know how it feels to hate someone all the way to your bones." Jeremy then explained how his own father had been killed in a car accident staged by his uncle, Bill Mortson, who succeeded some years later in administering an overdose of insulin to Jeremy's mother Tiffany, causing her death as well. Jeremy shyly added that he'd been forced to kill Uncle Bill in self-defense after the man came after Carlo and Jeremy with a gun.

That evening was the first and only time Lazzaro disclosed the details of his past, and Jeremy never brought up the subject—or his own tragedy—again; it was enough for him to have knowledge that Lazzaro had experienced heartbreak similar to his own.

Later that night, the effects of the drug faded from their bodies, as did their synthetic intimacy, and their relationship settled back into its listless tug-of-war, with neither man pulling hard nor letting go of the rope—or rather, the string—connecting them.

Lazzaro traveled frequently and sometimes wouldn't arrive home from "meetings" until the middle of the night or nearing dawn, his breath sharp from alcohol, his clothes stale from cigarettes, and his hair perfumed from shampoo . . . bearing no explanations or apologies.

So Jeremy would throw Lazzaro the cold shoulder, which would inevitably result in receiving an intimate morning e-mail that included some thoughtful link:

> I missed you last night. Then I saw this resort in the Maldives and imagined how wonderful it would be for us to stay there.

Or:

> Do you like this watch? I usually do not like the Rolex but this model is stunningly handsome, like you. Say the word and it is yours.

Jeremy would click on the links and think, *Wow, he really does think of me.*

And with furry, friendly Skipper providing Jeremy with her own reliable companionship, he didn't mind the time spent without Lazzaro.

Until one night.

During a grocery-shopping trip to Trader Joe's, Jeremy had spotted his ex-girlfriend Reed in line at the free tasting station. After exchanging pleasantries over teeny-tiny portions of couscous and red bean salad topped with molecules of crumbled feta cheese, Reed disclosed that she had been seeing someone on a regular basis and things were growing serious. Jeremy likewise brought Reed up-to-date on *his* new relationship, realizing that, as he was issuing the glowing adjectives from his mouth, he was probably building up Lazzaro to be more suitable for him than he actually was.

They both agreed that a dinner for four should be arranged.

Upon returning home, Jeremy made a reservation that coming Saturday night at Stakayu, the storied sushi restaurant frequented by paparazzi-seeking celebrities and actors on their way up—and down—the Hollywood A-B-C-D-F List.

Saturday arrived. And because Lazzaro had an afternoon business meeting that could likely elbow its way into dinnertime, Jeremy and he agreed to rendezvous.

At a few minutes after eight, Jeremy—outfitted in his tallest boots, sexiest jeans, tightest white V-neck T-shirt and black Armani blazer—rolled up solo to the restaurant and handed off his Jaguar to the valet. Once inside he spotted Reed at the bar with a spectacular blond stud whose identity stopped him in his tracks . . . a guy he immediately recognized from *Vanity Fair* and the tabloids as the charismatic head of his own strange new religion.

Why didn't Reed tell me she was dating Sebastian Black?!?!

Jeremy wove his way through the crowd up to the bar and kissed Reed on the cheek. "You look so gorgeous, you could *almost* turn a gay man straight."

"I know someone dumb enough to have tried that once," Reed replied.

"Jeremy," he announced to Sebastian, extending his hand.

Sebastian squeezed his hand, grinning through flawless white teeth. "Reed's told me a lot about you." He pulled out a barstool for Jeremy. "What're you drinking?"

"Anything but water." Jeremy turned to the bartender. "Goose martini with a twist, please." He slid up onto the barstool. "So you're Reed's new boyfriend?"

"I hope so," Sebastian replied. "They tell me she has great taste in men."

"Then her taste has gotten better over the years," Jeremy laughed, scanning the crowded, elegant room for any sign of Lazzaro.

But he was nowhere in sight.

Then nearly an hour—and another martini—later, with Jeremy receiving an education about Sebastian's fascinating spiritual movement and the group of fanatics who were hell-bent on either killing Sebastian or bedding him, the trio was shown to their semi-private banquette, where they settled into the white chesterfield sofa and ordered their favorites: Crispy Rice with Spicy Tuna, Yellowtail Sashimi with Jalapeno, and Salmon Sashimi with Black Caviar.

But even after their food arrived there was still no sign of Lazzaro . . . so Jeremy, knowing it would irritate Lazzaro, sent him a text: Where the fk are U?

After their initial orders were devoured they ordered four more dishes, and Reed and Sebastian decided to split a bottle of wine.

Jeremy opted for another martini.

And while picking at the scant, artfully assembled food with his chopsticks, Jeremy resisted the urge to roll his eyes as Reed and Sebastian glanced adoringly at each other while speaking with the abbreviated simplicity of a couple in love and destined for a long relationship.

Unlike Jeremy and Lazzaro.

Jealousy nagged at him. And resentment built while he did his best to hide his feelings by nodding and smiling and asking an endless stream of questions about their upcoming trip to Big Sur and the launch of Sebastian's world tour after that.

And as the check was delivered atop the unused fourth place setting—with its pristine folded napkin and unopened chopsticks—it was painfully clear that *Jeremy got stood up*.

The evening ended with Jeremy sufficiently hammered but having the good sense to take a cab back home to Ballena Beach, where he found Skipper anxiously waiting for him at the front door and Lazzaro glumly tapping away at his computer upstairs.

"What happened to you?!" Jeremy hollered as he swayed in the upstairs hallway with his dog panting happily by his leg. "All night I sat there waiting for you and you stood me up? In front of my ex-girlfriend and her famous boyfriend and all of Beverly Hills and those Neanderthal paparazzi? *Thanks so fucking much!*"

Lazzaro didn't even turn his way. "My father unexpectedly came into town. I had to meet with him in Marina del Rey where he is staying on a business associate's yacht. I am truly sorry, Jeremy, and I hope you will soon forgive me for being so rude."

"You stood me up to be with the man who *murdered your mother?*" Jeremy fumed, while looking around for something within reach to throw at Lazzaro . . . but then decided instead to sulk off to the kitchen to pour himself a glass of wine, which he carried upstairs to their bedroom.

There he sat down with his laptop and composed what he considered to be an impactful e-mail to Lazzaro, in spite of the booze that was making his thoughts slip like wet, wriggling worms through the mud of his besotted consciousness:

> You have no idea how furious I was sitting there waiting for you and you didnt have the respect or consideration for me to call or eventext me back and let me know you werent coming? Next time your father visits I hope you put a bullet in his

head and throw his body into the marina because that's what he deserves + and that's what I would do. I won't ever forget tonight. You owe me big time, Lazzaro.

With Skipper stretched out by his side of their bed, Jeremy locked the bedroom door and then fell onto the sheets.

CHAPTER

six

The next day Jeremy awoke, hungover and furious and sporting a heavily bruised ego, to a bouquet of white roses—on the carpet outside the bedroom door—with an apology note attached, as well as an invitation to brunch at Jeremy's favorite seaside restaurant, Jeffrey's in Ballena Beach. Lazzaro also let Jeremy know that he had arisen early, taken a cab into West Hollywood, and retrieved Jeremy's Jaguar from the valet at Stakayu.

It was downstairs in the driveway being detailed at that very moment.

At the restaurant Lazzaro was exceptionally charming and attentive. Jeremy treated his hangover with a Spanish omelet and roasted potatoes washed down with his very own bottle of Veuve Clicquot, and afterward they came home, ingested a bit of Sueño Gris, waited for the drug to peak, and then romped and heaved together in bed with the French doors open and the sea breeze cooling their sweat.

All appeared to be well.

:::::::::

Two days later Lazzaro returned visibly upset from one of his nightly meetings but would not discuss what happened.

Over coffee the next morning he explained to Jeremy that one of his family's European financial dealings had soured and he needed to fly home to salvage what he could; apparently, his father had fallen victim to some men who'd coerced him into a deal and then disappeared with his money. Hence, Lazzaro confessed, he desperately needed cash to help save the family's ancestral lands in Italy, so he was willing to quitclaim his beachside chateau to Jeremy for less than half its market value . . . with the Maserati thrown in as a bonus.

Plied with mimosas and eager to demonstrate to Aunt Katharine that he had finally grown some business chops, Jeremy sat next to Lazzaro while the man compared neighboring property values on various real estate websites and then Googled "Quitclaim Deeds" to show Jeremy how easy the process could be and what a common transaction it was.

Less than an hour later Jeremy had agreed to the transaction, which was signed and sealed a little before noon at a Mailboxes Etc. in Malibu, the closest notary.

From there they went to Jeremy's bank, where—as trustee, and with the quitclaim deed in his pocket—he was able to wire the money from his trust account to the Banca Monte Dei Paschi Di Siena in Italy, where Lazzaro's family held its accounts.

That afternoon a proud and excited Jeremy rode alongside a preoccupied Lazzaro to Los Angeles International Airport—though first stopping briefly to pick up some papers from Lazzaro's father in nearby Marina del Rey.

There Lazzaro surprised Jeremy by insisting he come meet his father. "You will see he is not the monster I sometimes paint him as," he said. "It is my fault you think him such a beast. Come, I want you to meet him and shake his hand. Please?"

Jeremy agreed.

After nodding to the two grim bodyguards stationed at the boat's entrance and then tottering up the gangway to the expansive, varnished teakwood deck, a slight, well-dressed, elderly man with a shock of white hair appeared, and Jeremy was introduced.

Francesco Sforza shook Jeremy's hand warmly—*a bit too warmly*—upon their introduction. "You be . . . *good* . . . to . . . *mi Lazzaro*," he told Jeremy, his voice graveled. "And you make . . . him be . . . good . . . to you."

"Oh, I will," Jeremy replied, catching the salacious gleam in the elderly man's alarmingly clear eyes. And he thought, *He looks more like an old queen than a murderer. But then again, neither did most of those guys on the* Sopranos. *Maybe it's just because he's European.*

That was the extent of their exchange before Lazzaro stepped behind closed doors with his father and then emerged a short time later hefting a black Gucci briefcase.

The pair hurried off to make Lazzaro's flight.

Curbside at the Bradley Terminal, Lazzaro assured Jeremy he would be in contact soon—in the next day or two.

Jeremy returned home to wait.

One day passed, then two days . . . then a week and then three.

In the meantime, the ugly truth about the mansion—and the Maserati, which was also upside-down in value—became evident.

"How could you do this?" Katharine demanded, her face the shade of raw cauliflower and her hands trembling as much as her voice. "We keep a law firm on retainer specifically for real estate transactions!"

"I thought—"

"You got a quitclaim instead of a warranty claim!" Katharine shrieked. "There's an outstanding mortgage on this property that's now payable in full! Didn't you learn anything in college? *Oh, that's right. You were kicked out!*"

After promising Katharine he would do everything possible to fix everything, Jeremy slinked back to his rotting chateau . . . but instead of following through, as the days and weeks passed, he did nothing.

Nothing at all beyond devoting himself to the tug-of-war between the reality that he'd put his trust in a lover who would rip him off and the hope that there must be *some* logical explanation for all this.

So the letters from the lending agencies accrued, and one Thursday morning a flatbed truck crept its way—air brakes farting loudly—down the steep private drive and then honked for access to the Maserati.

Jeremy unlocked the gate to let the truck into the courtyard and didn't even stay to watch as the voluptuous red sports car was cabled up the tow truck's greasy, tilting, groaning bed.

Then a letter from Lazzaro arrived, with no return address, explaining that he was in an area of Europe that did not have Internet access; he also claimed that he missed Jeremy very much and understood something had fouled Jeremy's end of their business transaction, so he would soon return to straighten out everything.

So Jeremy aimlessly rode out each day, which was easy to do without a job to report to or classes to attend or papers to write; he had few commitments except to his dog and no family except the old woman who'd made him feel even worse about himself than he already felt—which admittedly was her right to do. He'd fucked up *magnificently*.

Each pointless day of Jeremy's life drifted into the next, as if he were a boat with neither fuel nor sail nor anchor nor ballast, and completely vulnerable to the storm gathering just beyond the horizon.

CHAPTER

seven

During this time when Jeremy was neither in school nor employed, he spent his nights getting liquored up in clubs, online for horny men to hook up with, or getting high and then pleasuring himself on cam for anonymous—albeit highly appreciative—audiences.

Then on the morning of his Ides of March birthday, upon rising with a thundering headache, he discovered that a shame-faced Skipper—her head resting atop her paws and those mournful brown eyes watching him—had done her business inside on the floor by the French doors, because he'd overslept by nearly three hours and had neglected to let her outside per their agreed-upon schedule.

And as he gathered paper towels and a nearly empty spray bottle of 409, the thought occurred to him that although he was about to turn twenty-four, his life already felt as if it were over.

Might as well be dead. No one would miss me—except for Skipper . . . maybe.

She deserves so much better than me.

That afternoon he took his beloved retriever out on the beach for what would be their final walk together—at least for some time.

After allowing Skipper to meander some distance through the sand, sniffing this shell or that seaweed clump or this rock or that cigarette butt, the time came to advise her of what was to come.

He bumped his butt down in the sand and she collapsed next to him, panting contentedly.

"I love you," he said massaging her head, "but I'm too fucked up to give you what you need, and I don't want you to go through what I went through; I promised myself I'd *never* do to anyone what my mom did to me, but here we are. You deserve a *real* family—someone's side to sleep by, and someone to be there for you to open the doors when you need to pee or poo."

Skipper glanced appreciatively at him with her penny-colored eyes and then steadied her gaze back at a battalion of sandpipers charging the waves, her ears cocked to attention.

He leaned over and hugged her. "I promise I'll come back for you, *I promise.* But in the meantime, you'll be so much happier with Aunt Katharine and Carlo."

Upon returning to his home, Jeremy and Carlo texted each other about that night's dinner. Then he drove Skipper in the Jaguar up the road to Aunt Katharine's, dropped her off with a twenty-pound bag of food and a note on the kitchen counter to please understand that he could no longer take care of her, and then traveled down to Jeffrey's, the same seaside restaurant in Ballena Beach where Aunt Katharine had taken him years before for his first decent meal.

Carlo—who'd been downstairs working with Aunt Katharine in her office when Jeremy dropped off Skipper—arrived on time but then refused to have a drink with him, so Jeremy ordered a Grey Goose on the rocks, then another, and after that had a frosty bottle of Cristal with his medium-rare steak béarnaise.

"Katharine was livid when she found Skipper downstairs," Carlo told him after their chitchat ran dry, dabbing his fork into his scampi with linguini. "She'll only keep her for a month and then she's finding her another home if you don't take her back."

"I figured she wouldn't mind having another bitch around the house," Jeremy joked, but it came out sounding meaner than he'd intended.

"If you're referring to me, that's not funny."

"If the foo shits . . ."

"Speaking of shit, have you looked in the mirror lately?" Carlo asked, leaning in. "Would you like me to start composing your obituary tonight when I get home, or should I put it off until next week when your unemployment check arrives and you blow it on more booze or that other shit you've been taking, that Sueño Gris? People overdose and die on that crap, you know. And from what I've heard, some people even get flashbacks after they've stopped using it."

"Why are you lecturing me when I'm just trying to have a good time?" Jeremy slurred. "It's my birthday, remember?"

"You've reminded me seven times," Carlo snapped. "You need help, baby."

"And you need to get laid," Jeremy muttered into his empty champagne glass.

"They'd better put all twenty-four candles on your cake tonight," Carlo shot back, "because you're gonna need all the help in the world making your wishes come true. Too bad your missing boyfriend isn't here to help you *blow*." Then he pushed aside his dinner, got up from the table, asked the maître d' to call a cab, waited outside for it to arrive, gave the driver the number of his American Express, and the request to wait for Jeremy. He also specified that if Jeremy didn't take the cab home, the driver should call him immediately.

Predictably, Jeremy refused the cab upon staggering outside, his uneaten slice of complimentary birthday cake smashed inside the Styrofoam container clutched in his hand.

The cab driver called Carlo.

Carlo called the California Highway Patrol.

Some miles down Pacific Coast Highway the neon red and blue swirling lights in his mirror sobered Jeremy up . . . but not quite enough to pass the field sobriety test.

He blew a 0.12.

After spending the remainder of the evening in jail he came back to the Tyler Compound, but only long enough for Katharine to find a suitable rehab for him, located just down the road in Malibu.

Over the next thirty days Jeremy did sufficiently well there, finishing the course with praise from his counselors and an offer to return and work there, if he chose.

He did not choose.

Instead, he drove back to his beachside ruin and found it ransacked: His laptop was missing and everything had been pulled out of the drawers and closets and cabinets before being hastily tossed back into them.

So Jeremy celebrated his homecoming amidst the hurricane-like chaos with a fine bottle left over from Lazzaro's collection, a 1991 Chateau les Ollieux Corbiéres that went down as smoothly as its musical name implied. Then he made his way upstairs, gathered some sheets from the floor, and fell onto his bed.

And he began to cry.

He cried about his mother and he cried about his father.

He cried about his lack of hope, his inability to accomplish anything, and how completely he'd ruined the extraordinary opportunities given him.

Then he cried about giving up Skipper.

And he sobbed about Arthur.

Have you completely forgotten about me?

:::::::::

That was two—three?—weeks ago, during which time Jeremy had somehow gathered the wherewithal to put his house back together, order a new laptop from Amazon on his iPhone, and field questions from some terse detectives who came to the door wanting to know anything he might tell them about Lazzaro Sforza's whereabouts.

"We just want to ask him a few questions," the skinny member of the somber pair—who reminded Jeremy of Laurel and Hardy—told him. "If there's anything you could tell us, we would greatly consider your cooperation at a later time."

"Like what 'later time'?" Jeremy asked. "And where's my laptop?"

"We don't know anything about your computer," Laurel lied. "But your cooperation would be noted when your DUI court date comes up."

"Look," Jeremy began, his hangover headache pounding, "Lazzaro's father supposedly had some investment go bad in Europe, so he left to fix everything and I bought this house from him, but then he disappeared. I don't have any idea what's going on or where he is. *Really*. But I'd really like my computer back. It's the black HP notebook, and it's got files on it that I need."

Hardy spoke up. "What's your relationship with Lazzaro's father, Francesco Sforza?"

"I only met him once, and he's kind of an asshole from what I hear. Why?"

"Are you aware that Mr. Sforza passed away recently?"

"Really? He looked fine when I saw him. For an old guy, that is."

Laurel had been scribbling more notes, but looked up now. "Was this on the night of February twentieth?"

"That's over two months ago, so I'd have to think about it . . . but if I had my laptop I could look at my calendar. Why?"

"Do you know anyone named Sasha?" asked Hardy.

Jeremy thought about it and then shook his head. "Never heard of him—or her. Why?"

Laurel squinted at him. "Are you aware that Lazzaro Sforza had an alias?"

Jeremy's stomach clenched. "No . . . what was it?"

"Has Lazzaro Sforza contacted you?"

"I got a letter last week," Jeremy told them, suddenly lightheaded with anxiety.

"Can we see it?" they asked in unison.

Jeremy considered their request. "Will you *please* bring back my laptop? It'd only take you a minute to copy everything onto an external hard drive. But you won't find anything illegal on it, just some embarrassing stuff."

Laurel and Hardy glanced at each other.

"We'll look into it," Hardy replied.

"OK. Hold on." Jeremy shut the door, retrieved the letter, and then presented it to them along with the postmarked envelope.

"Do you mind if we keep this?"

Jeremy told them he didn't.

They thanked him, seeming genuinely appreciative, and just before leaving handed him an official-looking letter in a sealed envelope.

"What's this?" Jeremy asked, turning it front-to-back-to-front.

"A subpoena," Laurel said. "Court date's coming up in June, so you'll probably want to get yourself a lawyer."

The men about-faced and began trudging back up the driveway.

Jeremy was surprised to see Hardy take the lead.

"Hey!" Jeremy yelled to their backs, but neither turned around. "Don't forget my laptop!"

At this point, Jeremy knew he was sinking deeper faster, and he needed to start being proactive . . . even if it meant abandoning his property and going back to live at the Tyler Compound with Aunt Katharine—at least for the time being.

But he knew he couldn't go there.

Anywhere but there.

So he decided to batten down and ride out whatever situational hurricane might be heading his way.

:::::::::

Then this afternoon he'd heard the gate bell ring, hoping it might be Laurel and Hardy returning his computer.

He checked the security monitors and at first didn't recognize the man . . . probably because Jeremy was already more than halfway through a six-pack of Bud Light and Arthur was sporting more gray hair. Then by the time Arthur's lantern-jawed profile and broad-shouldered build registered, Jeremy was too embarrassed to greet him in his present state. *He'll think I'm just like my mom*, Jeremy thought, *and I look like shit.*

But he yearned to go to him. *Should I?*

Jeremy sprinted into the bathroom to check the mirror, where his reflection revealed exactly what he feared: an unshaven man with swollen eyelids, scummy teeth, messy hair, and swaying shoulders.

Deflated and resigned, Jeremy lurched to his office to study the security monitors as the ex-Marine and only man he loved trudged back up the steep driveway, slipped a note into Jeremy's mailbox, and drove away.

Jeremy waited a few minutes and then retraced Arthur's steps, pulled out the note, and read it.

At first he was filled with heart-swelling optimism . . . but then the specificity of Arthur's words sliced hatchet-like through his beer buzz: . . . *sounds like we should talk.*

Jeremy realized it only *sounds like* something if someone says it.

The realization stung.

Katharine convinced Arthur to rescue me. Is she paying him by the task or the hour?

He crumpled the note and threw it onto the highway.

Then Jeremy staggered back down the driveway and into the chateau, snatched his new laptop off the coffee table, and typed a message:

To: ablauefee@ballenabeach.com
Subject: SOUNDS LIKE WE SHOULDNT

Contrary to what you've heard I dont need you rescuing me. Tell Katharine nice try. Funny you still answer her summons. I thought she fired you.

Have a nice life. PS Hi to Jess.

He hit the SEND button before he could change his mind, got up from the sofa, grabbed another icy Bud Light bottle from the fridge, and twisted open the cap.

But as the fizzy, bitter draft slid down his throat, he began regretting his words.

He went back to his laptop, opened his Sent folder, re-read his message, and cringed.

That wasn't nice.

Maybe I should contact Carlo and find out what's going on—if he'll even talk to me.

CHAPTER

eight

The white yacht—a gleaming sixty-five foot Rybovich—had set out just after midnight from the bustling port in Bizerte, Tunisia, on the north coast of Africa, headed for Palma de Majorca. Lazzaro had taken a bottle of his favorite Turkish wine—a ripe Sarafin Cabernet Sauvignon—with him to bed, but the voices in his head were complaining louder than the elixir could hush.

Finally, around three in the morning, the throaty drone of the diesels below deck knitted a hazy coverlet along with the wine that cozied Lazzaro off to sleep.

Around dawn, with the first rays of sunlight glowing through his narrow porthole, Lazzaro awakened to hear the hum of the yacht's motors drop from alto to bass. With aching head and soured mouth he crouched up on his stateroom's bed to peer at the approaching marina's tangle of tall ships' masts—like a forest of white toothpicks—and the imposing amber-stone edifice of the Catedral Palma de Mallorca, its spires tickling the brightening sky.

As the reversing engines rocked the yacht to a halt, Lazzaro heard a quiet knock on his door. He reached over and unlatched it.

"We need to refuel," the crewmember advised him. "They will do an inspection of the boat as a formality. You must now take your place."

Lazzaro wriggled into his jeans, zipped up his hoodie, laced his Nikes, and then made his way down the tiny hallway and up the stairs to his now-familiar place in the storage bin beneath the banquette seats in the galley.

Once he was in his luge-riding position—flat on his back with legs extended and arms at his sides—the same crewmember covered him with a blanket and some life jackets, lowered the seat cushions and snapped the hatch shut. The first time he did this, days ago, he was nervous, but now it caused him no more stress than sitting on the toilet in an airport restroom.

Minutes later the boat bumped the dock.

After a short time, he heard footsteps and voices on the deck above him.

Then it became quiet, so Lazzaro figured that many of the euros he'd paid his smugglers were now changing hands.

He drew up his wrist to his nose, barely able to make out the time.

Ten excruciating minutes passed. Then twenty. Then thirty.

What's happening?

He pushed down his anxiety and told himself not to worry; the captain was probably having a cigarette with the inspector and would be finished in a moment or two.

And Lazzaro began to wonder: *Will I actually get away with this?*

He began sifting through the events that had brought him to this cramped cell: his parents' death; his stolen adolescence; the clumsy sex with strangers and the drug-fueled hours trying to forget it . . . then plotting and scheming and working to make it all end.

And now the murder of his adoptive father.

So he'd fled.

First to his family's seaside home in Capri. But soon after his arrival he'd discovered Interpol was hot on his trail, so he fled across the Mediterranean to Akhisar, Turkey.

Interpol began closing in again.

In a panic he called clingy Tristan, his former lover now living in Greece, and swore him to secrecy before selectively debriefing him.

"I always knew you would come back to me!" Tristan sang over the phone. "Our villa in the countryside has many unused rooms. I have horses and a motorcycle and my own barn overlooking the vineyards, and we have a full staff. I will leave my flat in the city, meet you at the marina, and drive us to the villa."

"Who else lives there?"

"Only my mother is expected there sometime soon. I will check when she plans to arrive."

"She and I have never met," Lazzaro said. "Surely she will find me an imposition. Can she be trusted with my secret? She must not tell anyone she knows where I am."

"She would never betray the only man I love, so it is settled. When will you arrive? Please tell me it will be soon."

Lazzaro estimated a date and henceforth began his secret journey across the Mediterranean to the Grecian countryside.

:::::::::

Lazzaro checked the time on his watch again and saw nearly an hour had passed. His legs were twitchy, his armpits trickled, and the air in the compartment shrank with each breath.

I can't do this any longer!

Just as that panic began ricocheting through his mind, he felt footsteps approaching.

The hatch was cracked, and Lazzaro gasped at the rush of sea air.

"A few moments longer," the voice whispered.

Lazzaro, grateful for the oxygen and the update, settled into his nest. He heard the muffled voices of men . . . more footsteps . . . more talking and footsteps, and then the shouts of the crew as they began readying the vessel for the final leg of her voyage.

The lid was inched up and propped open with a rumpled magazine.

"We leave soon but they still watch; do not move until we are at sea."

With the sliver of sunshine now illuminating—and the sea air curling—inside the compartment, Lazzaro calmed, returning to his usual flurry of worries . . .

What if I am too late? Will everything I've worked for be destroyed? I need to take back what is mine! I will rot in jail for the rest of my life if they find me . . .

At last one engine—and moments later a second—burbled up to a rumbling hum, and the yacht began rocking and swaying as it turned toward the ocean.

Lazzaro threw open the hatch, climbed stiff-jointed out from underneath the life jackets, and stepped out from the galley onto the deck—just in time for the port's security cameras to catch his movements.

A guard inside the watchtower observed the tiny figure on his monitor as it appeared and then vanished back down inside the ship. He picked up the phone and relayed to his superior officer what he'd seen.

"It's only a crewmember," the inspector lied, fingering the lump of euros in his pocket. "But to be safe I will call ahead to the port in Athens."

The man thanked his superior, hung up the phone, and gave it no more thought.

:::::::::

Lazzaro had been loitering on the windswept deck since their morning stopover in Palma de Majorca, alternately studying the translucent turquoise water rushing underneath the long white fiberglass hull or the zigzagging rocky hillsides drifting along in the distance, having no desire to leaf through a magazine or fiddle on his computer or eat or sleep. Occasionally the unending monotony of the voyage had been interrupted by a school of dolphins racing alongside the yacht or a cluster of seagulls trailing behind—suspended above the deck like kites—but eventually even these creatures grew bored and veered off to find adventure elsewhere.

He was tired of this voyage, tired of fleeing, and tired of being worried about what might meet him next week, next month, next year . . .

Then a creamy thought assuaged his chapped anxiety: *Tristan will do everything he can to help me. He would happily take a bullet for me, especially after I draw him into—*

"Would you like something to drink, Signore Sforza?"

The sonorous voice startled him. "No, thank you. How much longer?"

"About three hours until we reach Athens, Signore."

Lazzaro once again studied the young man's swarthy face, thinking he might be extraordinarily handsome if not for the somewhat weak chin. But his Turkish features were otherwise flawless: strong nose, even teeth, full lips, intense black eyes, bronze skin. *Perhaps a little beard growth might help.* "That long, even still?" Lazzaro considered this. "Perhaps I will take some wine."

"It will be my pleasure."

Lazzaro watched him turn and stride back into the galley, his shoulders rocking and his soccer-hewn buttocks shifting confidently in spite of the heaving and pitching of the speeding yacht.

He locked his elbows against the railing and sighed, once again considering Jeremy: He felt the tiniest guilt about having swindled him, but he also took satisfaction in knowing Jeremy had ultimately gotten what he'd deserved. Lazzaro's own mother—for some time before her death—had already begun washing away her health in a flood of Raki, so any weakness in this regard not only repelled Lazzaro, but also awakened his predatory instincts. And the trust money had been *given* to Jeremy; it wasn't as if Lazzaro had made off with any cash that his lover had actually *worked*—or even schemed—for.

Plus, my former chateau could someday be worth a small fortune . . .

The steward returned with a tumbler of deep red wine garnished with a single slice of orange and one ice cube—as he preferred. "Thank you," Lazzaro told him, taking the glass.

"*My pleasure,* Signore Sforza."

Lazzaro noticed that the man scanned his body so hungrily his eyes were almost drooling.

Warmth flushed Lazzaro's skin. *Am I in the mood?*

The idea stirred him; it had been weeks since his last conquest and he was tired of his hand. His eyes swept over the sailor's body: strong neck, broad shoulders, flat stomach, narrow hips, ample crotch. He was a bit young—nineteen or twenty—but was certainly old enough to know what he desired.

And they would never see each other again.

"Your name again is—?"

"Gizem," the young man answered.

"Gizem," Lazzaro echoed. "Since we are so close to Athens, might you help me gather my possessions and pack my bags?"

"With *pleasure*, Signore."

True to Gizem's estimation, three hours later the yacht slowed while approaching the breakwater protecting Eleusina—a sleepy town with scant port security west of Athens.

As the dock drifted into view Lazzaro began feeling hopeful; the dalliance with Gizem had distracted him from his trepidations, and their rough intimacy recharged Lazzaro's drained psyche.

The yacht slowed to trolling while approaching its slip, and Lazzaro anxiously scanned the marina, wondering what he might do if an army of police awaited him.

Relieved, he only saw the usual compact cars: Fiats and Renaults and SEATs and Citroëns . . . and a glossy black vintage Mercedes 600 Pullman limousine—replete with red fender flags he imagined were embroidered with Tristan's family crest—in front of which stood a diminutive yet perfectly proportioned young man wearing a white suit.

Tristan . . . where would I be without you?

Lazzaro didn't wait for the yacht to be tied down; instead, when the vessel's bumpers thumped its slip, he threw his bag onto the dock and leapt over the bulwark.

Moments later he was trotting up the gangway.

They embraced.

Lazzaro touched Tristan's chin, tilting up his face. "How can it be that you are even more handsome than I remember?" He pressed their lips together, and Tristan's mouth opened to him.

Their tongues met briefly, but then Tristan pulled away. "We are short on time; lunch is waiting for us at home and we can discuss your situation on the drive over. Come."

Tristan began walking toward the Mercedes, but Lazzaro grasped his shoulder. "You are angry with me?"

"Of course I am only delighted to see you," Tristan told him. "But you are not safe where eyes can see you. We must leave here."

They scurried to the limousine, ducked into the rear of the car, and slammed the door, sealing themselves within the chrome and saddle-colored leather, burled walnut, and smoked-glass cocoon.

"I have prayed for your return each night," Tristan said, nestling himself within Lazzaro's arms. "You cannot imagine my tortured thoughts."

Lazzaro kissed the top of his head. "Thank you for being my savior."

Then the driver—a funereal woman draped in black—started the motor, eased the vehicle expertly away from the curb, and began threading the long car through the town's narrow streets.

Minutes later they were floating through the Greek countryside at nearly twice the speed limit—the scarlet and gold fender flags flapping regally in the wind—as they headed to Tristan's ancestral villa.

CHAPTER

nine

After traveling for the better part of an hour inland from the coast, Lazzaro spotted their destination straddling a distant rise surrounded by green, corduroy-like vineyards, its walls golden in the brilliant afternoon sun. Soon after this, the driver slowed the Mercedes and made a careful turn into a driveway and up through an *allée* of Italian cypresses whose scruffy emerald foliage pointed skyward, like an armory of evergreen missiles.

While pulling into the cobblestone driveway at the front of the villa, Lazzaro surveyed the patrician setting: hand-hewn limestone walls supporting a sloping terracotta tile roof; pairs of narrow windows framed by filigreed iron balconies; rotund potted topiaries guarding the sturdy wooden entrance door.

The driver stopped the car and shut off the motor, and the men grabbed their belongings.

"Are you tired?" Tristan asked as they made their way toward the villa. "Would you rather rest than eat?"

"More hungry than tired."

"Wonderful, because I ordered the lunch to your liking." He led Lazzaro around the side of the villa onto the stone terrace, where the staff had arranged their meal atop an old table: slabs of rosemary bread and bowls of goat cheese and platters of roasted chicken and melon and olives.

Lazzaro slid out a chair, sat down, and poured himself a glass of Tempranillo.

Tristan took his place across from him. "Tell me everything."

Lazzaro gulped a heavy draught from the glass. "As you may know, my father has been murdered and I am under suspicion. Interpol was close to catching me; and without your assistance they would have found me and extradited me to the United States to stand trial."

"Did you kill him?"

"The less you know, the better for you. I fear you will be implicated."

Tristan sipped his wine. "Do they know you are now in Greece?"

"I have no idea. I may have lost them—for the moment."

"You've paid off whomever you've had to, of course."

"And the money only went so far," Lazzaro said. "Now I am dependent on others."

"What about your investments and the beach property you owned in California?"

"I could carry only so much cash with me out of the country to avoid arousing suspicion, so I sold my home at the beach and had the money wired to me in Italy. Then I used my cash to pay for protection here in Europe, and the rest I lost in Bizerte at the blackjack table—to a corrupt dealer, if ever there was one. I am fortunate to have paid for my passage ahead of time."

"Do you have any other friends who might help?"

"Only Jeremy Tyler in Ballena Beach, but he will never speak to me again."

"Why?"

"I sold him my estate for a good price but neglected to tell him I owed a substantial amount on it, which I borrowed in preparation for my escape to Europe. He drinks too much." Lazzaro laughed as he mimed gulping liquid from a bottle, "—so having him sign a paper was not difficult."

"Where is this money you borrowed?"

"It is also in my bank in Italy, but I cannot access it because Interpol would immediately know of my location. I did not think they would be after me so quickly."

"This Jeremy was your friend . . . but was he your lover as well?"

"I have only done what I needed to do. But not what I wanted."

"If you lured him here he could have an accident," Tristan suggested darkly, "then his family would send money for his care, which will come to me."

"Your jealousy is appreciated. But I am finished with violence."

"And I am finished with drinking wine." Tristan toasted him with his glass. "It is clear that this situation needs to be resolved."

Lazzaro settled back into his chair. "Yes, I cannot continue to hide. I feel hunted. This is not how a Sforza was meant to live—not even one who was adopted."

Tristan leaned in. "You can trust me to help you."

"I am deeply in your debt." Lazzaro stabbed an olive with his fork. "And where is your mother? I am anxious to meet her."

"My mother?" Tristan laughed. "If you mean the rising actress Carmella Montes, she is here for a few days, but will soon fly to Los Angeles for a guest starring role on a novella, and then she is off to Colombia, and then back to Hollywood . . . and after that I cannot remember. New York, I think."

"You never mentioned before that she was an actress."

"A dream that died with my birth but was resurrected after I left for the university. And when you meet her you will at once understand why she is now in such great demand. I believe the directors are too terrified of Carmella to tell her 'no.'"

"I hope she will not resent my presence." Lazzaro stifled a yawn; the tiresome voyage and the sex with Gizem and the long drive and the meal and the wine had defeated his usually indefatigable stamina. He ate one more bite of his sandwich and drained his glass. "In which room should I sleep?"

"Any room you wish," Tristan replied. "I will visit you, but only as you desire."

"A rest first," Lazzaro grinned, "then a visit afterward. Yes?"

"I have waited this long."

"Thank you for taking such good care of me." Lazzaro scooted back his chair and stood. "I'll repay you. Somehow."

"There is no need. Instead, reward me by being careful—and by resolving this situation."

Lazzaro leaned over and kissed Tristan deeply, caressing his neck. Then he made his way into the house and trudged upstairs to find an empty bedroom.

:::::::::

The first door opened to reveal a bed tossed with rumpled sheets and tables stacked with movie scripts and dog-eared magazines and half-filled ashtrays. Neat stacks of clothing tilted atop a pair of toile-covered Louis XV fauteuils, and organza drapes billowed in front of windows open to the countryside.

Carmella's bedroom?

He pulled the door closed and then walked to the end of the hallway, where another door opened to a room furnished with drum-tight linens, bare tabletops, and locked windows.

Lazzaro pushed the door closed behind him, unlocked the windows, shed his clothes onto the floor, and slid inside the envelope of crisp linen.

At last, he relaxed. The breeze carried the fragrance of lavender and sage, and the sensation of lying in a bed that wasn't rocking on the open seas was positively blissful.

His eyelids sagged, and he drifted to sleep.

:::::::::

Sometime later he awoke.

Someone's here.

He looked around the room's now purpling walls and drew in a breath.

A buxom woman with long black hair was posed on the Louis XVI chaise opposite his bed, her long legs crossed elegantly, and an inquisitive expression molding her face. Her features bespoke centuries of Spanish nobility—Habsburgs, Aragons, Oldenburgs—but with pinches of Moor and Gypsy tossed in to dilute all that crazy inbreeding. She wore an almost transparent white gossamer gown, over which she'd draped a scarlet satin cape with a high, gathered collar and cuffs. Lazzaro also noticed she was wearing the most whorish, ruby-hued, high-heeled pumps he'd ever seen.

He blinked at her, raising his eyebrows. "Am I in the wrong room?"

"No," she replied, staring at him. "But clearly I am."

CHAPTER

ten

That evening as the sun was setting, Jeremy—after a sobering nap and a scalding shower—called a cab and rode it south on Pacific Coast Highway to meet Carlo for dinner at Duke's in Malibu. Just recalling their previous evening together at Jeffrey's—and figuring they'd be discussing Arthur's mailbox note from this morning—had sparked that unmistakable craving for intimacy with a highball, so he figured his Jaguar would serve him better parked in his driveway than once again strapped to the back of a highway patrol flatbed tow truck.

The homely #2 pencil-colored Prius taxicab whirred to a stop in front of the restaurant's portico almost half an hour before their scheduled meeting time, so Jeremy could get a head start on his buzz before Carlo arrived. He paid the driver and dodged the wandering, zombielike patrons through the restaurant to the outdoor seaside seating with their dusty palm frond umbrellas and wobbly wooden tables and chairs. But after surveying the frumpy tourists devouring their burgers and fries alongside their restless kids, he decided instead to sit inside.

After all, he'd seen that Beverly was tending. She poured hard.

"Heeey!" Beverly called out to Jeremy as he lifted himself onto the stool at the lonely end of the bar. "It's been too long. What brings you?"

Jeremy quickly scanned the patrons for any attractive men. "Meeting someone."

Beverly scooped ice cubes from the tub below the countertop and slid them into a glass. "Goose martini, or rocks with an orange wedge?"

"Rocks and wedge." Jeremy settled his elbows onto the slab of glassy oak. "Please."

"Who ya' meetin'?" Beverly poured a generous stream of vodka into the glass, pinched in an orange slice, and slid it down to him.

Jeremy caught the glass before it sailed off the end. "Ex-boyfriend from high school."

Beverly snickered. "Bet he's got some *interesting* stories."

"Everyone's got stories," Jeremy mumbled and then slurped his cocktail. *Mmmmm.* "But only lucky guys like me have their own soap opera."

Just then Carlo appeared, a wary smile brightening his features as he caught sight of Jeremy.

They waved to each other.

"You're early," Jeremy told him as he drew close.

"Talk about early—what's your excuse?" He leaned in for a kiss.

Jeremy pecked his cheek. "Took a cab. By the way, I hope you're in the mood to be bored."

"Why else would I be here?" Carlo cocked his head. "A cab? Is your Jag out of commission?"

"No, but my driver's license is. Restricted, in fact, *thanks to you.*"

"You're welcome." Carlo turned to Beverly. "Mineral water with lime in a wine glass, easy on the ice, please." He gave Jeremy a quick up-and-down. "You look . . . *good?*"

"You lie as bad as I look. Thanks anyhow."

"Again, welcome. What's going on?"

"Tell you in a minute." Jeremy gulped his drink. "But first . . . let me clear the air before I chicken out."

Carlo climbed onto the barstool as Beverly delivered his beverage. "Listening."

Jeremy twirled his cocktail atop the bar. "I'm sorry."

"For what?"

"For being such an asshole."

"Are you speaking in generalities or just about the last month or so?"

Jeremy's eyes drifted up to Carlo's. "Ever since I can remember, you've been there for me. You were my first friend at Ballena Beach High, you taught me how to dance, you helped bring me out of the closet, you . . . were the first person who truly loved me for who I was, and you even stepped aside for Arthur when that whole thing happened in Brazil between him and me—that is, after you saved my life. And for me to treat you with anything other than love and undying respect and appreciation was just wrong, wrong, wrong. I—" he sighed heavily, "—owe you so much, Carlo. And if I ever act like an asshole to you again, I want you to scream at me and slap me until I actually start listening to you. And if I don't listen, you have permission to strangle me."

Carlo struggled to assemble his thoughts. "You've gotta deal," he said at last, "and I mean that in more ways than one."

"How?"

"You've gotta deal with your drug use—with that Sueño Gris shit. You've gotta deal with your drinking. You've gotta deal with your financial disaster and the strain it's put on the relationship with your aunt . . . and you've gotta deal with the fact that your gorgeous, exotic boyfriend screwed you, in a less than fun way, and isn't ever coming back. And finally, you've gotta deal with the fact that you're still in love with Arthu—"

"—I've got some news there, if you'll let me interrupt."

"You just did," Carlo told him and took a sip of his mineral water. "I'll stop my tirade, but only for a moment. News?"

"Arthur stopped by my place today and left me a note. He wants me to e-mail him."

"And?"

"It means nothing."

"Why do you think so?"

"His note said 'it sounds like we should talk,' so I figure Katharine put him up to it."

"You should be a detective."

"What do you mean?" Jeremy searched his face as Carlo glanced at the ceiling. "*You're* in on this too?"

Carlo returned his glare. "Calm down."

Jeremy clutched his arm. "You'd better spill—"

"Well . . . apparently Katharine was taking her new dog Skipper for her morning stroll on the beach and they ran into Arthur, who was also walking *his* dog. She invited him up to the gazebo and, over crumpets and tea, told him what's going on with you. Very *Downton Gabby.*"

"Did she tell him everything?"

"No, but I did." Carlo smiled. "*Everything.*"

Jeremy threw back more of his cocktail and glared at Carlo. "Just when I was beginning to like you again."

"Arthur really cares about you, Jeremy. We had a good heart-to-heart."

"Is he still with that guy? Jesus or Julie or whatever the hell his name is?"

"Send him an e-mail and ask him yourself."

"You are *such* a bitch."

"Thank you," Carlo said, shooting him a dead-eyed stare. "Thirsty, by the way?"

"Actually I'm tense and worried and broke," Jeremy replied. "Other than that, I'm *fantastic*."

"And I'm sure that, just like the last time I saw you, that cocktail's making *everything* better."

"No, it just makes everything *seem* better." Jeremy raised his glass. "Cheers."

"So blah, blah, blah. Enough about you. Ask me what's going on."

"I'm sorry. What's going on with you? I've missed you and I want to know."

Carlo propped his elbows on the bar. "Still single, still holding together your aunt's villa, *and* your aunt. I'm getting along a little better with my father, and I'm still counseling my best friend Jeremy, who attracts drama the way mobile home parks attract tornadoes. I just wanted you to ask me in case *something* actually had changed, like . . . maybe I'd started writing my autobiography, *Confessions of a Naughty Muchacho*."

Jeremy laughed while caressing Carlo's forearm, and the intimate camaraderie, as well as the moist heat from his skin, flashed them both back to the first time they made love. Carlo's dark eyes startled up at Jeremy but then flashed away.

Jeremy withdrew his hand. "I'm sorry."

"Not going there," Carlo stated coolly. "Tell me more about Lazzaro. Any sign of your Prince Frightening?"

"No, but some cops came around telling me he's wanted for questioning in the death of his father."

"*His father died?*"

"On the night I took him to the airport, Lazzaro had me stop off at the marina to get some papers from his dad, and Lazzaro insisted I come meet him. He was on someone's yacht. Then apparently he died—of what I don't know."

"What was his father like?"

"Creepy. Old and bent over, with white hair and dark circles under his eyes like that Pope . . . *Eggs Benedict*, or whatever his name was, who resigned."

"I get that he was old, but what was creepy about him?"

"When he shook my hand he held on to it too long, and his eyes reminded me of that perv who came on to me in Bakersfield at the bus station. Remember, on my way here from Fresno?"

"You mean the guy who would make you a movie star if he could suck your cock?" Carlo laughed. "Mr. Pigeon?"

"Yeah . . . *Jed Stygian!* Anyhow, Lazzaro's father had *that same look in his eyes*—like he was picturing me naked and bound and gagged and whimpering for my life. And it occurred to me that Lazzaro went back into the room with him and closed the door, and the next thing I know the police are looking for Lazzaro and his father's dead. I saw the old man that night, Carlo, so if he died and they think Lazzaro was involved, it must've happened at that moment or right after we left!"

Carlo grimaced. "Kind of seems that way."

"They also told me Lazzaro had an alias."

"An alias?"

"Sasha."

Carlo took a sip of his drink, working to absorb it all. "So how do you think he killed his father?"

"Who knows. But however he did it, he planned it well. He had everything lined up: the cash I gave him, his deadly visit with his father and his flight to Europe, and then his disappearance."

"But why would Lazzaro have wanted him dead?"

Jeremy then relayed to Carlo his first night on Sueño Gris, and the story of Lazzaro's mother's murder.

"Retribution—not a new concept." Carlo paused, and then squared a look at Jeremy. "So are you still taking that Sueño Gris shit?"

"Actually, with Lazzaro gone I don't have any source."

"Good! So when are you going to give up the booze?" Carlo wagged his finger at Jeremy's empty glass. "I just can't help thinking of your mother—" he made the sign of the cross, "—may she rest in peace."

"I think of her every morning when I'm popping ibuprofen trying to get rid of my headache."

"Ibuprofen for one of your hangovers must be like using a blow dryer to melt an iceberg. I've seen how plastered you can get."

"Look, I'm just waiting for someone or something to cut down for."

"Are you even hearing what you're saying? How about cutting down for yourself? Or maybe even for another chance with Arthur? Would you consider it if he were single again?"

"I don't know." Jeremy took his fresh cocktail from Beverly. "After Arthur sent me away *for my own good*, it's like my life switched from color to black and white—like the ending of *The Wizard of Oz.*" He knocked back the first of his vodka. "And it's taken me a long time to recover from it. What if he did that to me again?"

"I think you guys are too intertwined to ever have that happen again."

"Intertwined?"

"Have you ever thought about your karmic connection?"

Jeremy rolled his eyes.

"I'm serious! You guys had this immediate bonding, you went from mentor-mentee to lovers, and here you are four years after splitting up and you're *still* talking about him? Why don't you e-mail him about his note, even if it's only to find out what he has to say?"

"Because I don't know if I could ever trust him again."

"Oh, come on—"

"I'm serious! Arthur and I both felt this incredible passion for each other and we made amazing love twice, but then he threw me aside because I'm only nineteen? What kind of a man does that and runs off with some guy named Julie?"

"One who's scared, and who loved you so much that he'd rather see you happy with someone else than unhappy with him."

"*Scared.*" Jeremy laughed, his eyes glazing over. "Let's not forget that, unlike me, Arthur got *exactly* what he asked for." Jeremy clacked his glass onto the bar top and spilled some of his drink onto his wrist. "And if what Arthur demanded wasn't what he wanted, that's his problem to keep him up at night, not mine. I've got my own problems to keep me awake."

"You sure do." Carlo slid off the stool and stood up straight. "Come on, baby. Let's get us a table and some food. You're gonna need to sober up. *Fast.*"

CHAPTER

eleven

How wonderful to finally meet you," Lazzaro told Carmella, "and to see where your son got his remarkable beauty. But how can you possibly be old enough to have given birth to him?"

"You flatter like a gigolo down to his last euros," Carmella told him in her smoky contralto. "How were your travels here?"

Lazzaro scooted himself up against the pillows into a sitting position while straightening the covers around his waist, keenly aware of his nakedness beneath the sheets. "Luxurious and restful," he replied sarcastically. "I must tell you, it's been a long time since I've awoken with a strange woman in my bedroom."

Carmella half-lidded her eyes. "Because they are usually strange men?"

"The men are usually *in* my bed, not across from it . . . *usually.* So you're the famous Carmella Montes." He reached up and ran his fingers through his hair, at the same time giving his ample bicep a flex.

"And you are the infamous Lazzaro Sforza, wanted—or so my son tells me—for questioning in the murder of Francesco Sforza, your father."

Lazzaro dipped his head. "In the flesh."

"So I see." Her eyes drifted over his form. "You're even more handsome in person than those pictures Tristan showed me on the Internet." She peered at him, raising an eyebrow. "Quite beautiful, to be frank: body by Michelangelo and face by Jacques-Louis David. You must have left behind you a dozen broken hearts in each time zone."

"Actually, I am saving Asia for my forties."

"Ha!" Carmella threw back her head and laughed. Then she leveled her gaze at him. "My son said I should speak with you. He tells me you are desperate."

"Did he explain my circumstances?"

"He did."

"Might you be willing to help me?"

Carmella smiled. "Desperate men are my specialty."

"Is your specialty helping them . . . or creating them?"

"Both." She rose up from the chaise, ambled over to the bed, and sat down on the mattress. "Tell me what happened." She leaned in. "When did all this trouble start? Tell me from the beginning."

"My mother," Lazzaro began, "was a Bolshoi ballerina who injured herself and was forced into prostitution to survive; she met my father who remembered her from the ballet and began an affair with her."

"Before you continue, will you please enlighten me about your father?"

"My family's ancestors can be traced far back before the Renaissance, but their fortune had long ago been lost to the Church and taxes, and was finally rebuilt through shipping."

"Like the Onassis family in Greece. Please go on."

"After my mother gave birth to me, she soon discovered how unseemly it was to raise her son in the midst of such a shameful profession, so she took her meager savings and bought us passage to Venice to find my father. She met with him privately, showed him photographs of me, and explained to him that she only wanted enough support to keep me and herself clothed and housed and fed, and in turn she promised never to disclose his fathering me, out of respect to the marriage my father enjoyed with his wife.

"My father doubted her story—as would any man in his position. With a whore for a mother, he argued, it was possible that I could be any garbage man's son. She became angry and threatened him with exposure, with blackmail. That night after she went out for bread, she never returned to the tiny room she'd rented for us, and her body was—"

"—Let me guess," Carmella interrupted, reciting her words in a sing-song manner, "discovered floating in a canal. She'd been shot in the back of the head and you were presented to the family as a street rat in need of a home. And after you grew to manhood and discovered what he'd done to your mother, you were so filled with grief that you sought revenge and killed him when the time was right." Her face was a sad mask, but then she sat up straight, her features steeled. "Now tell me what really happened. If I am to help, I need to know the entire truth. That story was lies upon lies."

Lazzaro studied the sheets before him, and then looked up. "How did you know?"

"I recognize that plot from an old movie," Carmella chuckled, "a black-and-white melodrama circa 1940. Wooden actors opposite forgotten actresses; too many raincoats and fedoras. Are you truly incapable of original thought?"

Lazzaro's features took on a hard, wicked edge. "I will kill Tristan with my bare hands should you ever betray me."

"Of this I have no doubt," she murmured. "But I want the truth. Otherwise I cannot help."

He sighed, his mouth a grim line. "Francesco Sforza smuggled narcotics all over Europe and the Near East—designer hallucinogenic drugs with chemical formulas altered to avoid drug laws and prosecution. He sent me to the United States to be his liaison there, and we are only now establishing a foothold in China."

"You did not murder your father only to overtake his little drug business," Carmella accused, raising one perfectly manicured finger. "Designer hallucinogens can be made anywhere, by anyone. There is little money in it, so there must be more to your story. And you will tell me, otherwise I cannot help you; after all, patricide is considered an unforgivable sin—unless," she laughed, "you are an ancient Roman."

"Francesco was actually my *adoptive* father."

Carmella smiled. "I am relieved."

"This information could send me to prison for life. Why should I trust you?"

"Because you are desperate and you have no choice. But more importantly, Tristan loves you . . . and I would sooner tap-dance barefoot on razor blades than watch my son return to the misery of his loneliness. I give you my word as Tristan's mother."

Carmella locked his eyes, and he saw she spoke the truth.

"Francesco . . ." Lazzaro hesitated, ". . . was also head of a large sex tourism ring that operates in Turkey, Hungary, Romania, Serbia, the Czech Republic, Slovakia and even Slovenia—"

"Now we are getting somewhere."

"—and since he is dead I am the operation's rightful heir; I have been his right hand for years."

"In more ways than one, I imagine . . ." Carmella muttered.

"But because I am wanted in questioning for his murder, I cannot emerge to claim my empire until a plan is in place to prove my innocence. In the meantime our operations are floundering, and a power struggle between my rivals has begun." He leaned forward and grabbed her wrist. "If I do not soon claim what is mine—what I have worked so hard for—it will be seized by someone else!"

"Your father did not provide for this possibility? He did not name a second-in-command who would support you?"

Lazzaro glanced away. "Not exactly."

"This is not how an elder statesman bequeaths the business he has been building his entire life! *Do not lie to me!*"

Lazzaro crossed his arms over his bare chest. "No one else knows this."

"Tell me."

"Last I saw my father, he had traveled to Los Angeles to see a specialist who told him his heart was failing. He advised me that he was withdrawing from our businesses and . . . had named a successor other than me."

"Why?"

"He said I had proven myself irresponsible: too many drugs, too many lovers, too much money squandered at casinos. As a result, he found a more worthy and intelligent heir whom he was in the process of adopting."

"Were his accusations true?"

"Not at all," Lazzaro lied. "I believe he was charmed into making this decision."

"By whom?"

"I will get to that. But after I made up my mind to poison him, I asked Jeremy to take me to see my father on our way to the airport; there I dropped the Sueño Gris into his green tea. I knew he would not survive it; an overdose of this drug can cause almost instantaneous death even in a strong young man. Then I flew to Europe hoping his death would appear to be of natural causes—he was old and frail—but his autopsy revealed this drug in his system."

"And you did not anticipate this autopsy?"

"I came to understand that in the United States when an elderly person dies of what appear to be natural causes they do not perform an autopsy unless it is requested."

"But an autopsy *was* requested—most likely by the man who was in line to succeed him and supplant you," Carmella guessed. "And who is this new successor? Could he now be under suspicion of Francesco's murder instead of you, since he had more to gain from his death?"

"He is someone I knew once: a truly evil man named Olivier who is not only my former lover but who also sold me that rotting beachside chateau I then sold to Jeremy Tyler. I've heard he is now staying somewhere in Armenia and was nowhere near Los Angeles at the time of Francesco's murder, so it would be impossible to prove him culpable."

"Where did you go once you were named a suspect?"

"I fled to Turkey, to Akhisar, purchased a rusty Fiat, and traveled to Fethiye in the hills where no one might look for me until more time would pass and I could move to a larger city. Eventually I made my way to Lastovo in Croatia, where I worked as cook and server in a small seaside restaurant; there I met a wealthy man with a yacht who promised me passage, for a steep price, here to Greece." He spread out his muscular arms, Leonardo da Vinci's *Vitruvian Man* in bed. "And here I am."

"You never told me how you came to meet Francesco Sforza. The circumstances of him adopting you."

Lazzaro looked out onto the darkened landscape beyond the windows. "My mother *was* Russian but my father was a Turk, and they were both killed in a highway accident. My mother was driving drunk. When I was but thirteen years old, Francesco took me from the orphanage and I became one of his boy whores. For old men, young men; old women, young women; anyone who would pay for my company. Eventually I became the favorite of his clientele, and this is why he adopted me: to keep me close and under his precise control. He was truly an evil man."

Carmella dropped slowly onto the bed to pose Cleopatra-style, propped up on one elbow. "Tell me more about your 'sex tourism.' How does it work?"

"Francesco finds young women and men—teenagers—who are pretty, naïve, and desperate. Then he has talented people with sophisticated equipment create counterfeit credentials for these victims making them appear of legal age, but his clients know they are human contraband—and if anyone should begin investigating his enterprises too closely, there is almost limitless money paid for their cooperation and silence."

Carmella pondered his dilemma. "Perhaps your best chance to end this situation is to come forward for questioning and take what the Americans call a 'plea bargain': you will testify that your father had abused you *horribly* for years and you took action to prevent his harming other children."

"I cannot do that without killing the Sforza enterprises and incriminating myself."

Carmella pushed herself up from the bed. "Then I'll see if I can conjure anything to help you, but in the meantime you should keep yourself well hidden—even if that means hidden in a well."

"But I need more money to live and to hide . . . otherwise I will hang!"

"They don't really *hang* anyone anymore—except in the barbaric Middle East," Carmella replied. "Tell me about your former lover, the one who drove you to the airport. What was his name?"

"Jeremy Tyler."

"He is wealthy?"

"His family is very wealthy, but Jeremy is near poverty—thanks to me."

"Did he have any involvement in the plot to kill your father?"

"No."

"But Jeremy drove you to the yacht, and then to the airport afterward . . . he was there the night your father was murdered. Could you convince the police he was responsible for your father's death?"

"But he had no motive."

Carmella sat down on the bed once more. "Has he been arrested for anything?"

"Drunk driving, as I read in one of the blogs that feature news from Ballena Beach." Lazzaro grinned. "Quite recently." He looked at Carmella and locked his hands behind his head, flexing his biceps and squeezing his abs. "What are you considering?"

"If I am able to conjure a way to get you out of this mess, you will give me one-third of your earnings once you are in your rightful place of power. Yes?"

Lazzaro paused. "I will," he said at last. "But how will you do this?"

"The Americans have a saying," Carmella began, eyes narrowed, "*guilty beyond a shadow of doubt*. All we need now is to find a way to cast that shadow onto someone other than yourself." She leered at him. "But in the meantime you should put on some clothes and come down for your evening meal before I undress and join you in that bed." She shot him a lascivious smile. "You might think me a woman beyond my prime, but I've been told I fuck like a man."

Lazzaro matched her leer and pulled the sheets lower to reveal more of his muscled torso. "And I am *fully* a man," he said, his soft baritone filling the room, "but I've been told I make love with the sensitivity of a woman."

Carmella bent down and inched her lips forward until her mouth breathed upon his. "You'll have to show me how a bull like you achieves that."

Then she snapped the sheets off him so he was completely exposed.

She looked down.

"My goodness." Her fingertips traced feathery circles on his sculpted, iron-like thighs. "No wonder Tristan missed you so."

"You cannot tell him about this," Lazzaro murmured, his eyes closing from the pleasure. "Just as you cannot mention one word about the drugs or my other . . . *endeavors*."

"What are a few more secrets to keep from him?" she asked, and then moistened his lips with a flick of her tongue.

CHAPTER

twelve

Arthur's cell phone rang atop the kitchen counter, and he looked down to read the screen: Margo.

He put down Bingham's bowl and snatched the device. "Hey! You're back in town?"

"Got in this morning," Margo replied. "But this time I hid my jewelry in my purse, took an Ambien with my martini, and slept the entire way. Why did it take me all these years of flying to discover what puts me out at home also works at thirty-thousand feet?"

"How was New York?" He reached down to give Bingham's head a calming pat; the dog had been expecting his meal and was now stamping his feet while staring imploringly up at Arthur.

"Maddening," she replied. "It was possibly the worst Fashion Week I've ever seen: Some kid hot-glues wallaby fur onto a pair of translucent palazzo pants and suddenly he's the next *enfant terrible*. I *so* miss Alexander McQueen—and Dior, for that matter. When can I see you?"

"How about dinner tonight?"

"Well . . ."

Arthur hesitated. "I have news."

"Good news, I hope?"

He made his way over to the dog food container in the pantry and scooped out some kibble. "Maybe, possibly, good news."

"There's nothing I can't get out of. How about seven? Stanley's?"

Arthur glanced at his watch and then scanned the condo, still topsy-turvy a week after Jess's hurried exit. He'd intended to devote the remaining hours until bedtime to putting things away and organizing his suddenly spacious closet. *It can wait.* "I'll get there as close to seven as I can. Jess is gone, by the way."

"Oh, I'm sorry," she told him obligingly.

"No you're not. And neither am I."

"You OK?"

"I'm OK, but that's not my news—let's save it for martini hour, OK?"

"Can't *wait* to hear what's happening. See you sevenish."

Arthur ended the call smiling.

::::::::::

Stanley's was a well-established restaurant on Ventura Boulevard in Sherman Oaks, one of Los Angeles's more upscale communities. The clientele was professional, lively, and generally over thirty, so the food was reliably good and the service was usually top-notch.

And there were some handsome waiters serving there.

After arriving and then leaving his Jeep with Habib, the friendly valet, Arthur hurried inside.

Margo was sitting at the crowded bar with an empty stool next to her and two martinis before her: one with olives for him, the other with a lemon twist. She caught sight of him and her faced bloomed into a delighted smile.

He wove his way through the other patrons to her, and they embraced.

"You're beautiful as ever," Arthur told Margo, meaning it; her blonde hair grazed her shoulders, the black T-shirt under her blazer hugged her breasts perfectly, and her understated makeup was flawless. "How did you stop time at thirty-five?"

"By divorcing my husband." She leaned in and kissed him lightly on the lips. "And you're handsome as ever, my Ken Doll. How was your week?"

"Good." He slid out his stool and hoisted himself up onto it. "*Really* good. Been waiting long?"

"Just got here. Now tell me *everything.*"

Arthur took the first sip of his martini. "As I mentioned, Jess is gone so I won't need to bore you with that drama anymore."

"I'll drink to that," Margo replied, lifting her glass and taking an airy sip. "Was it ugly?"

"If you're asking if there was a final blowup, the answer is 'no.' Apparently we'd perfected the art of fizzling out."

"Then what's your news?" She stared at him, her honey-colored eyes searching his face. "Don't tell me—"

Arthur grinned. "Yep."

"When did you see him? What's going on?"

"I haven't seen him—*yet.* I fled the house early on the morning Jess was moving out so I wouldn't have to witness Jess eviscerating our life together, and I took Bingham to the beach and ran into—you'll never guess—the ogress known as Katharine Tyler."

"*No.*"

"And there she was walking this golden retriever named Skipper, who's Jeremy's abandoned dog." He sipped more of his cocktail. "Of course I was reluctant to talk with her, but she was *almost* friendly and I was curious, and she said she needed to talk to me about something serious and would I mind following her and Skipper back to her lair on the cliff."

Margo wrinkled her nose. "What was it like being there again?"

"Sad—but not terrible. You know, aside from the ending where I screamed at her and got fired and almost drove my car off the pier, I had some really good times there. And you'll never guess who Katharine's personal assistant is."

"Carlo."

"You're not much fun."

Margo laughed. "We've been friends too long. What's up with Jeremy?"

"Well . . . he's kept busy. He got kicked out of USC for beating up some jerk; he's descended into alcoholism and drug abuse and sex-addiction; he's been arrested for DUI; and he's fallen under the spell of an evil Svengali boyfriend who swindled him out of his trust money, fled to Europe, and then vanished."

Margo grimaced. "Not exactly the happily-ever-after you were hoping for. Please tell me you're determined to let Jeremy be someone else's problem."

"And what makes you think I would do that?"

"Because the very, very, *very* last thing you need is more heartache. Or more stress."

"But it's *Jeremy.*" Arthur searched her face for any glimmer of sympathy but found none. *Change the subject.* "Do you want to eat here or get a table?"

"Actually . . . I'm glued to my barstool wondering why you would want to get involved with such a train wreck, especially now. You're finally free of one toxic relationship, so you're gearing up to get started on another? Is there a trampoline in that frying pan of yours?"

"You really think Jeremy's toxic?"

"You just told me he's a drug addict, a sex addict, he's got a hot temper, *and* he's been kicked out of school and ruined his finances. Sounds to me like he's got enough drama in his life for the entire cast of a bad reality show."

"But this might be my only chance to make things right with him, Margo—and to see if what I've dreamed of for years could actually work."

"I'm suddenly getting the idea that there'll be no reasoning with you." Sighing, Margo settled back into her barstool. "So. What happened after you spoke with Katharine?"

"She gave me his address and I drove over to his house and dropped a note into his mailbox asking him to contact me."

"What's the house like?"

"Kind of—" Arthur thought for a moment, "—Addams Family meets Manson Family."

"Did he respond to your note yet?"

"Unfortunately . . . *yes*. Sent me an e-mail telling me to stay away." Arthur picked the garnish out from his martini and slid one of the olives into his mouth.

"Sounds like he has better sense than another man I know." She signaled the bartender. "Kristoff, can we get some menus, please?"

Kristoff began rustling beneath the bar's counter.

"He's still angry at me. But I'll see that he gets over it."

"And *why* would you try to accomplish this?"

"That's what I need you to tell me," Arthur replied.

Margo laughed, shaking her head, and then Kristoff handed over the menus. After he turned away, Margo asked, "How did you respond to his 'stay away' e-mail?"

"I haven't done anything yet. What would you say?"

"Thanks for the memories."

"I'm serious. You know how much this means to me."

Margo sighed again. "Against my better judgment, I'll offer you this advice: write whatever's in your heart—or better yet, forget the e-mails and keep going back to his house until you can actually speak with him, man to man."

Arthur's features softened. "Do you think I should tell him about my—"

"The sooner the better. Let him know he's not the only poor soul who's had to overcome a crisis. Now, what are you having?"

"My usual chicken piccata. You?"

"Probably the hamburger, same as always." Margo quickly perused the menu and then slapped it down on the bar top. "Hamburger. So when will you try to see him?"

"Probably . . . tomorrow during lunchtime—if I can steal away. My clients have been especially crazy lately. You know, even though four years have passed, when I was walking down his driveway my heart was pounding—I was so excited, so *thrilled* that I might actually see him again. I felt like—"

"A recovering addict tiptoeing down crack alley?"

Arthur laughed.

"Listen," Margo settled a gentle hand on his forearm, "if it's *bashert*, or meant to be, it'll all work out. And maybe this is happening so you can help him win all these battles he's fighting."

Arthur smiled wistfully. "Who knows, maybe he could even help me win mine."

"Speaking of, when's your next big checkup?"

"Just had another MRI, so I've got a six-week reprieve." Arthur swirled his toothpick. "But I'm trying not to think about it."

"You'll be fine." She patted his wrist. "It's been almost a year since the radiation, right?"

"A year ago next month on the tenth," Arthur said. "Not that I'm keeping track."

"I'm relieved to see that all your hair grew back so quickly," Margo told him. "And because you've been working out like the Marine you'll always be, you're the picture of manly health. Jeremy will double over with lust when he sees you."

"But the last thing I want is to finally reconcile with him and scare him off with this."

"You need to be honest with him. Look"—Margo squeezed Arthur's hand—"even though it's never worked for me, I still believe in the old *for better or for worse* adage, just as I believe in fate, or predestination, or whatever you call it. Remember how you and I met, at Danny's funeral? Both of us sobbing by the punchbowl, all those years ago? And here we are still."

"Danny, Danny, Danny," Arthur said. "So much has happened and so much time has gone by that I forget how much I loved him. But even out of a tragic death like his came some good—our friendship. So certain things must be *bashert.*" Arthur gave her an adoring smile. "You know, if I'd been straight, maybe that *for better or for worse* business might have worked for us."

"You don't have to tell me, Mr. Ken Doll. Are you ready to order?"

"Suddenly, I'm starving." Arthur unwrapped his napkin and draped it onto his lap. "And I'm dying to hear all about those wallaby-fur palazzo pants you bought in New York."

CHAPTER

thirteen

How is it that you have no hair here?" Carmella traced her fingers over Lazzaro's buckled abs and heroic pectorals. "Are you so vain that you shave your chest?"

"I have always been this way," he answered and then yawned; he was still drowsy after dozing off. "And I do not remember receiving any complaints before now."

Her lips opened into a ruby smile. "And you have none still."

Lazzaro surveyed the flawlessness of Carmella's features, her caramel skin and firm breasts, and the way her black tresses were gathered into a casual knot. "And how is it that after fucking like a man you can still be such an exquisite woman?"

"I, too, have always been this way." She drew herself up to lean against the stacked pillows. "Would you be a love and get a Sobranie from the case in that drawer?" She pointed. "There should be a lighter in there, as well."

Lazzaro opened the night table drawer, pulled out a cigarette from the ornate silver case, placed it between her lips, and lit it.

Carmella took the case from him and placed it on her own night table. "Tell me *all* about yourself," she said, exhaling smoke. "I want to know everything about you, especially your past."

"I hope you realize I cannot be your lover."

"You showed me differently," Carmella replied. "Twice—or was it three times? In"—she glanced at her Cartier atop the bedside table—"two hours."

"What I mean is there is no chance for a relationship between us."

"Do you think me stupid? You are my son's beloved; all he spoke of while you were away were his plans for when you returned." She drew on her cigarette. "Tristan might forgive me for sleeping with you, but he would never speak to me again if he thought I was after your heart. He must be pacing the floor at this moment waiting for me to leave you."

"And I don't wish to keep him waiting any longer," Lazzaro replied, "so if you will please leave me I can shower and go to him . . . not that I have the desire at this moment to give him what he is craving."

"Before you go, will you tell me something?"

"That depends."

"How do you manage your endeavors—the Sueño Gris trade and the sex tourism—without getting caught?"

"I cannot tell you."

"But you need me to keep you safe."

Lazzaro scanned the room, his vision touching upon the gilded dressing table, the moody baroque portrait over the washstand, the armoire with its icy beveled mirrors. "We have a network. People in several countries. Their identities are closely guarded, and each would die before revealing another's name. That is all I can say."

"Even to me? We are entering into a partnership."

"You must first get me out of this mess." Lazzaro looked at her. "Have you any new ideas?"

"One I'm considering," Carmella replied, "that hinges on your guarantee that my son will be shielded from *everything*. If you and I, or any of your network, are ever caught, he must not be affected."

"That is not a problem," Lazzaro lied.

"Why should I trust you?"

"Because there is nothing to be gained by sharing any of this with Tristan. He would only be in my way. Besides, I love him."

"Did you also *love* Jeremy Tyler?"

"I have a business to operate. I am not a monster."

Carmella laughed. "I wonder if your late father would agree with you."

"Do you really believe I have no conscience?"

Carmella leaned up and kissed his cheek. "Said the murderer who distributes potentially fatal drugs around the world . . . *and sells children for sex.*"

"Young men and women, not children! In many cultures, once a girl has her period she is eligible for marriage! But you would rather see her working for a bowl of rice and then buried alive in some factory collapse? Or might you agree that she is better off provided with adequate food and clean water and healthcare and lovely surroundings where she is shown affection for a living wage?"

"You rationalize like an American politician," Carmella teased. "And you need not convince me; I am willing to join you in your endeavors, remember? And I . . . *think* I may already have the beginnings of a plan to ensure your safety."

"What do you propose?"

"You must promise me again that Tristan will be safe."

"You have my promise."

"Then let's discuss my plan over dinner." Carmella reached over, yanking the top sheet off Lazzaro once more. "But first you will shower. Quickly, because I'm guessing it's nearly time for that extravagant meal my son has been fretting over since this morning"—she raised her nose and sniffed the air—"and *you* reek of sex."

CHAPTER

fourteen

Excited like a boy on Christmas morning, Arthur awoke before the sun and before his alarm clock.

In the darkened bedroom he drew his legs from the tangled sheets, stepped over Bingham's humped-up form on the floor, and went into the kitchen to switch on the coffeemaker ahead of its preprogrammed time.

The first songbirds of morning were already tuning up outside his kitchen window as Arthur stood watching the coffeemaker drizzle and snore. Minutes later he poured himself a mug, hurried through his shower, took his pills, and ate two mozzarella sticks. Finally dressed, he retrieved Bingham's jingling leash. "Ready to go find Jeremy?"

Bingham, grinning, spun a circle and galloped to the front door.

With the lavender sky glowing and the sun tucked under the eastern horizon, they exited the condo, got into Arthur's Jeep, and began driving toward Ballena Beach.

Instead of parking near Jeremy's mailbox and making his way down the drive as before, Arthur continued up the road toward a path between two properties that led to the shoreline from the highway. He parked and began leading Bingham, who tested Arthur's patience by stopping to sniff each kelp bulb and mussel shell and cigarette butt and twig littering the sand that sloped down toward the water's edge.

Finally edging the waves, the pair began jogging toward Jeremy's ramshackle mansion.

At last, Arthur spotted the chateau's majestic slate-tiled roofline looming over its more humble neighboring cottages.

He slowed Bingham to a canter and drew up—panting—in front of the house. Looking up to watch a squadron of gulls drift overhead, he also scrutinized the building for any signs of life—but there were none.

Probably still asleep, or maybe he's not even home.

Should I climb up and peek inside?

What if he's got some guy with him?

But before he could conclude what to do next, Bingham began whimpering and straining his leash.

Arthur looked over and discovered why.

Huddled in the sand beyond reach of the sliding surf sat a bundled man. Arthur hadn't noticed him at first because his gray sweatshirt blended into the gloomy beach, and his head was down, his arms encircling his knees.

Could it be?

Bingham began pulling with the strength of an Iditarod sled team.

"Bingham!" Arthur pulled back on the leash. "Heel!"

The dog ignored him, straining harder.

Arthur allowed Bingham to drag him toward the man, and with each step closer, the man's identity clarified like a movie screen image twisting into focus.

Bingham's tags jingled, Jeremy wrenched his head over his shoulder, and their eyes caught.

A glimmer of a smile, and then a hard look steeled Jeremy's features as he looked away.

Whimpering, Bingham made the leash a tightrope, so Arthur let go.

The dog scrambled, feet kicking up gusts of sand. Then upon reaching Jeremy he tucked himself under the crook of his arm, and Jeremy kissed his head.

Arthur drew up and stopped. "Dogs are amazing judges of character."

Jeremy rubbed Bingham behind his ears. "People should be more like dogs." He looked up at Arthur. "Who's this?"

Arthur did what he could to hide his shock at Jeremy's appearance: puffy eyes, blotchy skin, and his once square jaw now indistinct. He'd been transformed—in a scant four years—from age nineteen to his early-thirties.

"Name's Bingham."

"Bingham?"

"After our gay hero who died on September Eleventh. Remember the hot rugby player?"

"Yeah." Jeremy petted Bingham as the dog nosed under his armpit. "I remember now."

"Have a second to talk?"

Jeremy coughed a short, bitter laugh. "If you came here to lecture me, I'm sure it'll take longer than a second—so the answer is *no*."

"I'm not here to lecture you."

"Then why are you here—again?"

"I heard you're having trouble. And I need to clear the air."

"Does your, um, *boyfriend* know you're here?"

"Jess moved out a week ago. It didn't work out."

Jeremy looked out to sea. "That's too bad."

"And on the morning the movers came," Arthur continued, "I went to the beach to walk Bingham and clear my head, and I ran into Katharine—with Skipper. She's a beauty, and Bingham loved her."

"Clearly you're referring to Skipper," Jeremy replied dully. "Did Katharine enjoy telling you everything I've fucked up, and what a bitter disappointment I am?"

"Not everything. Carlo filled me in on the rest."

Jeremy wrapped his arms around his knees again, scanning the ocean. "Didn't you get my e-mail? Thought I was pretty clear."

"You were."

"So . . . it's not about what Jeremy wants, it's about what Arthur wants: Jeremy falls in love with Arthur so Arthur vanishes, but then Jeremy hates Arthur so Arthur shows up, uninvited. I guess it just takes me a long time to figure things out." He laughed. "Stupid me!"

"Old buddy—"

"Hey"—Jeremy held up his palm, eyes searching Arthur's face—"I'm sorry. I don't hate you. You just . . . caught me drowning in Lake Self-Pity. I appreciate that you're wanting to help. But considering I've done such a stellar job of screwing up my life, I'm the only one who can make things right. As they say, 'You break it, you buy it.'" He laughed. "And *booooy* did I break it."

"Do you feel like talking?"

Jeremy gave him the side-eye. "What's there to say? I've turned into a . . . drunk, bloated . . . broke . . . drug-addicted college dropout and cybersex addict." A choked laugh. "Wow. Sounds bad when you say it like that." When Arthur didn't laugh, he went on. "Good thing your secret agent instincts kicked in and you leapt off the Jeremy train before the trestle blew up."

"I never said I didn't want to be a part of your life. You stopped returning my calls, my e-mails . . . so eventually I got the message and moved on."

"You mean 'moved in.' With Jesus."

Arthur crouched down in the sand. "His name's Jess—not that it matters. Anymore."

"So. Your man ran off, and you miraculously ran into Katharine, who convinced you to work your magic." Jeremy paused. "Tell me. If . . . if you and Jess hadn't broken up and Katharine hadn't sounded the alarm, where would you be right now? Breakfast at the Rectory or the warehouse sale at Pottery Barn?"

"I—"

"And how much did you tell Jess about me? Did I even figure into your breakup, or was it just boredom mixed with twin midlife crises?"

"Jeremy, I don't know if I'd be here if Jess and I were still together, but I believe some things happen, at *just the right time,* for a reason—and sometimes it takes a while before we discover what those reasons are. Yes, you *did* figure into the equation. Jess knew all too well how I feel about you. By the end, he said as much . . . that I'd always love you more than I'd ever love him. Which is true—and not because he was anything but a terrific guy. But what keeps me awake is that *you* don't know how much I love you, and that's the only reason why I'm here . . . on your terms this time, not mine."

Jeremy looked up at a lone seagull tracing wobbly air circles, while Arthur crouched mute and still. Waiting.

"My knees are killing me," Arthur said at last. "I should let you go." He pushed himself upright. "Thanks for hearing me out—"

"I've waited so long to hear you say that," Jeremy said, wiping his eyes on his sweatshirt sleeve. "No matter how nice you tried to make it for me at the time—the old *it's not you, it's me* routine—I figured I just wasn't what you wanted. So I spent a lot of time trying to figure out what it was I was missing—or had too much of. But now, hearing you finally say what I've dreamed you'd say, I'm just feeling . . . kinda numb."

"I get it. Really."

Jeremy peered up at him. "I've spent years being angry with you so I wouldn't miss you. So maybe the anger has . . . well, kinda Velcroed onto my heart. I'm sorry."

"I'm the one who's sorry, and I'm serious about wanting to help. If nothing else, to go back to being the guy who taught you how to drive and how to not overcook the pasta. Maybe I could be a shoulder for you to lean on—or punch."

Jeremy tried and failed to raise a smile. "Like I said, I appreciate that you're here, and I know you're probably hurting because of your breakup, but I'm . . . I don't know what I am."

"If there's—" Arthur stopped talking, suddenly realizing there was nothing further he might say that would make any difference. Now it was up to Jeremy.

Then something occurred to him.

"I've been trying to imagine what it must've taken for you to give away Skipper," he said, "and now I think I know. You gave away Skipper because you didn't want to neglect her the way your mother neglected you. And because you thought you were headed for a tragic ending."

Jeremy looked up at Arthur.

"But you'll come out of this. I know it. Just like I know this fog will eventually burn off, I know you'll come out a stronger man—with or without me or Katharine or Carlo."

"How?"

"Because you're too much like your dad to wind up like your mom," Arthur replied and clapped the side of his thigh. "C'mon, Bingham-boy."

Bingham scampered after him, and Jeremy—feeling drained, his emotions deadlocked—watched man and beast labor through the sand until they disappeared around a bend.

CHAPTER

fifteen

While refueling his Jeep at the 76 gas station on the corner of Sunset Boulevard and Laurel Street, Arthur pulled out his phone to check for any updates.

He found new contact info from an old client and a security query from someone new.

A message from his liability insurance carrier.

One Facebook notification.

Two junk e-mails.

Still nothing from Jeremy?

He pushed the device back into his jeans pocket and went back to watching the numbers change on the gas pump's digital readout.

What's it going to take?

And because he was uncharacteristically late this morning getting to his office—due to an early phone call from his mother—Arthur only allowed the meter to climb to twenty bucks before releasing the trigger on the pump handle . . . but then some vague, silent instinct urged him to continue filling his tank, so he squeezed the handle again and watched the numbers climb into the thirties and then the forties.

He switched it off just after fifty.

:::::::::

It was Friday, and Arthur had spent the bulk of his morning putting out yet another fire caused by a drunk actor, one of his least favorite celebrity clients, who'd pushed a paparazzo down the steps of a nightclub and then was arrested for assault. The actor's obnoxious attorneys were already churning a stink because Arthur's employee-bodyguard had allowed the photographer to get close enough to the actor for the son-of-a-bitch to push, so Arthur had put every other task on hold to interview sources, review the police report, and return phone calls.

Now that it was well after noon, Arthur decided to head out from his office on Robertson Boulevard for a quick salad and a chance to catch up on some unanswered e-mails.

He'd just started his Jeep when his Bluetooth rang: Margo.

"Hey!" Arthur notched the transmission lever into reverse. "What's going on?"

"Quick question," Margo's voice blasted from his sound system. "What kind of car does Jeremy drive?"

Arthur began backing out of his parking space. "I saw a Jaguar at the place where he lives, but I don't know if it was his. Why?"

"A black one? A convertible?"

"Yes!" Arthur hit his brakes. "Have you seen him? Where are you?"

"I'm pulling into the Chateau Marmont to meet Bobbi for lunch, and this guy who sort of looks like Jeremy just dropped off his car at the valet."

"Are you going in?" A car horn beeped behind Arthur, so he checked his mirror and saw a gay couple—heavyset, bearded, matching baseball caps—in a red Miata waiting for his space. He put the Jeep in drive and depressed the gas pedal.

"I'll call you," Margo replied.

"What're you going to do?"

"Help Bobbi find a dress for her daughter's wedding."

"That's not what I mean!"

"I love you and I'll call you later. Bye now!"

:::::::::

Margo pulled her black Bentley Continental GT up the steep, cobbled ramp of Chateau Marmont's driveway and handed off her keys to the valet, and then stepped up the few stairs to the ancient Valentino-era elevator, which lifted her to the lobby level.

Once the doors parted she looked around trying to locate the young man she'd seen, while hoping he'd gone into the restaurant instead of up into the tower or off into the secluded cottages and bungalows to the east.

But he was nowhere in sight.

Oh well.

Margo shifted her focus to locating her lunch date—Bobbi.

Probably on the patio.

She passed the hostess podium and made her way through the gothic great room with its assemblage of ornate, overstuffed sofas and chairs and heavily carved tables and high-arched picture windows, but there appeared to be no sign of either her lunch date or the man-who-might-be-Jeremy.

She sat down at one of the tables, took out her phone, and waited.

"May I bring you something to drink?"

Margo looked up into the almond eyes of a statuesque young woman. "Iced tea. Please."

"It will be my pleasure." She smiled, turned, and stepped purposefully away.

Moments later Bobbi rounded the corner. They waved to each other, and Margo stood up to greet her.

"Been waiting long?" Bobbi asked as they embraced.

"Just got here."

They took their seats as the waitress appeared with Margo's iced tea.

"Sauvignon Blanc," Bobbi told her. "The house is fine." She turned to Margo, smiling brightly. "*How are you?*"

"On a mission—but first of all, are the colors *really* burgundy and apricot?"

"I know." Bobbi rolled her eyes. "The bridesmaids will look like some high school homecoming court. How about dark plum for me?"

Margo wrinkled her nose. "Aubergine is the nearest I ever get to plum."

"Good enough. You mentioned a mission."

"Did you happen to see a good-looking guy wearing a black T-shirt and jeans?"

"That describes every guy here . . . and most of the girls. Why?"

"I think I saw Arthur's Jeremy come in—oh my God, I think that's him." Margo tracked Jeremy as he made his way across the courtyard to a lounge chair under the high gothic colonnade and then sat down. "Oooh, and he's by himself."

"What's going on?" Bobbi whispered.

"I'll explain later. Just wait here, OK?" She scooted back her chair. "And order me a burger if the server comes—medium rare but not raw; no pickle, no onion, and a side of thousand island. Small salad with bleu cheese, no fries. I'm starving."

Margo began retracing her steps down the walkway, her mind trying to discern whether or not the young man matched the picture of Jeremy she dimly recalled from Arthur's photo collection. But as she drew nearer, she became neither more nor less certain.

Finally, she was standing next to him.

"Excuse me?" Margo asked, her voice as confident as it was apologetic.

Jeremy looked up just as the waitress placed his cocktail on the chair side table. "Yeah?"

"Are you Jeremy Tyler?"

He picked up his drink. "Unfortunately."

She held out her hand. "Margo."

Without releasing his right-hand grip on the drink he held out his left and clasped her fingers. "May I offer you a seat?" He motioned toward the chair next to him.

"Such charming manners." She folded herself down onto the chair. "It's refreshing."

"Actually, if I had any manners I'd have stood up before you sat," he laughed. "Do we know each other?"

"I feel like I know you," she said, straightening her posture. "Margo. Margo Selznik."

Jeremy settled back into his chair. "The famous Margo." He took a deeper sip. "Arthur's best friend that he inherited from Danny. I always wondered why he kept us separated."

She mirrored his smile. "Wives should never meet their husband's mistresses."

"So which was I? The wife or the mistress?"

"Well, I've never slept with him." Margo laughed. "So I must be the wife."

"What brings you here?"

"Perhaps fate—but actually, I'm meeting my friend Bobbi here and saw you and thought you looked familiar. It took me a moment, but then I figured out who you were."

"What can I do for you?"

"You can start by giving the only man I love a phone call."

"Why? Did your car break down?"

"I'm referring to Arthur."

"Yeah, I knew that. Why should I call him?"

"He believes he needs you in his life."

Jeremy thoughtfully jingled the ice cubes back and forth in his glass. "I'll think about it."

"And I'd like to go on record," Margo continued, "by telling you I am opposed to this."

"And your stake in this is?"

"None—other than my desire to see Arthur get what he *thinks* he wants. It seems clear to me that your priorities have been mislaid, along with your good judgment, and I don't want to see him buried by your self-inflicted avalanche of crises while attempting your rescue."

Jeremy put down his glass and crossed his arms over his chest. "It's comforting to know that so many people are familiar with my stupid decisions."

"Look." Margo moved in closer, her eyes searching his. "Arthur has suffered through the tragic death of one partner and the ruin of a relationship with another, and on top of operating a stressful business, the last thing he needs to worry about is someone who's hell-bent on destroying himself. Or have I been misinformed?"

"For your information, I'm meeting a Calvin Klein model here for lunch at one of the coolest places in LA—"

"As I was saying about mislaid priorities—"

"Shouldn't Arthur be the one to decide who he gets involved with—or throws away, in my case? You're sounding like someone's mother . . . or great aunt."

"You know," Margo began, leaning farther forward, "he didn't send you on your way to hurt you, or because there was someone else. Arthur wanted—and still wants—you and only you. And when he sent you off to grow up, he honestly thought he was doing the right thing *for you*. So why continue this silly grudge of yours?"

Jeremy sat back in his chair, feeling more content now that the vodka was taking effect. "Because of my mislaid good judgment, for which I am apparently famous?"

Margo looked over to see the waitress deliver their salads. *Speed this up*. "I may be wrong, but you seem miserable. My guess is you're lonely and you don't have many friends left. It's lunchtime and you're having a cocktail—which means you're not even looking for a job—and from what Arthur's told me, your shady boyfriend's vanished and your dog is living with your great aunt. But I think you should *definitely* go on ignoring Arthur and skipping along your yellow brick road to destruction, because it all seems to be working so very well for you both." She stood up from the chair and smiled. "I'm sorry to have bothered you." She held out her hand. "Have a *wonderful* day—but don't drink too much because I hear you're driving on a restricted license."

Jeremy looked down and began fiddling with his napkin. "Wait."

"You know, my friend Bobbi is waiting, and our food—"

"Please." He looked up at her, eyebrows raised. "Is he really that unhappy?"

Margo briefly considered enlightening Jeremy as to Arthur's health crisis of last year, but decided against it. "He's ached for you since the day he sent you away."

Jeremy sighed. "Look, I know what you're saying, but I can't stand the thought of going through that again." He scanned the crowd, suddenly hopeful that his lunch date wasn't coming after all. "Arthur was all I ever wanted, so it took me a while to learn how to live without him. But if I opened myself up again and he dumped me—even for another *noble* reason—I don't think I could handle it."

"And how well are you handling being apart from him now?"

Jeremy glanced down at the drink in his hand and looked back up at Margo.

"The universe will implode before Arthur lets you go again."

"But my life is a disaster. Why would he want to get involved with someone who's so screwed up?"

"Ask him yourself." She handed Jeremy a slip of paper with a phone number already scribbled on it. "Give him a call."

Jeremy looked at her, surprised. "I thought you were opposed to this?"

"Sometimes I like to be proven wrong." Margo smiled. "I should get back to Bobbi, but would you like to join us? You could probably use a burger, and"—she made an obvious scan of the room—"apparently your friend was the one with the broken-down car."

"I guess if he shows up I could still meet with him."

"So you'll join us?"

"Would it be OK?" Jeremy scooted back his chair. "I *hate* eating by myself."

"Come." She reached for his hand. "We've got so much to talk about."

CHAPTER

sixteen

Arthur, exhausted from both the labors of his day and waiting for a call from Margo that never came, shoved open his condo's door to find Bingham waiting for him, tail wagging and expression expectant.

"No, boy, I'm too tired."

Bingham growled playfully.

Arthur sighed. "OK then."

Bingham hula-danced his rear while following Arthur into the bedroom, where the man shed his work clothes in favor of some old jeans, his favorite sweatshirt, and his running shoes.

The delighted dog trotted off to wait for him by the front door.

:::::::::

An hour or so later, as Arthur was folding a load of laundry, his phone vibrated atop the nightstand. He picked it up and squinted at the screen, but he didn't recognize the number.

One of those asshole attorneys? "Art Blauefee speaking."

Silence. And then: "Um . . . it's—it's me," sputtered the faint voice. "Jeremy."

Arthur dropped the T-shirt from his hand onto the coverlet and sat on the edge of the bed. "I can't believe you actually called."

"I promised Margo I would."

"She can be rather persuasive. How are you?"

"Good," Jeremy replied. "Went out for happy hour but only had some sparkling water."

"Where'd you go?"

"The Rectory. Same old boring shit."

"I hate that place," Arthur said. "You need a chainsaw to cut through the attitude, but the only thing I arm myself with is a friendly smile. Stupid me. "

"Tell me about it."

"Sounds like you're in your car. Going someplace special?"

"Kinda. I'm, uh . . . headed outta town."

"Where're you headed—if you don't mind me asking?"

"The chalet," Jeremy replied. "Up at Lake Estrella. Remember?"

"How could I forget?" Arthur grabbed the T-shirt he'd dropped, fiddled with it, and then tossed it back onto the bed. "By yourself?"

"You know how I hate being alone—especially up there, after what happened with my dear Uncle Bill. His ghost roams the halls rattling chains and moaning for his gold pieces."

"Oh," Arthur said, deflated by the thought of Jeremy with yet another man. *Could he be going there with Carlo? No, he would've told me if it were Carlo.* "So what're you guys going up there for? Rest and relaxation or to do some work on the place?"

"Actually . . . Skipper's been complaining about the salt water at the beach, and she says she misses swimming in the lake. It's just the two of us, a trunk full of frozen pizzas from Trader Joe's, and my new laptop. I'm gonna . . . try to get my thoughts together. Long overdue. And if I can't do that, I'll write some filthy haikus."

Arthur felt his shoulders relax. "Sounds nice."

"So . . . what're you up to?"

"I'm still trying to get the condo back in shape after Jess left. I need to buy some furniture, but I just can't bring myself to do it yet, so I'm reorganizing the closets and cupboards. Really exciting stuff for a Friday night; I've discovered lots of orphaned Tupperware bowls I've got to find lids for."

"Too many bottoms and not enough tops," Jeremy laughed. "The story of my life. I hate to tear you away from your breathtaking evening."

"It's no trouble." Arthur laughed too, although he was momentarily embarrassed by the hint of giddiness in his voice.

More silence.

"Do . . . you . . . w-want to . . . come and join us?" Jeremy stammered. "You and Bingham?"

Arthur coughed. "You're joking."

"Actually . . . it was Skipper's idea. I think she's got a crush on that black dog of yours; he was all she could talk about on the way up here."

"As a matter of fact, Bingham was just telling me he's sick of the salt water, too—although you might want to warn Skipper that he has a thing for another dog we know named Princeton; I caught them recently perusing pictures of combat dogs online."

Jeremy giggled. "So what time do you think you can be up there?"

Arthur glanced at his watch. "About an hour to gather things and two-and-a-half hours driving up. How about by . . . oh, eight or nine, depending on traffic?"

"Did you already eat dinner?"

"I was just perusing my selection of miserable leftovers."

"Then I'll, uh, have something for you . . . but I can't promise anything amazing. I'm still a really bad cook—not like you."

"Jeremy," Arthur began but stopped himself. *Did Margo tell him?* "I don't get it; you made it pretty clear that you didn't want to see me again."

"Hold on, I've gotta pass this car."

Arthur heard the faint roar of an engine accelerating.

"OK," Jeremy continued, "Margo gave me lots to think about, so I think we should at least talk about stuff. And I—I could use your perspective . . . I've got a lot going on."

"That's very generous of you, considering my perspective caused us to not see each other for years."

"That was my fault too. But people can fix their mistakes. Right?"

"I sure hope so." Arthur paused. "Is there anything you need, or anything else I should know before getting on the road?"

Jeremy hesitated. "Only that . . . I've missed you. More than I thought I would."

Arthur closed his eyes as his memory rewound to their phone conversation they'd shared so many years ago. *Those same words.* "I've missed you too," he finally managed, his voice hoarse. "More than I thought I would, too."

⁝⁝⁝⁝⁝

Arthur spent the better part of an hour rummaging through the already disheveled condo gathering anything he might need for himself, for Bingham, and for his work should any pressing situations arise over the weekend; he assumed Jeremy had Internet access at the chalet, so communication with his employees and clients would be as simple as working from home.

He snatched some clothes and smashed them inside his overnight bag. After grabbing his meds from the fridge and filling a large Ziploc with Bingham's food and packing away his laptop, Arthur clipped Bingham's leash onto his collar, locked the condo's door behind them, and began making their way down to the parking garage with his kitchen garbage bag in his hand.

They crossed the garage floor to the dumpster, and as Arthur hefted the bag over the steel rims he noticed through the translucent white plastic—near the bottom—the lid to the Stouffer's Lasagna that had been his last meal with Jess.

My own archeological dig.

He dropped it in.

:::::::::

Sometime later, after traversing the highways of Los Angeles, Arthur transferred from the eastbound 210 freeway onto the steep and precipitous switchbacks that would deliver him to the Tylers' chalet at Lake Estrella.

The sun had settled below the horizon so he switched on his headlamps and glanced over his shoulder to check on Bingham, who was stretched across the Jeep's backseat dozing, nestled between Arthur's battered overnight bag and the groceries he'd hastily collected from his pantry and fridge.

Glad I put that extra gas in my tank.

At last he drove up the final rise, rounded a corner, and then coasted down toward the lake. And there it was: SHORELINE DRIVE.

He caught his eyes in the rearview mirror and smiled.

I'm doing this.

I am really doing this.

CHAPTER

seventeen

The gates were open, so Arthur slowly piloted his Jeep down the long gravel driveway—its oversized knobby tires munching pebbles—and pulled in behind Jeremy's sleek black Jaguar. He was surprised to see so few lights burning inside the immense Modernist structure, but then he recalled how Jeremy sometimes preferred to sequester himself in small spaces when alone—a throwback, perhaps, to that miserable little apartment in Fresno.

Arthur switched off the engine and ratcheted the emergency brake as Bingham got up from the backseat, panting and fogging the window with his breath. Arthur opened the door and the dog leapt down as the home's entrance door swung open, and Skipper loped out to greet them.

Jeremy stepped through the doorway—head down and hands jammed into his pockets—and began strolling toward Arthur.

Three paces away, Jeremy stopped.

Arthur felt himself glow.

"How was your drive?" Jeremy asked in a voice deep as it was hushed; leather speaking velvet.

"Hardly any traffic."

Their eyes found each other in the darkness, and Arthur held his arms wide.

Jeremy nestled into his embrace, Arthur breathed his scent, and a rabble of bittersweet memories fluttered between them.

They broke their hug to watch Skipper and Bingham romp and growl.

"We should take the dogs inside before they make a dash for the lake," Jeremy said. "Need help with your stuff?"

"I got it." Arthur reached in and pulled out the grocery and overnight bags. "Place still looks pretty much the same."

"I haven't been here very much over the years."

Arthur scanned the indigo sky with its tiny, fiery diamonds. "It's so beautiful here."

Jeremy likewise tilted up his head. "Sometimes I forget those stars are up there." He looked at Arthur. "Remember that dream I had about the Father's Star? And then you found out there was a Roman myth about Castor and Pollux that was similar to what I dreamed?"

"Seems like a lifetime ago. But I remember. The story of a father and son who prayed to the Gemini constellation for protection before going into battle. Did you ever figure out where you'd learned about that before you dreamt it?"

"Nope." Jeremy took Arthur's overnight bag and hoisted it over his shoulder. "I used to think someday I'd fall asleep on the deck watching those constellations drift overhead, but I never have. Guess I've gotten old."

Arthur laughed. "If you're old, I'm prehistoric."

"But we're not going to talk about age tonight, are we?" Jeremy headed toward the chalet, a dog bookending each leg.

"Deal. At least not tonight."

Jeremy turned to Arthur. "Are you really here?"

"Only because you invited me."

"I . . . need to take this slow."

"I'll take you any way I can."

Jeremy stopped and turned. "Your being here, I . . . wanted to call you so many times and had the phone in my hand. But I couldn't . . . I needed to wait—"

"For me to come find you?"

Jeremy dropped his head. Then he looked up and Arthur saw his brimming tears.

Arthur opened his arms, and they embraced again.

"I missed you so much," Jeremy said, hugging Arthur's waist. "Each birthday, each Thanksgiving and Christmas . . . each date with some guy when I'd be comparing him to you in my head—wondering what you were doing and hoping you were completely miserable."

"I missed you too, especially when I made dinner and Jess would hide in his office, and I'd think of how you'd watch me cook every night and we'd talk about cars or Aunt Katharine or men or something that was bugging you. I guess Jess figured that if he sat there watching the onions caramelize with me, we'd run out of things to say."

"But now we're home. We're together, we're safe, and we're home . . . where it all ended."

"I'll never forget that night, lying alone in my bed wanting to break down your door and take back everything I said."

Jeremy laughed. "I was awake all night hoping you would."

"Thanks for giving me another chance."

"And thanks for convincing me to." Jeremy felt the phone in his pocket vibrate. *Probably Aunt Katharine—again.* He ignored the call and they began making their way into the house.

The men crossed the threshold into the flagstone entry hall, and Arthur looked up at the massive wooden buttresses crisscrossing the cathedral ceiling. "This place is amazing. I wonder why no one's ever lived here—happily, I mean."

"*We* could live here happily." Jeremy squeezed Arthur's hand. "It doesn't need much structural work, and the kitchen and baths are so out of style now they're almost back *in* style. A while ago, Katharine earmarked some cash for a remodel but I convinced her to leave it as is so we could do a less expensive restoration instead, which I started years ago but kind of forgot about."

"Let's talk more about that later," Arthur said. "You know how I love architecture. Hey, are you hungry? I brought up some crackers and cheese and grapes."

"Hay is for horses, and I'm starving." Jeremy felt the phone pulsate once more, alerting him to a new message. "Do you mind setting it up at the bar? I just got a voice mail from Katharine and should probably listen to it."

"Go for it." Arthur crossed the foyer toward the kitchen, trailed by Bingham and Skipper.

Jeremy drew out the phone from his pocket, tapped the voice mail button, and held the device to his ear. *What does she want now?*

"Jeremy," said Lazzaro, "I need to speak with you immediately. But I will only be at this number for the next hour and then I must leave. I miss you. And I have something very important to share with you. Please call . . ."

Lazzaro recited the international phone number twice, and then the message ended.

Jeremy looked up and saw Arthur—a serving tray in his hands.

"What's wrong?" Arthur asked. "You look like you've just gotten a voice mail from the moaning ghost of Uncle Bill."

"It's probably nothing. Just . . . Aunt Katharine with something she needs to talk with me about."

"Is she OK?"

"I'm sure she is. But she needs me to call her back within the hour."

"Call her now; the cheese will be too cold to eat, anyway. Brie is always best at room temp."

Jeremy glanced away from Arthur, hoping he'd missed the dishonesty in his eyes. "Yeah, I'll give her a call. Oh, and I've got a pizza in the oven that's almost ready. Can you make sure it doesn't burn?"

"Yeah. Smells like it's almost done. Pesto and shrimp?"

Jeremy grinned. "I hope it's still your favorite. Do you want me to take your stuff upstairs to the master?"

"I got pretty used to sleeping on the couch these last couple of months, so that's fine with me—if you'd prefer."

"Forget what I said earlier about taking it slow," Jeremy told him as he hefted Arthur's overnight bag from the floor and began trekking up the stairs, his other hand grasping his phone. "Be right down."

CHAPTER
eighteen

Jeremy padded along the upstairs hallway on his way to the master bedroom, his stomach nervous and his brain reviewing the questions he'd been composing for Lazzaro.

He opened the door, tossed Arthur's bag onto the bed, and then snatched a stubby pencil from the nightstand drawer while replaying Lazzaro's voice mail, trying to scribble on his Trader Joe's receipt the digits of the complicated international phone number, all the while considering his conversation about Lazzaro at Duke's with Carlo—in addition to his meeting with, and the subpoena from, Laurel and Hardy—while wondering if he should twist himself tighter within whatever new drama was knotting together, especially now that his life might be veering away from the head-on collision he'd been hurtling toward, seatbelts be damned.

I'll make this quick.

He tapped the numbers into his phone and waited . . . and waited . . . for the call to connect.

Finally, Jeremy heard the strange note of a foreign-sounding phone ringing.

And then a click.

"*Yes-es?*" asked Lazzaro, his voice echoing from the satellite lag.

"Why didn't you tell me about the mortgage on your house?"

"Thank you for calling. It is so good to hear from you."

"Did you *hear* me? Why didn't you tell me about that mortgage?" His glance happened to fall upon a conspicuous lump on the side of Arthur's bag. *What's that?*

"That mortgage was to have been paid off by my father months ago," Lazzaro began, "but he lost all his money to those men I told you about, and he was too proud to tell me he had been cheated. I had no idea of this when I sold you the property for that inexpensive price, but now I have the money to reimburse you for the outstanding mortgage, and this is why I am calling."

"OK then." Jeremy felt himself relax. "Where are you? What's going o—"

"I am well enough," Lazzaro interrupted, "but I cannot tell you where I am. I want to explain everything to you, but I must not over this phone."

"Some detectives came to our place. I know what happened to your father. When are you coming back to—"

"You do not know what happened, I can assure—"

"—straighten out this mess?"

"—you of this. But I cannot yet return to America. This is why I need you to come here."

Jeremy coughed a laugh while waiting out the maddening satellite lag to make certain he would not be interrupting Lazzaro. "And where is that?" he asked at last.

"My location is secret until my attorneys can straighten this out, but I can meet you in Greece. Athens would be best."

"*Greece?* Why the hell would I meet—"

"There I will pay—"

"—you in Greece?"

"—you in cash for the mortgage when you get here."

"No fucking way! Wire it to me, like I did for you!"

Lazzaro waited until he was certain Jeremy was not speaking. "This is impossible," he said, "because of the situation with the detectives you mentioned. For now I need to keep my location to myself, and using a bank for the wire transfer would jeopardize my safety. But when you leave tomorrow you will be in Athens the next day; you could have in your possession all the cash I owe you by Monday or Tuesday to remodel your grand estate. Of course you would like this, yes?"

"Get someone else to wire me the money." Jeremy pressed the mysterious bulge in Arthur's bag. *Little plastic bottles—Vitamins? Pills?* "I'm sure you have at least one or two friends in Transylvania, or wherever the fuck you are."

"This situation has become difficult," Lazzaro replied, "and along with the money I owe you I have information that will keep you immune to the charges against me, as well as making you a strong witness on my behalf. I need to explain my circumstances to you, should you have the opportunity to testify for me in court. *I need you*, Jeremy."

Jeremy laughed. "Look, you've got to give me more than that. I already know about you having something to do with your father's death." Jeremy unzipped the bag's side pocket, withdrew two clear brown plastic prescription containers and examined the labels: TEMODAR, and . . . something else with an indecipherable name containing the simple instructions: FOR NAUSEA.

The silence on the other end made Jeremy think he'd lost the connection, and exactly at that moment he heard the telephone ringing downstairs. "Lazzaro? Are you—"

"Yes."

"—still there?" Jeremy, growing increasingly annoyed with their connection, hastily returned the medications to Arthur's bag and zipped it closed.

"That night," Lazzaro said, "after we met with my father at the marina, when we left to the airport, something happened to him and he died. But he was old and had been using the Sueño Gris, and now the police think I had something to do with this and they want to arrest me. And I don't care so much for myself as I am concerned for you, because the guards who were on duty identified you as there with my father at the same time I—"

"But you were the only one who went inside—"

"—entered my father's quarters with him and he was—"

"—that room with him," Jeremy told him, exasperated now with how their words were overlapping. *Fuckity fuck!* "So what happened?"

"—absolutely in fine health. He gave me the briefcase with the documents I would need in Europe, but now the international police, who are in league with these same corrupt men, are looking to capture me. Jeremy, I have everything I need to prove that my father was killed by the very men who stole his money—the very money my father intended to pay the mortgage on your beautiful home—but since I am your lover and the police wish to link me with his murder, I am afraid you will be implicated. You were there that very night!"

"But why would anyone think I wanted him dead?!"

"There is so much you do not know, but I must see you. I will not—*I cannot*—tell you one more word unless we speak face-to-face."

Jeremy paused, trying to calm himself. "I need to think about this, Lazzaro. Call me—"

"*You must be on a plane tomorrow—*"

"—tomorrow and I'll let you know."

"*—you must give me your answer now!*"

"Then the answer is 'no'! I've got a lot more important things to do than fly halfway across the world to hear something that could be said over the phone."

Silence.

"Then I will call you tomorrow," Lazzaro said at last. "Please, Jeremy, I care too much about you to let you be pulled into this mess."

"Yeah, well there's something else I need to tell you."

Long pause.

"Yes?"

"The man I told you about from a long time ago. Arthur? We're together again."

"Ah, the handsome soldier you showed me in your pictures." Lazzaro chuckled warmly. "Your news is good news; I cannot expect you to wait for me, and I wish you both happiness. Believe me when I say I am not jealous, and I want you to discuss this trip with him. Perhaps he will accompany you to Greece? I would enjoy meeting him; something tells me we have much in common."

Jeremy heard the rustle of fabric and looked up.

Arthur was standing in the doorway.

"I need to go," Jeremy said. "Call me tomorrow after Arthur and I've had a chance to talk about it." He ended the call and shot Arthur what he hoped was a guiltless smile.

"Is everything all right with Aunt Katharine?" Arthur asked, his voice lilting with sarcasm.

"It's, um, a long story."

"Because she sounded fine to me when I hung up with her a minute ago downstairs," Arthur continued. "I told her all's well and we were about to have dinner, and how strange it was that she could be talking to her nephew on a cell phone while speaking with me on the land line." He crossed his arms. "Isn't technology *amazing*?"

Jeremy rolled his eyes. "That was Lazzaro."

Arthur waited.

"After all this time with no contact, wouldn't you know he left me a voice mail tonight, but I didn't know what to tell you. I'm sorry I lied, but at least I was honest with him about you—and me."

After regarding him thoughtfully for a long moment, Arthur crossed the room, eased himself down onto the edge of the bed, and slung an arm around Jeremy's shoulder. "Want to talk about it?"

Jeremy dropped his head onto Arthur's chest. *What are those medications for?* "How about tomorrow? We haven't even had a minute to eat or enjoy that you're here." He smiled up at Arthur. "With me."

Arthur kissed his cheek. "Tomorrow, then." He stood, pulled Jeremy up from the bed and led him toward the stairs. "Dinner's ready, but it can wait if you're not hungry."

"I'm starving, then after we eat I want us to come back up here. OK?" Jeremy slipped a caressing hand down the backside of Arthur's jeans, then palmed his solid back and shoulders inside his T-shirt. "I've had a lot of sex over the past few years, but I can't remember what it feels like to make love."

"Then I'll just have to remind you." Arthur slapped Jeremy playfully on the butt and then began leading him downstairs, where Jeremy discovered a cheerful blaze inside the huge stone fireplace, and pizza and appetizers artfully arranged atop the bar.

"What do you want to drink?" Arthur asked, heading for the kitchen.

"There's some mineral water in the fridge. Where are the dogs?"

"In rug-mode by the fireplace."

Jeremy saw that, indeed, Skipper and Bingham were impersonating two lumpy, shaggy rugs in front of the hearth.

"You don't want wine?" Arthur asked. "I brought some up, just in case."

"Didn't bring up any on purpose. Trying to cut down."

"Then I won't have any either."

Jeremy sat on a barstool, spread some brie on a cracker, and took a bite. "So what's happened over the last four years?" he mumbled. "Your turn to talk."

"Besides pretending I wasn't missing you, I started a bodyguard company. They're trained in firearms and mixed martial arts, and we've got a really weird client list."

"Like what?"

"Celebrities, rich people, religious figures. My office is up on Robertson in WeHo."

"What's it like working with celebrities?"

"Like dealing with the gods and goddesses of Mount Olympus. And the Underworld."

"How so?"

"They're worshipped like they're beyond human, they don't age, they act like children, they have too much power and money, and when they get bored they cause trouble."

Jeremy paused, thoughtfully chewing. "Isn't there some fancy word for when humans become gods? Apollo-*something*? Is it like that?"

"*Apotheosis*. Where did you come across that?"

"Once upon a time Ancient Greece and Rome fascinated me," Jeremy replied. "After I had that Father's Star dream I did some research, mostly about mythology."

"I would've liked to live back then. What about you?"

Jeremy shook his head. "No way."

"Why not?"

"Waaaay too violent. So when did things start to fall apart with Jess?"

"About a year into it we both smelled that the relationship was souring, but we plugged our noses and kept going for three more years. We did have a lot in common and we really cared for each other, but we just didn't have the chemistry—"

"As opposed to you and me," Jeremy giggled, "where all we had was chemistry."

"If I remember, we had—and I believe we still have—more than that."

"Remind me."

"Like . . . love of dogs. And the beach. And going for walks. And great food. And exercising. But most of all, what I missed was your sense of humor; no one's ever made me laugh as much as you. But you're right about that chemistry; I've never forgotten how mind-blowing our sex was . . . even if it was only twice."

"Speaking of blowing . . ."

"Are you reading my mind?"

"There's that damn chemistry." Jeremy slid off his barstool, curled his arms around Arthur's neck, and drew their lips together.

CHAPTER

nineteen

The wet heat of each other's tongues quickened their heartbeats as the hard ridge in Jeremy's jeans chafed frantically against Arthur's.

Jeremy reached up inside Arthur's T-shirt and palmed his chest. "How is it that you're in even better shape than you were four years ago?"

"Four years of daily pushups." Arthur kissed a trail down Jeremy's neck. "And your ass—"

"Guess all those years of swim practice are still paying off."

They kissed again. Then Jeremy unbuttoned Arthur's jeans, slid his hand inside the man's boxers, and made contact.

They both gasped.

Jeremy began caressing him. "Has it been a while?"

"How could you tell?" Arthur put his arms around Jeremy's neck as the younger man pushed both hands inside his pants, cradling him in his palm and stroking him with his fingers. "Oh, God," Arthur whispered in his ear. "Stop, stop, *stop!*"

Jeremy stopped and began leading Arthur by the hand across the room to the stairs just as Skipper and Bingham arose wide-eyed from the living room floor, curious to know where their pack was migrating to. And as they climbed the stairs Arthur fell back, allowing Jeremy to move up ahead of him.

Jeremy stopped and turned. "What's wrong?"

"I love watching you move—the way your ass shifts and your shoulders rock from side-to-side is poetic . . . lyrical . . . sexy as hell. I should film you sometime so you can see what I see."

"You're crazy."

"Crazy about you . . . and hopefully, that's the last corny thing I'll say tonight."

At the top of the stairs, Jeremy led Arthur down the hallway—the dogs sleepily trailing them—and released his hand only to peel off his shirt.

Inside the bedroom, Skipper and Bingham took their places on each side of the bed as the men shed their clothing and fell onto the coverlet.

Arthur pressed his full nakedness on top of Jeremy . . . kissing him deeply, wrestling his hard musculature, tasting the salty musk of his skin and licking the gritty, erotic sandpaper of his beard stubble.

Jeremy reached back and grabbed Arthur's buttocks, and Arthur turned Jeremy's head to the side and smeared a line of kisses down the sinews in his neck.

"I have . . . to tell you . . . something important," Arthur murmured between kisses.

"Anything."

"I want us to savor this. Really savor it."

"I'm doing that already," Jeremy growled. "Aren't you?"

Arthur dropped to Jeremy's side and propped himself on an elbow. "It just hit me that . . . *everything* in my life has been building toward this moment: my sad childhood and my relationship with your father; the Marines; Danny's death and getting discharged and working for the FBI; even that crazy trip to Brazil and the failed relationship with Jess has brought me to this moment with you. And

I'm not afraid anymore. I don't have any reservations. All I want is to push forward and conquer the world with you by my side.

"And no matter what happens," Arthur continued, "if I died tomorrow I'd do so happily, knowing we were able to come back together—even if it was only for a short time."

"Well, I wouldn't be happy about it," Jeremy said, a bit crossly. "Why would you say something like that—especially right now? You just killed my hard-on."

Arthur was aching to tell Jeremy about the medical crisis he'd survived but decided to wait. "I guess it's just an overused expression . . . and an overly dramatic way of saying I want to spend the rest of my life with you."

"Me too. And maybe it *was* important for you to send me away so I could learn from what's happening now, the bad and the good. I've got to admit I've grown up a lot, thanks to you."

They kissed, and Arthur drew his hand down from Jeremy's chest to the pipe rising again from between his legs. "So you finally forgive me?"

"No."

"No?"

"I finally *understand* you. No forgiveness necessary." Jeremy kissed him on the chin. "So now that that's out of the way, will you please fuck me?"

"Something tells me you're ready."

The men tumbled into position, Jeremy on his back and Arthur kneeling between his legs.

Slowly . . . slowly . . . slowly they joined.

"You're good at this," Arthur gasped.

"Been practicing."

Jeremy whispered ecstatic complaints as Arthur muttered his own lovely, nasty desires.

Their moaning seesawed.

Arthur grabbed the back of Jeremy's ankles and Jeremy whimpered—his hand and arm blurring piston-like.

Then with Jeremy's babbling signaling his own climax, Arthur's urge crested as his thrusts lifted Jeremy off the mattress.

:::::::::

After their breathing calmed Arthur withdrew himself, and each man fell back onto his pillow.

"You need to trim your toenails," Arthur told Jeremy.

"I don't own any clippers."

"You own a Jaguar and a chateau, *but no nail clippers?*"

"You can take the boy out of Fresno," Jeremy giggled. "Can I borrow yours?"

"You may."

"Is that weird noise coming from Bingham? He sounds like an old car trying to start up."

"He's dreaming." Arthur smiled into Jeremy's eyes. "I love you so much."

Jeremy gazed back at him. "So all the practice paid off?"

"I don't know if you're ready for Carnegie Hall," Arthur yawned, "but there's always tomorrow for more practice."

"Then I can't wait for tomorrow. Till death us do part?"

"Not even then, old buddy."

:::::::::

Arthur awoke to the racket of blue jays squawking at the dawn.

Momentarily forgetting where he had been sleeping, he tried focusing on different parts of the room: ceiling—windows—floor. Nothing made sense.

He stifled a rising panic: *Is it happening again?*

Then he looked over at the form sleeping next to him and everything swirled into focus.

Jeremy.

At that moment, Bingham's bright eyes rose up from the side of the bed, an orange tennis ball with the wool peeled halfway off clenched in his jaws.

Arthur rubbed his head. "G'morning, Bingham-boy."

The dog dropped the ball onto the sheets and nosed it toward Arthur.

"Not yet, Bingy," he whispered. "Lay down. We'll play later. OK?"

Pretending not to understand, Bingham panted cheerfully.

"*No.*" Arthur rubbed the dog's head and Bingham, clearly disappointed, lay back down with a snuffle.

Arthur rolled over and enveloped Jeremy in his arms, and his sleeping form began to stir. Arthur secreted a hand down between his legs and felt him already hard and moist.

Jeremy's eyelids fluttered open, his mouth curling into a smile. "What a nice—" he yawned, "—alarm clock you are."

"Good morning." Arthur grasped Jeremy harder and began stroking him.

Jeremy's hand likewise found Arthur. "I . . . love—" he yawned again, "—you."

"Did you sleep well?"

"Not only did I sleep well," Jeremy's eyelids dipped from the pleasure, "but I woke up not hungover. No cement-head, no toilet mouth."

"Has it been a while?"

Jeremy nodded.

"Guess I'm good for you, after all."

Jeremy smiled. "Guess you are."

They kissed, the faint taste of each other lingering from the night before. And as their mouths opened more deeply, their hands tugged faster until first Jeremy, and then Arthur, spent himself.

They embraced in a musky hug.

:::::::::

After showering, dressing, and enjoying a breakfast of coffee, scrambled eggs, and bagels, Jeremy and Arthur took Skipper and Bingham for a walk by the lake. The clear white sun was already blazing through the branches of the green-bristled pines, and the morning chill had well burned off.

As Bingham and Skipper zigzagged from boulder to boulder, Jeremy—doing his best to not leave out any important details—recounted to Arthur his conversations with the detectives, and then with Lazzaro from last night.

"Of course you shouldn't go," Arthur sternly told him. "The best thing you could do is stay away from him and let the police do their jobs. You don't owe him a thing, and you're absolutely correct about insisting he wire you the money. This stinks to high heaven."

"I figured you'd say that, because I feel pretty much the same way." Jeremy stepped atop a hump of moss-covered granite and looked out over the placid blue lake. "But what if I could get information from Lazzaro that might help the police with their case? They haven't been able to catch him yet. And if Lazzaro's innocent, I could help clear his name and get my money back. Sounds like a win-win."

"What's your gut say about him being innocent or guilty?"

Jeremy's eyes scanned the cloudless blue sky. "Probably . . . guilty."

"Why?"

"Lazzaro told me his father had his mother murdered. He was already married and she blackmailed him after Lazzaro was born and he had her killed. So Lazzaro had reason to kill the old man, and if he did, it sounds like he got what he deserved—like when I killed Bill."

"Your uncle pulled a gun on you and Carlo, so there was no question of it being self-defense on your part. Did Lazzaro tell you anything about his father threatening his own safety?"

"No."

"Then even if Lazzaro's actions were somehow morally justifiable, they were still highly illegal. And in any event his proposition to meet you in Greece is dangerous and we both know it—especially after what we went through in Brazil. You've got very little to gain and a lot to lose. It's not worth the money."

"You're right." Jeremy crouched down to pick up a fragment of fool's gold gleaming in the shallow water. "But I'd still like to see Greece with you—sooner than later."

"And we will. But in the meantime let's have a good time by forgetting about Lazzaro, and if he calls again we can alert the authorities. I still have contact with Agent Singer from the FBI. Remember him?"

"I'll never forget." Jeremy slipped the rock into his pocket. "He's the one who put things together for you with my kidnapping in Brazil—"

"And since so many of my clients get into trouble internationally," Arthur added, "I run into him from time to time. He's got contacts at Interpol he works with. Would it be OK with you if I gave him a call and told him about your conversation with Lazzaro?"

"Sure." Jeremy jumped off the boulder. "But—and not that I believe it—what if Lazzaro *is* innocent?"

"No matter how convincing the rationale, innocent people rarely flee. So the last thing you should do is run over to Europe so he can 'give you information that will help keep you out of this mess.'"

"But wouldn't you like to use this situation as an excuse to see Greece? Years ago you told me how much you wanted to see Mykonos."

"I'd almost forgotten about that," Arthur said. "I used to picture myself holding a young, sun-darkened man in my arms on a high cliff overlooking the Aegean. Then as the sun sets we'd gather friends around a fire and make offerings to the old gods and the Fates."

"And then run off for some hot gay sex," Jeremy added cheerfully.

Arthur laughed. "There is that."

"And . . . what would this young man with the sun-darkened skin look like?"

"I always pictured him with hair that curled over his ears, like yours did when we first met"—Arthur put a hand on Jeremy's neck—"and dark, gentle eyes . . . like yours, a strong nose like yours, full lips like yours, and a hot, muscular body. Like yours."

Jeremy paused, thinking. "We could always take a trip to Greece, Lazzaro or no Lazzaro—but I don't know where you're going to find that beautiful boy. My body isn't what it used to be, but . . ." he held out his arms, ". . . at least I could get a tan."

"Even when you're seventy and I'm *eighty-nine*, you'll still be my beautiful boy."

"Promise?"

"Cross my heart and hope to . . . live forever."

CHAPTER

twenty

Tristan and Lazzaro soaked together in the bathtub on the second floor of the villa, the French doors opened to the rocky hillsides and chartreuse grapevines below.

"Is the water hot enough?" Lazzaro's bronzed arms swirled the water, causing the milky ripples to ebb and flow around the muscles of his chest, the white suds clinging to his nipples like snowflakes on rose petals. "Does the bath agree with you?"

Tristan rested his head on the edge of the Roman tub. "It is perfect—and the perfect way to begin the morning." His feet found Lazzaro's sex underneath the foam and began dabbling him with his toes. "Have you any more thoughts on Carmella's plan?"

"Only that your mother is a savvy woman."

"Savvy as a Babylon whore," Tristan laughed, delighted by the effect his touches were having on Lazzaro. "She never fails to surprise me."

"We are in agreement there." Lazzaro drew Tristan into his embrace and kissed the back of his neck. "Do you prefer that I take you here, or in the bedroom?" He nudged himself against the base of Tristan's muscled buttocks.

Tristan leaned back into his arms and raised himself out of the water so Lazzaro could witness his arousal. "As much as I am desiring you, instead I prefer that you save yourself for the old stable." He pointed toward the distant barn. "I was disappointed that you were not interested in being there with me after our meal last night. I thought you rested."

"Your meal was wondrous, but the voyage was more tiring than I realized," Lazzaro replied, pushing out thoughts of Carmella. "Why is it important for me to make love to you there instead of here, in this villa?"

"When you left for America, I came to live with my mother; as an actress she travels constantly and asked me to oversee the vineyards and grounds. Hoping you would once again desire my company, I began building a place for us in the loft above the horses. There I spent time imagining the life we would build together. It is my sanctuary, and the perfect place for lovemaking, because Carmella will not set foot inside."

"Why not?"

"She says the ancient structure is haunted."

"Haunted?" Lazzaro laughed. "What sort of ghost would scare Carmella?"

"Not a ghost," Tristan replied, rubbing his backside against Lazzaro under the warm, soapy water. "As a girl, she claimed to have witnessed a mythical creature emerge from the hayloft one night. A siren—half woman, half bird. This creature chased her through the moonlit vineyard until she was delirious."

"Aren't sirens supposed to sing?"

"She also sang songs about Carmella and her secrets—and she had many, even as a girl. No one believed her . . . but the experience was enough for Carmella to avoid that barn ever since."

"And now this is the one place you can be absolutely free from her."

"Exactly."

"Have you . . . seen this creature, this siren?"

"Not that I can say."

Lazzaro caressed Tristan's compact, sculpted torso. "I will look forward to being with you in this sanctuary of yours, but we have much to do this morning. Shall we sleep there this afternoon?"

"Only if we do not waste time sleeping." Tristan turned around to bite Lazzaro's nipple and Lazzaro arched his back out of the water.

Tristan inched down the muscles of his torso, carefully tracing each ridge and swell with his tongue—from clavicle to Adonis belt.

"I am afraid I cannot wait for the stable," Lazzaro panted.

"Then you must promise me to be ready again later."

"*I promise.*"

Tristan nodded and then eased his mouth down upon Lazzaro, kneading and caressing.

"Tease me," Lazzaro commanded.

Tristan brought Lazzaro to the edge and back three times until the man was moaning, rocking, and splashing the water from the tub onto the marble floor.

"*Faster!*"

Tristan obliged, and moments later Lazzaro spent himself.

Tenderly, they kissed.

"Now it is your turn," Lazzaro said.

Instead, Tristan pressed himself back into Lazzaro's arms. "I am happy just being here just like this. I love you."

"And I love you," Lazzaro lied. "Now let us dress and eat, and I want you to tell me your thoughts about Carmella's ideas; you have a cooler head than she."

Tristan—breathing hard—stepped out from the tub, snatched a towel, and began rubbing himself dry. "My thoughts are," he said, tousling the water from his hair, "that crossing the street carries risks, so if we agree that the dangers involved are reasonable, I will support her plan . . . even if it means giving up our time together here to travel back to Athens."

Lazzaro grinned as he pushed himself up from the tub, water streaming down his muscled flanks like the Aegean cascading off Poseidon. "But we need to anticipate everything that might go wrong—we need to examine her scheme from every angle."

"But Carmella's proposal is simple," Tristan insisted, tossing Lazzaro a dry towel.

Lazzaro smiled. "Passionate women sometimes do not see their own follies."

"No," Tristan countered. "Passionate women—like passionate men—always see their follies . . . but sometimes not until it is too late."

Lazzaro laughed, handing Tristan a robe. "It sounds as if you speak from experience."

"This Jeremy," Tristan began, slipping his arms into the garment, "what makes you think he will actually make the trip to Athens? Last night you said he dismissed your request."

"Jeremy is intelligent, but his judgment is warped by his anger at life and his love for vodka. He is of Irish and Italian blood—an easy man to fool. I believe he will decide to make the trip here."

"When will you telephone him again to ask if he will do this?"

Lazzaro paused to check his watch. "After our evening meal. With the ten-hour time difference he will have been awake for some time—" he laughed, "—trying to appease his hangover. And if I call around lunchtime, he'll already be drunk and missing me."

"You've thought of everything," Tristan said. "But how unfortunate for him to have trusted you."

"One man's purpose in life is to learn such lessons," Lazzaro said, drawing Tristan into his arms, "while another man's purpose is to teach them."

CHAPTER

twenty-one

From his redwood chair on the deck, Arthur put aside his crossword puzzle to watch Bingham observing a flock of ducks rising up from the water's surface, his furry black head tracking the creatures as each rose aloft, like a little boy watching fighter planes launched in succession at an air show.

The phone pressed to Arthur's ear had just completed its fourth ring, so he was expecting to get a voice mail prompt on the other end when the call unexpectedly went live. "Agent Singer speaking."

"Hey, it's Art Blauefee. Formerly of the FBI and the United States Marines."

"*Aliquando Fidelis* vs. *Semper Fidelis*." He laughed.

"Aliquando?"

"Latin for *sometimes*. What can I do for you, Art?"

"I may have something for you."

Arthur reached down and massaged Bingham's head while debriefing the agent on Jeremy's conversation with Lazzaro from the night before.

"You got that phone number handy?" Singer asked.

Arthur recited it slowly from the back of the Trader Joe's receipt.

"We'd been on the trail of Francesco Sforza for years," Singer told Arthur, "and just when we'd gathered enough evidence against him to have him indicted, the son-of-a-bitch dies . . . And, hold on . . . just as I thought, that phone number's already disconnected. By the way, the evidence is stacked so high against his son Lazzaro that Interpol believes his case is open and shut, so your pal Jeremy shouldn't feel guilty about turning him in."

"That's what I was thinking. Can you believe he wanted Jeremy to go all the way to Greece to meet with him to hear 'his side of the story'?"

"My guess is he also needed Jeremy to bring him some cash, and he just hadn't made the request yet."

"I hadn't thought of that."

"Anyhow, thanks for the tip—hey, and if he calls again, will you let me know ASAP? Especially if he discloses any information we might use later on."

"He's supposed to call Jeremy back sometime today, so that's not a problem." Arthur watched as his lover emerged shirtless from the house carrying their lunches on a tray, followed by Skipper, sniffing the wake of scents.

"You know—" Agent Singer paused, "—I've got an idea, but I'll need to run it by my boss. Can I get you at this number in an hour or so?"

"I'm not going anywhere."

"Talk to you then."

"Thanks, man." Arthur ended the call.

Jeremy placed the tray atop the coffee table and Bingham sat up, eyeing the twin turkey wraps. "More secret agent stuff?"

"When did you learn how to cook?" Arthur examined the offerings. "And yes, more *secret agent stuff*; he's going to call me back with some ideas he has."

"What's going on?" Jeremy asked, sitting down.

"Needs to run something by his boss." Arthur picked up his wrap and bit into it. "This is really good," he said, chewing. "What's in it?"

"Turkey and Swiss and basil pesto, a little mayo and tomato, and some avocado."

"Clearly, you're the perfect man. So what's on your agenda for today?"

Jeremy eyed Arthur's abandoned newspaper. "Not watching you do crossword puzzles. I can't believe you do them in pen."

"I like using pen. Agenda?"

"You see that cove *waaaay* over there?" Jeremy pointed to the distant side of Lake Estrella, while at the same time taking a bite from his own wrap.

Arthur checked the wall of emerald pines mirrored upside-down in the water. "The one with the big granite boulders?"

"The one next to that, to the right." He swigged some mineral water. "I've been wanting to take the Chris-Craft out all year to explore that side of the lake but didn't want to do it by myself. Curious?"

"With or without the dogs?"

"I . . . think it might be better to leave them here; wild gnomes and forest trolls and all."

"Good idea. When?"

"How about after we finish lunch?"

"Perfect. I'm already showered, so I'll pack us some afternoon snacks and some drinks, and we can be out of here in an hour."

:::::::::

Jeremy had gone upstairs to get ready; Arthur was washing their dishes when his phone rang: SINGER.

Arthur put down the plates and wiped his hands on his jeans. "What's going on?"

"Are you alone? Sitting down?"

Arthur leaned against the countertop. "I'm listening."

"I made a few calls and discovered some troubling info: the DA is getting her ducks in a row to indict your Jeremy on some very serious charges."

"*What?!*"

"Look, it could be a false alarm, but if it isn't, they could put him away for a *long* time."

"OK." Arthur breathed deeply. "Tell me everything."

"How well do you know Jeremy?"

"*Really* well."

"Has he mentioned to you anything about a drug called Sueño Gris?"

"No. What is it?"

"One of these new 'designer' hallucinogens." Agent Singer paused. "How about human trafficking and sex tourism?"

"Singer, what the hell are you talking about?"

"I can only tell you so much, but . . . the police found some incriminating files on Jeremy's computer; it was seized during a search of his home. And we don't know at this point if the files are truly Jeremy's or if someone was using his computer as a mule, but here's what I can tell you: Sforza and his father were both trafficking drugs and kids, and right now it looks—from these files—as if Jeremy was in on the action. They've got Jeremy's laptop in line for examination by some techies, but with budget cuts these forensic exams can take longer than autopsy results—we've got a backlog like you can't believe. In the meantime, if the DA has enough evidence to tie in Jeremy with the Sforzas, he'll be brought in soon. Like *tomorrow*. Aiding and abetting."

"*Aiding and abetting?* There's no way, man. Not Jerem—"

"Hey, does he have anyone who could bail him out? I mean, if they press forward with the charges? That would be the easiest way until forensics come back and the charges are tossed. He could be booked and released an hour later, but the bail on these charges'll be huge."

Arthur thought back on the conversation he had with Katharine and her insistence that Jeremy was absolutely and completely on his own from now on. "Not a soul."

"Too bad." Singer paused. "I've got another idea . . . so don't mention a word of this to him until I call you back, OK? I'm only telling you this as one agent to another."

"You're asking the impossible, but I'll do it."

"Hang onto your hat and give me twenty minutes."

"Done."

Arthur spent the next half hour cleaning the kitchen and then vacuuming scattered clumps of dog fur—all the while trying to put his fears on hold—when his phone rang.

"I just got an approval for this from high up," Agent Singer said, "but I understand if you might be uncomfortable with it. It's risky."

"Go ahead."

"First of all I want you to know I believe you, and I think Jeremy's been set up . . . but the DA's gonna need proof. So we'd like to use Jeremy as bait: we'll send you both to Greece to meet with Sforza; we'll have Jeremy wear a wire while being completely protected and surrounded, and after Sforza acknowledges Jeremy's innocence, we'll have our people take him down. We have some of the very best agents Interpol has working on this case right now—they've been trained in *Krav Maga,* and they're excellent marksmen; Sforza makes one wrong move and he's dead before his face lands in his kabobs."

"I don't know—"

"Jeremy's safety has been guaranteed," Singer continued, "you'll be staying at the best hotels, and I'll see that his DUI disappears because he already completed rehab; good thing it's his first offense."

"What else?"

"That's it. For now."

Arthur rubbed his temple as a headache began to bloom. "I've got to talk with Jeremy and see what he thinks. Can I tell him everything you've told me?"

"The less he knows about the sex tourism the better, unless he brings it up. If he does that, call me immediately. In the meantime tell him we've been trying to catch Sforza on drug trafficking charges and to question him about his father's death, and Jeremy's cooperation will help with his DUI case. Can you do that?"

"Can I trust you to get Jeremy off the hook, that is, if he's clean?"

"I'll do everything I can. Just know we're in a time crunch here. Let me know tomorrow if you can't tonight."

"I'll call you back—" Arthur squinted from sudden pain, "—maybe tonight."

He ended the call as Jeremy rounded the corner.

"What's up?"

"They want to send us to Greece to have you meet with Lazzaro, where they'll swoop down and nab him on some drug charges and to question him about his father's death. Singer says your safety is guaranteed, but there's really no such thing."

"What's in it for me, for us?" Jeremy asked, hoping Arthur wouldn't ask him what he knew about Lazzaro's bizarre hallucinogens.

"A free trip. And he might be able to make your DUI disappear."

"How much time do we get to think about it?"

"I need to call him back tonight or tomorrow."

"*Let's do it!*"

"Baby, let's think about this. It's dangerous."

"But we could hold each other while gazing out at the turquoise Aegean, we could stroll around the Parthenon, we could have a spy adventure, and I could finally get back at Lazzaro for screwing me over. Why would I possibly say no? Because I'm *scared?*"

"Jeremy, I've almost lost you before—and if anything happened to you now, I'd never forgive myself."

"Then let's not call Agent Singer back just yet, so we can both try to think of a really good reason not to go to Greece. OK?"

"That would be best."

"But what if Lazzaro calls me back before then?"

Arthur paused. "I guess you'll just need to tell him whatever your gut tells you."

"OK." Jeremy went to the fridge and pulled out two water bottles. "So while we think about all this, are you ready to head off to that deserted cove"—he tossed his head in its direction—"for some wildlife exploration and a swim in the lake? It'll kind of be like when were at that gorgeous beach in Brazil. But remember, a little innocent skinny-dipping sometimes leads to forbidden blow jobs."

"There's no such thing as innocent skinny-dipping," Arthur told him. "And clearly, blow jobs aren't forbidden anymore. But what about tomorrow? If we're even considering this trip, we should get back to Ballena Beach first thing in the morning. Thankfully it's been a quiet weekend for me, but I'll need to prep my managers if I'm going to throw all my responsibilities onto them for a week."

"Of course—and I'm anxious for you to see the inside of my scary mansion. No one else has seen it but Carlo, because Aunt Katharine was too scared to get out of the car."

"Then tomorrow morning we'll pack up early and head home?"

"That sounds *so* nice."

"What does?" Arthur asked.

"*Home*."

:::::::::

They had barely finished putting away their lunch dishes and were getting ready for their boat trip to the cove when Jeremy felt his phone vibrate. He slipped it from his pocket and answered the call. "Hello?"

"I need to keep this brief," Lazzaro said. "Have you made your decision? Because if you do not come here, I will need to find another use for the money I have to repay you."

"I have." Jeremy glanced over at Arthur. "We're coming."

CHAPTER

twenty-two

The next morning, after a hurried breakfast, Jeremy and Arthur left Lake Estrella.

Then a few minutes before noon they pulled each of their cars into the cobblestone driveway of Jeremy's run-down chateau.

Arthur opened the back of his Jeep to grab his overnight bag, and Bingham jumped down. "It doesn't look so bad. When was this place built?"

"Nineteen twenty-something." Jeremy opened the door of his Jaguar to let out Skipper. "You know the huge fire that destroyed the north end of Ballena Beach around the turn of the century? This place was built on the site of some big old Victorian mansion that burned down."

"I remember seeing the pictures taken after that fire. So sad." Arthur stood back to admire the architecture of Jeremy's mansion, his head tilted back. "Is that a real slate roof? It's gorgeous!"

"Is that something special?"

"Slate roofs—they're actually built from hand-chiseled slate rock—are fireproof and waterproof and usually last hundreds of years. So whoever designed this place held true to the Norman style:

the steep mansard roof, the fieldstone exterior, and the limestone door and window surrounds are very exacting." Arthur looked over at the east side of the house. "And it's even got a turret and a garret and double-stacked chimneys! So . . . tell me again what it was that your aunt didn't like about this place?"

"I paid twice as much for it than it's worth. In fact, I'm so upside-down on the mortgage now that the slate roof you like so much might as well be covering the basement." He punched him on the shoulder. "Let's get settled."

Jeremy fitted his key into the castle-worthy door and shouldered it open.

Skipper trotted inside, but Bingham stopped at the door—a growl rumbling in his throat.

Arthur scratched his head. "Bingham, what's going on?"

Bingham's hackles bristled as if staring down a wolf.

"What's wrong with him?" Jeremy asked.

Arthur, now on one knee, curled an arm around his body. "I've never seen him like this."

Bingham growled and curled his lip.

Jeremy backed into the entry. "Why don't you see if he'll follow you in."

Arthur entered the house and Bingham crept alongside him, skulking low, and pressed against Arthur's leg. Jeremy kept the door open until Bingham's posture began to relax; then after the dog began his usual behavior of sniffing floor moldings and trotting after Skipper, Jeremy closed them all inside.

Arthur stopped to scan the interior. "Whoa."

Beyond the formal marble-floored foyer on the right, a flying staircase swept up counter-clockwise to the second story, and to the left a magnificently scaled great room with high, narrow windows reaching almost to the beamed ceiling flanked an immense carved, marble fireplace mantel befitting a Florentine villa. Straight ahead stood a long bank of French doors overlooking the shimmering Pacific, and to the right a long, formal dining room adjoined an outdated, railcar kitchen.

Clearly the scale, architectural integrity, and genteel style of the home bespoke a once gracious and glamorous lifestyle. But now the structure was clearly in disrepair: the ceilings and walls were absent the chandeliers and wall sconces that had glittered so long ago; there were crooked, dirty cracks spiderwebbed along the dingy marble floors; more than a few of the doors suffered broken moldings; patches of wall plaster were missing, and even some of the window panes had been patched with rectangles of plywood and even cardboard.

But worst of all was the wall color: *Greenish brown.*

"It's almost grand enough to be a chateau in the Loire Valley," Arthur remarked. "Too bad no one cared enough, or had money enough, to fix the place up."

"And so the tradition continues." Jeremy dropped his bags onto the floor. "Apparently Lazzaro bought some new lighting and furniture and art for the place, but that all got repossessed after I moved in. That's where all the holes in the walls came from." He laughed. "I like to think of my little palace here as *Architectural Digested.*"

Arthur put an arm around Jeremy's shoulders. "I think it's magical."

"You do?"

"Of course! The possibilities are amazing!"

"Like . . . what?"

"Well—" Arthur began pacing, pointing here and there, "—for one thing, this turtle-shell green on the walls needs to go; it would suck the light from a nuclear blast, and you need lots of light coming in. And you could switch out half of those broken French doors with double-paned ones that aren't mullioned, to open up the view. And get rid of those drapes." He grimaced at the ratty panels drooping over the living room windows. "And have someone come in to buff and patch the marble floors so they shine like glass again. And I'd love to see everything painted white: the walls flat white, the moldings glossy off-white. With the white marble floors, it would look incredible!"

"Umm, so what else?"

"I'd . . . probably go with white leather upholstery. Modern. With a few signature pieces like Le Corbusier and Mies van der Rohe—knock-offs, of course—and the rest you could buy at a basic furniture store. And I'd stick with really simple, natural finished modern case goods, but throw in a few reproduction Louis XV pieces—gilded, of course—and some contemporary art . . . just poster copies for now, like Picasso and Franz Kline." He pointed to the ceiling. "And chandeliers. *Lots* of crystal."

"Who's Franz Kline and Meese Rander Voe?"

"I'll show you pictures later." Arthur drew him into a hug. "We'll look at magazines and websites together . . . fix up one room at a time, and do most of the work ourselves. I can show you how to paint, to install new hardware, and fix these broken moldings and windows and everything!"

"You wouldn't mind?"

"Are you kidding?" Arthur laughed. "What's the outside look like? The deck and the grounds?"

"That's the best part." Jeremy rolled his eyes. "Come on."

He took Arthur by the hand and led him outside to where the dogs had already escaped.

"Look." Jeremy pointed.

Arthur looked. "At Bingham doing his business?"

"To the right of him."

Arthur saw where a cavernous, rectangular swimming pool lay empty—but for a few inches of algae-green water festering at the bottom—surrounded by dried weeds and a long stone balustrade and a cracked and lifted concrete patio on the edge of the property overlooking the ocean.

"There's something so sad about an empty pool," Arthur said.

"Especially with piles of dog crap around it."

"Do you think it's OK structurally?"

"Nothing else here is. Why should this be any different?"

Arthur turned to him. "Because it's your pool—and you're a champion swimmer and you love to swim, so we can get it fixed up!"

"And you're a champion dreamer." Jeremy hugged him. "You're somehow forgetting I don't have any money. I think it makes more sense to start hauling up sand from the beach to fill in the fucking thing. Then all the feral cats in Ballena Beach can poop in it. Yippee!"

Arthur kissed him. "Were you serious about what you said up at the lake . . . about us spending the rest of our lives together?"

"Is this house making you change your mind about saying 'yes'?"

"I'm serious."

"Arthur, do you really need to ask me that?"

"I just want to be sure you haven't changed your mind."

Jeremy's eyes searched Arthur's. "I'm ready to spend every day of my life with you. Starting with yesterday."

"And I with you." Arthur reached up and mussed Jeremy's hair. "So the minute we get back from Greece I'll put my condo on the market, and we can use whatever money I make from it to fix this place up."

"*Do you really mean it?!*"

"Old buddy, do you really need to ask me that?"

:::::::::

After dinner the men were yawning from the long day, and the dogs were snoring quietly atop the cold marble floor, so they decided to retire upstairs early.

They'd been perusing various websites looking for remodeling ideas for over an hour when Arthur's eyelids began dipping, so Jeremy quietly shut down his laptop and switched off the table lamp next to him.

Arthur drifted off almost as soon as his head hit the pillow, and then Jeremy glided asleep a few minutes later, a smile upon his lips.

:::::::::

Sometime later Jeremy's eyelids blinked open in the darkness.

Something's here . . . watching me.

His eyes searched the room and saw the comforting silhouette of Arthur's slumbering form rising and falling under the covers, while the muffled thrash of waves breaking on the shore assured him no windows or doors had been opened.

Then he caught sight of her.

Graceful as a swan skimming the surface of a pond, the woman materialized out of one dark corner of the room, drifted across the floor, and stood facing him. Jeremy saw she wore a floor-length dress of a dark textured material—black feathers?—and black velvet, opera-length gloves. But her shoulders, neck, and face were bare, and Jeremy noticed her skin was as white and translucent as moonlight. And no tresses flowed down upon her shoulders; instead, her hair had been pulled up underneath some sort of sequined hat . . . a matador's hat, he determined.

Jeremy had gradually slid himself up into a sitting position against the pillows when the room's air suddenly chilled his naked chest . . . as if the French doors had blown open.

His flesh bloomed goose bumps as he watched her slide above the floor, her dark eyes never leaving his, her silent red mouth poised as if about to say something important.

Is this one of those Sueño Gris flashbacks Carlo mentioned?

At last Jeremy summoned the courage to speak. "Who are you?" he whispered. "What do you want?"

Her expression remained unchanged and completely impassive. Instead of answering, she slowly held out one gloved hand while drawing closer to him.

In this glove he now saw she held an object like none Jeremy had seen before: something like a small axle with only one wooden wheel attached, and wound tight with pale thread so fine it might have been pulled from the back of a tarantula. At first she held up the object for him to see, but then she slipped it back into her pocket.

Nearer and nearer she came, and Jeremy considered shouting to awaken Arthur. But just as quickly as this thought formed itself in his mind, the wraith shook her head once as if to say "No."

Closer still the being came to him until he caught whiff of her scent.

Roses. Roses and lavender. And . . . sage, like the summer countryside.

Now near enough to kiss him, the apparition laid one gloved hand on his bare chest and the other on his forehead. Then Jeremy watched, his heart beating frantically, as she dipped her mascara-lined eyelids closed.

At once his vision was flooded with images of a sun-blanched landscape . . . olive trees and oaks and cypresses scattered amidst lumpy, dusty hills, while in the distance a mighty compound of ruined buildings and pools and gardens and orchards sprawled under a clear, cloudless sapphire sky.

Jeremy somehow felt himself standing there . . . standing amidst those ruins by himself.

He inhaled the scents and felt the desert-like air caress his forehead, neck, and chest.

Then her hands withdrew from his body, and the vision faded and morphed back into the reality of his bedroom.

He watched the entity glide backward and melt away into the darkness.

The bedroom's air cooled his skin once more, and the intoxicating botanical scents dissipated. He looked over. Arthur was still asleep.

Jeremy stared at the ceiling—troubled and preoccupied but still as a statue—until the first rays of sunlight urged him from his sheets to begin preparations for their trip to Greece.

CHAPTER

twenty-three

The US Air flight from Los Angeles made an uncomfortable but ultimately forgettable two-hour stopover in Philadelphia, and then finally descended into Athens International Airport more than twenty hours after Arthur and Jeremy had dropped off Bingham and Skipper at the Tyler Compound to be watched over by a nervous Aunt Katharine. "Don't think I've forgotten about the last time you two traveled internationally," she told them, her moony eyes shifting from one man to the other. "Please be careful."

After the couple landed, Jeremy and Arthur lurched stiff-kneed and zombielike up the aisles of the 767 to enter the jetway. They followed the signs to the baggage terminal, where they waited impatiently shoulder to shoulder with the other clustered travelers for their belongings to materialize.

After what seemed an interminable wait, their bags finally tumbled down the conveyor belt. Then, possessions in hand, they wended their way through the wandering hordes to the tiny Bank of Greece depot, where they exchanged credit card swipes for cash euros.

Finally replete with currency and all their traveling possessions, they headed outside to the curb.

"God, it's smoggy," Jeremy observed, curling his lip. "You never see skies this polluted in Los Angeles—thank God."

"Thank the EPA and the AQMD." Arthur scanned the dirty air and then slipped his Ray-Ban Aviators onto his face. "I think it's all the secondhand smoke from the Germans who come to visit. Did you see everyone smoking in that terminal?"

Jeremy placed his bags down onto the curb and stretched. "I was surprised when that French baby in the stroller at the baggage claim didn't light up with her parents. Hey, is this a cab?" A dirty yellow Mercedes four-door with its windows rolled down pulled up to the pair and stopped, its diesel engine idling like a metal pail swirling with gravel.

"Taxi?" the craggy-faced man behind the wheel asked.

The pair nodded, so the man exited the driver's door and made his way to the back of the car to open the trunk. "You go hotel?"

"The Hotel Philippos," Arthur told him as the driver hefted their bags over the bumper and laid them inside the trunk. "Downtown Athens, near the Acropolis."

The man drew a cigarette pack out of his shirt pocket. "Philippos Hotel."

They spent the next half hour or so speeding northwest along a freeway bordering dry fields and occasional farms, passing commercial centers and grove after grove of olive trees.

Finally they came to the outskirts of Athens, lurching, bumping, and threading their way through the early afternoon rush of Athenian traffic, with the taxi driver alternately taking drags off his cigarette and barking gibberish into his cell phone.

"What time are we meeting with the detectives?" Jeremy asked. "My brain is marshmallows and I can't remember."

"They're coming to the hotel tomorrow morning, so at least we can do whatever we want for the rest of today and tonight. What's on your agenda once we get to the hotel?"

"Grey Goose martinis and a sexy bath?"

Arthur laughed. "Are you . . . really craving a martini? I could use a nap; I hardly slept at all on the plane."

"I'm always in the mood for one—a martini, that is." Jeremy flashed Arthur a wan smile. "But don't worry, I'm OK. It's just that I didn't sleep either, and I'm feeling just as exhausted as I am keyed up." Jeremy checked out a group of athletic men pedaling bicycles as they wove through the cars stopped for the traffic light. "But I'd really like to explore; I mean, here we are in the land of some of the most gorgeous guys on the planet."

"Too bad the city's not so gorgeous," Arthur said as the light changed and they began passing through yet another block of haphazard architecture crisscrossed with power lines and cable wires, and long rows of dusty, filthy cars that appeared to have been parked at the curb for years. "It's not how I pictured it at all. This looks more like . . . Beirut, especially with all the graffiti and the soldiers carrying machine guns."

"What's that about?"

"You haven't heard of the riots they've been having? The austerity programs and the neo-Nazis and the anti-fascists?"

"I'd forgotten about all that. Hey!" Jeremy pointed. "The Acropolis!"

Arthur ducked his head to follow Jeremy's line of sight out of the bouncing cab's roof. "Well, there it is. Now *that's* exactly how I pictured it!"

The high, flat-topped mountain in the center of the city looked to have been built from countless mammoth stones assembled like chimney bricks, atop which the Parthenon crumbled majestically above the roofs and undulating streets, as if Zeus himself had snatched it from Mount Olympus and hurled it down onto that rise in the center of Athens.

The driver stopped in front of the hotel, got out to unload their bags, and shifted from foot to foot awaiting his fee. Arthur paid him, after taking some time to estimate a decent tip in euros.

After checking in and riding the elevator up to their floor, they located their room, sorted their clothes inside the dresser and closet, and then took a moment to freshen themselves.

Finally, Arthur turned to Jeremy. "You know what I said about taking a nap?"

"Yeah?"

"I'm feeling like I could really use some air. How about a walk?"

"I'd love that. We can acclimate to the time change and have an early dinner and go to bed; that way we won't be so jetlagged tomorrow for my big confrontation with Lazzaro."

"Do you feel like . . . maybe even hiking up to the Parthenon?"

"My thoughts exactly."

Arthur clapped him on the shoulder. "Let's go!"

:::::::::

Since no one could miss the Acropolis they had no need to ask for directions; instead they walked up Kallisperi Street up to Mitsaion toward the ancient monolith, and then followed the series of hand-painted signs directing them up the hillside past the bustling Plaka marketplace. They made their way along tiny, winding alleys suitable for vehicles no wider than a small scooter, and then passed by modest stucco-covered houses that looked to have been built into the hillside. Around each corner loomed overgrown bushes and paths that seemed to head nowhere, but whenever they suspected they'd taken a wrong turn and were about to give up and head back down, another hand-painted sign pointing farther up the path would miraculously appear.

Finally, they found themselves at the ticket gate at the base of the great monument.

"Yikes." Jeremy appraised the long stairway of stone steps before them. "Maybe we should do this tomorrow."

"*Acropolis* is Greek for 'high city.' Or hadn't you figured that out?"

Jeremy glared at him. "I'm game if you are."

"I just wish we'd brought some water with us." Arthur was feeling another headache coming on and was concerned it might be more than routine fatigue. "It's the hottest part of the afternoon."

"Hold on a sec." Jeremy scampered toward a nearby souvenir vendor, and then returned with a frosty bottle in each hand. He handed one over to Arthur. "Healing waters from the gods."

"Thank you." Arthur cracked the cap and took a long draught, and Jeremy did the same.

"After you," Arthur said, now optimistic that his headache might go away.

After paying the entrance fee, the couple spent the better part of an hour dodging batches of overheated tourists both ascending and descending the seemingly endless path; then at one point they stopped to rest and examine the ancient open-air amphitheater identified by a plaque as the Theater of Dionysus.

"Just give me a jar of wine and one of those high-backed throne chairs up front, and I'd even sit through a Justin Bieber concert here," Jeremy said. "But look how uncomfortable those benches are that go all the way to the top."

"The cheap seats. So nothing's changed in two thousand years"—Arthur scanned the amphitheater—"except all of the decorative stonework's missing. Wouldn't you have loved to watch a production of *Oedipus Rex* or *Antigone* on a warm summer night? I can almost see the actors in those weird masks, shouting like crazy so the poor folks at the top could hear them." He held out his arm. "It gives me goose bumps thinking about it."

"I picture all of the wandering eyes of those hunky Greek men checking out the other guys," Jeremy laughed. "Come on, we can fantasize more about that later."

Arthur and Jeremy continued proceeding up the stairs leading to the Parthenon, while taking several opportunities to stop under the narrow afternoon shade of a random olive or cypress tree to scan the panorama.

Somewhere near the top of the climb, as they were approaching their destination, Arthur turned and looked out over the city. "It must have been fantastic to live in Athens all those years ago knowing it was the greatest civilization of its time. The sculpture, the plays, those philosophers we still talk about today like Socrates and Plato, and"—he swept his arms in the air—"all of this phenomenal architecture."

"Was it really that utopian?"

"There were greedy bastards back then, too—and slavery was a part of life and children were exploited and women weren't treated equally; except for those living in Sparta, where they could own property and beat up suitors they didn't like, and they were trained and schooled as rigorously as the men."

"Then why aren't we walking around Spartan ruins?"

"Athens is on the bay and Sparta's inland, which allowed the Athenians to trade and make more money—and money buys beauty and power."

"Also just like today. But it's cool how at least some of the positive parts of their culture have transcended time."

"You're pretty much right about that. Anyhow, I'll bet the view here is pretty much the same as it was back then—at least from this distance."

Jeremy also looked out and saw the bay glimmering mirage-like in the distance. But then something closer caught his eye. "What's that?" He pointed to a grassy area below with a series of columns surrounded by scattered white discs, like the remains of giants' spinal vertebrae.

"It's been years since I studied this, but I think that open area with the columns is what's left of the Temple of Zeus, and beyond that's the site of the original Olympic stadium." Arthur put his hand on Jeremy's shoulder. "And that little gate near the boulevard is Hadrian's Arch. Can you see that?"

"Hadrian, the guy who built Hadrian's Wall?" Jeremy asked, squinting in the direction Arthur's finger pointed. "So is that part of the wall that was brought over from England?"

"Actually, whenever the emperor came to an important place, he commissioned something to commemorate his visit, so that must've been built when he was here. We should definitely check it out."

Finally, they made their way up the few remaining flights of stairs and found themselves standing in the shadow of the mighty Parthenon.

Arthur examined a sign printed in various languages. "*Built by Pericles in the Fifth Century BC to honor the gods for their victory over the Persians at Eurymedon.* I thought the Acropolis was older than that."

Jeremy tilted his head back. "I can't believe they were able to build this without power!"

"Don't forget, they had slave power."

"I'd rather not think about that. Let's see what else is up here."

The pair spent the better part of the hour wandering between the various temples, examining the carved motifs and reliefs and coffered stone ceilings, while Arthur did his best to put his mind at ease about the throbbing pressure building inside his head.

Then as the sun slid toward the western horizon and they began making their way back down toward the city, Arthur put a hand on Jeremy's shoulder. "Old buddy?"

Jeremy turned to him. "Yeah?"

"Do you remember that day when we first met? We had a conversation where I told you that knowing you're in love is as easy as knowing when you're hungry or realizing when you're full?"

Jeremy beamed at Arthur, recalling those very words. "And being in love with the wrong person is like convincing yourself you're full when you're still starving, or that you're hungry when you've eaten too much. I'll never forget it. Why?"

"Because just now my heart started feeling starved, and I know the only thing that'll fill it is a big hug. Or a kiss. From you."

Jeremy looked around. "There's a group of chubby tourists waddling our way, but I don't care if you don't."

Arthur grinned. "When in Greece—"

"Do as the Romans?"

Tears began gauzing Arthur's vision. "I can't believe I'm here with you."

"Why did we put this off for so long?"

"Guess we had to wait for just the right time."

With the sun securely nestled below the Athenian hillsides and the sky dimming its tangerine tint, the men kissed; but instead of becoming lost in this moment, Arthur was surprised by the single thought echoing through his mind, as if broadcast by a silent, insistent bullhorn:

I need to see a doctor.

"Let's go get some room service and some sleep," Arthur said as the pair turned and began footing their descent. "Tomorrow's going to get here fast."

CHAPTER

twenty-four

Arthur?" He felt a hand gently nudge him. "We need to get going." Arthur opened his eyes and found Jeremy standing over him, fully dressed although he sensed it was still very early. "Ummm . . . what time is it?"

"Already after nine."

"Wow." Arthur began moving upright but suddenly felt dizzy. "My body clock is way off." He waited for the dizziness to pass.

"Are you OK?"

"Just a little . . . tired. It must be the jetlag and the time change."

"The detectives'll be here at ten," Jeremy said. "Can I get you anything?"

"Coffee. Please?"

"Room service already delivered some. I'll get it ready for you." Jeremy made his way toward the kitchenette. "Want me to start your shower?"

Arthur closed his eyes. "That'd be great—just give me a minute." He swung his legs over to the side of the bed, took a breath, and stood.

The dizziness passed. *Good.*

After showering and dressing and downing three mugs of coffee along with two Motrin, Arthur felt ready for the day.

The detectives didn't arrive until almost eleven o'clock, but by the time they left—after showing Arthur and Jeremy a diagram outlining where the armed agents would be positioned, and teaching Jeremy how to conceal his bulletproof vest and use the voice transmitter disguised inside the arms of a pair of dumpy sunglasses—it was time for lunch.

"Where do you want to go?" Jeremy began gathering their wallets and sunglasses and phones.

"I'm thinking we avoid the Plaka today and head down toward the old Olympic coliseum and the Temple of Zeus. We could probably find a great place for lunch on the boulevard there, and do some sightseeing." Arthur grabbed two bottles of water and held one out to Jeremy. "I almost forgot: that place you sent me the link to looked like it could be good."

"What link?" Jeremy asked, taking the bottle from him.

"The one to that little café—with the view of bay."

"I don't . . . remember sending you a link," Jeremy said.

Arthur pulled his phone out of his pocket and held it for Jeremy to see. "This e-mail you sent me last night, it had a link to this restaurant. Here, look."

Jeremy examined the picture while suddenly recalling the hallucination of the drifting woman in black that he'd seen the other night in their bedroom. *Am I losing my mind?* "Oh, yeah," Jeremy laughed. "I forgot. I'm game if you are."

"OK then." Arthur slipped his phone back into his pocket. "Did Lazzaro call you yet?"

"He did when you were in the shower, and we're set to meet at six for dinner at a restaurant in the Plaka nearby where the agents'll be stationed."

"So everything's all set."

"He also told me he has the cash and can't wait to see my face when he gives it to me."

"Just like I love seeing your face when I give it to you. Nervous?"

Jeremy tried a smile. "A little."

"I was too until we met those detectives. Those dudes are impressive."

"I know it," Jeremy agreed. "At first I thought they were just skinny, but then I got a glimpse of their lats and forearms. Those guys are ripped!"

"It's all that *Krav Maga*. They're trained in Israel before they can work here, and they make my mixed martial arts bodyguards back home look like donut-eating NASCAR dads."

"Do you really feel comfortable letting them handle all this? After all, you're the guy with the bodyguard business."

"Judging from their answers to every question I asked—cloaking, surveillance, firearms, communication . . . even crowd control—I'm convinced that they're total pros." Arthur leaned over to tie his shoes. "And I can understand why they don't want me to participate; they've been training for years as a team, so I might only get in their way."

"Why?"

"Cops act the same way with the FBI—they'll hand off a case completely from one to the other to ensure fluidity of tactical operations as well as clarity of jurisdiction."

"So what'll you do?"

"I'll just . . . hang around the Plaka while you're meeting with Lazzaro. Maybe I'll even find a café close by so I can jump in *just in case* I'm needed. You're going to eat with him, right?"

"I can't imagine I'll be hungry."

"I'd feel the same way." Arthur stood up. "Jeremy, I hate to ask you this but . . . did you know anything about the drugs Lazzaro is accused of trafficking? Some kind of new hallucinogen?"

Jeremy looked down and then brought his eyes up to Arthur's. "Yeah."

"Did you . . . ever take any of it?"

"A few times."

"Are you still using it?"

"Absolutely not."

"Did you ever help him sell or distribute it?"

"*Never.*"

"Good enough. So are you ready to go explore?"

"Yep." Jeremy grinned. "I'm ready."

:::::::::

The pair set out on foot with their water bottles in hand and began making their way down the streets and boulevards in the direction of the temple and the coliseum while relying on Arthur's sense of direction, instead of maps, to guide them to their destination.

Eventually they made a right on Filellinon Street and walked down to Leoforos Vasilissis, where the taxis and scooters and trucks and tiny sedans zoomed noisily by at reckless speeds.

Moments later they were looking across the street at the ruins.

"Isn't that the structure of Hadrian's you were talking about?" Jeremy asked, pointing at the narrow, flat wall pierced by an arch, with another light-scale structure balanced atop it.

They waited for traffic to stop for the signal and then began crossing the street.

"That's it," Arthur replied, quickening his step. "It's easy to see how it represents ancient Greece being supported by modern—at the time, I mean—Rome."

Jeremy cocked his head and laughed. "Oh yeah? Easy for you, maybe. What are you talking about?

As they strolled along the grass toward the gate, Arthur helped him see it.

"The top half—" Arthur pointed, "—those columns forming the three rectangles and the pediment in the center? They look like what we saw yesterday at the Parthenon, don't they?" Jeremy nodded. "Even the Corinthian columns are similar to the Doric columns except for the very tops, the capitals," Arthur went on. "But the bottom half, the base, almost looks like part of a Roman aqueduct. It's got a typical Tuscan arch in the center held up by Corinthian pilasters and surrounded by solid marble blocks. It's an interesting melding of two very different architectural and cultural styles."

"I can see it, but just listen to you," Jeremy said. "How do you know so much about this?"

"I studied Greek and Roman architecture in high school; I guess I was transfixed by the idea of thriving civilizations that encouraged our kind of love."

"It kind of . . . reminds me of a big, strong guy with his younger lover riding on his shoulders," Jeremy told him. "Almost like—oh my God, remember how I jumped on your back when we were skinny-dipping in that lagoon in Brazil?"

"An act that will live in infamy. But I think you might be on to something there."

"What else do you know about Hadrian?"

"Not much," Arthur replied. "I was more interested in his buildings: the Pantheon in Rome; his villa at Tibur . . . and others, but I can't remember the names. As I recall, though, Hadrian was quite a guy: an architect, a poet, a soldier, and a commander, and he's considered to be one of Rome's best and fairest emperors. And he was openly homosexual."

Jeremy looked adoringly at Arthur. "He sounds a lot like you."

"I'm guessing that, also like me, he had his faults."

"So he wasn't married?"

"From what I recall he did have some sort of loveless marriage with a woman named, what was it, *Sabina*. But the love of his life was—"

Suddenly Arthur was hit with a dull pain in his head and a wave of dizziness so strong he thought he'd fallen into a hole. Knees buckling, he reached out to grab Jeremy's shoulder. *God, no.* "I gotta sit," he gasped.

"You OK?!" Jeremy took his arm and Arthur eased himself down onto the grass. "What's going on?!"

"It's . . . I'm not sure." His eyes followed Jeremy as he sat down next to him. "I guess the heat and the long trip yesterday and the climb up to the Parthenon were harder on my old bones than I thought."

"Could it be something you ate?" Jeremy pointed at the half-empty bottle in Arthur's hand. "Did you drink enough water?"

Arthur downed a swig from his bottle. "I'm sure that's all it is," he said, praying it was.

A few minutes later Arthur began feeling better. He looked over at Jeremy. "What were we talking about?"

"You were about to tell me who the real love of Hadrian's life was." Jeremy scrutinized him. "Your skin's got its color back."

"But now I can't remember what his name was."

"Can you make it back to the hotel?"

"Sometimes I get this, and it just comes and goes. Just give me a minute and I'll be fine."

"Are you sure? Should we take a cab?"

"I'll be fine." Arthur looked up at Jeremy, glanced over at the arch, and sighed. "Promise."

CHAPTER

twenty-five

The tiny old woman scrutinized Lazzaro suspiciously. "Is this a joke?" she asked in Greek, looking around. "Where are the cameras?" Straightening as much as her bent spine would allow, she adjusted the bright blue scarf wrapped around her head.

"I am in need of employment to pay for my mother's medicines," Lazzaro told her, gazing wistfully into her beady, milky eyes. "I worked as a seafood chef and waiter in Lastovo, Croatia, for many years, where I became the favorite of many tourists; I speak Greek, Spanish, French, Turkish, and English—and just enough Arabic to get me into trouble; and I can cook whitefish so well you might think you are eating lobster."

She wrinkled her nose at him and threw him a dismissive gesture with her shriveled brown hand. "You too handsome." *Ptuh!* She pretended to spit onto the floor. "I never saw a good-looking man as you do an honest day's work."

He tried out his most hopeful smile on her. "Won't you give me a chance? I will not charge you one euro. And if you do not like my work"—he made the obscene *moutza* sign with his hand—"*I* will pay *you* for my time here."

The *moutza* caused the old woman to giggle, and a faint blush crept into her prune-like cheeks. "You got an apron?"

Lazzaro shook his head. "No, Yiayia."

She looked him up and down. "You need apron. I no want you coming out to the tables with blood on that shirt."

Lazzaro smiled. "I will use a big towel."

She squinted at him. "Tell me . . . what is the secret of cheese pies?"

"Saffron."

"What you put into *soumatha* to give it flavor?"

"*Masticha.*"

She glared at him in silence, and then finally nodded.

He grinned at her. "When can I start?"

She glanced up at the dimming sky and then scanned the bustling marketplace. "The Plaka will get too many hungry people here in, oh, three hours . . . more people than my granddaughter can handle. You go right now into back and find out where is everything: the knives, the oven, the food." She paused. "I'm hungry, so you go make me some *dolmadakia* with *tzatziki*. If it's good, you can work tonight." Her eyes scrutinized him. "And do not get any ideas about my Adonia; my granddaughter is already betrothed—he is stupid, but a good worker."

Lazzaro leaned in close to her. "You will have no worries, Yiayia. I only like the men," he lied, thinking of his frenzied romps with Carmella.

A big, nearly-toothless grin opened her face. "A *pousti?* You shoulda tell me before!" She laughed, clapping him about the waist. Then in an instant her smile vanished and her face darkened. "You keep your hands off my grandson Iapetus, OK? He only seventeen."

Lazzaro laughed. "OK."

"I just hope he keeps his hands off you." The old woman turned and began hobbling toward one of the tables by the walkway. "Where are my *dolmadakia*?" she shouted at him as she sat down, drawing a crinkled cigarette pack from her tattered apron's pocket. "And a little ouzo—the cold bottle on ice, not the cheap one for the customers." She pinched out a cigarette, lit it with a match, and began watching the tourists amble by as Lazzaro slipped—grinning—into the kitchen, satisfied now that the final obstacle to the success of his scheme had just been overcome.

All he had to do now was wait for Jeremy to arrive and for Arthur to wander by—something he was certain would happen before the dinnertime rush was over. And when Arthur did wander by, Lazzaro knew precisely the ruse with which to garner his attention—a trick taught to him by a veteran prostitute he knew who could lasso just about any man from a crowd.

And although he'd never met Arthur . . . this was no longer a problem: Last night, while Tristan slept, Lazzaro had reviewed the files copied from Jeremy's computer onto his cloud and discovered pictures of Jeremy laughing alongside an older, handsome man—clearly Arthur—on the beach. Even though the pictures had been taken several years ago, they gave him enough information to work with . . . as did the link he'd sent Arthur about the sea view café from Jeremy's computer that, once opened, allowed him access to all of Arthur's personal files.

Lazzaro drew his iPhone out from his pocket, swiped the screen, and examined the photo once more: Arthur looked to be just over six feet tall, wide shoulders and chest, bulging biceps, cropped hair, prominent nose, kind gray eyes, easy smile.

Poor man. I'd know him anywhere.

:::::::::

At about half-past five Jeremy located their appointed restaurant, *Medusa's Garden*. Lazzaro had given him specific instructions so the place was easy to find; it was a bustling outdoor café making up the

Plaka's hub, with tables covered in red-and-white checkered cloths and sheltered by olive trees and thick stands of potted lavender and rosemary.

Jeremy had been told to pretend that the Interpol agents were nowhere in the vicinity. To help him with this, they instructed him to imagine he was being filmed in a movie or television show, and like any actor he had to block the presence of camera equipment and boom operators—and anxiety—from his mind because of the possibility that Lazzaro would smell it on him and figure out that their meeting was a setup.

Which apparently he did.

Six o'clock came and went.

Then a few minutes later, Jeremy's ears pricked at the sound of police sirens wailing and squabbling with each other somewhere in the near distance.

Just after six-thirty, with Jeremy growing more and more frustrated and his mind hamster-wheeling about his damn mortgage and what Arthur's dizziness might have to do with the medications he found in his luggage, and why hadn't he just asked him about it and could it be that Arthur was hiding something from him, he spotted a statuesque blonde rounding the corner. She was wearing sunglasses and a white, pleated, halter-top Marilyn Monroe–style dress that showed off her ample bosom and graceful arms, and she carried a large purse in one gloved hand and a bottle of red wine and two glasses in the other.

She stopped in front of his table.

"Jeremy Tyler?" she asked, her voice low and suggestive.

Jeremy looked up at her, wondering if she were a drag queen. "Who're you?"

"Lazzaro sends his regrets," she told him, and placed the wine bottle and glasses atop the table. "Do you mind if I join you?"

Unsmiling, Jeremy pointed to the chair. "Sure."

She continued standing, as if not having heard him.

Jeremy got the message. He stood and quickly yanked out her chair.

"How has your trip been so far?" she asked, folding herself down into the seat and scooting herself up to the table.

"I asked who you are."

She cracked the metal cap on the bottle and carefully poured two glasses of wine and presented one to Jeremy. "And I asked how your trip has been."

"I don't drink anymore," he said, sliding the glass back to her.

They stared at each other in silence.

"Your trip?" she asked once more, and then sipped a little of her wine.

"We haven't seen much yet," Jeremy finally replied, noting the large smudge of red lipstick on her glass. "But our hotel is close to the Acropolis and to Hadrian's Arch, so we've seen those."

"The Hotel Kristos? I simply adore their rooftop lounge."

"The Hotel Philippos," Jeremy responded, at once regretting he'd divulged where they were staying.

"Not the most luxurious," she noted, taking a small silver case from her purse. "But not the worst, either." She snapped open the case with her gloved fingers and drew out a cigarette. "Lazzaro tells me—"

"By the way, where is the son-of-a-bitch?"

She calmly lit her cigarette and blew out a cloud of smoke. "As I was saying, Lazzaro tells me you and your former lover are back together. He and my son are very happy for the two of you. They are also together—actually, they were never apart, except for his unfortunate visit to America. Lazzaro is everything my son has ever wanted and he loves him more than life itself, and once this mess is resolved they can finally begin making a reality of their dreams."

"I really couldn't care less. So where's the money from him? I hope you brought cash because I'm not sure I'd take even a cashier's check from that asshole."

"Unfortunately, there's been a change in plans." She took another taste of her wine, and then an especially long drag off her cigarette. "Lazzaro's financial advisor is very, very, *very* unhappy with the real estate deal you two made. He insists Lazzaro hastily undervalued his property by a million of your dollars. But because Lazzaro is a man of his word, he is willing to split the difference with you and only wants two hundred thousand euros, or about five hundred thousand dollars, depending on the daily exchange rate. How long will it take you to gather the money?"

Jeremy felt his heart race and his face flush. "That house still had a fucking mortgage on it that he didn't tell me about! I've already paid twice for that goddamn teardown. Tell him no fucking way!" he shouted. "*No way!*"

"Please, please calm yourself." She shook her head at him, her face still obscured by the huge sunglasses. "People will think you a poorly behaved American shouting at a lovely lady."

Jeremy clamped his mouth shut.

She leaned forward, elbows on the table. "Lazzaro told me to remind you that you had been drinking heavily and were quite insistent that he accept the amount you offered, because you told him that although the property was undervalued, someday it would be worth three or four times what he was asking. Lazzaro tried convincing you that he only wanted a fair deal, but you insisted on taking over the house and the mortgage, and he honored your wish in spite of his objections. He told me you are a man of great character"—her mouth bent into a pout—"but your terrible problem with alcohol clouds your judgment."

"That fuck-head Lazzaro is a goddamn liar!"

"When should I tell him you will be able to deliver the money, the two hundred thousand euros?"

"Tell Lazzaro I'll bring the money to him in jail." Jeremy bolted upright from the table and threw his napkin down . . . but then remembered that this conversation was being recorded, and every word might make a difference.

I wonder if her ugly glasses hold a voice transmitter, too.

She sighed, holding up a gloved hand. "I'm sorry to do this, Jeremy, but he warned me you might react this way." She gestured to Jeremy's chair. "I suggest you sit down and hear what I need to tell you. Would some of this wine help you to relax?" Once again, she slid the brimming glass toward his side of the table.

Jeremy slowly sat down, thinking the wine probably would help. *No.* "I told you I don't drink anymore."

"A noble notion." She nodded slowly, patronizingly. "Now, Lazzaro told me how he did not want me to bring this up unless it was completely necessary, but apparently it is."

Jeremy rolled his eyes. "What is it?"

"I'm afraid I must discuss with you your role in the plot to kill Francesco Sforza."

CHAPTER

twenty-six

Arthur, seeing that Jeremy was securely in place at his café table while presumably being watched over by the loitering covert agents, began ambling about the Plaka. Unsettled by his headache and bouts of dizziness that morning, he had some hard thinking to do about how and when to tell Jeremy about his health issues.

In spite of the cacophony of police sirens wailing somewhere nearby, the Plaka seemed to be getting more crowded by the moment now that night had come and the dinner rush was in full swing; when Jeremy and Arthur had arrived at the marketplace the majority of the tables were empty, now most were occupied.

Arthur found it interesting to eavesdrop here and there, trying to figure out what languages were being spoken and what stage of happiness—or dissatisfaction—the couples and families eating together displayed. And he was enticed by the exotic scents of the food cooking around him: bubbling tomato sauces and fresh oregano, and sizzling, spiced meats and baking bread.

What would it hurt to get something to eat?

Arthur strolled easily from café to café, examining menus while being beseeched by the waiters or hosts who stood at their respective restaurants' entrances. "Come in! Come in!" each man importuned. "Very authentic food. Best in Athens!"

Arthur smiled at each, shaking his head. "No thank you," he told them, one by one, knowing that Jeremy might be finished earlier than expected with his meeting and would come looking for him.

He finally decided to find a café close—but not too close—to the location of Jeremy's meeting place.

Arthur had just begun to peruse the menu of a tiny, empty café when a gentle hand on his shoulder startled him. "Excuse me," asked a sonorous voice with an intoxicating accent. "But did you drop this?"

Arthur turned and found himself staring into one of the most handsome Mediterranean faces he had ever seen: bronzed skin, Roman nose, full lips, and square jaw. And even behind the man's eyeglasses, his huge, dark eyes were as soulful as they were hypnotic.

The bandana-headed waiter was holding out a wallet, grinning at him.

Arthur felt for the lump in his front pocket. "No, thanks. I didn't."

"Are you sure?" the waiter asked. "I thought I noticed you drop something just now."

"I'm sure." Arthur smiled. "But thank you."

"You have that hungry look," the waiter said, his suggestive gaze never leaving Arthur's, "and I just brought some pita out from the oven—it is hot and fresh—and we have a fantastic sundried tomato pesto and the freshest feta in all of Athens. Would you like to try a taste? No charge." The tall man pulled out a chair for him at one of the nearby tables. "Please. You look like you could use a rest from walking."

What the hell, Arthur thought. *I could just sit here and look at this guy.* He made his way over to the chair and sat.

"Would you like something to drink? Wine, mineral water, coffee?"

"How about some white wine?"

"You must be an American," the man laughed. "Only Americans ask for white wine in Greece."

"Yep." Arthur laughed as well. "We have very predictable taste."

"I have just the perfect *Moschofilero* for you. It is a bit spicy," he said, briefly pinching together his thumb and index finger, "but it is also floral. You will like it."

"Sounds great. Thank you."

While he was waiting, Arthur sat back in the hard metal chair and performed a mental body check: Did he feel dizzy? *No.* Tired? *Not really.* Headache? *Nope.* Depressed? *Thankfully, no.* Hungry? *Starving.*

Everything's fine.

But that dizziness this morning . . .

I'd better have that MRI the moment we arrive home from this trip.

And then his anxiety began wrenching upward—the thought of driving to the hospital, the waiting, trying to lie in that contraption without moving, the machine's awful racket . . . and then the interminable waiting for the results!

He felt panic rising within him, despite his efforts to stifle it.

What if I have another dizzy spell?

I've got to tell Jeremy about the gamma knife surgery and the chemo and the possibility of another brain tumor. It's not fair to him.

The waiter arrived with a tray, atop which teetered a frost-covered glass of wine, a basket of bread, and two saucers—one containing red pesto and in the other a clump of white, crumbled cheese.

The handsome man put these in front of Arthur. "Is there anything more I may bring you?" He leaned in closer. *A little too close.* "We have some very savory kabobs that are on the fire right now; when they are cooked you might be ready by then for more food?"

"That's OK. I'm meeting someone in a little while."

"That is a coincidence," the waiter said, straightening up. "I was to meet someone here too, tonight. My ex-lover. But something unforeseen happened with him so I called off the meeting."

Arthur dabbed his pita bread into the pesto, and sprinkled some feta atop it. *So this gorgeous creature is gay?* "That's too bad." He took a bite. *Oh, that's good.*

"May I tell you what happened?" the waiter asked. "Something tells me you will find it interesting."

Arthur took a leisurely sip of his wine. "Sure."

"This ex-lover of mine," the waiter continued, "he is now with his lover before me. An older man who is very sick."

Arthur stopped chewing and looked up at the man. "Really?" he mumbled.

"Yes." The waiter pulled out the chair opposite Arthur and sat. "This older man has a tumor"—he pointed to his temple—"in his brain. He had treatments and many medications to correct it, but sadly tumors of this nature always come back. The older man is afraid to tell his younger lover because he is scared he will leave him." He frowned at Arthur, shaking his head. "I suppose no one wants to die alone, and this older man is no different. Especially not a death so horrible as cancer of the brain."

Arthur's hands had dropped to his side and he somehow managed to swallow the lump of food in his mouth.

"So I found this older man and I talk to him," the waiter softly continued, "I tell him, 'Do you really want your lover to see you waste away and die? Wouldn't you prefer to send him away now—tell him you don't love him anymore, tell him *anything*—so you won't need to put him through the torture of seeing you turn into bones stretched with skin?' Then I tell him I will take good care of his lover . . . I will see that he has everything he needs to be happy and he will get fucked hard by me"—he pumped a clenched fist into the air—"the way he likes, and when the time comes—after the older man is dead and buried in the ground and he no longer needs his diapers changed—I will tell this lover about the sacrifice he made by sending him away. I will tell him that his love was so strong that he made the very best sacrifice for him, and he only wanted for his younger, handsome lover to live a long and happy life."

And still Arthur found himself unable to speak, or even think.

"But this older man is foolish," the waiter went on. "He told me I was wrong and it was none of my business and he would tell his lover about his disease only when he was ready, so I went ahead and told the young lover about this older man's disease to do them both a favor. And when I told him about my telling his lover the truth, do you know what this older, sick man did?"

Arthur could only stare blankly at Lazzaro.

Lazzaro launched a maniacal laugh. "He looked at me just the way you are looking at me now!"

At that moment an old, shrunken, wrinkled woman stuck her head out from the kitchen. "Σας! Σταματήσουμε να μιλάμε με τους πελάτες!" she yelled at him.

"You were right about me, Yiayia!" he called back to her in Greek. "I am no good for work here!"

Lazzaro got up from the chair, clapped Arthur amiably on the shoulder, unwrapped the kitchen towel from around his waist, and laid it carefully on the back of his chair, and then swaggered off into the bustling Plaka, its dinner rush now in full, noisy bustle.

CHAPTER

twenty-seven

As I was saying," Marilyn Monroe continued, "Lazzaro was a bit disturbed about how much you resented Francesco Sforza for killing Lazzaro's mother, but he understood this had something to do with your uncle killing both your parents—what the psychologists call 'transference' or something like that. He told me how you said people should get what they deserve, and since you killed your uncle in retribution, you would be happy to help him do the same to Lazzaro's father."

Jeremy blinked wildly, shaking his head. "What . . . what kind of a joke is this? I don't know what the hell you're talking about!"

"You've forgotten this as well? You must have been drinking very much each day." She shook her head, clucking her tongue. "Even the guards from the boat will attest to your having been onboard that very night."

Jeremy leaned in close. "But I'm sober enough to know I didn't kill his father! I don't even know how he died, but I'm guessing he choked on a dildo!"

She sipped more of her wine. "Are you insisting that you never held any conversation of this sort?"

Jeremy paused. "I told him about my uncle killing my parents, but that was all."

She inhaled more of her cigarette. "Lazzaro told me he never wanted any part in your plan, but you did what you wanted to anyway. He said you used his fragile mental state—his grief at losing his mother—to play up the need for revenge on Francesco. He tried to reason with you, but you were drunk with that Grey Goose vodka every day and crazed with hallucinations from the Sueño Gris."

Jeremy sat back in his chair, his arms folded over his chest. "This is insane."

"Did you not wire a tremendous sum of money to Lazzaro in Italy, only days after Francesco was killed, to buy his silence?"

"That was for the sale of the house!"

"I have a copy of the wire transfer safely in my possession," she said, "which I am ready to hand over to the police. This will implicate you in Francesco's murder, where your rage and your drug abuse caused you to think you could recruit others to carry out your hateful desires."

"So that's the best you could come up with?" Jeremy laughed. "It's a good thing you don't write scripts—or novels. Tell Lazzaro he's a big disappointment."

"OH! *Thank you* for reminding me; I nearly forgot," she muttered while pulling her iPhone from her purse. She swiped the screen a few times and then held up the phone for Jeremy to see.

Lazzaro's tiny, electronic face popped up and began speaking. "Hello Jeremy. I was truly looking forward to meeting with you today. But when I discovered you had been sent here with police agents to arrest me I decided to record this message for you instead, which is why your beautiful dinner companion was a little late. And for this, I hope you will please accept my apology.

"I am disappointed that you felt you could not trust me, and you betrayed me. I worry for your safety here in Athens, and I worry about what will become of you back in Ballena Beach. Why? I will tell you now.

"Do you remember the e-mail you sent me the night after you met with your friends at the restaurant and I was unable to attend? Let me read it slowly to you—omitting your drunken errors in syntax, of course—in case you have forgotten what you wrote: *You have no idea how furious I was sitting there waiting for you and you didn't have the respect or consideration for me to call or even text me back and let me know you weren't coming? You have no idea how furious I was sitting there waiting for you.* Now here," Lazzaro continued, "is the most important favorite part: *Next time your father visits I hope you put a bullet in his head and throw his body into the marina because that's what he deserves and that's what I would do. I won't ever forget tonight. You owe me big time, Lazzaro.* But now I am the one paying the price—I am a fugitive from the law for your role in killing my father. So please know that if you assist the authorities again I will bring you to prison with me; I have the proof I need between this e-mail and the money transfer and the conversations we had where you coerced me into providing you the opportunity to murder my dear father, Francesco Sforza.

"All I am asking for is another two hundred thousand euros, which I know you can afford; I have access to your bank accounts, so I know how many American dollars remain in your trust. I will call you tomorrow to let you know where you can deliver the cash.

"I will always be grateful for the time we spent together, and I wish you and your lover whatever happiness you might enjoy. I hope someday you will wish the same for me."

She put her phone away and looked at him expectantly.

"Greek jails," she began, "are very different than American jails. Here you don't even need to 'drop the soap' to be raped." She cocked an eyebrow and leered. "But before you get excited by that possibility, you should know that your cellmates are usually fat, smelly Turks or insane North Africans. And even if you are eventually acquitted, the trial will be long and difficult and costly."

"This is blackmail." Jeremy glanced around to see if the agents were closing in. "You know and I know these are nothing but lies! You and Lazzaro are thieves!"

"That is all I have to say," she said, scooting back her chair. "I cannot sit here and listen to you say such untruths about Lazzaro. He and my son will be together forever, and I trust him completely." She smiled. "I will tell Mr. Sforza that you will have an answer for him within the hour. And if the answer is no, be assured that you will be named as the perpetrator of this murder; this wire transfer and a copy of your e-mail will go to the Hellenic police and they will arrest you at, now where were you staying, the Hotel Philippos?"

"You are harboring a criminal," Jeremy said darkly, watching the night sky glow orange in the distance. *What's burning?* "You'll be charged as an accessory."

She laughed. "This is Greece, handsome one. The austerity programs most now suffer through have unintentionally provided special privileges for those of us with deep resources and extended government connections. It may be unfair, but this is how it now is." She stood. "Lazzaro told me that as trustee of your trust, you can have the money wired to any bank in Athens. Or should I send the police to the Hotel Philippos?"

"Send the police," Jeremy snarled. "Tonight even. The sooner the better."

Her phone began ringing, so she retrieved it from her purse again and held it to her ear. "Yes, my love?"

Jeremy watched her as she listened.

"Jeremy said 'no.' He is refusing to pay you more money, and he told me to send the police to his hotel to have him arrested."

She listened some more.

"You are certain you wish me to tell him this?" She paused. "If this is your desire then I will let him know." She ended the call and dropped the phone inside her purse. "Lazzaro will give you one more chance and will call you in the morning out of sympathy because . . . your lover, the older man? Lazzaro wants you to know that he has . . . a brain tumor, but has not told you because he is afraid you will leave him. Good night."

She turned and vanished into the nighttime crush.

As the frenetic hubbub of tourists and shopkeepers and food servers and musicians swirled around Jeremy—in a state of shock over Lazzaro's spiteful revelation—a single notion bubbled up from the depths of his unconscious like the final exhalation from a drowning man:

An . . . tin . . . ooooz.

Jeremy, his mind numbed into another dimension, said it aloud by melting together the syllables.

"An*tin*—noos."

He tried it one last time, a word now . . . *or perhaps a name.*

"Antinous."

CHAPTER

twenty-eight

"I can't believe you didn't tell me this," Jeremy told Arthur, his eyes spilling tears. "What were you afraid of?"

Arthur examined their hotel room's cheap blue carpeting, his dirty cross-training shoes on the floor by the bed, the lumpy stucco walls—anything to avoid looking into Jeremy's eyes. "I was going to wait until my next MRI, which is scheduled for a few weeks from now. I figured the test would be clear and then I could break this all to you with some great, brilliant news." Arthur sighed, looking up. "I didn't want to worry you, especially with all this drama—your house debacle, being suspended from Tyler, Inc., all this craziness with Lazzaro . . ."

"Will you please level with me? How bad is it? What's the prognosis?"

"They found it almost a year ago and I went in for treatment immediately. It's called a *craniopharyngioma multiforme II*, and mine was supposed to be benign—at least I thought the gamma knife surgery, which uses radiation the way a surgeon uses a scalpel, took care of it."

"What makes you think it's come back?"

"Because I'm starting to have the same symptoms: headaches, dizziness, some disorientation. I . . . I guess I was in denial about it, because there's always something else I can attribute the symptoms to."

Jeremy began pacing. "Maybe this time they *are* attributable to other things, like traveling to the other side of the planet and getting stressed out about everything that's fucking going on, thanks to me."

"Actually . . . I started feeling this way even before we left on the trip."

"Well at least I know now what those medications are for."

"You found 'em?"

"When we were up at Lake Estrella."

"You were going through my things?"

"I was curious about the bulge in your luggage, so I unzipped it and looked inside."

"There you go, getting into trouble with bulging zippers again," Arthur told him with a grim smile. "I'm just sorry you had to hear it from Lazzaro by way of that awful woman. If only I'd had the balls to tell you myself."

"Serves me right for snooping." Jeremy stopped pacing and stared at Arthur. "We need to get you back home—I'm changing our flight reservations to tomorrow." He grabbed his iPhone from the desk and began scrolling through its screens.

"But what about Lazzaro's demand for more money?" Arthur asked, recalling the conversation with Agent Singer and the possibility that Jeremy might be swept into the drug and sex trafficking charges. "Does he have anything on you that I don't know about?"

Jeremy hesitated. "It's too hard to explain."

Arthur steeled himself for the worst. "*Tell me.*"

Jeremy took a moment to explain to Arthur about the e-mail he'd sent regarding Lazzaro's father, the wire transfer to "buy his silence," and having been on board the yacht the night of the murder.

Arthur got up from the bed and crossed the room to where Jeremy stood. "This guy is dangerous in a way I've seldom encountered."

"How so?"

"On top of putting everything together the way he has, somehow Lazzaro gained access to my medical history. I was sitting there wondering, 'How am I going to tell Jeremy about my tumor symptoms returning' and thinking about the gamma knife surgery I had and how much I hate going in for this MRI, and he was already a step ahead of me! *How did he know?!*" Arthur began pacing the length of the hotel room. "At least when they question your . . . *Marilyn Monroe* character, they'll get a better idea where they can find Lazzaro. And wouldn't you know he was hiding in plain sight at that café! If only I'd been thinking clearly, I would've tackled him! If only I hadn't been in . . . such a state of *shock* when he told me what he did—it's like my brain completely short-circuited." He continued pacing. "Let me think about this. I want to have this chapter in your life closed for good, *especially* if I need to have treatments again."

"I'm scared, Arthur. Really scared!"

"Look . . . when I was a teenager, the AIDS epidemic hit and I figured I'd never make it past twenty-five—but here I am. You never know what the future holds. And baby, you're stronger than you realize. This is just one of those wobbling bridges that we'll cross together. And I think the timing is fortuitous; once we come through this we'll be golden! You'll get this situation settled with Lazzaro and your house; Aunt Katharine will reinstate you with Tyler, Inc.; I'll recover from this health scare and we can enjoy our time remodeling that crazy mansion with Bingham and Skipper chasing tennis balls through the cracked marble hallways."

"But—"

"No buts, Jeremy. And I know what you're thinking, that Lazzaro said I was dying." Arthur faced him, his hands squarely gripping his shoulders. "He might be clever enough to access my medical records, but he's not a doctor reading an MRI. Let's leave all the prognosticating to the surgeons, OK?"

Jeremy's eyes began filling with tears again. "OK."

"Don't cry." Arthur drew him into a hug.

"I'm just so mad at myself."

"Why?"

"Because I want to be strong for you, and here I am all crybabyish." He sighed against Arthur's chest. "Tell me. What's it like for you going through this?"

"It's like . . . having your brain go from being your friend to your greatest enemy. Like being in a dungeon with a dragon, but you're both the prisoner *and* the dragon."

"How've you kept your sanity?"

"I've had a lot more time getting used to all this than you." Arthur squeezed him. "And having you here makes me stronger."

"We're going to get through this."

"You bet we are."

Arthur's phone began ringing. He released Jeremy, crossed the room, and picked it up. "Art Blauefee."

Jeremy watched as Arthur's hopeful expression melted into one of disappointment.

"I understand, and I hope they recover soon. Thanks for letting us know." Arthur put down his phone and looked up at Jeremy. "They lost Marilyn Monroe."

"*How did they do that?*"

"Interpol was set to take whoever they needed into custody, but just before your meeting tonight, a riot broke out down the hill from the Plaka—"

"So that's what it was! I saw the sky light up and heard the sirens! What happened?"

"Yet another conflict between the neo-Nazis and some anti-fascist squatters at the Villa Amalia, about a mile away. Any Hellenic police in the area not tending to acute situations were ordered to pacify the disturbance."

"My situation wasn't acute enough?"

"Well . . . Lazzaro never showed up to meet with you, and, at the riot, two police officers were injured—one pretty badly, from what the inspector told me—"

"That's terrible."

"—so the officers assigned to you were yanked over to the riot, which was turning ugly, quickly. People have been killed and entire city blocks have been torched."

"Oh God."

"At least the man on the phone assured me that they went back and lifted fingerprints from your table. No results yet, though."

"It wouldn't matter anyway," Jeremy glumly told him. "Marilyn was wearing gloves."

:::::::::

After their room service dinner, Arthur was feeling wiped out from the day's stresses and decided to head off to bed early; Jeremy, too antsy to sleep, turned on the television and began channel surfing: vapid American reality shows; frenetic Greek soccer matches; stoic news programs that highlighted the evening's riot—apparently started by a Molotov-cocktail-heaving motorcyclist—along with the conditions of the injured police officers; and a few dramas and situation comedies where Jeremy tried to ascertain what was happening, but the indecipherable gabble being spoken prevented him from extracting any viewing pleasure.

He switched off the TV, and then, sometime before midnight, Jeremy's eyelids closed and he fell into an uneasy sleep . . . but then spent the next couple of hours waking and dozing and twisting the bedsheets and trying to find a position on the hard pillow where his head felt comfortable.

Eventually his body surrendered to its exhaustion just as a scene began flickering through his dimming consciousness . . .

:::::::::

"Jeremiah?"

The gentle hand on his shoulder startled him awake, and the doctor sat down on the wooden stool facing the bed. "Oh . . . sorry I fell to sleep," Jeremiah said, and rubbed his eyes.

The dawn's dim blue light glowed against the closed curtains behind the doctor's head. The old man's eyes were bloodshot, and his jowls and eyelid bags seemed to sag even lower than usual.

Jeremiah made himself ask the question. "Is . . . she doin' any better?"

"We did everything we could, son."

Jeremiah stared at the doctor, and the doctor stared at Jeremiah.

"My mother . . . she's dead?"

The old man nodded. "The consumption ran its course. It seemed as though she'd just lost the will to live, after losing your father and sisters. I'm sorry."

"But I'm still here," Jeremiah told him. "Weren't I enough?"

"Grief does strange things to the body." The doctor picked up his cracked black leather bag from the table, stood with a sigh, and began shuffling toward the door. He stopped and turned before opening it. "I'll speak with the undertaker and see when's the soonest he can come gather her. She's still in the bedroom if you'd like to say good-bye—passed just this last hour. I cleaned her up best I could. Who'd you like for me to notify?"

Jeremiah swiped away a tear and gave his head a single, hard shake. "Ain't no one left to tell. And we ain't got no money for a casket, nor to pay you."

"Undertaker's got a way of working these things out," the doctor assured him. "Don't give it another thought. Your daddy did a lot for folks in this

town and people remember that." He reached for the door handle, but again stopped and turned. "What you gonna do with yourself now, boy?"

Jeremiah sat up on the edge of the bed he'd been sleeping on. He sighed, thinking. "Guess I could join up now. Got nothin' left to lose."

"You eighteen yet? Not that it matters anymore. Confederate Army'll pretty much take anyone now who can stand on his own two feet—or one foot, I 'spect, if that's all he's got." The doctor placed his hat atop his head and opened the door.

"Doc," Jeremiah called out.

The man turned.

"Thank you for all you done for us."

"Wished I could do more."

And then he was gone.

:::::::::

By midmorning, Jeremiah had gathered into a pillowcase a few items of clothing along with a tangle of dried beef, a heel of bread, and a stoppered half pot of strawberry jam. He figured he could slake his thirst at the wells of abandoned farms along his trek into Charleston—provided the Union hadn't fouled them all. There were reports of typhoid and cholera stemming from some such wells, though how he was supposed to tell the good from the bad, he couldn't guess.

Feet heavy and heart heavier, he slung the pillowcase over his shoulder and headed out. Jeremiah figured it would take him two or three days walking, but maybe he'd be able to hitch a ride with someone—provided there was still a wagon rolling somewhere in South Carolina.

After a long day's march and a miserable night curled up on the hard floor of an abandoned plantation house—mourning deeply for his family and cursing his bad fortune—Jeremiah was awakened by the distant clip-clop of hooves. He snatched his pillowcase and skittered down the front steps of the house just in time to hail the wagon and its driver, a surly woman named MacBride, who was hauling cotton bales from Orangeburg to the last working mill in Charleston.

With the afternoon sun obscured by a chilling fog, MacBride dropped him off near the outskirts of town, and Jeremiah walked along the city blocks toward the induction office, his disbelieving eyes taking in the widespread destruction while his mind struggled to comprehend it all: city blocks reduced to piles of brick and rubble; hollow stone facades blackened by fire and reeking of smoke; carriages abandoned on the sidewalks and wide streets; Grecian columns holding up nothing but air. What were once Charleston's lush, shady maples and magnolias were now mere skeletons looking like huge, crooked slingshots lining the desolate avenues.

As the streets dropped down toward the vacant harbor, Jeremiah scanned the scarred skyline for the Methodist church, which according to MacBride stood next to the induction office. Finally he spotted it: spires pointing to heaven atop a remaining trio of walls.

Next to that church he found the induction office. Jeremiah lied about his age, signed his papers, and moments later was handed his uniform, a scratched-up rifle, a deflated leather knapsack, and some worn-out boots.

After changing into his gear—faded trousers that were too large for him and hung from their braces; a matching shell jacket and stained white shirt that were too small—he was introduced to his commanding officer, a stout and stately man with an air of hopelessness simmering beneath his friendly gray eyes and accommodating smile.

"Jeremiah Murray," the induction officer said, "this is Captain James Finnegan."

Captain Finnegan handed Jeremiah his unadorned forage cap and then saluted him. "Welcome to the Army of the Confederate States of America, Private Murray."

At once Jeremiah fitted the cap onto his head, straightened his spine, and returned the salute.

:::::::::

Loud voices in the hallway followed by a door slamming awakened Jeremy.

He looked around the dim hotel room, the dream fading into darkness like the flare from a camera flash.

That was weird.

Weird and sad.

The faint hubbub of Athenian traffic drifted up from the street below.

He looked over at Arthur's sleeping form, switched on the television with the remote, turned his head into his pillow, and tried to conjure something that might soothe his mind.

CHAPTER

twenty-nine

The sunlight outside the hotel drapes reeled Arthur slowly awake at a little before seven. He lay on his back with the pillow squarely behind his head, his nose pointed toward the little white smoke detector.

How do I feel?

Arthur took inventory of his bodily sensations—*lift . . . breathe . . . focus . . . twiddle . . . concentrate*—just as he had each morning since finding out the cause of his squeezing headaches and dizzy spells last year. Then after a few moments he decided that, aside from a slight pressure at his temples, he felt OK.

He looked over at Jeremy slumbering on his side and smiled.

I'll conquer this for you, my love.

Arthur got out of bed, used the restroom, and was just about to call room service for their coffee when Jeremy's phone began vibrating atop the dresser.

He looked over at Jeremy to see if the noise might awaken him, but he continued sleeping soundly. Arthur grabbed the phone. "Hello?"

"Who is this?" Lazzaro demanded.

"It's your new best friend," Arthur pleasantly replied. "I certainly enjoyed meeting you yesterday. And I loved that sundried tomato pesto, but the wine tasted like piss."

"Your taste buds are remarkably precise," Lazzaro said. "Let me speak with Jeremy."

"I'm afraid he's asleep. May I take a message?"

"I'll call back—"

"I'm not asleep," Jeremy called out, pushing himself upright against the pillows. "Who's that?"

"Just a moment please, he's awake now," Arthur told Lazzaro, and then held up the phone. "It's that charming friend of Marilyn Monroe's."

Jeremy held out his hand and Arthur handed him the phone.

Then he watched Jeremy argue about evidence leaked to the Hellenic police and Greek jails and mortgages and Francesco Sforza and blackmail . . . and . . . and . . . and. And for the first time Arthur realized how useless and powerless he felt. *How the hell do you catch a criminal who's always one step ahead? I've got to think of something . . .* But his mind kept shooting blanks:

We could . . . No.

I could . . . No.

They could . . . No.

And then Arthur flashed on what was waiting for him back home: the hospital visits and chemo and more gamma knife—or *worse*—and how destructive this all could be to Jeremy's hatchling sobriety. Then he recalled Agent Singer's warning that Jeremy might soon be charged with aiding and abetting Lazzaro in drug trafficking and sex tourism.

We need to get back home to find him a good lawyer. We're fucked if we stay here. We're just wasting time.

Arthur waved frantically at Jeremy. "Hey!"

"Hold on," Jeremy barked at Lazzaro. "Arthur wants something." He put down the phone.

"Tell him you'll give him what he's asking for."

"*What?! But—*"

"You've got just about that much left over in your trust. Right? And remember, I'm putting my condo on the market when we get home, so we'll have that money when it sells." He glanced at his watch. "The banks should be opening in about an hour. We can meet him at noon."

Jeremy just stared at him.

"Baby," Arthur pressed, "we're tired, and I'm sick. We need to get home so I can get well, and you can finally get this asshole off your back. OK? The last thing in the world we want to do right now is dick around with the Greek police. And yes, they might just recognize this for what it is and let you go, but I'm guessing they won't—at least not until they do some investigating, and that'll take time. He's got us."

"But—"

"*Just get it for him*, Jeremy. Find out where he wants to meet, and assure him we won't tell anyone."

"Why *not?*"

"Because we know now he'll only smell it and it'll backfire on us. Tell Lazzaro he won and we've got to tie this up and get home quickly. Life's too short. End of story."

Jeremy's eyes narrowed as he put the phone up to his ear. "I'll have the cash to you around noon—and we promise not to tell anyone, because Arthur says you'll figure it out, you motherfucker." He paused. "Yeah, hold on."

Jeremy handed Arthur the phone.

"What?" Arthur snapped.

"I need to hear it from you."

"We won't tell anyone where we're meeting. I give you my word."

"No one but Jeremy there to meet me," Lazzaro specified. "I don't want you to come."

"I'll stay away—no problem. But I need your word that you won't hurt Jeremy, so the exchange will only take place in a very public place—like the Acropolis."

"Jeremy will be safe. You have my word."

"Fine." He handed the phone back to Jeremy. "Time and place."

"What time and what place?" Jeremy asked. After a moment he turned to Arthur. "Do you know where the old Roman Forum is?"

"I . . . think it's on the north side of the Acropolis." Arthur pointed to the far wall of the hotel room.

"Can I meet him there at twelve and still get us to the airport in time for the five o'clock flight?"

"Not a problem. Where specifically?"

"Where specifically?" Jeremy listened and then turned to Arthur. "There's something called the Gate of Athena. Do you know it?"

"Four columns and a pediment," Arthur replied. "I know it well. Tell him you'll be there, twelve o'clock on the nose. *By yourself.*"

Jeremy relayed the message and ended the call. Then he glared at Arthur. "That's all the money I have!"

"And as completely wrong as this is, it'll be worth it to have this over with. Just allow yourself to concentrate on how glad you'll be when we're on that plane back home. You can't put a price on certain things. Now why don't you get showered and dressed and I'll go downstairs to find us something to eat. OK?"

"This makes me so angry!" Jeremy stormed up naked from his side of the bed and crossed the room into the dressing area. "This is just wrong, wrong, wrong!"

Arthur watched Jeremy's muscular ass shift enticingly from side to side as he began getting washed up at the bath counter. "Let it go, old buddy," Arthur called out to him. "Trust the Universe."

As soon as Arthur heard the shower spray thrumming the bathtub, he picked up his phone and headed to the door to get them both some coffee and a little sustenance for breakfast.

And to make a couple of phone calls.

CHAPTER

thirty

Arthur and Jeremy hastily packed their belongings and took a cab to the closest bank, where it took less time than expected for Jeremy to withdraw the funds from his account back in Ballena Beach and have them converted to euros. Then the pair wrapped the clusters of cash in a plastic bag, and with their luggage stowed in the taxi's trunk, wound their way around the Acropolis toward the north side of the hill, where the old Roman Forum—and the Gate of Athena—awaited.

Jeremy was in an especially foul mood during the transaction, taking the opportunity more than once to open the plastic bag and look wistfully at the stacks of 500-denomination bills with their printed lavender numbers and letters and maps of Europe, their vermilion stars, and fascinating three-dimensional holograms.

"Can you imagine what we could do with all this?" he asked Arthur.

"What would you rather do with all that money?"

"Anything but give it to that ass-wipe."

"I know . . . but tell me. What's one thing you'd do with almost half a million dollars?"

"Go on a real vacation, for one thing. And I'd drive a bulldozer through that stupid mansion and use this money to help us build a modern house on the site—glass walls, an infinity pool that looks out over the water, all white leather furniture, and great artwork on the walls—and a big green lawn for Skipper and Bingham to chase each other on."

"That sounds perfect—but you'll need a lot more money than what's in that bag for a house like that," Arthur laughed. "Hey, I think that's the Forum up ahead." He pointed.

"So where will you be during my lovely transaction?"

"I'll have the driver take me around the general area until you call me, and then we'll swing back and pick you up and zoom back to the airport."

"How do you feel?" Jeremy asked.

"Healthy, a little nervous, but absolutely convinced we're doing the right thing here."

"I wish I were as sure as you."

The taxi slowed, pulled to the curb in front of the Gate of Athena, and stopped. "Good thing it's crowded," Jeremy said. "I'll call you the second this is over with." He squeezed Arthur's hand and scooted out of the cab.

As expected, there were gangs of tourists milling about the site taking pictures and gabbing and pointing at this acanthus detail and that chipped marble scroll, so Jeremy wasn't as uneasy as he had imagined he would be. But he felt sadness as the taxi pulled away from the curb with Arthur alone in the backseat, wishing his beloved was standing by his side, and dreading the medical crisis waiting for them to grind through back home.

One step at a time.

He looked around, clutching the bag, scanning the crowd for any sign of Lazzaro.

His phone vibrated inside his pocket.

Jeremy pulled it out. "Fuck you."

"I see you're alone," Lazzaro told him. "Do you have my money?"

"No, but I have mine. I hate you for doing this to me and Arthur."

"You'll get over it." Lazzaro paused. "Tell me what's inside the bag."

"Two hundred thousand euros."

"Where did you get it?"

"At the bank this morning. Attica Bank, about four blocks from the Acropolis. Why?"

Lazzaro paused. "And you have the entire amount I requested."

"Yes, you stupid fuck! So are you going to come get it or should I take it home with me where it belongs?"

"Did you or Arthur tell any of the authorities you would be meeting me here?"

"I promised you we wouldn't. Arthur gave you his word."

"Is the money counterfeit?"

"Of course not. We just got it from the Attica Bank, like I said."

"Does it have a tracking device attached, or is it rigged or marked in any way?"

"*No.*"

"Is your lover watching this transaction?"

"No!"

"Do you miss making love to a man who is not terminally ill?"

"Fuck, fuck, *fuck* you, Lazzaro! *I hope you die.* Now come and get this bag before I give it to one of these chain-smoking Germans."

"Put the bag on the bonnet of that blue Citroën in front of you."

The call went dead, and Jeremy looked around.

Indeed, there was a dirty blue car just to his right, but he wouldn't know a Citroën, or what its "bonnet" was, if it mowed him down in a tunnel.

Why doesn't anyone in Greece wash their cars?

Jeremy stepped around the vehicle and saw from the badge on its hatchback that it was, in fact, the identified car.

That's kind of cool looking.

Gently, so as not to scratch the paint, he placed the bag atop the hood.

Moments later he heard the popping crescendo of a motorcycle engine—like a string of exploding Chinese firecrackers—heading his way.

Jeremy looked around and saw the motorbike zip round a corner and then skid to a stop in front of the Citroën.

The motorcycle's driver, a diminutive yet athletically built young man—who was clearly not Lazzaro—dressed in tight black leathers and a black helmet, reached over and snatched the package from atop the car's hood. Then he flipped up his visor to expose his turquoise green eyes and a band of finely molded face.

"I am sorry to do this to you," he told Jeremy, and then sputtered off with the bag under his arm.

Jeremy watched the bike rider until he could no longer see or hear him.

It's done.

Jeremy took out his phone and called Arthur.

CHAPTER

thirty-one

They landed at LAX just after midnight and then found a car service to take them back to Ballena Beach.

"Do you want to go to my place?" Jeremy yawned, once he was buckled securely into the back seat of the Cadillac Escalade. "Or would you rather go to Aunt Katharine's, or to your condo in WeHo? You decide, because I'm brain dead."

"Let's go to Katharine's. I know it's a longer drive, but I'm dying to see Bingham, and maybe if Carlo's still up we could talk him into making us some dinner." He looked out the car's window at the familiar sights of the San Diego Freeway's uneven, curving lanes and the cars rushing along beside them.

Jeremy looked over at him. "You're still hungry?"

Arthur wrinkled his nose. "That chicken sandwich on the plane was so dry I couldn't eat it. How do you suppose airlines manage to squeeze all the texture and flavor out of everything they serve and still insist on charging top dollar for everything?"

"I'll call ahead and alert Carlo that you're hungry *and* grouchy," Jeremy said. "And I think Katharine's is the best place to go; especially after everything that's happened, I can't imagine setting foot in Lazzaro's castle of horrors just yet." Jeremy scrutinized Arthur's features. "How're you holding up?"

"I'm OK." Arthur shot him a wan smile. "Just exhausted. And to know that first thing tomorrow I need to get to the ER at Cedars for another MRI makes me delirious with glee."

Jeremy took his hand. "We're doing this together, remember?"

"That's the only thing that's keeping me from opening this door and throwing myself out into the fast lane. Thank you."

:::::::::

Nearly an hour later the Escalade pulled up to the Tyler Compound, Jeremy leaned out and punched the numbers into the keypad, and the gates motored open.

As the driver slowed to a stop in front of the servant's entrance, Carlo stepped out from the side door to greet them, followed by an ecstatic Skipper and Bingham, tails sweeping furiously.

"You guys made it!" Carlo exclaimed, pulling their luggage from the back of the SUV as the dogs spun circles around the homecoming pair, sniffing their pants and shoes and vying for head massages.

Carlo scanned Jeremy and then Arthur. "Was it a hurricane, a tornado, or an earthquake?"

"I'm sorry?" Arthur bent down to kiss Bingham's head.

"You guys look like you've been through a natural disaster."

"It's good to see you too." Jeremy pulled him into a hug.

"I'm glad you called when you did, I was able to get this twenty-four-hour pizza place to deliver a couple of large vegetarians—and no lesbian jokes, please."

"Is my aunt awake?" Jeremy asked, patting Skipper's side as she leaned her weight against his leg.

"She tried to stay up but went to bed about an hour ago," Carlo replied. "She was sitting in front of the TV, nodding off with her crossword puzzle practically falling into her ice-cold tea, so I shooed her upstairs with a promise to wake her early enough to talk with you guys in the morning."

"Anything new around here?" Jeremy asked, watching the SUV turn around and drive off.

"Not really," Carlo yawned. "But speaking of tired, would you guys mind if I went to bed? I've been up since six this morning, and I put a lot of effort into cleaning up that filthy guesthouse: mold in the shower and spiderwebs full of bugs everywhere. Fully stocked fridge, by the way."

Arthur put his arm around Carlo's shoulders. "You're amazing."

Carlo yawned again. "No problem. The pizzas are warming in the oven in the guesthouse, and I got some good stuff for breakfast tomorrow. Spanish omelets with salsa and guacamole homemade by my sister Carmen—she said to tell you guys 'hi' by the way."

Jeremy grimaced. "We've kinda got an important appointment tomorrow morning. Could we, maybe, save it for the next day?"

Carlo shrugged. "Sure, it'll keep. So what's the big occasion? I figured something was up for you to come back early."

Arthur and Jeremy gave each other a furtive glance.

"I've got a doctor's appointment," Arthur replied. "Part of my journey into geezer-hood."

Carlo's eyebrows knitted. "Nothing serious, I hope."

Arthur shook his head. "Anyhow, thanks for everything. We've got some sleep we need to catch up on and some jetlag we've gotta get rid of." He began leading Jeremy toward the door, with Bingham and Skipper trotting happily behind. "Good night, and thanks!"

:::::::::

Once inside the guesthouse they looked around.

"Carlo did do a great job cleaning this place," Jeremy said, surveying the pristine carpet and clean surfaces and fresh flowers. "God, that pizza smells good." He went over to the oven, grabbed a pot holder, and slid out one of the pizzas. "Is eating here at the bar OK?"

"Sure." Arthur made his way over to a barstool and sat, and Jeremy served them each two large slices while the dogs negotiated the stools' legs and curled themselves at the men's feet.

"I hate to ask," Jeremy began, "but we need to talk about tomorrow. What should I expect?"

Arthur was about to take a bite, but instead placed the pizza slice down on his plate. "It's all pretty routine, but the waiting is awful. We'll get there, tell the ER what's going on, and wait for them to pull up my medical history; we'll wait in a room to be called for the MRI; then they'll prep me with a Valium drip and put me in a machine so loud it sounds like a freight train blasting off to the moon. Then we'll wait forever for someone to come and read the damn test results, and the next thing you know it's five p.m. and another precious day has vanished." He bit into the pizza. "That's if we're lucky," he mumbled, chewing. "We might not even get the reading until the next day."

Jeremy scooted in closer. "What about after that?"

"You mean, how do we deal with the prognosis?"

Jeremy stared at him.

"Until we know what the situation is, there's no point in thinking about what's next."

"So we'll just wait and see." He bit into his pizza.

"Yep. Wait and see—and then figure it out. After all, these symptoms could still be something else . . . even a reaction to the meds. So we're just going to push a diagnosis and prognosis out of our minds until we have something concrete to deal with."

"How do you feel? Besides tired."

"No headaches today," Arthur lied. "And no dizziness—and I'm hungry as hell."

Jeremy put his head on Arthur's shoulder. "Maybe we've got nothing to worry about."

"That's where I'm putting my money."

"Speaking of money—" Jeremy took another bite, "—will you finally tell me why you were so insistent that I give Lazzaro my cash? I've been so worried about *you* today that I forgot to be pissed off about *that.*"

"It just seemed like the only sane thing to do under those insane circumstances." Arthur yawned. "You'll just have to trust me. Are you about ready for bed?"

"I guess we'd better try for some sleep. Tomorrow's a—"

"Big day," Arthur cut in. "And no matter what the tests tell us, nothing's for certain."

"I'm just glad to have you with me tonight. Fuck tomorrow."

"You said it." Arthur pulled him in tight. "*Fuck tomorrow.*"

:::::::::

Sometime that night Jeremy awoke with a start.

He thought he'd heard that strange word again—that foreign name that came to him in the Plaka—but now it seemed as if someone in the room had uttered it.

"*Antinous,*" Jeremy whispered to hear if the words matched—and they did.

Jeremy stared up at the ceiling, his heart beating hard in his chest. Then he looked over to see if Arthur was awake and had muttered something, but all he saw were the sheets on his back slowly rising and falling.

And then a fantastically vivid series of scenes flashed through Jeremy's consciousness as his dream rewound:

Bearded, robed gentlemen gabbing with younger, unclothed men.

Vast buildings. Geometrically inlaid stone floors. Lush gardens.

Himself: naked, lounging in a chaise by the edge of an expansive pool hemmed in by an arched colonnade; the splashing of fountains nearby and the lemony tang of lavender cutting the air. He glanced down to survey his glistening musculature, wet from his dip in the pool. Then his thoughts circled back to his worries.

"And what is taking my beloved so deep inside his pretty head?" a deep voice asked.

Jeremy looked up into Arthur's bearded face. "I did not hear you approach."

"You were so transfixed that a stampeding horse might have escaped your attention," Arthur laughed. "What concerns you so?"

Jeremy brushed wet ringlets from his eyes. "How are you feeling?"

"Looking at you, never better."

Jeremy frowned, sitting up. "Are you still fatigued, as you were this morning? How is that pain in your legs and arms?"

Arthur sat next to him and gently pressed a finger to his lips. "Quiet your worries, Antinous. With you by my side, I am strong as any soldier."

:::::::::

Suspecting now that the hamster-wheels in his mind would prohibit any further sleep, Jeremy sidled silently out of bed and padded his way to the living room.

First that weird Civil War dream and now this? Maybe I'm the one with the brain tumor.

Their luggage still rested where they had dropped it earlier by the door, so Jeremy located the bag containing his laptop, opened it, and started the machine.

He typed the words *brain tumor* into the field and pressed the Enter key; and while the search engine sifted through its trillions of digital bits, Jeremy tiptoed into the kitchen to see if there might be a stray bottle of wine tucked somewhere inside the cabinets.

CHAPTER

thirty-two

God, why is it taking so *long*?" Arthur, wearing a paper robe, slumped atop the examination table, while Jeremy looked up at him from where he sat in the gray plastic chair by his side.

Jeremy scrutinized the red hazmat needle receptacle with its ominous, triple scorpion-pincer logo on the wall. "I'm sure it won't—"

The door swung open, and the doctor—a petite woman with blonde hair pulled up into a bun and reading glasses dropping off her nose—entered. "Mr. Blauefee," Dr. MacTavish began, examining the report, "you have a growth that appears to be similar to the one we treated with the gamma knife last year. It's in a different site, and it's grown to about the same size. If you'll recall, at the time of your previous treatments we discussed the possibility of another tumor recurring."

"That's what we were afraid of," Arthur told her. "What's the prognosis?"

"I'll need to consult with the multidisciplinary team, the neuro-oncologists, radiation oncologists, surgeons, and rehabilitation therapists, before we make any decisions."

"Can you give us *some* idea of what might happen?" Jeremy asked.

"My first inclination is to treat this with more aggressive radiation and chemotherapy. Again, this could all change after the team has been consulted, but this would mean radiation every day for six weeks, and Temodar, which you're currently taking, for twenty-eight day cycles—five days on and twenty-three days off. We might even ramp things up with an Avastin drip to cut off the blood supply to the growth—and there are some new, targeted therapies that attack the specific genes of this tumor; we'll certainly explore those options. Then, after six weeks, another MRI will tell us if we need to reconsider treatment."

"So then . . . no surgery yet?" Arthur asked.

Dr. MacTavish looked from Arthur to Jeremy and back. "I'll need to consult with the team, but this is the way I'm leaning at the moment. The tumor is in a part of your brain that presents more challenges for excision than the site of your previous growth."

"Is that good or bad?" Jeremy asked. "Not having the surgery, I mean. I'm confused."

"Even the chemo and radiation are brutal," Arthur explained. "Last time I lost my hair and dropped twenty pounds from the nausea, and I was so tired I slept on and off during the day. It's a grueling process, and I'll need to hire some additional help again at my agency . . . but I'd gladly give that another try before having my skull cut open and having someone root around in there with pliers and scissors."

Dr. MacTavish smiled. "We can help manage your discomfort during the process by giving you some stronger meds for the headaches and nausea. You're not experiencing any seizures at this time, is that correct?"

Arthur nodded. "That's right."

"That's a good sign. So today I'm sending you home with some new prescriptions, but before you leave you'll need to make an appointment so we can meet again in two days, after the team has evaluated your test results. As you know, time is of the essence, so I want you back here just as soon as we're ready to move forward."

:::::::::

After thanking the doctor and then waiting yet another hour to fill Arthur's medications at the hospital's dreary and crowded pharmacy, the couple drove home in silence, not wanting to discuss the various scenarios popcorning inside their heads.

Then about a mile from home, Jeremy's middle-of-the-night computer session sprang to mind, and an intense craving began creeping down his spine. He slowed for a red light and turned to Arthur. "Hey, I'm in the mood for enchiladas suizas for dinner. Would you mind if I stopped at the market to pick some up?"

"Do whatever you'd like. But do you really feel like cooking? Carlo stocked that fridge pretty good."

"Yeah, but I figured some bungled meal prep might help me get my mind off stuff."

Arthur looked at him. "Black beans and Spanish rice?"

Jeremy grinned. "And no gummy bears this time. I promise."

"Don't forget the sour cream. Or the hot sauce."

"I've already got some down at my place, but it's not like another bottle of Cholula will ever go to waste. Look"—he pointed—"there's a Fresh & Easy up ahead; I'll stop there instead of the Vons in Ballena Beach. They have stuff that's all prepared and ready to cook." Jeremy accelerated with the green light and then wheeled into the parking lot.

Once inside the market and with Arthur waiting in the car, Jeremy collected a package of ready-to-bake enchiladas, a can of green sauce, an envelope of shredded cheese, a bottle of Cholula, one tub of sour cream, a box of Rice-A-Roni, and a can of black beans. He also bought three bottles of sparkling water and two bottles of good chardonnay from the vintner he preferred: un-oaked, hints of apple and melon with a caramel finish.

:::::::::

Upon their arrival back at the Tyler Compound's guesthouse, Arthur brushed past Carlo with a perfunctory "Hey," and Jeremy began unloading their groceries from the trunk of his car.

Carlo sidled up to Jeremy. "What's the trouble?"

"Why do you always assume there's trouble?"

"Because Arthur just crept into the guesthouse without insulting me, and I heard some wine bottles clank together in your bags, so something's up. Come on. *You can tell me*—and there's nothing you can say anymore that would surprise me."

"I can't talk about it right now," Jeremy replied, slamming his trunk.

Carlo leaned against the wall of the guesthouse, his arms crossed. "Well, now I *am* surprised. I figured by now you two would've had every argument there was to have."

"It's not that," Jeremy said. "I wish it were that simple. Let's . . . just say Arthur's having some health issues and I'm trying to figure out how I can get us both through this."

Carlo leaned in and clutched Jeremy's arm. "So the doctor's appointment you guys came back early for *was* for something serious! My God, he doesn't have AIDS, does he? But there are all kinds of great treatments for that these days."

"I wish it were that simple—not that AIDS is simple." Jeremy adjusted the grip on his grocery bags. "Carlo, I don't know what the hell I'm saying."

"Please"—Carlo's eyes bulged—"Please tell me it isn't cancer."

"I . . . um, Oh God, Carlo I don't know what to do."

"Baby, where . . . ?"

Jeremy turned to Carlo, closed his eyes, and pointed to his head.

"Jesus . . . Jesus. Oh, Jeremy. Jesus. Is there *anything* I can do?"

"Did prayers help when your mom was sick?"

"I wouldn't know; I was too pissed off at God to ask him, or her, for help. What's the prognosis?"

"It's too soon to tell. They did some tests this morning, but we won't know the course of treatment until the end of the week, so we're taking this one day at a time."

Carlo sighed. "I've come to understand that whenever someone invokes the *one day at a time* phrase, things are looking kinda bad. Are you OK?"

"I guess so—except for the permanent tear-jerker movie headache I've got, and my stomach feeling like I just drank a big cup of wet cement."

"I remember that exact feeling from when my mom was sick."

"What'm I gonna do, Carlito?"

"Just like you said: Take it one day at a time. And will you please keep me in the loop?"

"Of course." Jeremy sighed. "And when this is over I want us all to celebrate." He swallowed and despite himself added, "I just hope it's not at Arthur's wake."

Carlo gripped his shoulder. "Look, everything's gonna be fine—it has to be! You guys didn't get back together after all this time just for . . . for . . ."

Jeremy felt a lump blooming in his throat. "I . . . gotta go. Just don't tell Arthur I told you. OK?"

"I'm glad he knows," Arthur said, stepping out from the darkened doorway. "Jeremy, my love, when are you going to stop hiding things from me?" He waved Carlo inside. "You deserve to know exactly what's going on." He opened the door wider. "Come on in."

Carlo followed Jeremy inside the guesthouse but then only stood inside the open doorway.

"It's not contagious," Arthur laughed. "Please, close the door and have a seat."

Carlo shut the door. "So?" he asked, sitting down.

Arthur filled him in.

After he was finished, Carlo brightened. "Thank God no surgery."

"We were pretty relieved, too," Jeremy said. "But the chemo and radiation are going to be tough—"

Carlo leaned forward. "When do you start treatments?"

"In a couple of days," Arthur replied. "After that, I'll be going to Cedars every morning for six weeks."

"*Every morning?*" Carlo asked. "Even on weekends?"

"Every morning," Jeremy and Arthur said in unison.

Carlo leaned back. "Can I help you by taking him there, Jeremy? That'll get old for you real soon—especially with the traffic down by Cedars; it's like driving in Mumbai. We can trade off."

Jeremy smiled. "Thanks, but I can't imagine getting tired of helping Arthur with this."

"I know, I know," Carlo said. "Just remember that the offer stands."

"Thanks, pal." Arthur smiled. "So now that you know everything we know, let's talk about something else."

"Like?" Carlo asked.

"Like . . . how are you?"

"Lonely and horny," Carlo replied. "But what else is new? Plus, your aunt is driving me nuts, so I'm considering a career in taxidermy—starting with her."

"Where is she?" Jeremy asked. "I haven't broken this news to her yet."

"Probably in her office."

"I'll go find her," Jeremy announced. Then after scanning the empty kitchen counters he turned to Arthur. "Did you . . . already put the groceries away?"

"I did."

Their eyes met.

"Thanks." Jeremy looked away. "After I'm done talking to Aunt Katharine, do you want to go for walk on the beach? I'd like some time with you and the doggies."

A smile glimmered on Arthur's face. "I'd love that."

"I'll be back in a few." Jeremy turned and left them to find his aunt.

"So what's *really* going on?" Carlo asked Arthur, once they were alone.

"Jeremy has no idea how tough this'll be. It'll get ugly, Carlo. And I'm not sure he's strong enough to handle it—especially with his fragile sobriety and what we just went through in Greece, which . . . let me just say . . . didn't go so well."

"What do you mean *fragile*? I thought he was doing so well."

"I just put the groceries away, which surprisingly included two fairly expensive bottles of wine. I'm more than a little worried about him."

"Yeah, I worry about him too. I remember the whole thing with his mom's sobriety and relapsing like it was yesterday. You'd think he'd know better."

"Any suggestions?"

"*Therapy*. I think you could both use it."

"I'd thought of that," Arthur said. "But I don't know if Jeremy will be amenable to it."

Carlo stood up and began straightening the throw pillows on the sofa. "You know, I saw this great therapist who helped me through that time when my mom was sick and my father and I were ready to murder each other. I can get his number for you."

"Could you? I'd appreciate it."

"Anything for you guys. I love you both so much, and I just want you to know that—" Carlo stopped, unable to finish his sentence. "I'm sorry, I—"

Arthur crossed the room and pulled Carlo into his arms. "We both love you too. And it makes me feel so much better knowing you'll be there for Jeremy, no matter what happens to me."

"*Forever*, Arthur. I'll be by Jeremy's side forever." Carlo wiped his eyes and began making his way to the door. "Oh, and before I forget, two sour-faced detectives came sniffing around here earlier and I told them you'd be back later. I guess they wanted to talk to Jeremy about that psycho he used to date. Here's their number." He handed over a business card. "I was *really* hoping your trip would be wonderful. Was it that bad?"

"It was perfectly, colossally, fucked up," Arthur replied, examining the business card in his hand. "Just like everything seems to be these days."

:::::::::

"You're back, safe and sound." Katharine, sitting at her desk, pulled off her glasses with one hand and smiled at her nephew. "And looking healthier than I can recall in recent times!"

Jeremy went over to her, bent down, and kissed her cheek. "It's good to be home."

"How did your trip to Greece turn out?"

"It was . . . just OK."

"Did you get reimbursed for that terrible secret mortgage?" Katharine asked, and Jeremy could almost hear the wheels of judgment squeaking in her head.

"Yeah, I need to talk to you about that."

"I'll take that as a 'no.'" She sighed. "We all make mistakes, my dear. So what's the next step in your plan for rectifying yours?"

"There's only one thing I can do—and that's to fix up that place so it'll be worth what I paid for it, even if it means replacing one floor tile at a time."

"With what money? Last you told me, your trust contained little more than half a million dollars, and it would be too risky to sink what little you have into that tear-down. Your only other choice would be a second mortgage, but, as we both know, you already have one."

"I agree, so I was thinking, well . . . you know that money you set aside for the chalet's remodel up at the lake? We agreed on the cheaper restoration, so what if I use what's left over for the mansion? My place is oceanfront and nearly as big as the chalet, and as an investment I still think it's a good one; we just need money to put in a good kitchen and some new baths. Arthur knows how to do the painting and some of the repairs himself, and he's already promised to use the money he'll get from the sale of his condo." He stared hopefully at her. "You've never even been inside, so why don't you take a look at it with me and see what you think? You could loan us the money and we'll pay you back with interest, then you can take that interest money to make another investment."

"That's not a bad plan." Katharine tapped her lips with her pen. "I've just checked my calendar a moment ago and, thanks to a cancellation with our accountants, I happen to have the morning after tomorrow free. We can go see your house then."

Jeremy grimaced. "Unfortunately, that's when Arthur and I need to be—"

"If you're not willing to compromise your personal time," Katharine cut in, her voice brittle as glass, "then there's no point in including me in any of your business dealings."

Jeremy felt his anger rise, so he took a deep breath. "I didn't want to tell you like this, but the day after tomorrow I'm taking Arthur for his first round of chemo and radiation."

Katharine hesitated, clearly taken aback. "I see," she said at last. "Where . . . what . . . ?"

"He's got a brain tumor. His second one. Arthur went through radiation and chemo last year, but another one's just started giving him trouble."

She shook her head. "Poor man. What's the prognosis?"

"Too soon to tell. I took him to Cedars today because he started showing symptoms on the trip. There's still a lot we don't know."

Katharine got up from her desk, made her way over to Jeremy, and put her hand on his shoulder. "I had a dear friend who went through this with her husband. The doctors did all they could for Debbie's husband, Bobby, but the disease ran its course." She moved her hand to his chin and lifted his face to hers. "She only survived the ordeal because his death was something she was prepared for even from the beginning."

"Arthur's not—"

"My dear, I am a firm believer in the power of positive thinking and today's amazing advances in medicine and even prayer, if that's your belief, but are you ready to face the possibility of Arthur succumbing to this illness, even while hoping and praying and doing everything your wits advise you for a complete healing?"

"I am," Jeremy lied. "Yeah, I'm . . . prepared for the worst."

CHAPTER

thirty-three

What are your plans," Tristan asked Lazzaro, "now that you have your money?"

"I am not sure yet," Lazzaro replied, looking out the barn's hayloft window at the sandy horse paddock and thinking of the used Ferrari he'd recently seen advertised. "But I know I must find somewhere else to live—most likely back in Turkey . . . or Croatia. But I must not stay here."

Tristan sat upright in the straw. "Why not?"

Lazzaro leaned against the bale behind him. "Because I am my own man. And although you have been generous to offer me this place to stay, it is only a matter of time before they find me here."

"I will go with you," Tristan said, settling into Lazzaro's arms.

"You cannot." Lazzaro embraced him and kissed the nape of his neck. "I do not want you to be running like me. You deserve better."

"But I *need* to be with you," he pouted. "I *love* you."

"And I love you as well."

"What . . . what if we found you a place . . . somewhere in the hills, where no one would look for you? Or by the sea on a cliff overlooking the ocean? I have my own money. I could help—it would be for the two of us."

"Perhaps when the time is right . . . but for now I am sorry I must leave you again."

Tristan's eyes filled with tears. "I have so patiently waited for you! I waited and waited and dreamed of our time together and made plans! And now you do this to me? Why do you enjoy tormenting me?"

Lazzaro wiped Tristan's tears. "What would you have me do? I am a fugitive."

"This villa is many kilometers from any other estate or town," Tristan reminded him. "We could see anyone approaching and could well hide you; we have cellars and outbuildings where no one would find you, and any could be modified for an extended stay should the need arise."

"But what about your mother? This would happen only with her approval."

"Carmella is always traveling. It would make no difference to her. She only wants to see me happy."

Lazzaro pushed down a smile. *I can think of a few other things she wants.* "If you think it would meet with her approval, then I will ask her tonight at dinner."

"Will you, please?"

"Only if it means this much to you."

:::::::::

Because the evening was warm, the house staff once again laid out their evening meal atop the old farm table on the fieldstone terrace: woodstove pizzas with goat cheese and fresh herbs culled that afternoon from the kitchen garden; marinated and fire-roasted chicken; chickpeas with fresh basil and balsamic vinegar; sundried tomato croquettes with Crème fraîche. And accompanying this feast, a few of the better wines from the well-stocked cellar.

Lazzaro had just taken his place, alone, at the table when he spotted Carmella jabbering orders to the staff. She had her long black hair pulled up in a loose upsweep, and was dressed in a gauzy pink floral dress that showed off her cocoa shoulders and long, shapely legs, which she'd accentuated with high-heeled sandals. Watching her graceful approach, Lazzaro marveled: this woman—most likely past fifty years of age—was the embodiment of youthful femininity and grace, yet her manner exuded absolute confidence and command of her companions and environment.

At last she made her way down the path toward the table and stood by her chair; Lazzaro jumped up and pulled it out for her. "Your skin looks even more radiant than usual," he whispered into Carmella's ear as she sat. "How is that possible?"

"Something special the abbot gets from his altar boys," Carmella replied. "There is a seminary just up the road. They send me a vial each Sunday afternoon. Funny word, *seminary.*"

"That is hardly amusing considering Sforza's actions after snatching me from that orphanage," Lazzaro snapped. "Why do you insult me?"

"And why are you so humorless? I should imagine you to be in a fantastic frame of mind, now that some of your monetary troubles are finished—thanks to me."

"Forgive me." Lazzaro sighed, sitting down at his place across from her. "I had a conversation this afternoon with your son, and it is weighing heavily on my mind."

"But this conversation took place during time you should have spent *with me*. I would remind you to never deny me my simple requests—or have you already forgotten what we discussed the other day?"

"And I do not need to remind *you* that Tristan is my priority." He looked around. "Where is he?"

"He will be down in a few minutes." Carmella unfolded her napkin upon her lap and sipped from her wine glass. "I asked him to give us some time alone because there is something I need from you."

"Anything." Lazzaro drew a long draught from his own glass.

"Since I am now one-third partner in your business venture, you will give me one-third of the cash I secured for you."

Lazzaro choked on his wine. "Except for that."

"I'm completely serious, Signore Sforza. This ancient villa is in need of much repair, and appearing in an occasional Mexican novella or selling a bottle of Tempranillo here and there isn't going to replace that tile roof." She pointed upward. "You should be glad that there is no rain presently expected; during a storm, you would be drier in the shower with the faucet at maximum than lying in that bed you've been buggering my son in."

"I am sorry to disappoint, but I have already made plans for my money."

"Thus you will need to amend those plans." Carmella tore a large chunk of bread from a swaddled loaf. "You are under suspicion for murder, you are integral to a sex tourism ring, and you've been trafficking illegal drugs. In the meantime there are only two people in the world who know where you are. Would you care to guess the names of your two protectors?"

Lazzaro set his glass down, staring at her incredulously. "You would turn me over to the police if I do not give in to your demands? What happened to *tap-dancing barefoot on razor blades to shield Tristan from his loneliness?*"

"You're the smart one." Carmella smiled. "You tell me."

Lazzaro stabbed at one of the roasted chickens in the center of the table and hoisted it over to his plate. "You disappoint me."

"My *exact* thoughts about you." Carmella sat back in her chair and pinched out a cigarette from its case. "Aren't these riots in Athens *terrible?* Those poor injured police officers and the loss of property; all of this continuing political unrest?" She fitted the cigarette between her lips, placed her elbows on the table, and flicked him a packet of matches.

"I couldn't care less." Lazzaro picked up the matches, bent forward, and lit her cigarette. "Why bring it up?"

She blew out a drag. "You knew, of course, that we—or, more accurately, *I*—was under surveillance during my meeting with Jeremy."

"Of course."

"But somehow, *magically*, the police were too inept or stupid to detain me."

"Of course—because they were looking for me." Lazzaro paused. "At least . . . it would appear that way."

Carmella sucked in a heavy drag and blew it out in an obscuring cloud. "Stupid police; stupid men—lured into danger, as it were, *by sirens*."

Lazzaro glared at her. "Will you please get to the point?"

Carmella chuckled. "Last night, yet another riot in Athens was ignited by some purported neo-Nazi on a motorcycle who tossed a Molotov cocktail into that notorious anarchist squat, the Villa Amalia, and then sped off, causing every available police officer in the vicinity to report to the site of the disturbance. Hence, I was able to fully explain your demands to Jeremy and then leave unmolested."

"And?"

"Have you asked Tristan where he drove last night on his motorcycle?"

Lazzaro's mouth dropped open. "*Your son began last night's riot as a diversion?!*"

"No, *your lover* began last night's riot as a diversion. Yesterday I explained to Tristan that it was your wish for him to carry off this task because it was your only assurance of a clean escape . . . but you were too concerned about his safety to ask him to do something so dangerous. I also told him I was *completely* opposed to his doing this. He really is quite devoted to you—for what reason, I cannot imagine."

"He could have been arrested—or worse!"

"This is not child's play we are engaged in, Signore Sforza." Again she drew heavily from her cigarette. "Without me you would not have been able to carry off that stunt in the Plaka. I served you well, I have allowed you to stay here, and now you show your lack of gratitude by denying my very reasonable request for . . . *half* the money and *half* the control in your enterprises, as well as the names of your most important business contacts?"

"*You said one-third!*"

"I've changed my mind." Her features cocked into a half-smile. "Otherwise, as the Americans say, it is your bed, you've made it, fucked in it, and now your bed will be your prison cell."

"Funny that I never heard the Americans say those words when I was there. But speaking of fucking in it," Lazzaro began, "will it not be a shock for Tristan, your only child, to learn of how you seduced his one, true beloved?"

"Not at all." Carmella's dark eyes flashed. "But it *will* be a tragedy for him to learn of how you raped me and I covered up the horrible truth to protect him—but he is a young man of character and strength, and I am certain he will eventually overcome this hideous revelation."

"*Raped* you?" Lazzaro laughed. "I still have your claw marks on my back!"

"I am the trained actress; you would be wise to never forget this. But if you would like a free performance tonight to remind you, deny once more my request and tomorrow's news feeds will be ablaze with the story of Lazzaro Sforza, wanted for murder, drug and human trafficking, and inciting a riot, discovered in a country villa in Greece holding the great actress Carmella Montes, whom he raped, and her son against their wills. Police photos will show how Sforza's back was striped with scars from the fingernails of the unfortunate lady who so bravely fought him off."

Lazzaro opened his mouth to speak, but found himself suddenly mute.

Carmella, seeing his hesitation, closed her eyes and touched an index finger to each of her temples. "I am now sensing your thoughts. I feel now that you . . . have reached a new conclusion that there . . . is no choice other than to graciously . . . agree to my request." She opened her eyes and grinned, and then dabbed her chunk of bread in a nearby plate of olive oil and balsamic vinegar.

Lazzaro felt his skin flush. "You are a demon."

"You flatter me," she said, and then turned to follow her son's path as he wended his way down from the villa toward their table. "And what is your answer?"

"Forty-nine percent," Lazzaro spat. "But no more; I'll give myself up to Interpol myself before giving you a controlling share in my life's work. And no names, *yet;* I will need to contact them first to introduce you."

"That is fair, and you know it. I could have demanded entire control. You will pay me the cash you owe me following dinner tonight, when you'll also give me the contact information for those I should notify about this shift in ownership, and tomorrow *we* can begin regaining control over *our* enterprises." She ground her cigarette into a bread plate. "And you can forget about visiting my bed from now on; I've rekindled my . . . *friendship* with a Portuguese soccer star whose libido better matches my own."

Tristan approached the table dressed formally for dinner, in a fitted white suit and a black shirt unbuttoned nearly to his navel.

"*Hola mi guappito.*" Carmella lifted her cheek to him and he pecked it. "Thank you for joining us."

Tristan made his way over to Lazzaro and kissed him on the mouth. "My love—did I miss something?" He began gently massaging Lazzaro's shoulders.

"Only . . . that I have offered just now to give half the money I received from Jeremy to your mother"—he smiled warmly, nodding at Carmella—"and she has graciously accepted. I want to do my part to help you with the expenses, especially now that this will be my permanent home."

Carmella's eyes bugged and Tristan smiled broadly.

"This is so wonderful!" Tristan exclaimed. "My dream has come true!"

"*We did not—*" Carmella began with a snarl.

"It is the least I could do," Lazzaro interrupted, holding up a hand, "for the two most important people in the world to me."

Lazzaro glared at Carmella and she looked away, fuming.

"Certainly this is something we must celebrate," Carmella darkly added, clapping her hands for one of the servants. "Some champagne perhaps?"

"We should drink . . . to *family*," Lazzaro announced, his eyes sparkling.

"To family," Tristan breathlessly agreed as a servant approached the table.

"Champagne," Carmella told the servant, giving him a short nod. "*For my family.*"

CHAPTER

thirty-four

Jeremy had just finished folding a load of whites in the bedroom, and was arranging them inside the dresser's top drawer, when he heard the guesthouse door squeak open and then slam shut.

"Arthur?" he called out.

No answer.

Jeremy recalled how Arthur had barely eaten any of the bland risotto he had made him for dinner and had been complaining of feeling sleepy, so there was no reason for him to be anywhere but stretched out on the sofa watching one of their many Netflix selections.

Jeremy slid the dresser drawer closed. *Better go find out where he's off to.*

Bingham's and Skipper's eyes tracked Jeremy from their positions on the floor by the front door, muzzles resting atop paws and ready to spring into action should a leash be jingled or the refrigerator door be opened.

Jeremy carefully stepped over them and walked outside to survey the grounds.

No sign of him.

He crossed over to the main house and had just opened the servant's entrance door when—

CRASH!

He launched himself into the house in the direction of the sound.

"Arthur?! Carlo?!" he called out, looking around. "Aunt Katharine?"

Jeremy quickly determined that the noise was the explosion of a fragile object—not the tinkling shatter of glass, but a lower concussion—porcelain, perhaps. He did a quick mental inventory of ceramic artifacts in the house and made a deduction: the Chinese vase on the demilune table at the top of the stairs.

Aunt Katharine's favorite Chinese vase.

"Arthur?" Jeremy called out again. "Are you OK?"

"I'm fine!" Arthur's distant voice answered. "Bumped into something."

"Where are you?" Jeremy began quickly making his way through the house.

"Stairs!"

Jeremy found Arthur on his knees at the top of the staircase collecting large shards of porcelain, but seemingly unsure of what to do with them. "Hey, let me take care of that."

Arthur looked down at him, his face awash with uncharacteristic shame. "I'm sorry. I just . . . bumped into it. I didn't see it—my vision, it's not what it . . ."

"It's OK." Jeremy began climbing the stairs, scanning the area for remnants.

"Was this expensive?"

Jeremy knew it was—and he also knew Arthur had dusted this same vase at least a hundred times during his assignment as an FBI agent posing as butler in this very home. "Probably not," he lied. "Aunt Katharine bought some fakes, so don't worry about it." He bent down and began picking up the pieces. "You're probably dehydrated;

you were throwing up a lot after we got back from Cedars—or maybe it's just the new meds."

"Could we glue this back together?"

"We'll try. I'll go grab a trash can and get this cleaned this up."

"No, I'll get it." Arthur pushed himself up, groaning. "Be right back."

Jeremy scrutinized his partner as he strolled down the hallway. He looked a bit unsteady but still had that Marine's virile build and swagger. No one would ever look at Arthur and be able to detect the trouble brewing inside the man's handsome head.

Arthur reappeared a few minutes later with the wastebasket. "Sorry it took me so long. I thought I had to pee but barely did at all, so I guess I am dehydrated."

"What were you doing in here instead of in the guesthouse?" Jeremy asked, placing the broken pieces carefully inside the steel pail. "I was folding clothes and all of a sudden you disappeared."

"I wanted to ask Katharine something, but I couldn't find her."

"Why didn't you use the intercom?"

Arthur paused. "Guess I forgot about it."

"She's probably down in her office." Jeremy tried a reassuring smile. "What did you want to ask her?"

Arthur stared blankly at him. "Now I can't remember."

Jeremy gave him an appraising look. "You look really tired—why don't you just go get ready for bed?"

Arthur checked his watch. "It's only just after eight."

Jeremy flashed on the bottle of chardonnay chilling under the stalks of celery in the crisper drawer of the fridge. "You need your rest."

"Will you come in and lay down with me for a while?"

"After I finish cleaning up, I'll be right there."

Arthur turned and began heading toward the hall closet. "Be right back."

Jeremy cracked his neck in a futile attempt to alleviate the tension clustered inside. *How can this be happening to us?*

"Carlo?" Aunt Katharine's voice crackled over the intercom. "Jeremy? Who's there?"

Jeremy stepped over to the device in the wall and depressed the button. "It's Jeremy. I'm up here on the second floor."

"I heard something crash all the way down here in my office. Are you all right? What was that noise?"

"I'll explain when I come down; right now I'm cleaning it up." He let go of the button just as Arthur appeared with the vacuum.

"It's just about the dogs' dinnertime," Arthur said. "Do you want me to go ahead and feed them?"

Thank God he remembered feeding the dogs! "You go feed 'em and I'll clean up. Are you OK? Should I take you to the hospital or the urgent care?"

"I'm fine—I mean I'm obviously not great, but I'm OK."

"Drink as much of that fruit punch Gatorade as you can when you get back to the guesthouse. I'll be over in a few minutes; I need to go talk with Katharine. I love you."

"I love you, old buddy." Arthur smiled, turned, and left.

Jeremy determined that cleaning the remainder of the mess would take some doing, so he pressed the intercom for Carlo's quarters. "You there?"

"Serf's up," Carlo replied. "Who's this? You sound kinda cute."

"Listen, I need for you to help me clean up a mess so I can go talk to my aunt. Arthur just destroyed her favorite Chinese vase at the top of the stairs. You busy?"

"I thought I heard something, but I was on the phone. Be right there."

Knowing Carlo was on his way, Jeremy left the vacuum leaning against the wall and began making his way down to Katharine's office on the bottom floor of the estate.

He found her working at her desk.

"I'm sorry, but I broke your favorite vase—the gilded one on the Louis XVI demilune."

Katharine looked up from her computer screen. "The Canton Baluster?"

Jeremy nodded.

"I'm sure Arthur couldn't help himself. Don't give it another thought." She nodded at him. "Nice attempt covering up for him, by the way. I'm proud of you."

"This is so hard." Jeremy collapsed into a leather wing chair and put his head in his hands. "Every day he gets a little weaker, a little skinnier and there's more of his hair on the pillows and less on his head. And he's more forgetful . . . it's like watching him die by inches—"

"And it's going to get worse," Katharine interjected. "At least, that is, before it gets better." She took off her reading glasses and stared at him. "Jeremy dear, you are going through one of the most trying sets of circumstances anyone can endure. And you're holding up *very* well—but have you considered seeing a therapist to help you get through this rough patch?"

"That's what Arthur suggested."

"You really should consider it. And if there's anything I can do to help locate a good one, will you please let me know?"

"Yeah, sure."

"On an unrelated subject, there's one piece of news I thought might please you: I received a call from a realtor wondering if your old house is for sale; he's representing someone who's interested in tearing down the structure and building something new. Would you like his contact information?"

Jeremy hesitated. "I guess."

"You're not excited?"

"Actually, I was kinda hoping to fix up the place once we're finished with this crisis." He glanced up, his eyes searching hers. "Arthur really likes the house and he's got some great ideas on what we could do." He sighed. "His condo's in escrow, so we'll be getting some of the money we need soon . . . so we . . . um . . ." Jeremy looked down, unable to finish.

"So it's Arthur's and your dream to restore the place. And the money's on its way?"

Jeremy swallowed hard. "I know you've never been crazy about the property and I'm pretty much broke—"

Katharine held up her hand. "Sometimes wonderful things happen." She tipped her glasses back onto her nose and turned her attention back to her computer. "I'll tell the man the property is not for sale. And please know that I'm still considering your idea to loan you the money earmarked for the chalet at the lake."

"Thank you . . . Aunt Katharine. I—"

"Don't mention it, my dear."

:::::::::

It was just before midnight when Carlo found Jeremy reclining on one of the chaises around the swimming pool by himself, a nearly empty chardonnay bottle by his side.

"So it's only you," Carlo said. "I saw something move down here from up in the kitchen, so I got my hopes up that my stalker was finally out of jail. Are you OK?"

"Arthur's finally asleep," Jeremy slurred. "But he'd been throwing up almost all day since we got back from Cedars, and even after taking the anti-nausea pills he couldn't keep anything down. I can't stand seeing him like this; it's only his fourth day and I'm already feeling beat-up. How're we gonna get through this?"

"I can't tell you," Carlo replied, easing himself down onto the adjoining chaise. "But since people have no other choice, somehow they do get through it."

"Arthur's the sick one, but I feel like—I'm going crazy. We've gotta go through this every day for five more weeks? And all the time we're waitin' and waitin' and waitin', bein' glad the fuckin' treatments are drawin' to a close, but worried all the same that the 'Judgment of the Almighty Fuckin' MRI' is just around the corner? Not to mention my upcomin' court date with that mysterious fuckin' subpoena."

"Do you even have an attorney yet?"

Jeremy dropped his head into his hands and began massaging his temples. "I've been . . . kinda puttin' that off."

"You've got a lot of balls in the air, including your own, baby—and I've got just the person to help you sort them out, but her name isn't Miss Chardonnay."

"Mr. Daniels, perhaps?" Jeremy laughed sourly. "Jack?"

"A therapist."

Jeremy sighed. That made it unanimous: everyone in the house wanted him to see a shrink. "And you just happen to have one handy for me?"

"It's the same therapist who helped me get through all the crap when my mom was dying and my dad was being such an asshole and my sister Carmen ran off and was nowhere to be found. *Smart girl.*"

"I remember that. What's his name? I remember . . . it was . . . something hilarious."

"Dr. Studski."

"Now I remember!" Jeremy bellowed. "Do I have to be a *naughty muchacho* like you to see him?"

"No, but you've got to have an open mind. He's got some . . . *unusual* approaches to therapy." Carlo narrowed his eyes. "Are you ready to give him a call? You know, Arthur's really, really concerned about you."

Jeremy raised the bottle to his lips and threw back the last of his wine, blinking in the darkness. "He told you that?"

"We're old friends—or enemies, I can't remember which; he did steal my boyfriend some years ago. By the way, you would have loved the kid: hot, handsome, hung, and horny." Carlo looked around. "I wonder whatever happened to him?"

"I heard he's had a string of bad luck," Jeremy muttered. "He's broke and he drinks too much."

"Then what are you waiting for, another DUI—or worse?" Carlo wagged his finger at the bottle. "Arthur's aware that you've somersaulted off the proverbial wagon, and we all know the last thing that man needs to concern himself with is you taking out some Korean family in their Mazda minivan on Pacific Coast Highway after drinking a small flock of Grey Geese. Speaking of, how did your phone call go with the detectives? Are they helping you with the DUI charge?"

"The phone call went OK I guess. They're collaborating with Interpol, so they know all about what happened in Greece and told me what I need to do if Lazzaro contacts me again. And I let them know what Lazzaro threatened—about his accusing me of masterminding his father's murder—and they said they'll look into it . . . which could be good or bad." He blew out a long sigh. "As for the DUI, since I already finished rehab the judge'll consider that in deciding my probation—"

"As long as you don't get yourself into trouble again," Carlo interjected. "So you'll be needing Dr. Studski's number. *Riiiiight?*"

Jeremy sat back in the chaise, staring up at the stars. "Everything seems to be pointing that way."

"I'll e-mail it to you tonight."

Jeremy looked over at him. "I don't know what I'd do without you."

"Somehow, I do always wind up playing Jiminy Cricket to your Pinocchio." Carlo pushed himself up from the chaise. "I want you to call or text me the moment you've made the appointment with Dr. Studski so Arthur and I can stop worrying about *you* and can concentrate on *him*. And tomorrow I'm taking Arthur for his treatment; Margo and I've come up with a relief schedule for you."

"Since when did you two get so chummy?"

"She's Arthur's best friend and I'm yours," Carlo replied. "Duh."

"Well . . . that's great, but no. You don't have to do that."

"We want to, baby. We *want* to. She loves him like I love you. We're here for you, and I want you to remember that."

Jeremy tried to speak but was suddenly overcome. "Why do I keep crying when someone does something nice for me? What's wrong with me?"

"Because you're going through something horrible, dummy." Carlo reached down and took the empty wine bottle from Jeremy's side. "And besides, only real boys cry . . . so I guess this proves you're not Pinocchio anymore." He turned to head back into the main house but stopped himself. "But we still need to do everything possible to save your fairy godfather. Happily-ever-after this time. Right?"

"That's right," Jeremy sighed. "Happily ever after."

CHAPTER

thirty-five

How do you feel today?" Jeremy asked as they strolled along the sand.

"Much better," Arthur replied, making a detour around a large fork of twisted driftwood. "I think the anti-nausea meds are finally working and my head is a little clearer. What did you do after I fell asleep?"

"Went out by the pool to get my head together, where Carlo and I had one of our chats."

"You mean where he does most of the chatting?" Arthur laughed.

"Exactly."

"What about?"

Jeremy looked out at the waves breaking far from shore, and the bank of fog farther up the coast inching its way back out to sea. "About everything you'd expect—oh, and Carlo brought up his old witch doctor. Dr. Studski."

"Carlo also mentioned him to me. Are you going to call him?"

"I told him I would. Did you sleep all right?"

Arthur paused. "Yeah . . . but I had weird dreams."

"Me too. In fact, I've been having a lot of strange dreams lately. Like from a long time ago."

"When you were a kid back in Fresno?"

"Like from some movie that takes place in ancient times. Naked guys sitting around a pool talking to men in white robes and things like that. Then another one where my mother had just died, so I went to enlist in the Confederate Army during the Civil War. *Bizarre*. What about your dreams?"

"Nothing as elaborate as yours. More like frustration dreams where I'm driving that old Taurus again but it dies on the freeway and I'm stuck in the fast lane waiting for a collision . . . or I'm back in that furniture store I worked in during high school but no one will buy anything from me . . . or Bingham gets out and I can't find him." Arthur slowed his pace. "Tell me more about your dreams."

"Do you remember when we were at Hadrian's Gate and you were describing the different architectural elements and you started feeling sick and almost fell over?"

"Unfortunately, I remember it quite well. Why?"

Jeremy stepped around a lump of seaweed the size of a gathered bedspread. "You were about to tell me the name of the guy Hadrian was so in love with. Do you remember it now?"

Arthur paused. "Can't think of it."

"Antinous?"

Arthur grinned, eyes bright. "That's him. How could I forget? There are hundreds of statues of the young man in museums all around the world. He was gorgeous and built like a porn star—"

"—and Hadrian was completely devastated when he died."

"What makes you so interested in this, all of a sudden?"

They resumed their strolling. "All right. Now this is weird: The name 'Antinous' came to me in Greece when I was in the Plaka, and I didn't know who it was or what it meant, so I forgot about it. Then it came to me again the other day after I woke up from a dream, so I Googled it and found out that he was connected to Hadrian. Well, more than just connected. They were the loves of each other's lives."

Again, Arthur stopped walking. "You're saying you'd never heard of Antinous before the Plaka, and now you've had a vivid dream starring him and Hadrian?"

All Jeremy could do was shrug. "I told you. Weird."

Arthur blinked at him. "I should say so. I'll bet you just forgot that you learned about them in high school."

"I took ancient history in ninth grade," Jeremy said. "Do you really think a teacher in Fresno would devote any instructional time to a gay couple living in Ancient Rome? *That* I would remember."

"Good point," Arthur said, as they began walking again. "Hadrian and Antinous were a happy couple, as I recall. You find out anything else about them?"

"That's it. I've had more important things on my mind than Googling anything other than treatments for cancer."

"Do you think your dreams have anything to do with this situation of mine?"

"Well . . . in one of them, I see you as this older man with a beard and you actually call me Antinous. I'm naked by a pool with some other guys, like I told you. And in the dream I'm worried about your health . . . something to do with pains and numbness."

"I can see why your subconscious would have us play those two roles."

"What do you mean?"

"Because of our age difference—and because we were just in Greece. But the part about all the naked guys sounds tasty." Arthur wiggled his eyebrows up and down. "Does anything fun happen?"

"No," Jeremy replied. "Actually, I think my brain's been on overload, so it's just spinning random thoughts off, like a merry-go-round on spin-dry."

Arthur rested his hand on Jeremy's shoulder. "I'm sorry my situation is affecting you."

"Please don't ever apologize." Jeremy stopped walking and turned to him. "I'm so glad to be with you during this time, especially after Jess abandoned you. It kills me to think you might have had to go through this on your own! I'm *honored* to be by your side—and I wouldn't have it any other way."

Arthur sighed and squeezed his shoulder. "Your father would've been so proud of you. You know that, right?"

"I know he'd be so glad to know we're finally together. I can't think of anyone else he'd have rather seen me with."

They continued walking along the beach without talking, soothed by the boom-and-fizz of the waves upon the sand, and the ghostly daytime moon overhead half-shrouded behind a scrim of platinum-tipped clouds.

Finally Jeremy had the courage to spring the question that had been crouching in his head. "Will you tell me something?"

"Anything."

"What do you think happens after we die?"

"For some strange reason I've been wondering that lately." Arthur chuckled. "When my father died I wondered where he went, thinking he wasn't the kind of guy I could've seen getting into heaven—or at least the kind of heaven I was raised to believe in. And when your dad was killed in that car crash and your mother overdosed years later, I wondered the same thing; I suppose having someone die or living with a disease makes everyone examine their beliefs about eternity a lot more closely."

"So what conclusions have you reached? Anything?"

"Basically . . . that nothing matters except today," Arthur explained, "and how you treat others each day matters a lot. We need to live our lives honestly and bravely, and we have to take chances and believe in ourselves and find love everywhere we can and then nurture it. And if there *is* something out there after we die, then it'll be a bonus—I guess . . . but if there isn't anything beyond this world, then we'll feel content when we're drawing our final breath, knowing we lived a good life and made life happier for some people and animals. And finally, I think love lives on forever, even if we don't."

"But what if we *do* live on somehow after our bodies die?"

"Then each of us should . . . get ready for what I'm guessing is a really big surprise."

They continued ambling along in silence for a few moments, both men lost in their thoughts.

"I also wanted to discuss something else with you," Jeremy said.

"All ears, old buddy."

"Do you really think a therapist will do me some good? Because with everything happening with Lazzaro and my upcoming court date and various financial disasters, going back into rehab isn't an option right now and I'm scared of winding up like my mom . . . but more than anything I want to be there for you. I mean, what if you need me to rush you to the urgent care, or one of the dogs gets injured and needs to go to the vet, and I'm drunk or totally hung-over? I'm kinda stuck here."

"I'm a great believer in therapy," Arthur said. "And if there's anything that might make this period easier to get through, you should do it—for yourself and for us both. I'm guessing Doctor Studly—"

"Studski."

"—*Studski* could give you a new perspective on all this. Something you wouldn't ever think of yourself."

Jeremy shot him a hopeful smile. "I'll e-mail him when we get back."

"Sounds like a good idea." Arthur hesitated. "And . . . there's something I've been meaning to discuss with you, as well."

Jeremy waited.

"For me to sleep at night, I need to know there's a plan in place for you after I'm gone . . . that is, if things don't turn out the way we all hope."

"I'm not talking about that," Jeremy snapped. "You're going to make it through this and we're going to live happily-ever-after. *End of story.*"

"Baby, listen: I need to be real with you here . . . we need to talk about all possible scenarios, from the very best to the worst—for my sanity, if nothing else. Do you understand?"

Jeremy's mouth made a grim line. "OK then."

"Have you thought about this, too?"

"No," he lied.

"Then let's talk about it."

Jeremy took a deep breath. "If something happens to you . . . I'll sell our house and sell the Jaguar and buy a Prius and move in with Aunt Katharine and Carlo at the Tyler Compound. The dogs will be fine and I'll be fine and everything'll be fine." He glowered at Arthur. "How's that?"

"Will you . . . look for love again?"

Jeremy squeezed his eyes shut, shaking his head.

"Baby, don't cry. I need to ask you this."

"That's not a fair question!" Jeremy yelled as tears spilled down his cheeks. "Why would you ask me that?" He bent over and clutched at his stomach. "I can't do this, Arthur. I can't think of you . . . *dying* and then finding someone else to be with. I just can't!" He began hyperventilating, his eyes wild.

Arthur lowered himself onto the sand and patted the area next to him. "Sit down. Please."

Jeremy began pacing the beach. "I can't sit down—and I'm sorry. I should be strong for you. I told myself I wouldn't do this. I'm sorry, Arthur. *I'm so sorry!*"

"It's OK! Will you please just sit?"

"I'm sorry," Jeremy's voice creaked, as he folded himself down next to Arthur. Then he wiped away his tears, sniffling. "I'll never do that again. I promise . . . I'll never have another meltdown like that." He managed a blotch-faced smile.

"What's gotten into you?"

Jeremy saw the kindness in the man's eyes, and he almost began bawling again . . . but instead, he drew himself up straight. "I . . . I started thinking about everything we haven't done together that we've talked about: going to Pebble Beach this August and then to Spain next summer and actually getting married, and on and on. And I thought, all my life it seems like I've been waiting for you; I've been waiting for things to be safe between us so we can just breathe for a minute and look around and say, 'OK. Everything's finally the way it's supposed to be, so now we can start planning for the future.'" He took Arthur's hand. "But now I'm scared that there's no future anymore."

"Baby, there's never a future. But we *do* have today." Arthur smiled, looking deeply into Jeremy's glistening brown eyes. "And that's what we're going to concentrate on, because no one knows how much time they have left; all anyone can count on is today, and *maybe* tomorrow. And I know that sounds like some sappy greeting card with a sunset and a lone seagull on it, but it's true."

"I've lost both my mom *and* my dad, so you don't need to convince me."

Arthur threw an arm around him. "I just want to know, more than anything right now, that you'll find happiness with someone else if I don't make it through this."

"No!" Jeremy exclaimed, jumping up. "I won't look for love again because it's never worked with anyone but you! And you need to get better and get beyond this, because without you *my life is shit!* And I'm sorry if my saying this gives you more stress and this'll sound like the most selfish thing you've ever heard, but *you* are my life and I can't imagine myself ever being happy again if you die. *Do you get that?*"

Jeremy jammed his fists down into his jeans and hung his head, sniffling quietly.

Arthur slowly pushed himself up out of the sand. "I shouldn't have asked you that. My mistake."

"You've got to get better, Arthur."

"I see that."

"Can we go home?"

"You mean to the guesthouse?"

"I mean, to that stupid haunted house."

"I was hoping you'd say that," Arthur replied, smiling. "In consideration of your aunt's smashable art treasures, I was thinking that place of yours has nothing in it that's worth very much—"

"That place of *ours*—" Jeremy corrected.

"OK," Arthur chuckled, "*ours* . . . it's empty, and I think we could really use our privacy and time together. I think it might even do us some good to repair whatever we can . . . at least vacuum the ghosts from the closets, things like that. How about if we go pack up the guesthouse and take the dogs home with us this afternoon?"

Jeremy smiled, eyes glimmering. "There's nothing I'd like more."

"Hey—"

"Hay is for horses." Jeremy appraised him. "What?"

"Whenever I get really depressed I plan something to look forward to. So let's plan something fun. Will that make you feel better?"

"I guess."

"What would you like?"

"Aside from a threesome with Daniel Craig?"

Arthur laughed. "Aside from that."

"Maybe we could . . . be proper homosexuals and host an intimate brunch at our chateau that would give us something to work toward; we could have Carlo and Margo over and dress up Bingham like the butler and Skipper like the maid. Like, in a couple of weeks?"

"Some Eggs Oscar and roasted potatoes and a little non-alcoholic champagne?"

"I'll e-mail them when we get home—right after I e-mail Carlo's witch doctor."

"Cancer or no cancer, as long as we're alive we've gotta keep living, old buddy."

Then with Arthur's arm around Jeremy's shoulder, the pair made an about-face and began making their way through the sand back toward the Tyler compound.

CHAPTER

thirty-six

"What brings you here?" Dr. Studski asked Jeremy.

Jeremy stared zombielike at the heavyset, middle-aged man, thinking, *After throwing away the last four years trying to avoid him, the only man I've ever loved is going to die—but only after I've watched him waste away.* "Um . . . we just found out," he blandly replied, as if reporting the weather, "that my partner has another brain tumor."

"I'm sorry to hear that," the doctor replied. "What's your partner's name?"

"Arthur."

"Has Arthur received an official prognosis?"

Jeremy studied the inexpensive oak reproduction Arts and Crafts lamp table by the loveseat's side. "We've got five more weeks of chemo and radiation, and then an MRI to figure out if he needs surgery."

"How is Arthur weathering his treatments?"

"He's adjusting, but it's pretty brutal."

"And how are you faring?"

Jeremy squinted over at a tangle of black extension cords hidden behind the artificial, potted ficus tree in the corner, and then up at the cheap framed print of a forested brook. "I guess I'm OK."

"Can you put into words how you feel?"

Jeremy squared his gaze at him. "Sick to my stomach. And sometimes I feel like going postal, and other times all I can do is cry. But I feel guilty because I'm not stronger and I'm usually craving a Grey Goose martini the size of a fishbowl. But other than that I feel great."

"Sounds like you're feeling anger and sadness and helplessness," the doctor said, scribbling notes onto a yellow legal pad.

"Actually, *furious* and *totally depressed* pretty much sums it up."

Dr. Studski clicked the tip of his pen rhythmically with his thumb. *Clickety-click-click—click; clickety-click-click—click.* "Are his treatments causing you stress?"

"Could you please stop doing that with your pen?"

The doctor stopped clicking. "Is that bothering you?"

"Thanks. We've kinda settled into a new routine: scheduling meds and doctor appointments and trips to the pharmacy and all that. And we're trying to strike a balance between what we'd really like to do on some beautiful afternoon and what we're actually capable of doing . . . while each morning I wake up wondering if this is going to be the day the other shoe drops."

"What do you mean?"

"I've started scrutinizing everything Arthur does: every sentence, every step he takes, whether or not his hands are shaking or if he remembers something that happened last week." Jeremy looked up at the ceiling, searching the water-stained acoustical tiles. "Then at night I lie in bed wondering: could Arthur go blind or have a stroke or die in his sleep, or will he look at me some morning and ask who I am?"

"This uncertainty must be a huge burden to live with—"

"But I don't have a choice, so I've decided that whatever's going to happen, I'll handle it. Nothin' else to do."

"What made you decide to seek therapy?"

"Because . . . well, beyond the fact that everyone I know suggested it, I'm finding it harder to be cheerful and optimistic around

Arthur. And I'm really scared of what's down the road; there are all these sad pictures online of skinny, frail, bald people smiling bravely even though they're dying. And I drink too much."

"When do you feel this sadness most, Jeremy?"

"Mostly when I'm alone, when I'm driving . . . I'll think of something like how everything's changed. Like, now we have a BC: *Before Cancer*. Or I see something that makes me think that the last time we did it everything was fine: 'last Sunday' or 'last time we had sex' or 'last time we filled up at that gas station.' And when I think of all the time we could've been together but weren't, I want to kill myself."

"What's this feeling of anger toward yourself?"

Jeremy shook his head.

"Perhaps we should begin with the history of your relationship. Tell me as much or as little as you'd like."

"It's complicated," Jeremy muttered.

"Then just the most important parts first—I'm pretty good at filling in the blanks."

Jeremy drew in a breath while looking around the room. "Things were never easy between us, but no matter what happened it seemed like we were destined to be together."

"Go on."

"When I was two my father was killed in a suspicious car crash, so I was brought up by my alcoholic mom; then in my senior year of high school she went into rehab again, so I went to live with my great aunt and her husband in Ballena Beach, where I met Arthur, their butler. Aunt Katharine tried to control every part of my life, but Arthur got me through all that. Then when I came out, she freaked out, and Arthur helped me get through that, too. Then it turned out Arthur was actually an FBI agent who was undercover and trying to protect my aunt and me from my uncle Bill—the one who had my father killed in the suspicious accident." Jeremy sighed and rolled his eyes toward Dr. Studski. "You getting all this?"

"Sounds like a novel," Dr. Studski noted.

"Oh, there's more. My mom, who was diabetic, got out of rehab and started drinking again, so my uncle Bill shot her up with extra insulin one night when she was drunk."

"Did she survive?"

"No. But she'd been really sick with kidney failure and diabetes, and since she started drinking again I figure that even if Bill hadn't killed her, she would've died soon anyway."

"That's extending a very generous point of view to your uncle, if I might say so," said Dr. Studski. "And where is your uncle now?"

Jeremy smiled. "In hell."

"I'm sorry?"

"I killed him. He was coming after me and my boyfriend Carlo with a gun, so I jumped him and cracked his head open on a rock fireplace. Do you remember Carlo Martinez?"

"Of course. He recommended me to you."

"Yep."

The doctor nodded. "Where does your relationship with Arthur come into play?"

Jeremy settled back into his chair. "Just when things were getting good with Carlo and we were celebrating graduation in Hawaii, Arthur called to say my aunt needed us to go to Brazil to check out a real estate deal my uncle invested in before he died. Arthur also told me he missed me, more than he thought he would—and I took this to mean he was falling in love with me."

"But his role was your protector. Did you take this revelation as a breach of trust?"

"No. I was totally in love with him but was too scared to tell him."

"What's your age difference?"

"How'd you know there's an age difference?"

"You'd just graduated high school and he was an FBI agent."

"Oh yeah," Jeremy laughed. "He's nineteen years older than me—"

"Which seems unusual for two men, but not for heterosexual relationships; my wife is considerably younger than I."

"The age difference never mattered, at least to me, but it bothered Arthur and my aunt."

"So then what happened?"

"We went to Brazil and I got kidnapped and almost died. It was the scariest thing I'd ever been through, until now. And as it turned out, my aunt was behind the kidnapping because she'd taken out kidnapping insurance on me and needed the money—remember how the economy tanked really bad?"

"She did *what?*"

"It was all supposed to go really smoothly, but the guy who was handling the fake kidnapping double-crossed her. She didn't mean for anything bad to happen to me. The guy was just a greedy fucker, and when she found out what was happening she did everything she could to get me back home safely."

"And how was Arthur involved in this?"

"Arthur and Carlo—remember, he was my boyfriend and even now we're still friends—rescued me."

"Carlo once mentioned shooting and killing a man . . . yes, this is sounding familiar." Dr. Studski began scratching more notes onto his pad but then stopped. "Was this when you and Arthur became a couple?"

Jeremy shook his head. "No. We had sex a couple of times, but Arthur got all guilt-ridden and decided our age difference was too big. He said I needed to experience life and go to frat parties and stay up all night and I shouldn't be tethered to an older man."

"How did you react to this?"

"He devastated me—and I was so angry at him I didn't talk to him for four years. In the meantime Arthur found some guy to move in with, but they broke up and Arthur found me on the beach, hungover and depressed. I told him I wanted nothing to do with him, and he said I was all he ever wanted . . . and he said he'd do anything in the world to get me back."

"How did it feel to finally hear those words?"

"After I got over my anger at him, it was like I'd . . . just been given wings. I knew this was what I'd been waiting for and we'd finally be together for the rest of our lives. And we've been together ever since—which hasn't been very long."

"And how's it been going?"

"It was great until I found out about Arthur's diagnosis—which was told to me not by Arthur but by this sociopath named Lazzaro who I dated and who screwed me over in a real estate deal. I thought I was going to get my money back, so we traveled to Greece to meet with him, but then he blackmailed me for something I never did and got even *more* money out of me."

"Maybe we should save that part for another day," Dr. Studski suggested, rubbing his temples. "You mentioned wanting a martini the size of a swimming pool."

"A fishbowl, actually. I forgot to tell you that I quit drinking before I found out about Arthur's diagnosis and then started up again, so Carlo told me he's worried about me and so's Arthur, so I figured I should call you before I do something stupid again." He paused. "I also forgot to tell you that I got a DUI and completed thirty days of rehab."

"Are you here today on your own volition, or because of Arthur and Carlo's requests?"

"I'm here because . . . I kinda need to be. Too much is at stake."

"Of course." Dr. Studski nodded. "And presently, how old are you and Arthur?"

"I'm twenty-four now and Arthur's forty-three."

"That's very young to be dealing with a life-threatening disease."

"You mean for me, or for him?"

"For both of you." He paused. "When were you first aware of your attraction to Arthur?"

"Well, the moment I saw him I thought he was hot. There's really no question about it. He's an ex-Marine, and it shows on him, even today. He's handsome, with salt-and-pepper hair, crow's feet, big arms and chest. He gets more looks on Santa Monica Boulevard than even the hottest twinks—like how a restored sixties Mustang can make even a brand new Porsche seem invisible. But more than that, it's his personality and his character. He's a strong, loving, generous, and patient man, and I—" Jeremy looked down.

"It sounds like you're very proud of him."

"I love him." Jeremy's mouth curled into a sad smile. "Like you can't believe."

"Can you tell me about Arthur's decision that you shouldn't be together? What led up to that?"

"How much time do we have left?"

"I'll let you know when our time is up."

"When we were in Brazil, I balls-out seduced him. We had sex and it was like nothing I'd ever felt before; we were both shaking, we both wanted it so much. And before I could figure out what to tell Carlo, I got kidnapped, and Carlo and Arthur rescued me, like I said. Then Carlo and I broke up, and Aunt Katharine fired Arthur and told him she'd disinherit me if Arthur came anywhere near me again."

"You stopped seeing each other because of the money?"

"God no," Jeremy laughed. "I didn't care about the money. Actually, at first Arthur left because he didn't want to ruin my relationship with Aunt Katharine, but then he came back and told her off. And everything looked like it was going to be OK until Arthur's conscience kicked in; he started freaking out about 'stealing my youth' and told me we weren't meant for each other and needed to find mates our own ages. And at first I went along with it, because I didn't have any choice; I started dating guys my age but kept comparing them to

Arthur. So Carlo encouraged me to go after Arthur again; he said we were destined for each other and relationships with anyone else were a waste of everyone's time."

"It sounds as if you value Carlo's perspective."

Jeremy grinned. "He's the best. And we had fun together as lovers, but it always seemed like we were better brothers—*or sisters*—than lovers."

"Perhaps you were," Dr. Studski suggested. "Or perhaps you were intimately involved in some other way."

Jeremy furrowed his brow. "What do you mean?"

"Without violating Carlo's confidentiality, I'm going to suggest something that I'd like you to consider. I believe in cases like yours there might be something more at work here than mere happenstance."

"Like what?"

"I specialize in something that might be therapeutic to you: *past-life regressions*. I use hypnosis to go back into other lifetimes to understand what's happening today. And in a case such as yours and Arthur's and Carlo's, and the rest of your family and what's his name—Lazarus? It sounds to me as though you have very strong karmic ties."

Jeremy stared at him for a long moment. "'Past-life regressions'?"

Dr. Studski nodded.

"And 'karmic ties.'"

"That's right. Do you know what those mean?"

That you are, maybe, crazier than I am? Or you're joking? But Dr. Studski was dead serious, Jeremy could tell. "I've heard that 'karmic ties' phrase," he admitted, "but no, I don't really know what it means. And his name is *Lazzaro*."

"Oh yes. Lazzaro. Sorry." He made a fresh note, then looked up at Jeremy. "Those terms refer to the notion that events from your past lives are tied to events happening today . . . and from what you've told me, you all seem bound—doubly bound, from the sound of it—by karmic 'strings' attached to one another."

"But I thought you were a doctor."

"I *am* a doctor—and I completely understand your skepticism. Jeremy, I'll do my best to help you through what might be the most trying period in your life either way: by looking at today only, or by factoring in events from long ago. The choice is yours, and I won't pressure you. I'm merely offering more than one course of therapy."

It seemed crazy to Jeremy—but he had to admit he also felt a strong compulsion to learn more about it. If nothing else, it might help him make sense of those vivid dreams he'd been having. "When would we start this—that is, if I decided I want to go forward with the hypnosis?"

"We'd begin next week."

"Why not after I tell you more about what's happened in the past? That's how it was when I was in rehab: we talked and talked and talked about all the shit that's happened."

"Therapeutically, my approach is in the same vein as Freudian therapists, who examine their client's first childhood memories and then move forward—but in this case we go even further back than childhood. I . . . like to think of this method as inspecting the foundation of the house before examining the warped floors, the shifting walls, and the short-circuiting electrical. Do you understand?"

"Just like my creepy chateau. I—" Jeremy paused, "—guess I'd need to do some research first before I went under hypnosis, if that's OK."

"That's a terrific idea." Dr. Studski glanced at his watch. "There are plenty of resources on the Internet to explore. In the meantime, our hour is up. Same time next week?"

"Sounds good. But—" Jeremy pushed himself up from the loveseat, "—I just thought of something."

"Yes?"

"Having a past life means dying at one point. Right?"

"That's how it seems to work."

"But what if something comes up that's traumatic? Like if I was beheaded or set on fire or . . . fed to the lions?"

Dr. Studski began fiddling with his pen again. *Clickety-click-click—click.* "We look at a past-life crisis similarly to one that's happening right now—with one major difference."

Jeremy withdrew his keys from his pocket and jingled them. "What's that?"

"We know how it ends."

CHAPTER

thirty-seven

Upon arriving home, Jeremy found Arthur fiddling with his laptop in the chateau's dilapidated breakfast room, a half-eaten turkey sandwich on the table in front of him, and the French doors open to the *allargando* bass drum and cymbal snare of the waves beating the sand.

Bingham—looking like a big black pillow—was curled at Arthur's feet in front of the chair, while Skipper lay prostrate on the floor within a trapezoid of sunlight framed by the doorway.

"Hey," Jeremy said.

"Hay is for horses," Arthur replied absently, still focused on his computer.

"What're you up to?" Jeremy slid his keys and wallet onto the kitchen's tile counter.

Skipper looked up at Jeremy for a moment, and then lay her head back down with a yawn and a tinkling of tags.

"Just looking for some information that might give us more hope. Oh, and I picked up some paint chips." He pointed to an area of the countertop where a series of paper color samples were lined up.

"Did you find anything new? About treatments I mean?"

"And how did it go with the therapist?" Arthur asked.

"Pretty good, I guess." Arthur had ignored his question, so Jeremy let it drop. He made his way over to him and put an arm around his shoulder while gently nudging Bingham with his foot. The dog fully stretched out his legs, and Jeremy reached down to rub his furry belly. "The guy's nice enough, but he had some . . . unusual ideas that he wants me to think about."

Arthur looked at him, fatigue simmering in his eyes. "Like what?"

"He thinks we might have a karmic connection that's figuring into this newest drama of ours, so—get this—he actually wants me to consider investigating our . . . *past lives.*" Jeremy wiggled his fingers in the air. "Ooga-booga!"

Arthur went back to studying his computer's screen. "Actually, I've always wondered about that myself."

Jeremy's hands fell to his sides. "You're joking."

"Haven't you?"

"I've had enough drama already to count for three or four lives, so I'm usually just trying to wrap my head around what's going on right now." Jeremy turned and made his way to the counter and began examining the paint chips. "Have you actually looked into this reincarnation stuff? And why haven't you told me before now?"

"I've done some research," Arthur replied. "Most of it while we were estranged."

"Did you discover anything? Like . . . were you Napoleon?"

"No, but I love them for dessert. I was looking for answers, Jeremy, like . . . why did I have such a shitty relationship with my parents, and why was I gay, and why as a gay man was I drawn to the military, and why did I have this immediate and very strong love for you . . . things like that. It seems to me that there are too many coincidences in life for things to happen by chance, and I do believe there are karmic ties involved in relationships—*especially* relationships with too much drama." He glared at Jeremy.

Still surveying the paint colors, Jeremy picked up two. "So do you believe in it?"

Arthur closed the lid of his laptop. "I never reached any conclusions one way or another, so I kind of filed the information away—but I did come across some very compelling stories . . . a boy who remembered being a fighter pilot in World War II who crashed into the Pacific; a woman who recalled a life as Anne Frank and living in the concentration camp; a retired police detective who discovered in a regression that he'd been a portrait painter in the nineteenth century. Fascinating accounts, and each from a highly credible source—at least, they seemed credible to me."

"Huh," Jeremy said. "By the way, I love these two colors; this ivory or this dove gray would look great in the living room, huh?"

"Uncanny." Arthur looked up at the samples in Jeremy's hand with a wry smile. "Those are *my* two favorites, as well."

"*Karmic*," Jeremy said, with mock solemnity. Then he glanced over at Arthur's discarded sandwich. "Is that all you've had to eat today?"

"Not really hungry."

"No surprise—that sandwich looks awful. Can I make you something else, like mac 'n' cheese, or at least put some mustard and mayo on that thing?"

"Just not very hungry, old buddy. But I'll want something later. Promise."

Jeremy made his way over to Arthur's side and leaned against his shoulder. "OK. But if you decide in the meantime that you want something, you'll let me know. Right?"

Arthur reached out and took Jeremy's hand. "All I want is you."

"Hey! How about a walk?"

At hearing this, Bingham lifted his head and stared at him.

"Are you up for that, Arthur? That'll get your hunger up and you could tell me more about all your freaky reincarnation research."

"I've got some things I need to take care of," Arthur replied, knowing that a walk while fighting his nausea was precisely the last thing he was in the mood for. "Do you mind if I stay back? I've gotta pay some bills, and I'm falling behind with the business; I've been leaning hard on Greg and John, and it's not fair to them. Our liability insurance premiums just shot through the roof, so I've got to research other carriers. Plus we're hiring two new guards, and background checks are time-consuming."

"I can help you, if you want."

"This is my work, old buddy."

They looked into each other's eyes.

"I'll be back in about an hour," Jeremy told him at last. "The dogs already had their walk today. Do you mind if I leave them with you?"

"It's just about their dinnertime, anyway—and I'd like their company."

"I'll stay with you if you want."

Arthur smiled wistfully. "You look like you could use some fresh air and 'Jeremy time.'"

Jeremy jingled his keys. "Forty-five minutes then."

"Be counting each one," Arthur told him, opening his laptop.

:::::::::

After negotiating the warped and wobbling wooden stairs down from the chateau, instead of making his usual left to head down the beach toward hip and trendy Malibu, something compelled Jeremy to turn right toward the north end of Ballena Beach.

There was something unsettling about this ribbon of sand and its string of ancient estates, which dated back to the turn of the twentieth century. The grand pier and boardwalk—now history, but for an assemblage of piling posts sticking up from the water like a giant submerged hairbrush—heralded the new wealth and prosperity of Southern California in the Roaring Nineties, until a deadly Ferris wheel fire decimated the tourist attractions before spreading to many of the waterfront homes and cliff-top estates overlooking the bay.

Jeremy had always felt out of place here . . . he supposed because this stretch of Ballena Beach more resembled pictures he'd seen of a stuffy New England enclave than the more casual beaches of Los Angeles. Up the shoreline tilted a now defunct lighthouse atop a jetty of monstrous boulders. The remaining Victorian mansions were as imposing as they were silent, and there seemed a hostility or sadness in the air that said, *Go away. You're not welcome here.*

It was late afternoon, and although the sky had been a bright, arching sapphire since morning, now the fog was settling in: the clay-red cliffs were paling pink behind the mists, and the shoreline topography—the iceplant drapes hanging from the cliffs; the acne-scarred sandstone precipices, tunnels, and caves; the tangles of iced-tea colored seaweed—was taking on a ghostly pallor, as if viewed from behind scrims of ultra-fine white lace.

Jeremy continued trudging through the sand, his feet heavy and his mind whirling. He had just noticed a pair of perfectly good neon-pink flip-flops someone had discarded in a cluster of sea grass nearby when he looked up to see a column of light blistering out from the fog.

At first he couldn't tell what he was seeing and thought perhaps his eyes were playing tricks on him . . . until he began to ascertain that the light looked somehow like a radiant shadow—if such a thing could exist—drifting ashore out from the listless waves. As the form drifted closer, Jeremy began perceiving the shape of a woman . . . wearing a flowing white dress . . . and some sort of high, gossamer veil held up with tree branches atop her head like the sail on a makeshift raft.

Jeremy blinked hard. *Am I actually seeing what I'm seeing?*

The being drew closer to him, her expression placid and her body skimming over the beach—although the side-to-side shifting of her dress indicated limbs ambulating in slow-motion, as if she were somehow roller skating over the sand.

He was about to dismiss the approaching woman as one of those eccentric performance artists from down the beach in Venice—or perhaps a fashion model outfitted for some French magazine's photo shoot—when it became apparent that the being was actually transparent.

Could this be a flashback from the Sueño Gris . . . or is this somehow real?

His spine feathered with goose flesh as he realized he was experiencing something otherworldly.

The apparition drew up to him and stopped, floating, or so it seemed, nearly two feet above the sand and about a car's length away.

Jeremy squinted at her, his brain scrambling to make sense of this. "What do you want? Who are you?"

"I have a message for you," she told him in a richly resonant voice seemingly synthesized from perhaps a dozen people—female, male, adults, and children—speaking in perfect synchronization, like a well-practiced Greek chorus.

"What . . . w-what is it?" Jeremy stammered, fighting the urge to turn and flee.

"You don't remember me?" Her pale, glossy irises searched his.

He examined her face, trying to find any feature that might trigger recognition. "Not really, but I—"

"You may recall my sister, the spinster; she told me you are having trouble sleeping. Perhaps these scenes will look familiar?"

While Jeremy was trying to remember any women he'd recently met, there was a sudden flash of light above the apparition's head. He looked up into her suspended veil and saw faint images projected upon it—or within it, he couldn't quite tell. At once he was mesmerized by the translucent slideshow: A bearded man sobbing. A beautiful, aristocratic woman. A grand villa. Naked bodies coupling. A battlefield lined with smoldering cannons and corpses. A uniformed gentleman bent doubled with grief. Prancing horses and a tethered dog. Pyramids. A long funeral procession. "What the hell—"

"Just as one man knows not the length of his spring," she said in her chorused voice of a dozen, "neither do three men know the lengths of their summers, autumns, or winters."

"Aren't they each three months long?"

She stretched open her red, painted mouth and a cacophony of storm-thrashed waves thundered from her throat as the veiled images dimmed and vanished.

"You're fucking scaring me," Jeremy told her, backing up.

"Are you not a companion to the stars," she asked, "south of Aquila the Eagle?"

"I don't know anyone famous," Jeremy answered. "Except for maybe Sebastian Black."

"Eta, Theta, Delta, Iota, Kappa, and Lambda Aquilae," she said, her breath misting. "You must remember these: Eta, Theta, Delta, Iota, Kappa, and Lambda Aquilae. You know these better than you know your name."

"I've got no idea what you're talking about."

"They say your spirit has not changed." She smiled. "He must love having you by his side again."

"Arthur?" Jeremy froze, wide-eyed. "*What do you know about Arthur?!*"

"Eta, Theta, Delta, Iota, Kappa, and Lambda Aquilae. Take your string and measure the stars, but take care not to snap the thread."

Thread.

And then he remembered: *A small axle with only one wooden wheel attached, and wound tight with pale thread so fine it might have been pulled from the back of a tarantula.* The apparition in their bedroom, the night before their trip to Greece.

"Your spinster sister!" Jeremy shouted. "Does she dress kinda like a Spanish bullfighter and carry a little—I don't know what it is . . . thing with"—he was gesticulating frantically—"you know a little wheel on the end with thread wrapped around it?!"

The apparition smiled as she began to vanish.

"Hey, don't go!"

She evaporated, and Jeremy found himself alone on the beach—his mind wobbling from what he'd just experienced.

Was it real?

I saw what I saw.

"I'd better go check on Arthur," Jeremy told the empty beach as he turned and began trudging toward home, muttering *Eta, Theta, Delta, Iota, Kappa, and Lambda Aquilae* as he hurried through the sand.

CHAPTER

thirty-eight

"You know," Jeremy began, "I've always wondered why people who believe in reincarnation always think they were someone famous."

"We call those 'landmark cases,'" Dr. Studski replied, "where a soul remembers a famous person or an amazing event from their lifetime, because that person or event attracted tremendous attention. A typical landmark case might involve someone who thinks they went down with the *Titanic*, because it was such a huge event from the time when they lived before."

"So their soul remembers the event, but forgets that they only heard about it and weren't really involved in it?"

"Something like that."

"So then how do you know if you really are—were—someone else and not just one of those landmark cases?"

"Few actually recall themselves as famous figures. Though of course it happens. When it does, there are other indicators that can help establish authenticity: shared facial architecture; attraction to geographic locations; anniversary phenomenon; innate talents; gravitation toward similar professions; even precise memories that one's soul remembers under hypnosis or meditation or dreams . . . or even spontaneously in a waking state. But one of the most significant indicators is when soul groups are reincarnated together. *Reunited,* as we say."

"How does that work?"

"People somehow locate each other from one lifetime to the next, as if they'd planned a vacation to meet up in a foreign country. For example, coupled souls from one lifetime might find each other and become involved in their next lives, and members of one's family can be reborn within the same, or related, lineage. Even people who've worked to effect positive social change in one era can come back together in future incarnations to accomplish more as a team than they could alone."

"That's interesting," Jeremy told Dr. Studski while actually thinking it wasn't, "but I've been having hallucinations and I'm really freaked out about them."

"Hmmm." *Clickety-click-click—click.* "Of what sort?"

"Women ghosts wearing what looks like Alexander McQueen couture saying things that don't make any fucking sense."

"Alexander McQueen?"

"Crazy-brilliant designer who committed suicide—hanged himself after his mother died of cancer. Lots of sequins and matador hats. He designed dresses that celebrities might wear to the Academy Awards—*in hell.*"

The doctor paused. "What did these entities tell you?"

Jeremy's eyes searched the ceiling as he tried to recall specifics. "Riddles about not cutting thread, and Greek letters, and saying I was a companion to the stars; showing me pictures of people I don't know, and war scenes with cannons and dead bodies, or teasing me with strange little objects that they hold out for me to see and then put back inside their pockets."

"That must be troubling. Or annoying."

"Tell me about it."

"When do these manifest, and how often?"

"Just twice so far: I saw one in our bedroom when Arthur was still asleep, and the other one I saw on the beach when I was walking by myself. The first one was all in black like a matador and the second was dressed in white with a weird veil on her head held up with branches—or were they antlers?"

"What was your mental state at the time?"

"Same as usual: on the brink of a nervous breakdown . . . my brain hamster-wheeling with one doomsday scenario after another. But I thought this might be happening because I took this drug a few times that's similar to LSD. Do you think I could be having flashbacks?"

"What's the name of this drug?"

"Sueño Gris, which means 'gray dream,'" Jeremy explained. "It's a designer drug that's supposed to make you awake and dreaming at the same time."

"Were you on this drug at the time of your hallucination?"

"I haven't taken any in months."

Dr. Studski tapped his pen on his knee. "These new drugs can be extremely dangerous, but I'm betting there's no literature yet on their long-term effects. I'll look up this 'gray dream' drug just to be sure . . . but even those much-purported LSD flashbacks of old were revealed to not actually exist—and I don't think your alcohol dependency would have caused you to experience *Delirium Tremens*, or DTs. This sounds more like your distressed mental state enabling entities from the spirit world to make themselves known to you."

"You're joking."

"Such things happen; there have been many documented cases where spirit messengers have been sent to warn or to comfort those in crisis." Dr. Studski cleared his throat. "Did you get a feeling of doom or evil from these beings?"

"No." Jeremy shook his head. "They startled me, but it wasn't like *The Exorcist*."

"Then I wouldn't be too concerned about it. But in the meantime, if something further happens, I'd recommend you write down the details of your visitation as soon as you possibly can; we might analyze the messages and try to extract some significance. You said she mentioned you are a 'companion to the stars.'"

"Yeah, but I don't know anyone famous except for Sebastian Black—and I barely know him; he's my ex-girlfriend's boyfriend and we only had dinner once. She, the ghost lady, said the words *Eta, Theta,* and *Delta* . . . and *Lambda* something. Oh, and *Iota*, which are Greek letters. I looked them up."

"Greek letters, yes, but they also used these to denote the stars and their constellations, so we might already be headed somewhere. What were they, once more?" Jeremy recited them again and Dr. Studski recorded the words. "I could do some work on these and see what they might spell or stand for. But in the meantime, I'd like to proceed with the regression. Are you still willing to try?"

Jeremy shrugged. "Sure."

"One more thing I should've mentioned."

"Yeah?"

"At times I'll ask you to clarify what you're experiencing, but because hypnosis increases suggestibility I won't lead you toward a specific answer, and I won't jump in with what I already know or may suspect. Everything needs to come from within you."

"So you'll be playing dumb," Jeremy said. "Even when you're not."

Studski chuckled. "Exactly."

"Fine."

"Then lay back and close your eyes," Dr. Studski told Jeremy as he stretched out onto the doctor's dark green corduroy sofa. "Be very conscious of your breathing. With every exhalation I want you to focus on pushing out. Push out the stress, and then every new inhalation brings in warm, relaxing energy. Release those stresses and allow your body to feel heavy with relaxation. Allow your body to go limp and loose and relaxed. Every inhalation brings in relaxation."

Jeremy began breathing in deeply and exhaling slowly.

"You may be aware of noises, but these only allow you to know that life is going on around you. Feel your shoulders relax; allow your shoulders to go limp. Bring in deep, relaxing warm energy, flowing down your shoulders into each arm, your biceps and elbows, in your hands, and moving into your fingers so there's no longer any tension in there. Relax your stomach, your solar plexus. Allow the deep warm energy to spread across to the tops of your thighs. Sink deeper and deeper into the couch. Every inhalation is deeper. I'm going to count backwards from five to zero; with the sound of my voice your muscles get more loose and limp. On zero you will feel maximum relaxation. Five . . . four . . . three . . . two . . . one . . . zero." The man snapped his fingers loudly. "Allow your mind to drift. Let it all float by. Visualize a beautiful garden, so special because it was created specifically for you. Everything here was created to make you feel relaxed and joyous. Every element was created for you. Take a moment and wander through the garden, look at the flowers and the plants. Now find a source of water. It could be a fountain or a waterfall or a stream. Now you can see the fresh, clear, beautiful water. Where is it coming from?"

"There's a stream flowing into a pool," Jeremy muttered.

"Put your hands in the water," Dr. Studski continued. "It feels cool and refreshing and lovely. See the droplets. Can you see the droplets?"

"Yes."

"Now walk along the stream. You're completely safe. Up ahead you'll see a beautiful golden gateway. The gate is closed, but it looks very inviting. You're going to walk through this gate, which can only be opened by you. You walk closer and closer and the golden gate gets brighter and brighter–more golden and inviting. You put your hand on the gate and feel the gate open. Know that what you are about to see is entirely, absolutely safe for you. It's a very important and beautiful place for you. I want you to walk through that gate. This gate is taking you back in time. You'll be aware that the environment is changing. You walk through and see a place that's chosen by you. Get yourself oriented. Tell me what you're wearing."

Jeremy hesitated. "Pants and a shirt. No, it's . . . a jacket over a shirt. My pants are torn. My pants are crusted with dried and wet blood."

"What's your name?"

"Jere . . . *miah*. Jeremiah." Jeremy cocked his head, eyes closed. "*Jeremiah Murray.*"

"Can you see where you are, Jeremiah?" Dr. Studski asked.

Jeremy paused. "Outside somewhere. In a field. It's hot, and I'm trying to drag myself under a tree. And I don't feel well."

"Why?"

"I'm . . . dying?"

"Why do you think this?"

"My leg is throbbing . . . parts of it are swollen and purple. I was shot a few days ago, and ever since then it's been bleeding and it hurts a lot. Plus, I'm really hot. I know I have a fever. My whole body aches—even my hair."

"Why are you in this situation?"

"I'm . . . a soldier. At least I used to be. I deserted and then I was shot. I don't want to see the doctors from the other side because I know they'll cut off my leg. For the enemy soldiers they cut off everything too soon so we can never go back to war; their doctors are under orders to use any excuse to cut off a leg or an arm. I have seen their stinking pile of legs, stacked like rotting logs. The stench." Jeremy wrinkled his nose. "You never get that smell out of your nose."

"You can smell it now?"

Jeremy nodded, eyes tightly shut. "And now it's coming from my own leg. I know I'm going to die soon because the purple is spreading to my man-parts, but there's nothing I can do. The fever makes me not care. But I'm so thirsty. All I want is to not die thirsty. I am . . . *crazy* with thirst."

"Where are you?"

"The forest."

"Are you close to any city or town?"

"My army was close to Owen's Crossroads at River's Bridge over Duck Creek. The stream that runs through the town is red with blood. I can't stand any more cannon fire. My head splits from the noise. I am young but almost deaf. You cannot be a soldier if you cannot hear the enemy coming—and it's hard to run if you have no legs." He laughed.

"What's the year?" Dr. Studski asked.

"Eighteen . . . sixty-five."

"How old are you?"

Jeremy thought for a moment. "Eighteen—no, seventeen; somewhere around there. No one cares about birthdays, so it really doesn't matter. A man is a man."

"What color is your uniform?"

Jeremy tucked down his chin, as if examining his outfit behind his eyelids. "Gray."

"So you're a Confederate soldier?"

Jeremy nodded. "And we are losing the war. Everyone knows it. And now I am losing my life for them and all I care about is General Lee. So I deserted."

"Is that also why you don't care about dying?"

"Yes," Jeremy said nodding. "My family is dead. My farmland is dust. All my friends have vanished. There is nothing for me back home, and with only one leg, why would I want to live? When I die there will be no one to miss me—well, almost no one."

"Who will miss you?"

Jeremy paused. “Only General Lee and my captain,” he said in a somber voice. “My captain showed great kindness toward me.”

Dr. Studski tapped his pen on his notepad. “Tell me more.”

“He is Captain James Finnegan from Charleston, South Carolina. In this life I know him as Arthur.”

“What was your relationship with him in this lifetime?”

“He was my commanding officer, and he took a special interest in me. He is patient and noble. He is a good leader, and he has the respect of his men. He is why I am sorry for deserting my post; I know I have disappointed him, and he will take my desertion personally.”

“What else can you tell me about your relationship?”

“Captain Finnegan is like a father to me. He speaks kindly and shows me the proper way to do things. He is fierce when angry with others but patient when I make mistakes. He taught me the correct way to use a bayonet and tie knots and march and ride a horse into battle.”

“Can you see him, this Captain Finnegan?”

“He’s broad of shoulder, and he rides better than the other men. His uniform is . . . different from mine. It’s gray, but has yellow cuffs and a yellow collar with stripes on it. Plus, it’s got some scroll-y kind of threadwork on the sleeves and two rows of brass buttons, where mine only has one going down the middle. Everyone’s uniforms look worn-out, though; mine is muddy and there’s a big hole in the right arm. We’re in the cavalry—or at least we were before we had to kill and eat our horses.”

“Do you . . . have a romantic or a sexual relationship with him, with Captain Finnegan?”

“In this lifetime such a relationship would have been completely unacceptable,” Jeremy replied. “But there is a feeling of great affection between us, and our eyes seek out each other in a crowd. His gaze never leaves mine when we talk. He puts his arm around me and makes me laugh, even under these terrible circumstances. He has a wife and two children at home in Charleston. I can tell he is very worried about his family. He is a good man, and I see why his wife would love him so much."

"Does he know you are injured?"

"No. I . . . was shot in the night after deserting my post for the sake of General Lee. Now I'm on my third day out and the wound has bugs crawling inside it, but I cannot go back for help because deserters are shot on the spot. And I am too weak to walk."

"Did your captain know you were thinking of deserting your post?"

Jeremy shook his head. "He understood we were all considering it, because we are losing the war and no one wants to be killed for nothing. He came to me the night before I left and told me after the war is over I can come live with his family. He knows I care for no one but him and General Lee."

"What did you tell him?"

"I thanked him very much for his offer, and said I would most certainly consider it."

"Couldn't you have gone back to him and asked for his assistance? You might have told him you were injured in battle and were just now making it back to camp."

"But that would be a lie," Jeremy answered. "We are men of honor."

"Of course. So what happened after that?" Dr. Studski waited a few moments but Jeremy said nothing; only tears creeping down his cheeks told Dr. Studski he was still concentrating on his vision. Finally Dr. Studski asked again, "Can you tell me what happened next? If you're not comfortable doing so, it's fine."

"I died. Underneath a large oak tree. I was suffering greatly, so in an act of desperation I tried to remove my dead leg but could not accomplish it. The first slice from my knife allowed me to bleed to death."

Dr. Studski winced. "That must have been horrible for you."

Jeremy sighed. "I was ready, but I was also very worried about General Lee. About his safety."

"And where are you now?"

"Light. Peace and warmth. Light."

"Are you between lives?"

"I don't know. I only know that I am all right. And I'm given the knowledge from those around me that Captain Finnegan has been made aware of my death, and he grieves heavily for me—but General Lee is fine. The Captain is considering ending his own life but will not do so as long as he is standing; he feels a strong sense of duty to his family in Charleston . . . but should he become injured he has already made the decision to fall onto his sword."

"How does knowing this make you feel?"

"I want to comfort him. I feel badly about his grief for me. It is of my own doing, and I only lightly considered him in my decision to desert. This was wrong, especially—"

Jeremy stopped.

"Especially what?"

"I don't want to talk about it yet."

"You don't need to. Are you in this state for long?"

Jeremy shook his head. "There is no sense of time here. But I'm made to understand that I need to comprehend what's happened."

"In your life as a soldier?"

"Yes . . . but in a life before this one."

Clickety-click-click—click. "Before we move backward, Jeremy, do you know how your experience in the Civil War affected your affiliation with Arthur in this current lifetime?"

"This explains . . . the dual nature of our relationship when Arthur and I first met in Ballena Beach."

Jeremy paused.

Dr. Studski cleared his throat. "How so?"

"Because . . . he had been my mentor and protector during the Civil War, he easily stepped in to continue that role by mentoring me and protecting me from Uncle Bill. Then after we successfully tied up what was unresolved from that previous lifetime, we were free to move even further back to resolve what had taken place a long, long time ago, when we were each other's beloved . . . and when all of the *real* trouble started."

"And are you ready to explore this lifetime now?" Dr. Studski asked.

"I am."

CHAPTER

thirty-nine

So you're going backward in time?"

"A long time back." Jeremy's features pinched together, and Dr. Studski could see that an important transition was taking place. "Still a soldier and still fighting, but in a different place."

"You're moving backward in time, and you're perfectly safe."

Jeremy shook his head, his usually even features contracting and relaxing, like the bellows of an accordion. "No I'm not." He panted heavily. "Oh no! No, no, no, no!"

"You're perfectly safe," Dr. Studski reassured him. "Leave the pain behind and tell me what you see. No pain, no emotion."

"Death." Jeremy's breathing began to calm. "Everywhere. Everywhere I see bodies. My friends. *My beloved friends!*" he wailed.

"Who?"

"My friends," he whispered.

"Where are you? Can you see where you are?"

"Big field. Trees around the edges. Green trees. Tall—those tall . . . cedars. And grass. Tall grass."

"What is your name in this lifetime?"

"Kleon."

"Why are your friends dying?"

"A battle. Too many against us. Outnumbered, but we were holding them off until . . . until they used long poles. With a knife on each end." Jeremy began hyperventilating. "Where's Arthur? I'm hurt! I need him!" His head began thrashing side to side. "Gods, don't let him be dead too!"

"Arthur's there with you?"

"I can't see him—but there he is! He's running and yelling something; I can't understand. The noise. The shouting! The screams!"

"You're safe. No emotion, no pain. Can you determine where you are? What part of the world?"

Again Jeremy calmed. Took slow breaths. Nodded. "A long, long, time ago. In Greece."

"Can you get any other names or details?"

"Arthur's coming—he looks like Arthur but also doesn't. He's got a beard and a bigger nose. Dark skin, like coffee. He's running to me because I'm injured. My arm is bleeding. It's been cut open, I can see the bones and I can't stop the blood."

"Do you have any idea what this is about? The battle, I mean?"

"They're here . . . to take our city. There's a general and his men up on the rise; their army is huge. Unstoppable. We are a small group, one mouse against a pack of wolves. Our city will fall to them, we see that now. But we'll fight until death."

"What city? Do you know that name?"

"*Theeeeeeebs*," Jeremy whispered. "Thebes. We have so many in the city who are depending on us to save them. But now we know the end is coming for us and for them. We do whatever we can to kill or hurt or injure as many as possible. We fight without fear. We fight hoping for death. We have nothing to lose."

"What's happening now?"

"Arthur's . . . running to me. He screams a battle cry. His face is fierce. A soldier charging me with a long spear. This is the end. I look at Arthur as the sword takes me—the metal coming into my side and out from my stomach. Arthur swings his sword and slices the man's neck open. He falls backward, blood spraying from his neck, and Arthur collapses onto his knees, shouting at me . . . calling my name. Everything is gray. My . . . vision is fading, but I hear him say he will be with me again before the day is over. His face is tender; he cradles me in his arms—and . . . as my last breath rattles from me, Arthur, still holding me, is run through with a spear. He makes no noise. It is as if he has already died.

"Then the strangest thing: I . . . find myself alone, standing on the plain by myself. It's almost night. The field is quiet, and a young man stands alone. He has golden hair below his ears. He's from the other army, yet he wipes away his tears."

"Tell me." Dr. Studski leaned forward in his chair. "Why is he crying? Did he lose someone he loved?"

"He cries . . . because he sees the waste, the tragedy. He sees the decimation of our brave men. The torn and broken bodies, and the few of us who found our beloveds to die with—to embrace our lovers in death as we embraced each other in the joyous moments of life."

"What happens then, Jeremy?"

"The young man's father is there, too. The king. The young man, the prince, argues fiercely with him. This king walks angrily away from him, shouting as he walks, waving his arms around. I know we are all dead but one, a very fierce and proud dark-skinned warrior who was the youngest of us—I know him as Carlo in this lifetime—he was the beloved of our leader and somehow escaped injury. He will not talk, and he will not meet the eye of the prince or any of his soldiers. But the prince bends to him, and sits beside him on the grass. He puts a hand on his shoulder and they talk. Carlo is furious and silent, knowing he will be taken as a slave. The prince keeps talking to him, and Carlo tells him he wants to die fighting like his brothers or he will take his own life. And the prince tells him he will allow him to take his own life, but has a task for him first.

"What is this task?" the doctor asked.

"There is already a huge pyre burning nearby, making the area bright as day, but the prince commands instead that a grave be dug—a huge hole, which is soon underway. This is what the king was upset by, because his soldiers are already exhausted and worn from the battle, so fiercely did we fight. But the grave is dug, and Carlo tells the soldiers who should be buried together. Then one by one each man is placed with his lover, their stiffening fingers intertwined as is our custom, so we can wake together in the underworld. And a coin is placed under the tongue of each man—these coins come from the prince's own royal purse—so the ferryman can take him across the river to the sacred fields."

"Do you see your body, Kleon's body?"

Jeremy nodded. "Yes, because Carlo ensured that I am placed beside Arthur. He was close to us both, so it is difficult for him to contain his emotions as our fingers are joined. His mouth is grim and tears stain his cheeks, but he says nothing."

"But you don't see any of the other souls standing there with you?"

"I cannot see any of the others, but this does not alarm me. Each soul has somewhere specific to go that is not revealed, and Arthur is all I care about."

"Where is he?"

"After the dirt covers us I will go to him."

Dr. Studski paused. "Then what happens?"

"Carlo's lover, our leader, is laid in the grave by himself so Carlo turns to the prince. He demands a sword to kill himself . . . the short sword we are trained with since childhood. The prince throws him his royal *xyphos*; Carlo catches it effortlessly in spite of his exhausting day and lunges at the prince, allowing the prince to succeed in killing him. Predictably, the prince's own sword thrusts cleanly into his chest and takes his life—Carlo utters only a whimper as he falls—then the prince pulls out his sword, waits for Carlo to stop breathing, and then tells the men to lay him with his beloved. As the dirt is thrown onto the bodies—onto the frozen, upturned faces—the prince says a quick prayer over the grave, and then turns and begins making his way back to camp. He is furious, and he blames his father for this terrible waste."

"Waste?"

"It turned from battle to slaughter; many of these men might have eventually been trained to fight in the king's own army."

"And who's this prince?" Dr. Studski asked.

"Alexander of . . . *Macedon.* Son of Philip. Known forever as Alexander the Great."

"What happens after that? Where do you go?"

"I'm . . . standing there for a while not sure what to do. Waiting. There's a few men, soldiers, sitting against a tree drinking from a sack of wine. They can't see me, and I don't care about them. I'm numb and beyond emotion—no longer alive, but still standing there. Then . . . I see Arthur walking toward me and everything goes white—the brightest white, like the inside of a star—and we drift to that place that's in between lives."

"Do you remember what happens after that?"

Jeremy sighed. "I do, but I wish I didn't."

Dr. Studski glanced at the clock on the lamp table and started. His next client, the ever-impatient Mrs. Himes, had already been waiting in the lobby for almost ten minutes. "Jeremy, I'm afraid we need to end here, so I'm going to bring you back up by counting from zero to five, and when you awaken you will remember everything you've told me. Are you ready to come back?"

Jeremy tossed his head from side to side. "No."

"Why not?"

"Because I need to stop him before he can do it again."

"Stop what? Who? Alexander?"

Jeremy paused. "Lucius."

Dr. Studski looked at the clock again. "Unfortunately, we need to wait until next time. But you're all right. You're going to be OK. You're going to leave behind the emotion and the hurt, and come back into the present feeling calm and refreshed."

Jeremy lay motionless, his eyes tightly shut. "OK then."

"Take a last look around your garden," Dr. Studski said. "But just a last look for now, because we'll be coming back here. And know that on days when you need a break from what's going on at home, you can come back here and relax. Right now you'll become more and more aware of your body, you feel your body again. Feel your arms and your shoulders. Come back to the present time. I'm going to count forward from zero to five. You're going to feel relaxed and you'll remember everything, coming upwards from zero. Zero . . . one . . . two . . . three, moving into the present . . . four . . . remembering where you are in the world. Five." Dr. Studski snapped his fingers, and Jeremy opened his eyes.

They looked silently at each other for a moment, and then Dr. Studski handed over the Kleenex box.

"What the hell was *that*?" Jeremy asked, wiping his eyes and nose. "I've never even seen a movie about Alexander the Great, and there he was standing in front of me . . . as if I were Anderson Cooper reporting from Macedonia, and right before that from the Civil War: the colors, the sounds, even the smells were like I was standing right there! I didn't even sound like myself when I was talking."

"I must admit that your recall seems especially clear for your first regression, especially with regard to the specificity of events and individual names and locations." Dr. Studski momentarily considered this. *Clickety-click-click—click.* "Perhaps that strange drug you were taking has . . . *widened* the doorway of your subconscious the way years of practicing deep meditation sometimes does for others.

"In any case, this process can be as jarring as it is revelatory," he went on, "and you won't necessarily sound like yourself because it's your higher self speaking. I'm sure we'll find out more about these events next week, but in the meantime I don't want you to research anything about Lucius or Alexander on the web. I'd like our next session to be pure in its discovery. And I'll leave it up to you whether or not you want to tell Arthur about what happened here today."

"What about Carlo?" Jeremy asked. "Did he mention any of this Alexander the Great stuff in his sessions with you?"

"That is for you to discuss with Carlo, should you decide to ask him. As far as your sessions here are concerned, I have no inside knowledge whatsoever of Carlo."

"I get it."

"In any event, I'd advise you to begin a journal, because in many cases having a first regression unlocks a previously hidden part of the mind, and then seemingly unrelated memories will begin floating up to the surface of your consciousness—not to mention whatever's been done to your brain by this strange drug."

"I can do that," Jeremy said, pushing himself up into a sitting position. "So if this reincarnation stuff is true and I was a Greek soldier and then a Civil War soldier, why am I not in the military in this lifetime? Why don't we just pick up where we left off each time?"

"Each lifetime is *one* trip, *one* specific voyage—like a . . . multifaceted college course that lasts decades. And what we learn and how we learn it in each lifetime is up to us."

"I guess that . . . kind of makes sense." Jeremy fidgeted in his seat. "So when will I know if I've learned what I'm supposed to learn? In this lifetime, I mean?"

"Did you ever hear what Michelangelo said after unveiling his statue of David?"

"No."

"People were astounded by the sublime beauty of the sculpture, and how he was able to carve it from a single block of marble that was considered unusable because of its length and narrow width. And when asked how he accomplished this impossible feat, Michelangelo stated that he only needed to release David's form from the stone; that David was already in there the entire time."

"What does that have to do with past lives?" Jeremy asked.

"People sometimes believe if I buy this or accomplish that, my life will be how I've always wanted it to be. But the life you're meant to live is like David's figure in that stone, and you're the only one who can release it. It's a process that involves visualizing and practice and hard work and expertise and determination—"

"—and the right tools?"

"Absolutely—and a block of marble, which in this case is your karmic past." Dr. Studski squinted at him. "Are you all right? Do you think you're OK to drive?"

Jeremy rubbed his cheeks hard and then looked up. "I think there's a market down the street; we're having a couple of friends over for brunch this weekend, so I could do some shopping to help clear my head before I drive home."

"I think that's a good idea."

"Yeah," Jeremy agreed, swinging his feet down from the sofa onto the floor. Then he pushed himself up into a standing position. "Because I've gotta figure out what I'm going to tell Arthur about all this. He's got enough on his mind worrying about his own brain without having to also worry about mine."

CHAPTER

forty

Just before midnight Lazzaro felt the Sueño Gris taking effect. Earlier that evening he'd been feeling bored and restless and crabby and horny—and especially irritated by Carmella after Tristan had indulged in too much Tempranillo and then lumbered up the stairs to bed, after which time Carmella insisted on pressing him for details about his sex tourism enterprises—so he'd hastily bade her good night and then gone upstairs to see if Tristan might scratch his itching libido.

But the young man was snoring contentedly.

So Lazzaro locked himself in the bathroom, tipped his head back, eyedroppered a tear of the sacred elixir into his nostril, and drew himself a hot bath.

About an hour later, as a delicious, rushing warmth was coursing through his veins and a veil of euphoria was settling down upon his head, he heard a noise outside the open bathroom window: a soprano's faint warble.

What was that?

Lazzaro raised himself out from the tub, ears pricked, listening intently.

Nothing.

He settled back down into the hot water, resting his head against the stone-like porcelain.

I'm just on edge, he told himself. *Nervous—always expecting the police now and losing control of my enterprises, more and more each day. I've got to get out of here . . . but where? Nowhere to go, and all that money just sitting downstairs in that lockbox . . . I should go check on it to see if Carmella's stolen it yet.*

Lazzaro lifted himself up from the water, toweled himself dry, and wriggled into his jeans and T-shirt.

On his way back through the bedroom he glanced over at Tristan asleep in bed, his fine features and alabaster skin even more striking in repose than awake; his perfectly defined—yet languid—athletic musculature entangled within the single bedsheet like the sculpture atop a Florentine prince's sarcophagus.

If only you didn't bore me so, I'd take you with me.

He heard the soprano's faint singing once again.

Lazzaro quietly pulled open the bedroom door and tiptoed out into the hallway and past Carmella's bedroom to the stairs.

Once in the kitchen he poured himself a tumbler of Tempranillo and stood facing the bank of French doors overlooking the moonlit vineyards, taking in the rows of grapevines gilded like hammered silver under the midnight sky.

And he began to wonder: *France? They'll find me there. What about Sweden? I've never been to Sweden—or should I give myself up and take whatever is coming my way? No. I'll never surrender.*

Lazzaro was about to descend the cellar stairs to check on the lockbox when, in the corner of his eye, he saw a movement outside.

Something was flying, gracefully flapping its huge wings as it fluttered from one row of vines to another. And whatever it was appeared far too large for an owl—the only species of nocturnal fowl he knew of.

He leaned in close to the French door to see the creature more clearly.

"Please tell me you're not here," he whispered, fogging the glass with his breath.

Predictably, the reply circled back to him with boomerang-like precision.

Why don't you come outside? the haunting voice sang in his head. *It's a lovely night and I have something to give you; something you'll want, too . . .*

"Go away."

A caress that makes one forget his burdens is more dazzling than diamonds and more precious than gold, this I've been told . . .

Completely forgetting that he was starting to ride the high of a powerful hallucinogen, Lazzaro felt a ball of paranoia ballooning in his head. He was familiar with this creature's temptations and his usual inability to resist her or her sisters' prurient advances—temptations that had sent too many men to their watery graves. "Are you alone, or are the others here as well?"

I've come by myself to help you. Hold you. Heal you. My feathers ache to caress your body, my talons eager to hold you in their gentle grasp.

"A siren, to help me?" Lazzaro laughed. "I'd sooner trust a harpy with my supper!"

I am Raidne, yet you judge me by the mischievous acts of my older sisters. How long must I endure such undeserved judgment and bigotry? Come out and speak with me!

"I shall judge you for as long as you deserve it, I suppose."

Would you care to come outside to enjoy the countryside's moonlight and to hear what I came to tell you, or should I return to my lair with my secret tucked inside my breast? My tongue aches to lick your body; I promise to tease you as no one has before, but your release will be granted only when you promise me something. . . .

Lazzaro felt himself through the fabric of his pocket and confirmed that he was already fully aroused. "Only for a moment, and then I'm going back to bed." He twisted the door handle and stepped outside.

The night air breathed gently onto his skin as he made his way down the steps of the country house toward the vineyards, with each step measured carefully and his defensive—as well as his predatory—synapses firing on high alert.

His eyes had little difficulty adjusting to the countryside, radiant for the full, white moon fixed upon the star-speckled black sky.

He swiveled his head from side to side. *No sign of her.*

"I am here," he announced to the empty night.

At once a sound caught his ear again—like a flag flapping before a brisk wind.

Lazzaro looked up and saw the being circle just once above the nearby olive trees before drifting to the ground, like a fully plumed hang glider—with a human tethered to its wings—riding a downdraft.

With her talons extended she landed and then folded her wings around her body . . . a fair-faced young woman wrapped inside a blanket of auburn feathers lustrous with moonlight.

"Worry bends your features," she told Lazzaro, while tottering ungracefully toward him. "Yet you are still as beautiful as I remember, a man to make Adonis weep for the gruesomeness of his own face." She reached out and traced the wingtip along his cheek. "It is deliciously warm tonight. Do you not wish to feel the air on your naked body?"

Lazzaro stepped back. "Shouldn't you be at sea, luring sailors onto your jagged rocks with your miserable songs?"

"Men who set sail weave ridiculous tales," she said, half-singing, half-chirping. "Those men craved our sex, our lecherous skills so enticingly complex. Odysseus, our most frequent guest," she continued crooning, ruffling her feathers and rotating like a ballerina, "having lost one ship, had himself lashed to the mast on his final trip."

"What's your particular specialty?" Lazzaro asked, standing his ground.

She stopped revolving and glared at him. "You've forgotten my skill with mouth and quill?"

In a single movement, Lazzaro pulled off his shirt and dropped it onto the dirt. "Why are you here?"

Her pale eyes ran up and down his naked torso. "Rumor has it you are vexed . . . as vexed as you are oversexed."

"Vexed." Lazzaro laughed. "Such an old-fashioned word."

She lifted her nose into the air. "I smell it on you."

"Well . . . who isn't vexed these days?"

"I know something I wish to share. Won't you please remove those horrid leggings? Might as well shroud a statue of Antinous in beggar's rags."

"Best to not mention him." Lazzaro unbuttoned his jeans and peeled them down his muscular legs. "Your kind has lied to me before, so I am understandably wary," he said while stepping out from the cuffs and caressing his nakedness. "I should have been emperor if not for your sisters' villainy."

"Lucius, Light-bearer of the underworld, you are exquisitely formed," she told him, her voice deepened by lust. "Easily the most beautiful man in this part of the world." She drew nearer, fluttered her feathers as she dropped onto her bird's knees, and then spread out her wings fully onto the ground.

She took him into her mouth.

"And you are very good at what you do," Lazzaro whispered.

I know you came into possession of treasure, she silently told him as she worked. *What are your plans for this gold?*

"I am not yet certain." Lazzaro began gently thrusting. "Any suggestions?"

I also know that the woman Carmella has claimed much of what should have been yours. She needs to give it back—but if she does not, you will kill her and share it with me, don't you see?

Lazzaro laughed. "Why would I share it with you?"

I have haunted Carmella since she was a girl; screeching and chasing her through the twilit fields, waking her at night with my talons tapping her window pane; invading her dreams with gristle and blood. But what Carmella does not realize is that the plans you carried out in the Plaka were mine.

"Yours?"

Just as you are reading my thoughts now, I planted those ideas in her head: your ex-lover's blackmail; the riot diversion begun by her son; her outlandish costume. Poor girl has no idea where her cleverness originates; she actually believes her ideas are her own when they are really mine—whose joke do you imagine it was about sirens luring the stupid policemen away? And now she has stolen our gold? It is time for her to die.

Lazzaro began thrusting faster. "You . . . tempt me with . . . the obvious, dear . . . Siren."

So where will you escape to with your paltry treasure? You needed each drachma to buy your freedom. My sisters and I will help you if you share your gold with us . . .

"I will think of something—and we don't use drachma anymore." He placed his hands onto her feathered shoulders. "These are euros—made from paper."

You will entice the woman Carmella with your plans; then she will contribute her share of the money, you can win her trust and then dispose of her. We will be close by, watching and ready to assist.

He began building a sweat. "And how . . . might . . . I accomplish . . . this?"

I have thus arranged it so she dreams of a life with you; each night I plague her sleep with your face so she awakens longing for you—each sunrise her womanhood quivers for your thrusts and her nipples prick at the memory of your touch. Carmella now believes she loves the ocean, so you will find a seaside home to buy together—Santorini here in Greece would be preferable, so you might be close to my sisters and me. Once your deal is set and you travel there, anything might happen: an unexpected taxi or a misstep on the steep cliffside or, my favorite: inexplicably stormy seas. Her share of this property will transfer to you, her business partner, and perhaps even her husband, or to her son, who will always remain by your side. Evermore you will enjoy your wealth and a stream of eager lovers to spend your passion with. Happily ever after, happily ever after!

"I will be discovered . . . in any city—even one by the sea."

You will most certainly be discovered here; I understand there are those who already know, already know. Are the . . . feathers to your liking?

Lazzaro quickened his thrusts. "By the gods, I am coming!"

But as Lazzaro felt the building of his orgasm at the base of his spine, she pulled her mouth from him and gently grasped his scrotum with her left claw.

"Why did you do that?" Lazzaro gasped, his neglected cock twitching before her nose.

"Promise you will share your gold with us," she demanded, beginning to squeeze. "Or did you not think me serious?"

"That hurts!"

Slowly, she released her claw.

Lazzaro stepped back, grasped himself, and began jacking himself furiously. "It—is—*my* gold," he growled as his back arched and spurt after spurt shot onto the dirt.

"You deny me what is mine?" Raidne snarled, her upturned face now ferocious.

"No, I deny you what is *mine*." Lazzaro stepped back from her and put one leg and then the other into his jeans. Then he pulled up his pants and buttoned the fly. "Now fly away, batwoman," he told her while bending down to snatch his T-shirt from the ground, "before I catch you pecking my spunk from the dirt like a bird groveling for breakfast. I shall never forget what you and your sisters did to me."

"You betray and insult a siren!" she screeched as her wings beat the air and she began gaining altitude. "I should never have told you what I did! This was my secret to give!"

“And as rightful emperor, it was mine to take,” Lazzaro laughed as he made his way back toward the house. “Now, be careful of those helicopters.”

“No one betrays a siren and lives!” she screeched, her voice growing fainter.

“No one but I,” Lazzaro snickered as he climbed the stairs to the house, unaware of Tristan’s curious stare peeking out from behind the window of the second story bedroom. “No one but I, but I.”

CHAPTER

forty-one

Is the table outside set?" Arthur was standing in front of the stove whisking a pan of hollandaise atop the ancient white porcelain range top. "I probably shouldn't have made this sauce yet, but I usually burn it and wanted to give myself time to make another batch in case I did."

"Table's set, so we're ready," Jeremy replied, wiping down the long kitchen counter with a wet sponge. "And the fog's finally burned off, so it should be a beautiful day. I'm gonna run upstairs and change, I found something kind of cool in the closet—" he paused, "oh, I . . . forgot to clean the powder room."

Arthur glanced at his watch and shot him a concerned look. "You'd better do that now."

"Right. Are you feeling OK?"

Arthur continued stirring the sauce. "Except for dreading Carlo's reaction to the overcooked asparagus, I'm fine."

"He just pretends to be picky, but he'll eat anything that's not nailed down. Is Margo bringing someone?"

"She said she wanted to come alone; I think she knows something's up."

"And . . . when do you want to tell them?"

Arthur stared at him, eyes moony. "When it feels right."

Suddenly the gate bell buzzed, and Skipper and Bingham scrambled up from the floor barking furiously—as if an army of zombies were staggering toward the front door.

Jeremy shot Arthur an alarmed look. "Powder room!"

"Grab your toilet brush and I'll grab the door." Arthur untied his apron, turned off the heat under the saucepan, and began making his way through the house to the entrance. Halfway there he stopped to check out his reflection in the decrepit Louis XV mirror they'd bought last week at a Malibu garage sale: his shoulders, arms, and chest had deflated and his pants hung a bit too low on his waist, but he didn't care. *I'm alive and in love.*

He yanked up his posture, smiled, stepped into the foyer, twisted the handle, and swung open the door.

"My Ken Doll," Margo said, smiling brightly up at him. "Handsome as ever." She glanced to his side at the empty house. "Am I early?"

"Right on time." Arthur stepped aside, admiring her petite frame, understated makeup, and flawlessly coiffed blonde locks. "And breathtaking, as usual. Come in!"

"You're too kind. I hope I'm not underdressed."

"Jeans and black angora never looked so ravishing together."

Margo stepped up into the foyer and presented Arthur with two chilled, foil-crowned green bottles. "I didn't know which to bring," she said as they embraced. "One's non-alcoholic and the other's the real stuff; I wasn't sure where Jeremy is with his sobriety."

"That makes three of us." Arthur kissed her cheek, closed the door, and placed the bottles atop the nearby console table.

"This place is stunning!" Margo slowly scanned the home's dilapidated interior as the dogs sniffed at her shoes and jeans. "Arched ceilings, marble floors, a flying staircase, and a medieval fireplace? It reminds me of that mansion in *Sunset Boulevard.*"

"Especially with me looking more and more like Gloria Swanson every day. Come on, I'll show you around." Arthur took her hand and they began walking.

"Where's Jeremy?"

"Last minute, uh, preparations," Arthur replied as a toilet flushed behind the nearest closed door.

The door swung wide and Jeremy appeared, drying his hands on his jeans. "The famous Margo!" They embraced, and he kissed her cheek. "Sorry to drag you from your usual lunch at the Chateau Marmont."

"You mean Burger King," Margo laughed. "What a grand home! Is this Capri or Venice?"

"More like Wilmington," Jeremy countered.

"Seriously, the last time I saw a place with this much potential was my first—and only—date with Calvin Klein," Margo replied. "He'd bought a grand yet rundown estate in the Hamptons that had this same faded grandeur."

"We've christened it *Welfaire* with an *a-i-r-e*," Jeremy stated grandly. "Can I get you a drink?"

"Whatever you're having."

"I'll get it." Arthur turned and made his way toward the kitchen.

Margo turned to Jeremy and mouthed the words *How is he?*

"Today's a good day," Jeremy told her, *sotto voce*, "especially because any talk of illness or chemo or radiation is strictly off-limits. We want to have a normal day just like normal people, so we're in a complete state of denial."

"If Denial is a state, I must be the governor," Margo muttered as she began strolling through the expansive home. Then she stopped, placing her hands on her hips. "This place needs chandeliers . . . and I've got two gargantuan ones in storage that belonged to my ex-husband's mother. French from the 1920s, bronze . . . with crystals the size of wine glasses." She turned to Jeremy. "Would you like them?"

Jeremy coughed. "Are you kidding? But I'm sure Arthur told you I'm broke."

"They've been sitting in storage for ten years since my divorce. And I'd much rather see them enjoyed by you two than by the spiders and mice. They're gorgeous, but they remind me of my ex, so I can't stand the sight of them, but neither could I have let him keep them in the settlement." She crossed her arms, pressing a finger to her lips. "How about if I send them over next week? Installation on me. But let's keep it a surprise from Arthur; he might think they're too *Liberace*, so we'll need to act fast."

"Whee!" Jeremy bent over and hugged her. "Hey, I'm gonna run upstairs and change. Be right back." He turned and bounded up the stairs.

"'Whee,' what?" Arthur asked as he returned with two fizzing champagne flutes, one of which he handed over to Margo.

"Thank you." Margo sipped from her glass. "We were just discussing what Jeremy preferred as a housewarming gift: liquid soap dispenser or paper towel rack . . ."

Arthur leaned in and kissed her cheek. "If it's from the Empress Margo, it'll be appreciated." They clinked glasses. "How's the fundraiser coming?"

"Why I get myself involved in these things I'll never know," she said. "Each time we get finished with another event I tell myself this is the last one, but when the Board gets another half-baked scheme for raising money, it seems that I'm the only one gullible enough to chair."

"It's very admirable how committed you are to your causes," Arthur told her as Bingham drew up to his leg, and he bent down to massage the dog's neck.

"You mean I *should* be committed," she laughed.

They both heard a sound and looked up to see Jeremy at the top of the stairs in a white tuxedo jacket, bow tie, and black slacks.

Arthur gave a low whistle. "Where'd you find that, Mr. Hefner?"

"You can call me Mr. Bond," he replied. "I found it the other day in the back of what had once been Lazzaro's closet." He began descending the staircase.

"Well I hope there's another just like it, because I suddenly feel terribly underdressed," Arthur complained.

Margo clapped her hands together. "Every time I see you together I'm reminded more and more of Cary Grant and Randolph—"

Bingham suddenly sniffed the air, sprang up onto his feet, and launched into a barking fit.

"Bingham!" Arthur snapped. "No!"

As Jeremy drew nearer the dog continued growling and barking and sniffing, as if he'd somehow forgotten who Jeremy was.

"What the hell's wrong with him?" Jeremy asked, a panicked expression on his face. "What am I, a grizzly bear?"

"I've no idea!" Arthur grabbed onto the dog's collar. "I've never seen him like this, except for—"

"When we first came to the house," Jeremy finished for him, clutching the banister as he inched backward up toward the second floor. "He acted the same way then. Remember?"

Bingham continued barking.

"I guess he doesn't care for formal affairs!" Margo yelled over the racket. "I should take a lesson!"

"I'll go change back into my jeans and T-shirt! It's too hot for a jacket, anyhow." Jeremy turned and hurried back up the stairs.

Arthur looked down and saw Bingham had finally calmed. "What the hell was that all about?"

"All I know is that dogs are a lot smarter than some people give them credit for being." Margo took his hand. "Come on. Let's sit outside."

The pair continued chatting as they sauntered through the house toward the open French doors, with Bingham and Skipper trotting happily behind.

Moments later Jeremy reappeared in his usual worn jeans and black T-shirt, and everyone was relieved to see that Bingham viewed his arrival happily, if not a bit indifferently.

"You two sit here and relax," Arthur said as Jeremy approached, "and I'll finish concocting my disastrous meal."

Once in the open air, Jeremy and Margo settled back into their chairs around the vintage iron, glass-topped table, decorated for the occasion with white linen place settings and a crystal vase choked with scarlet roses.

"You filled it!" Margo noted excitedly, pointing to the sparkling swimming pool. "Does it leak? I know you two were worried about that."

"Arthur knows how to do *everything*," Jeremy said, his voice silken with awe. "He showed me how to caulk the cracks, and then we replaced the missing tiles with some he found in the basement. Then I coated the plaster with epoxy paint Arthur ordered online. His energy's still zapped by the chemo, so he sort of points and barks at me when I do something wrong—like any grouchy husband—but then somehow he was able to get that ancient pool filter cleaned and running all by himself, so we filled it, and so far so good. I marked the waterline on the tile over there"—he pointed, wagging his finger—"with a red Sharpie and as of now it's holding."

"Clearly you two make a *wonderful* team." Margo relaxed back into her chair, scanning the miles of curving white sand cradling the wide expanse of glimmering blue water. "So what else is going on with the remodel? And what a perfect springtime afternoon! I could sit here all day."

"That's about it so far; Arthur's condo has just gone into escrow, and we're going to use whatever profits he gets to fix up this place. But I'm so excited about your chandeliers!"

"What about chandeliers?" Arthur asked as he reappeared from the house carrying a platter of fresh fruit and an iced bottle of champagne.

Margo and Jeremy side-eyed each other. "She wants us to look at a dreary little pair she saw in some store," Jeremy lied. "That is, after your condo closes."

Arthur chuckled. "Just nothing too *Liberace*."

"They probably came from some little old beauty parlor in Burbank, but you've got to hang *something* from that big, empty ceiling," Margo said, fitting her sunglasses onto her face.

"Besides spiderwebs," Jeremy added.

A sudden, faint chime sent the dogs up and scrambling back into the house, so Jeremy leapt up to answer the door.

Margo turned to Arthur. "Jeremy already told me we are on restricted content rules for conversation—and that's completely understandable—but I have to ask: How do you feel today?"

"Each morning I wake up knowing we're one day closer to the MRI—which I think of as God's version of an IRS audit—and that usually rattles me, but today all I care about are good friends and cold champagne. Thanks again for taking me to Cedars yesterday."

"I always look forward to our time together." Margo sipped from her glass. "How's Jeremy holding up?"

"He's been seeing a therapist who's kept him sober for a few weeks now . . . but something's going on that he doesn't want to discuss with me."

"Why do you think so?"

"He keeps asking me these strange little questions."

Margo settled back into her chair. "Such as?"

"Such as . . . how do I feel about the Civil War and Alexander the Great . . . and have I ever known anyone named Lucius . . . and do I believe in ghosts."

"What do you tell him?"

"I said I'm glad the Civil War is over but could see another one happening; I don't remember anyone named Lucius; and Alexander the Great would've probably been some really hot sex—especially if we could include Hephaestion and a dozen-or-so Greek soldiers."

"I'll drink to that." She speared a wedge of pineapple from the platter in front of her. "What about the ghosts?"

"Never seen one."

"Why do you think he's asking you these things?"

"I think it has something to do with his therapist taking him through—and I know some folks think this is crazy—*regression hypnosis for past lives.*"

"I had one of those once."

"You never told me that!" Arthur stared at her. "What happened?"

"Complete silliness. Supposedly I was some washerwoman in England to make up for a lifetime in Rome when I was the wife of someone very rich and powerful and unpleasant, and I didn't do enough to help the poor." She chuckled. "This might explain why I do so much philanthropy work now, but it doesn't explain why my unfortunate taste in rich and unpleasant men hasn't changed. So how's the day-to-day going?"

"Well . . . here we are in this kooky old house, scraping paint and fixing toilets and running back and forth to the local hardware store—or walking the dogs and watching *Mapp and Lucia* reruns and getting settled into our lives together. We're so domestic now that I sometimes forget about the head-on collision we're trying to avoid down the road."

"You're being fatalistic. And I thought we weren't talking about that."

"I know, I know. But what I'm saying is . . . somehow we're adjusting. And we're in love." He reached over and caressed her hand. "And when either of us gets stressed, we talk it out and cry or laugh or scream, and even though my sex drive is nonexistent we'll still cuddle, or I'll just watch him because that turns him on. And we remind each other that we're not lacking anything anyone else has in this world because no one has guarantees, and sometimes people don't come home from a five-minute trip to the post office because some idiot in a Navigator was texting and ran a stop sign."

"So you're actually living in the here and now."

"Yep." Arthur nodded, getting up from his chair. "Sorry, but I've gotta check on the meal." He turned and headed toward the house in time to greet Carlo—bottle and flowers in hand—stepping out from the house to make his way to the table.

"Hey, pretty lady," Carlo said, bending down to kiss Margo.

"How did your date last night go with—what did you call him—the prettiest nurse on the fourth floor?"

"It was just OK." Carlo pulled out a chair and sat. "But I've agreed to another date with him this Friday."

"Why didn't you invite him today?"

"I'm not sure how I feel about him yet; he's cute and all, but he's so gay he lisps when he yawns."

Jeremy punched him playfully on the shoulder while seating himself. "Which he must do a lot during a date with you."

Moments later Arthur arrived with the plates and placed one before each guest. "Crabmeat's a bit fishy, eggs are runny, the plates are cold, and the asparagus is overcooked. Otherwise everything's perfect."

"This looks delicious," Margo said. "And fresh hollandaise? My favorite."

"Arthur, do we need anything else from the kitchen?" Jeremy asked.

Arthur scanned the table. "Peppermill."

Jeremy jumped up and quickly marched into the house.

Arthur sat and took a sip from his champagne glass. "Thanks, both of you, for coming here."

"It's so great to see you and Jeremy looking so happy," Margo told him. "Who are the red roses for? They're gorgeous!"

"The roses were from me to a certain young man," Arthur replied, watching Jeremy as he returned with the peppermill.

"Speaking of roses, did Arthur tell you we have news?" He twisted the mill over each serving of eggs.

"Pregnant *again*?" Carlo asked.

"I was waiting for you," Arthur grumbled.

Jeremy grinned nervously at Arthur. "You tell 'em."

Arthur held up his glass. "Mr. Bingham Blauefee and Miss Skipper Tyler are pleased to announce the engagement of their human companions, Arthur and Jeremy, to one another."

"Oh!" Margo reached up, clutching her pearls. "That's wonderful!"

Carlo got up from the table and hugged both men. "I am *so* happy for you guys!"

Jeremy looked from Carlo to Margo. "And we asked you here today to be our best men."

"We want Carlo to give away Jeremy—" Arthur began.

"Again?" Carlo interrupted.

"And Margo, you'll stand up for me. That is, if you want to."

Margo smiled, her eyes glistening. "I'd be so honored."

"When?" Carlo asked excitedly.

"We've started planning for the week after the MRI next month, so we can really celebrate the good news."

"Now that's a positive outlook." Margo gave them each a decisive nod. "Any suggestions for where I can rent my tux?"

"Same place where I'm gonna buy my dress," Carlo replied.

"Now when's that MRI?" Margo asked, pulling out her iPhone. "I want to put it into my calendar."

"May thirty-first," Arthur told her.

"Then on June first we can start the countdown," Carlo added. "Where are you planning on having the ceremony?"

"Here," Arthur and Jeremy replied in unison.

"Will it be a large affair?" Margo asked.

"Only very close friends and family," Jeremy answered. "Probably twenty people, max."

Arthur sat back in the chair, scanning the grounds. "We've got a lot of work to do in the meantime, but it'll be fun getting ready for it."

Jeremy leaned over and kissed Arthur's shoulder. "Seems like I've been waiting a lifetime for this."

"For me, it's been an eternity," replied Arthur, a dreamy smile illuminating his face.

"I hate to be Dennis Downer," Carlo cut in, "but is there any word on Jeremy's creepy ex-boyfriend? Have they caught up with him yet?"

"Not yet," Jeremy replied, shaking his head.

"Not yet," Arthur echoed. "But today he doesn't exist. Now let's eat."

"Here's to that," Jeremy said, raising his glass.

"And here's to the happy couple," Margo added, raising hers.

CHAPTER

forty-two

How are Arthur's treatments progressing?" Dr. Studski asked.

Jeremy shrugged. "OK, I guess. It's been over four weeks now and his body's tolerating the chemo and radiation better. So far his symptoms are pretty much stable, but sometimes it's hard for me to tell."

"How do you mean?"

"He's not always honest with me; like . . . sometimes he gets this glassy look in his eyes or he'll reach over to steady himself, and when I ask him if he's OK he always just smiles at me and acts like nothing's wrong. And when he goes into the bathroom he runs the faucet full-blast or flushes the toilet five times so I can't hear him throw up. And after we had friends over for brunch last weekend he went to bed and didn't get up for almost a full day afterward."

"How does that make you feel, knowing he doesn't want to burden you with the severity of his discomfort?"

"It makes me sad to think he's always protecting me; that even in this horrible situation he's still putting me first." Jeremy closed his eyes, sighing, and then lifted an angry stare to the doctor's gaze. "And it makes me feel like screaming. All the time I feel like screaming.

We've only got two more weeks until the MRI, and I'm walking around with my stomach in knots and I can't sleep and I've lost almost ten pounds in three weeks, same as Arthur. And every day I wake up knowing we're one day closer and it scares the shit out of me."

"Have you thought about what you'll do if the MRI comes back positive?"

"Help Arthur die peacefully when he gets to that point, find the dogs a really good home together, and kill myself."

Dr. Studski eyed him critically. "Is this something you're actually considering?"

"Not really," he lied.

"Do you have a plan in place for suicide?"

"Can we just get on with the regression?" Jeremy snapped. "Isn't that why I'm here?"

"So you don't want to talk about your anticipated grief if Arthur's condition looks terminal," the doctor stated.

"Look," Jeremy began, wringing his hands, "if the MRI tells us things are bad, then I'll talk about it then. But I know some weird things came up last week that I'd like to find out more about. Could we do that?"

"Did you discuss your regression with Arthur?"

"Discuss it? No." Jeremy crossed his arms over his chest. "Somehow I didn't think having my guts get ripped out with a sword or burying dozens of corpses are what he needs to talk about right now. Plus, I don't know if I believe any of this Alexander the Great business. I'd believe it more if I saw myself as some old Chinese lady or a kid working as a chimney sweep, but doesn't this seem like one of those landmark cases you mentioned?"

"Actually, we might discover a previous life that at first seems completely unrelated," Studski replied, "but that usually happens only if it's pertinent to what's troubling you today. And as for the possibility of a landmark case, we'll just have to wait and see what's revealed. They're pretty easy to spot once we dig in. So do you still want to proceed?"

"How can I say no?"

"Then lay back and close your eyes, and we'll proceed as we did during the last session."

After the doctor took Jeremy back into his "mental garden" and was certain he had safely transitioned into his hypnotized state, Dr. Studski continued where they had left off. "I want you to move forward from the life we discussed last week, Jeremy, where you discovered your incarnation as Kleon and your encounter with Alexander the Great." He glanced at his notes. "You mentioned someone named Lucius and your desire to fix a situation he caused. Do you remember saying this?"

"Yes."

"Have you remained in your lifetime as Kleon to resolve this business with Lucius?"

"No. That was not Lucius's time. I'm there now, though. It's hundreds of years later."

"Where are you? Can you see your surroundings?"

Jeremy hesitated. "It's a forest—no. Not quite a forest. But there are trees around me. Pine trees and big shady trees and rolling hills. Not like Ballena Beach. I'm on the edge of a big valley with . . . a river below, and farmland. There are herds of goats and flocks of sheep. The sky is blue and there are good clouds overhead. I am heading back to town. To . . . Claud—Claudio . . . polis? Is that the name?"

"How do you feel?"

"Happy. Content."

"Are you alone, or are you with someone?"

"I'm walking alone. Going home after my lessons. Yes. But I hear something. I stop and . . . um . . . I listen."

"What's happening?"

"An army is coming."

"How do you know? Do you see them?"

"I see dust. Over the mountains. It's happened before, so I know."

"How does this make you feel?"

"Scared—and angry."

"Why?"

"The soldiers are cruel to the women and girls and the animals. I have a dog I love. I need to get back to my home to protect my mother and sisters, and my dog."

"Where's your father?"

"He died. I am the man of my family now."

"How old are you?"

"I'm not sure, but I'm tall and strong for my age."

"What's your name?"

Jeremy hesitated. "A-Antinous. Named for my uncle."

Why does that name sound familiar? "Where is the army now, Antinous?"

"They are still coming, so I am running to my home. I get there and my mother is preparing the evening meal. I tell her about the soldiers and she is afraid. She doesn't know where my two sisters are."

"Do you know?"

"No. They are at the age when they make a point of pretending to be busy somewhere they are not. I will search for them after my mother and my dog are safe."

"What happens next?"

"I bring my dog into our house and make a bed for him out of straw and then tie him next to the bed. He lies down, staring at me with those huge eyes as he settles into the hay. Then I hear noise—the noise the army makes is deafening and my dog begins barking. Carts and horses and wagons and men all yelling. Scrape of metal and creak of wood. Shouting. So much shouting. And the language is something clipped and harsh, not beautiful like the language we speak. Greek."

Clickety-click-click—click. "Where are you? Can you see where you are?"

"Bithynia is my country. And I'm on the rooftop. Our house is open at the top for sleeping during the hot nights, so I climb the ladder and watch the soldiers in the narrow street below. But for some reason I am no longer scared. There's something different about this group of soldiers, and something inside me knows what's coming. I am excited. I am shaking. I am grinning and shaking, as if I've just won a footrace and am waiting for the wreath. The soldiers, some are very cocky and handsome . . . but some look hardened and scarred from too many battles. Then I see tall flags coming. Bright purple. The most vivid purple I've ever seen. There is a grand chariot coming. Pulled by four horses. It's the emperor! I've heard of him but have never seen him."

"What does he look like?"

"He's tall and solid . . . short curly hair and a beard. His nose is prominent and his skin is sun-darkened, like before. He stands upright in the chariot. Everyone sees he is a great leader. His breastplate blinds me with the reflected sun"—Jeremy held up a protective hand in front of his closed eyes—"and his purple cape flaps behind him in the wind. Seeing him makes me want to cry. People shout to him. Women throw flowers and oak leaves. There is great celebration."

"Why do you want to cry? Do you feel scared? Sad?"

"No," Jeremy laughed. "I want to cry because my soul recognizes the love I have for this man. It's Arthur again, but not Arthur. And now he is my emperor."

"And you know this by seeing him in his chariot?" Dr. Studski asked.

"My *soul* knows it's him. My heart. I don't consciously know it, but we've been together before. He tried to save me in that terrible battle, in my lifetime as Kleon. And I think, *Will he see me? He must see me.* I stand up and just at that moment he shields his eyes from the sun and looks up at me on the rooftop. He pulls on the reins of his horses and barks a command at them. The chariot stops. The horses whinny and stamp the dust. Men yell to each other and the procession stops. *The entire procession has stopped for me.*"

Dr. Studski waited for Jeremy to fully immerse himself in the moment he was reliving. At last he cleared his throat. "What happens next?"

"I wave at him, and he calls up to me."

"What does he say?"

"He says, 'You there! What barbarian province is this that there is no wine or water offered to the Emperor of Rome?' At once I scamper down the ladder, my heart beating hard in my chest. I dash to where we keep the water jug down in the dirt below the floor and pull it up by its rope. Then I take it to him outside the door, and hand it to a nearby soldier to give to him. I do not look down as is customary, but instead meet his eye, man to man."

"But you are much younger than he."

"I am old enough." Jeremy grinned, eyelids tight. "The emperor snatches the jar from the soldier and takes a long look at me as he lifts the jar to his lips and tilts it back. I see the water run down his chin, but his eyes never leave me. His eyes take in all of me from head to toe and back again, as if he is trying to remember where he knows me from."

"And does he remember you?"

"The heart never forgets," Jeremy laughed. "The emperor yells at two soldiers near him to escort me to him. I go willingly. I am nervous meeting him—he is such a commanding man that I should be frightened. But his eyes—his soft, gray eyes—are kind. And his voice is quiet, as if every word spoken to me—in perfect Greek—is just between us."

"Where do you go from here?"

"I hug my dog and say good-bye to my mother, and her eyes fill with tears; she does not want me to leave. But I convince her this is something I want: to be a great soldier, and to be chosen personally by the emperor for his court. Arthur assures my mother of my care and then gives her a bag heavy with gold, and she is greatly relieved. He even tells her a joke that makes her laugh. She opens the bag and gasps; she has never seen such wealth before, and each piece has the profile of the emperor stamped upon it."

"What is the emperor's name?"

"Trajanus . . . Hadrian . . . Augustus. The emperor known as Hadrian."

CHAPTER

forty-three

Clickety-click-click—click. "Tell me more."

"I never left his side until the day I died. I became his favorite and his beloved, as he became mine. *As we are still.*"

"You mention being his favorite. Were there others?"

Jeremy's face darkened, his smile vanishing. "Two others. One was very jealous, but the other became my good friend and companion. He was like a brother to me."

"Do you know these other souls in this lifetime?"

"One is now Carlo. We immediately recognized each other and became lovers for a short time. During my lifetime as Kleon, he also lived as the dark-skinned warrior who talked to Alexander over our graves."

"I recall this. What about the other young man?"

"Today he is known as Lazzaro. We have a strong and timeless bond but not a good one. I still have a score to settle with him."

"And where you are now, is he the Lucius you spoke of?"

"Yes."

"And what do you need to settle with him?"

Jeremy began breathing heavily. "I don't want to say."

"You needn't tell me. Instead, why don't you go back to the day you met Hadrian."

Jeremy's breathing calmed. "I am . . . placed with an escort, a kindly older man who is also a tutor, to look after me while Hadrian tends his troops. Because it is peacetime there are only hundreds with him instead of thousands. Traveling with him are not only soldiers, but also guards, supply men, slaves, cooks, engineers, and mechanics."

"What time of year is this?"

"Just before winter. And night is coming sooner each day and the weather is getting cooler. I have only a tunic with me, and I am holding my arms for warmth. The emperor sees me, unhooks his purple cape, and throws it to me. The look on his face—he loves me already. I wrap myself in the splendid garment. It smells of him, and it is a scent my heart remembers. I know at that moment that I will never leave his side."

"What happens next?"

"A man comes for me . . . to escort me to Hadrian's tent. It is in the center of rows of tents, and looks like the others—nothing special. The encampment is on a rise overlooking Claudiopolis in Bithynia, near the area where I was earlier that same day overlooking a valley we use for farming. I know the mountains and the winding river below like my own hands and feet.

"Hadrian is tired, anyone can see this. But he is also restless, and I suppose he will need release to allow him to sleep. I am nervous; I have only been with others my age, and I have heard of powerful men abusing those who hold no social importance. But he advises me to not worry, that what is coming will happen only when I am ready, and he wants me near him only that I should feel safe on my first night from home with the protection of the guards inside his tent; the soldiers are not as considerate with their lust."

"Did he keep his word?" Dr. Studski asked.

Jeremy smiled. "Hadrian never broke his word to me, just as Arthur has never in this lifetime."

"How do you feel, being there?"

Jeremy took a deep breath and then sighed. "Peaceful . . . serene . . . and secure. As if I had finally come home. But this is also the moment when Lucius sees me. He enters the tent and I see envy burning like pitch in his black eyes."

"Lucius, the man you mentioned?"

"He is another young man chosen by the emperor, a dark Adonis and great athlete from an aristocratic family by the sea—he is . . . my age, yet more heavily muscled. He has gained the admiration of many."

"Does Lucius say anything to you?"

"He eyes me with a woman's jealousy and backs out of the tent. But the next morning he puts his arm around me and shows me the camp. He speaks kindly, but I do not trust him. And the feeling of his arm makes me uncomfortable. Nervous—like . . . having a viper around my shoulders, ready to sink its fangs into my neck."

"Who else is there with you?"

"Corydon, who is now my Carlo; he is also dark-skinned, but with a fine quality to his features. He is more . . . *delicate* and is appreciated for his sharp wit, whereas Lucius was already a well-known troublemaker." Jeremy cocked his head, as if listening to a conversation. "And Lucius is not as smart as Corydon; he does not understand our humor, our jokes."

"Jeremy, I want you to go forward in time. Are you living with Hadrian?"

"Yes . . . and we travel often. But we always go back to Rome. To his estate, built in the Greek style. The villa is sprawling with stables and palaces, libraries and baths. There is a constant supply of water that is heated before spilling into many pools and fountains. My emperor and I spend mornings strolling between the temples and libraries, staterooms and theaters. Each section of the villa has been modeled after a place Hadrian visited: Egypt and Asia Minor and Greece and parts of Africa. There isn't one corner in the villa that is not finished and decorated; architecture was one of my emperor's great passions—besides beautiful men.

"Hadrian would visit somewhere in the Empire, take detailed notes on what he saw, and then come home to replicate some new foreign grandeur. He never tired of delighting his eye. His gardens were specially designed to please the senses; on summer evenings the lavender and sage and gardenia would perfume the air, and there was never a shortage of delicious fruits from the farthest corners of the Empire—even from Asia. Everything . . . is stone and marble; the floors are inlaid with geometric tiles, and the statues are decorated with gold. These statues are amazing. Beautiful statues . . . mostly of men—gods and a few goddesses, painted to look real . . . real skin colors and hair and all. They look like frozen people, and their eyes follow me wherever I go. The roofs are open in places, and birds come in and out and sit on the statues' heads. It's funny."

"Where did you stay at the villa? Did you have your own quarters?"

"There is no need for my own quarters. We are one man. Hadrian makes me walk in back of him because he's the emperor, but tells me he would like me to walk before him because he loves to watch me move."

"What's your relationship like?"

Jeremy smiled warmly, eyes closed. "We talk all the time and I make him laugh . . . but he can be tense—which I understand. But if he speaks harshly to me I give him a look and walk away, and that makes him sorry. He's constantly adding to his villa; he says the noise makes him even more irritated, but he has a vision and he won't rest until it looks the way he sees it in his mind. He's . . . brilliant—interested in everything: art and poetry and languages; he's even learning to read hieroglyphs so he can argue with the Egyptian priests when we travel to Alexandria."

"When will you be doing this?"

Jeremy paused. "We're not sure. He says there's no reason yet to go and there is too much that needs his attention in Rome. Perhaps next summer."

Dr. Studski noticed Jeremy frown and his eyes squeezing together more tightly. "What's worrying you?"

"Lucius. He can be an asshole."

"What do you think he wants?"

"To become the emperor's beloved and to gain power."

"Does Lucius really care for Hadrian?"

Jeremy shrugged. "I don't know and I don't care. He's one of those people who thinks because he comes from a patrician family he's entitled to more than everyone else."

"I know the type," Dr. Studski said. "Go on."

"When Lucius looks at me his mouth smiles but his eyes do not."

"Can you tell me what Hadrian thinks of Lucius?"

"Hadrian is entranced by his beauty—as is anyone who is not blind—and Hadrian will need a successor; there can be only one who will succeed the emperor, as Hadrian did with Trajan. I am from a peasant family, so it will never be me; Lucius imagines it will be him because his family has longstanding ties to the Roman army: uncles and cousins and admirers in high positions."

"Is Hadrian married?"

"The Empress Sabina is a good woman. Although many think her dull, she notices everything: a glance, a hesitation, an insincere laugh. We are friends of a sort."

"How does that work?"

"We are married, in a sense, to the same man. But she is bored by him in bed the same way he is by her. She prefers to read and to keep company with her ladies."

"Is she a lesbian?"

"No. She is simply without physical passion."

"Do you know Sabina in this life?"

"Of course." Jeremy laughed. "She is now my great aunt, Katharine Tyler. She and Arthur have a very strong bond, which is why they have argued so much through the years—even after he came to be her protector. But this old relationship between Hadrian and me was also the reason for Katharine to keep Arthur and me apart. Of this she nearly succeeded."

"Is there anyone else from your soul group who is now with you and Arthur?"

"Margo, Arthur's best friend. She was the Empress Pompeia Plotina, wife of Trajan, the man who was Hadrian's lover and then became his father."

"*His father?*" Dr. Studski asked. "Trajan was Hadrian's lover *and his father?*"

"Trajan was his *adoptive* father," Jeremy clarified, "but only in the last hours of his life. In Imperial Rome, succession was based upon merit and not always by blood; this way the emperor might bequeath power to one who was worthy instead of one whose familial ties put him in line to the throne. That Hadrian and Trajan were once lovers was inconsequential."

Clickety-click-click—click. "Tell me about Pompeia."

"The . . ." Jeremy took a moment to think ". . . Empress Pompeia and Hadrian were friends for many years; they were trusted confidants. Such was their intimacy that people whispered about Hadrian having tastes both for men *and* for married women . . . but I never knew if the rumors were true. Their enviable intimacy spoke of a very deep love and commitment to each other. It was Pompeia who assured Hadrian's ascent to the throne."

"How did this come to pass?"

"Pompeia signed the letter to the Senate stating it was Trajan's deathbed wish to adopt Hadrian, which was true. Of course there were rumors that she posed as Trajan under the sheets and disguised her voice to impersonate her ill husband, but Trajan wanted no one but Hadrian to succeed him and he only stalled naming him to control him. Trajan and Hadrian maintained a love-hate relationship, and Trajan wanted to keep his 'son' beholden to him because he was afraid Hadrian might kill him, as was sometimes the custom for successors to usurp power."

"What was it like being the emperor's beloved?"

"I am treated like his queen, his prince, and his whore: whatever I desire is mine—but I'm also frightened, because every day I grow older our relationship comes closer to its end."

"I don't understand."

"If the emperor is seen loving a man who is his equal, he will lose the respect of his senate and the reverence of his soldiers. People already whisper because I am nearly as tall as he and broader through the chest, so Hadrian had his breastplates made larger to compensate for my musculature's growth. He needs to look more powerful than I."

"What will you do if, or when, you outgrow your role?"

"I've thought of that many times, and there are few answers. Of course Hadrian will provide for me—this is what he's promised. But for now everything is as it should be."

"I want you to go forward in time, Jeremy, and tell me when this changed."

"It changed a short time before I died."

"Can you tell me what happened?"

Jeremy paused. "Hadrian was . . . sometimes distant. Preoccupied—like in any marriage where one or both partners hold positions of importance. And I knew it would not be long before I needed to leave his court. I felt sad, because I truly loved him. But there was a significant change in Hadrian; something was happening."

"Can you explain?"

"Over the course of some months he'd been stricken with an illness that came and went: numbness in his extremities, and no appetite for days. He began to shed weight and he looked much older, similar to what is happening to Arthur now. Then, as mysteriously as the illness came, it would disappear; he would regain his appetite and strength and all was well.

"After he consulted the priests they told him he had angered Hera, wife of Zeus, by ignoring his own wife and having one in full manhood, me, as his beloved. They said the illness coming and going was a warning from Hera, and if he wanted his health to return he needed to appease her by casting me aside.

"Hadrian was frustrated by this and suggested the priests' prophecy was wrong; he insisted that Achilles was justified loving Petroclus just as Alexander loved Hephaestion, but then I reminded him that all those men were taken early in their lives, and Hadrian had already outlived Alexander by nearly two decades. But it bothered him that an end was being forced upon us and there was little to do—at least, that's what I thought until he had me deified."

"He made you a god?"

"He had the priests *declare* me a god, and because Hadrian was considered Zeus on earth and there were no laws preventing one god from loving another, we were the same as Zeus and Ganymede or Apollo and Hyacinthus."

"An astute strategy. Go on."

"Everything would have been great if not for Lucius. His ambition fucked up everything."

"How so?"

"Lucius mocked my deification and said if I were really a god I should defy death. Of course I told him if he had any problem with the emperor's decision he should take it up with Hadrian directly."

Clickety-click-click—click. "What was his response?"

"He looked at me and smiled, but said nothing more."

"Was that the end of it?"

"No. But I did not concern myself with what he was conjuring; the emperor had many plans to complete for our upcoming trip to

Egypt, and he insisted on including me in almost every aspect of this. But I never imagined Lucius had his own evil plans."

Dr. Studski checked his watch. "Unfortunately we need to tie this up, Jeremy, so I'm going to bring you back to the present. Are you comfortable doing this?"

Jeremy nodded, his head sunken into the sofa cushion. "I understand."

"When I count forward from zero to five and snap my fingers, you'll awaken refreshed and remember everything that happened. Are you ready?"

"I am."

"Zero . . . one . . . two—completely refreshed and relaxed—three . . . four—remembering what you've just seen—five." *Snap!*

Jeremy blinked open his eyes and took a few moments to reorient himself to his surroundings: the cheap lamp table; the worn brown carpet; the ficus in the corner with its tangle of electrical cords.

"It's . . . *amazing* watching this all unfold." Jeremy pushed himself upright on the sofa. "But what I want to know is how this Roman drama has anything to do with the Civil War, or with Arthur's brain tumor or Lazzaro stealing my money, or even with Margo and Carlo and some upcoming trip to Egypt that happened thousands of years ago."

"I have complete confidence that the significance of everything you've seen will reveal itself in its time." Dr. Studski scrutinized Jeremy's face and noticed his skin had paled. "Are you feeling all right?"

"Just kind of worn out—and sad." He swung his feet over to the floor and pushed himself up off the green corduroy sofa, and then began shuffling toward the waiting room door. "This all makes me feel really sad."

Dr. Studski, likewise, got up from his chair. "Jeremy, has the time come for you to share any of this with Arthur?"

Jeremy glanced down for a moment, shoving his hands deep into his jeans pockets. "Yeah," he said, finally looking up. "I think we're at that point."

CHAPTER

forty-four

Arthur put down the *Elle Decor* he'd been flipping through and looked up at Jeremy.

"That's the silliest thing I've ever heard of. *Me, the Emperor Hadrian?*"

"What's so silly about it?" Jeremy asked indignantly.

"Because I'm more the Cleopatra type?"

Jeremy rolled his eyes and began making his way over to the fridge. "Arthur, listen to me. Just—before you shut your brain to this possibility, will you please listen?"

Arthur barked a short laugh. "Sorry, old buddy. I'm all ears—and remember, having a past life is something I briefly looked into a while ago."

Jeremy opened the refrigerator door and scanned the shelves for something to eat; earlier there had been a few gloppy triangles of chicken pesto pizza left over from last night, but now they were missing. *Good, he's been hungry.* "How is it that the name 'Antinous' magically comes to me in the Plaka, and under hypnosis, why did I miraculously display this big storehouse of historical knowledge that

I never knew I had, including accurate details about the reign of a certain Roman emperor?"

"Which begs the question: Why does everyone who believes in reincarnation think they were someone famous?"

"That's *exactly* what I asked, so Dr. Studski told me those are called 'landmark cases,' where a soul remembers a famous person or important event from their lifetime"—he leaned back onto the counter—"because that person or event attracted a lot of attention. He says typical landmark cases involve people who remember going down with the *Titanic* or . . . they walked with Jesus or were Amelia Earhart, because those were landmark events from the time when they lived before. But famous people need to reincarnate like everyone else, so Ms. Earhart could actually be flying overhead right now."

"With Jesus as her copilot?"

"I'm serious, Arthur."

"I know, baby. It's just that the other day you told me you got interested in Greek and Roman history after your Father's Star dream," Arthur reminded him. "So you do possess *some* knowledge of the period."

"That had to more to do with mythology than history. Remember?"

"But you could've stumbled upon some Antinous information and taken it in."

"You're right. I could have. But even Dr. Studski told me ours doesn't sound like a 'landmark case.' He said I knew too many details, like Hadrian having a mysterious illness and Antinous being from the countryside where people kept their water jugs underground for cooling; he Googled that info at the end of my session."

"OK, I'll agree that it's highly unusual for you to know those things. But for me to be Hadrian? I'm a nobody!"

"But you've always been in some sort of military job, Arthur! The Marines, the FBI . . . even controlling your own little army of bodyguards for hire—"

"But there's not a royal bone in my body—"

"And Hadrian wasn't royalty either; he was adopted by Trajan—another fact I mysteriously knew." Jeremy grabbed a cheese stick and began peeling down the clear plastic skin, as if it were a tiny white banana. "And I also knew how Trajan's wife Pompeia helped Hadrian become emperor.

"Look, I know what happened today may be hard to believe, but I swear I wasn't making anything up. I saw the sheep on the hillsides and the emperor's chariot and the worn out soldiers as clearly as if I were watching a miniseries on hi-def TV. And I'd really like to read up on Hadrian and find out more things that you both have in common, but Dr. Studski doesn't want me to do any research yet; he wants the information we explore to come from my own little brain."

"Does that mean I shouldn't research Hadrian?"

"No . . . I don't know." Jeremy shrugged. "I guess you could do whatever you want."

"I was going to start dinner in a few minutes, but I suddenly have the urge to run to my computer if you're not that hungry."

Jeremy considered this while chewing his cheese stick. "Just don't tell me what you discover," he mumbled and swallowed. "I'll just wait a while longer to eat."

"Can I research Antinous, as well?"

"I don't see why not."

"When's your next appointment?"

"A week from today."

"Did the good doctor have any other advice for you?"

Jeremy folded his arms over his chest. "He said I should start keeping a journal so I could write down anything significant that comes up, and that regressions unlock a part of the mind, and weird stuff bubbles up—plus he thinks those hallucinogenic drugs, the Sueño Gris I was taking with Lazzaro, might have opened up my subconscious in a way he hasn't seen before."

"Why would he think that?"

"He says the clarity of the details I've been seeing are like those from someone who's been practicing this kind of craziness for years."

Arthur leaned forward, brow furrowed. "What else did you see? What other details?"

"Well . . . last week I saw myself as a ghost next to all these dead soldiers—Greek soldiers—and we were buried all lined up in pairs inside this big hole in the ground. Then Prince Alexander had an argument with his father the king, and he cried over us. But there was this one soldier who I identified as Carlo who didn't die in the battle; he told Alexander which of us needed to be buried together, because we were—"

"*Lovers?*" Arthur asked, wide-eyed.

Jeremy looked at him. "How did you know?"

"You've just described the battle between King Philip of Macedon and the Sacred Band of Thebes."

"*Thebes!* That's what I said! What was the Sacred Band?"

"The Sacred Band was a small army—around three hundred men, all couples—who fought fiercely because they were defending their comrades *and* their lovers. But they were no match for Philip's army, so the Band was decimated. But instead of their bodies being burned, which was customary, Alexander had a grave dug for them, and he wept over their corpses."

"I know." Jeremy nonchalantly chewed the remainder of his cheese stick. "You and I were soldiers then. And we died together."

"Now *that* I can believe," Arthur said with a curt nod, "being an ordinary soldier. Do you think that's why we recognized each other in that later life as Hadrian and Antinous?"

"Now you sound like Dr. Studski." Jeremy walked over to Arthur and sat down next to him on the leather sofa. "Margo and Carlo were with Hadrian and Antinous, too; Margo was Trajan's wife Pompeia and Carlo was a guy named Corydon. He's been with us for many lifetimes."

"Didn't you mean 'too many' lifetimes?" Arthur asked, chuckling—and then he stared at Jeremy wide-eyed. "What did you say about Margo?"

"She was Pompeia. Married to the Emperor Trajan. Why?"

"Probably nothing . . . just something she told me the other day at brunch about a lifetime as a washerwoman—I need to ask her more about that. I'm curious, but is there anyone else you knew back then?"

"There was this other hot guy—he was trouble even back then. Guess who he is now?"

"The prick who's walking around with your money?"

"Which means it's official—some people really *never* change."

"Are you referring to him or to you?" Arthur stretched an arm around Jeremy's shoulder and drew him into a hug. "Beautiful men are *always* trouble. Anyone else?"

Jeremy considered disclosing the troubled relationship between Hadrian and Sabina—now known as Aunt Katharine—but thought better of it. "I'll tell you the rest some other time."

Arthur started to push himself up from the sofa, but stopped mid-hoist.

"What's wrong?"

Arthur huffed a deep breath. "Just a little dizzy. Listen, I'm going to go do some research on this, if you don't mind."

Jeremy nudged his shoulder. "Go."

Arthur stood. "Do you know what you want for dinner? I was hoping you'd like some—"

"Mac 'n' cheese?" Jeremy grinned, looking suddenly a decade younger. "Really? We've been so good on our diet and exercise regimens."

"Bought some of the sacred blue and yellow boxes today at the market figuring we could go for an extended walk tomorrow; I'm feeling so much better now with my energy and appetite improving."

"Thank God we only have a week or so left of the treatments."

"Can you handle the cooking while I go online?"

"I don't know if someone formally of the emperor's palace should be relegated to such a mundane task," Jeremy replied.

"You're not suggesting the emperor himself should cook for you . . ."

Jeremy stood and pecked Arthur on the cheek. "I'll fire up the pasta pot."

:::::::::

In the course of an hour Arthur had learned that more than a few notable, highly educated people believed reincarnation was anything but conjecture and fantasy, and several scientific researchers had been applying precise theoretical methodology to their investigations for decades. And the overarching concept that the soul should learn from each lifetime's successes and failures to become more actualized appealed to Arthur. In fact, he remembered how this idea had resonated with him years ago when he'd considered the possibility of a botched past incarnation as explanation for his bafflingly tumultuous life.

As a result, the more case studies he read, the further his mind's frozen, FBI-trained logic and skepticism began to melt.

Especially with regard to Jeremy's revelatory assertion.

He saw now that the parallels between Hadrian and himself were startling: As Jeremy reported, the adopted Hadrian was of common blood (*how could Jeremy have known this?*); Hadrian was initially unpopular but then had won over his adversaries, just as Arthur had in the Marines; Hadrian had risen through the military ranks, but even at the height of power had slept and dined amongst his troops, as Arthur preferred to do as First Lieutenant; Hadrian spoke Latin and Greek, while Arthur had inexplicably excelled at Latin in high school, completing four years of intense study in only three; he and the emperor shared a passion for architecture; and Hadrian and

Arthur both—in spite of societal mores of the times—pursued *loving and committed* homosexual relationships. Finally, the men shared an eerie similarity in physical stature and facial structure—this at least from the busts and statues that had survived the past two millennia.

All coincidence? Perhaps. Arthur reasoned that there could likely be parallels drawn between just about any human and another, if you searched enough and conjured . . . or were delusional.

Delusional.

Arthur riffled his cerebral files back to his weeks of desk training at Quantico:

Delusions of grandeur: the belief that one possesses qualities such as omnipotence, fame, or wealth, or of having made some important discovery . . . or of being, or having a relationship with, someone extraordinary . . . these delusions are most often associated with bipolar and psychotic disorders.

Arthur decided to table that mental debate and to continue learning about those two lovers from so long ago. And what brought a tear to his eye was Hadrian's undying dedication to Antinous: that young man from the humble countryside known for his spectacular beauty and unassuming manner . . . beloved of the emperor until drowning in the Nile, after which Hadrian was reported to have "mourned like a woman."

Drowned? But Jeremy's a champion swimmer!

And then it occurred to Arthur that perhaps Jeremy's passion for swimming sprung from some deep-seated fear of drowning.

Could it be?

He Googled and downloaded more images of the numerous sculptures Hadrian had commissioned of Antinous, and felt his excitement explode as the resemblance to Jeremy became starkly evident. Of course Arthur had to do a little imagining, because each marble or bronze bust or statue was blank-eyed and eyebrow-less and monochromatic—but he knew enough to imagine how these features would appear when painted in a lifelike manner, as the Romans preferred.

Then after he'd gathered about half-a-dozen images, he began zipping through pictures of Jeremy from his own digital photo albums—if only to prove to himself how uncanny the likeness was.

It only took one side-by-side comparison for his forearms to bloom goose bumps.

Jeremy looks just like him!

The same wide, gentle eyes.

Pensive brow.

Ruler-straight nose.

Sensual full lips.

The pair even shared Olympian musculatures, and when Jeremy had first come to Ballena Beach his tousled hair had been styled—or rather *un*-styled—in a similar, carefree fashion.

Could this be true?

Then a dark thought deflated Arthur's excitement.

If we've come back to learn from our mistakes and to reap the benefits of having treated others with love, kindness, and consideration in our former lives, why would I be suffering from this brain tumor, and why would Jeremy be an alcoholic, and why would Lazzaro cheat Jeremy out of his inheritance, and why would I forever be doing battle with Aunt Katharine, with Carlo playing shortstop and Margo cheering—alone—from the sidelines?

Shouldn't we all be living happily ever after by now?

Or is our karma so very, very damaged?

CHAPTER

forty-five

Jeremy answered his phone on the third ring. "Hey, girl."

"You OK?" Carlo asked.

"Margo just called and asked me the same thing. We really appreciate your checking in on us—both of you."

"Um, you didn't answer my question."

"Considering the MRI's tomorrow, I'm holding up OK—and so's my fiancé."

"Has anything changed with tomorrow's schedule?"

"Still set for ten a.m. And it's Margo's day to drive to Cedars, so you should start planning your outfit to coordinate with her Bentley's red leather."

"Already talked to her," Carlo said, "and she's picking me up on the way to your place."

"You're so good to go with us," Jeremy told him. "For once, we could use the distraction of your flat jokes and bitter observations."

Carlo laughed. "I love you."

"I love you too. But hey, I've gotta get running; I've got an appointment with my witch doctor that I'm gonna be late for. We're trying something new."

"You want me to bring you guys anything for breakfast tomorrow?"

Jeremy considered his offer. "Actually, I don't think anyone's gonna be hungry."

:::::::::

"You're going to concentrate on your breathing," Dr. Studski began, enunciating his words slowly. "Deep in, hold it . . . slowly out. Deep in, hold it . . . slowly out. Now feel your body relaxing. Your body is heavy, and you've never been more relaxed. Your consciousness is about to delve deeper than it's ever gone. You'll need to give your soul permission to more fully reveal itself, so if you feel comfortable I'd like you to say: 'I give my soul permission to reveal itself to me, and to go deeper into my psyche than I've ever gone before.'"

"I give my soul permission to reveal itself to me," Jeremy droned, "and go deeper into my psyche than I've ever gone before."

"You're going down a flight of ten steps in a darkened stairwell. Each step is covered in the thickest, deepest, most luxurious carpet. Your bare foot sinks into the nap of the first step, and you grasp the brass handrail. It's solid and secure. Can you feel the security of the handrail?"

"Yes. It's . . . cold."

"Can you feel your feet sink deeper into the carpet?"

Jeremy waited a moment. "Yeah."

"I want you to go down to the next step. Your feet sink deeper into the carpet. The handrail is firm in your grasp . . ." Studski continued taking him down the imaginary stairway until Jeremy was finally at its base. "Now when I count down from ten and snap my fingers, you will feel completely relaxed, and you'll be in a deeper state of consciousness than anything you've ever experienced. Are you comfortable with this transition?"

"I'm comfortable with this transition."

"Ten . . . nine . . ." The doctor hesitated. "Deep in, hold it . . . slowly out. Now feel your body relaxing. Deeper than you've ever gone before . . . eight . . . seven . . . six . . . five." He stopped again. "Deep in . . . slowly out. Your body is heavy, and you've never been more relaxed. You're completely at peace . . . four . . . three . . . your soul will reveal itself more deeply than ever before . . . two . . . one."

Snap!

Jeremy felt himself drifting down, down, down . . . as if he were falling slowly down a shaft inside the dark, damp earth. Scenes began flashing higgledy-piggledy before his mind's eye: Ballena Beach and his old elementary school in Fresno and learning to drive and the chalet in Lake Estrella and high school swim practice and his mom's dirty, chaotic apartment.

Jeremy heard a distant voice: "Deep in . . . slowly out. Your soul is now revealing itself more deeply than ever before."

Then a collage of now-familiar faces began flitting though his mind's eye, like a film alternating between quick rewind and fast-forward:

ArthurLazzaroCorydonPompeiaHadrianLuciusCarloJeremiahSabina FinneganKatharineCorydonHadrianPompeiaLuciusJeremiahKatharine LazzaroSabinaArthurFinneganCarloJeremy . . . Jeremy . . . Jeremy . . . .

The whirling faces slowed to a stop and Jeremy found himself studying a rippled glass mirror on the wall where someone stared back at him. The young man was Jeremy and *not* Jeremy: the facial architecture was the same, but his eyes were spaced a bit farther apart; his hair was longer and tousled and curled below his ears; his plump lips were slightly parted; and his expression was transfixed . . . as if beholding a spectacle he did not quite fully comprehend.

It was then that Jeremy realized he was watching himself *as* someone else; whereas in the earlier regressions it had seemed as if he were only reporting on Antinous of Bithynia, now he was actually staring into his eyes.

And Antinous of Bithynia stared back at him.

Jeremy blinked and Antinous blinked.

Antinous smiled and so did Jeremy.

This is real, Jeremy thought. *I . . . really . . . was . . . him.*

And then he felt himself drifting into the mirror, becoming one with his former self.

:::::::::

Antinous heard footsteps approaching, and then someone clearing his throat. He looked up from his scroll, his dark eyes narrowed and intent. "Yes?"

"The emperor wishes to see you," the page announced.

"Concerning what?"

The man glanced up at the ceiling. "The emperor has only now finished consulting with his priests, thus he would like to discuss his upcoming trip to Egypt."

"Are you joking? Surely we're not doing this again!"

The man's gaze drifted down to him. "Perhaps you should discuss this with the emperor. He wishes to see you."

Antinous hesitated, and then rolled up the scroll he was studying. He had been deep in his studies for the better part of the day, but now realized what a relief it might be to take a break and clear his mind. He stood up, stretched, and yawned. "Where is the emperor?"

"He can be found outside the library pavilion by the reflecting pool, near the men's baths."

Antinous judged that he was in need of sunshine and fresh air . . . and if it felt warm enough, he might even have a swim. "Please tell him I will be there."

The man gave a short bow, turned, and marched away.

For Antinous, the walk from their chambers to Hadrian's favorite poolside pavilion took some effort; the villa had always been more than expansive, but now it seems to be growing by the month. Thus Hadrian had been traveling more to avoid the endless construction noise and dust; and when the Emperor of Rome traveled, so did Antinous—alongside a small army.

As the summer heat wafted through the stone halls from the gardens and blazed down through the open-air atria, Antinous pulled higher the short, belted tunic he wore. If the heat in Egypt was worse than this, he would be in the Nile every day.

He found the emperor poolside, surrounded by the foremen of his construction crew.

Hadrian waved him over excitedly.

Antinous quickened his step underneath the long colonnade and its welcome shade, noticing the slaves laying brick or installing gleaming sheets of marble and alabaster, their dark skin glistening like rain-soaked sculpture as they grunted and strained in the midday sun.

"Come look at this." Hadrian swept his hand over the plans. "The designs for the retreat!"

The chief architect stepped aside to allow the young man to examine the series of scrolls laid out on a wide wooden table.

"It's beautiful," Antinous remarked, after allowing his gaze to sweep over the meticulous drawings. "And I love the idea of a small villa surrounded by a pool." He looked up at Hadrian. "But how will anyone get to it? By raft?"

Hadrian pulled the scroll aside to reveal another beneath it. "Retractable bridges we can raise and lower from within the villa. If we wish for complete privacy, no one will bother us—*not even the empress.*"

Antinous glanced up. "Has Sabina yet seen these plans?"

"Do I care if she approves?" Hadrian laughed. "The empress is only concerned with her poetry and pantomime, and her fat singing birds." He tossed his head in the direction of an approaching figure. "Lucius approaches."

As Antinous turned to see the young man approach, he was unnervingly captivated by his wicked beauty: the beardless perfection of his handsome, dark features; his sculpted musculature; the gladiator's swagger offset by his patrician arrogance.

Deciding to ignore him, Antinous refocused on Hadrian's plans. "The adjoining garden," he noted, leaning in for a closer look. "Tell me about it."

"The walls will be sheathed in marble like a luxurious coliseum," Hadrian explained. "And the flowers will soothe the senses: roses, azaleas, orchids, and perfumed gardenias." He tapped his finger on different areas of the schemata. "The aqueducts will empty from sculptures and fountains into the pools, so we will hear the music of water everywhere and at all hours."

Antinous looked lovingly at him. "I cannot wait to enjoy this with you."

"And you will. It is ordered to be complete by the time we return—"

"And what is this you cannot wait to see?" Lucius asked as he drew up to the table.

Hadrian stepped back. "See for yourself."

As one of the architects summoned the emperor to examine the details on some other plans, Lucius scrutinized the drawings. "What's this?" he laughed under his breath. "An island of debauchery for the emperor and his harem of beautiful, stupid boys?"

"Of which you are more than fortunate to belong," Antinous replied. Then he stepped over to Hadrian and placed a gentle hand on his shoulder. "May we speak in private?"

"Walk with me, beloved." They strolled away from the others.

"I am told you are planning another trip to Egypt soon," Antinous said. "But we have detailed plans for the remainder of this year here in Rome."

"Plans that have already been altered," Hadrian answered softly. "I regret this, but it is necessary. I hope you understand."

"But we have traveled to Egypt so many times already," Antinous said, "looking to cure your ills, but nothing there seems to help you."

"The priests assure me there will be an exceptional alignment of the stars next month and if we hasten to the waters of the Nile, I am *assured* of a cure. The omens are strong."

"But traveling exhausts you! Would you not rather stay in Rome and seek treatment here? The physicians in Greece could be summoned here once more."

"The omens are strong," Hadrian repeated. "But if you do not wish to accompany me, I am certain Lucius will indulge me with his usual presence—*and* his spectacular thighs."

"Thighs that have entertained more soldiers than the Coliseum has seats," Antinous snapped.

Hadrian looked at him with raised eyebrows and laughed. "What would I do without you?"

"Of course I will accompany you," Antinous replied, "if for no other reason than to protect you from surly courtiers with sticky knees."

:::::::::

After nearly seven days and nights of preparation they traveled from Rome to Greece on the emperor's barque, and from there sailed across the Mediterranean to Alexandria. Their journey to the Nile's delta was mostly smooth, with the royal flotilla enjoying good weather, ample food and water, and various pleasures each night.

On afternoons when land was within sight they turned toward shore, where the local merchants sailed out to them offering their wares: honeyed sweets, exotic wines, fresh fish, and beasts from sea and land. Hadrian—as generous commander—was enjoying himself, and his jovial mood made Antinous happy.

In Alexandria the pharaoh's palace was as sumptuous as ever. Antinous never tired of studying the strange architecture and the colorful way the people dressed; those in the royal court kept their heads shaved and decorated themselves with face paint and golden chains and elaborately woven linens; and the men and women were equally as beautiful, with high cheekbones, plump lips, and glossy dark skin. These were friendly people, and there seemed to be no discomfort with the role of Antinous in Hadrian's court; they lavished upon him the same reverence the empress would have received.

However, after their arrival in Egypt, Hadrian grew increasingly serious, as if something worrisome were occupying his thoughts; at the dinner banquet he appeared sullen and ill-humored, and everything Antinous attempted to cheer him with was met with indifference or disapproval.

Antinous had sulked off to bed.

Then at sunrise, he awoke determined to hear the truth.

He found Hadrian sitting outside on a shade-covered chaise, intently sketching architectural details of the royal Egyptian palace.

"Will you finally speak your mind to me," Antinous demanded, "or must I make myself crazy trying to guess what is consuming you?"

"There . . . is something of great importance I have been considering," Hadrian replied, his features at last displaying relief. "But only as of last evening did I reach a decision, and I apologize if my surliness has affected you. Please sit."

Antinous sat, glancing away from Hadrian and knowing he was about to hear the words he'd been dreading: He'd grown too old to be the emperor's intimate companion and would be quietly displaced from the royal court.

Hadrian placed a heavy hand on his knee. "Trajan waited until his deathbed to adopt me; and without my dearest Pompeia, I might have never ascended the throne. The truth is that my relationship with you, beloved Antinous, is causing a scandal in Rome and abroad."

"What does one have to do with the other?"

"I am getting to that. As you well know, it is perfectly acceptable for the emperor to bed young men who are almost girlish in stature and are no threat to my rule, but you are now as powerfully built as your face is handsome, and some claim that you conspire with my enemies to slit my throat when I sleep."

"And you listen to these lies?" Antinous laughed. "I'd sooner slit my own throat!" He lowered his voice. "The gossip I'm told is that the emperor is less a man because he clenches his legs to another."

"Rumors such as these tell me something must be done. You were—just as I was—a boy from the provinces born to a common family . . . although my father had been a minor Roman official for a short time before his death. And through tireless work you are now educated and have shown your generous character and wit and honor many times; during the hunts we've enjoyed together you demonstrated the bravery of a warrior, yet when one of our hunting dogs or horses was injured you showed the compassion and knowledge of a studied healer. Your high position in my court has not affected your treatment of commoners or slaves, and all who know you love you—even cold-hearted Sabina smiles when you approach, and Pompeia has often expressed her deep affection for you."

"What are you telling me?"

"The priests here have confirmed that my illness is a result of our public relationship. We have angered the goddess Hera, and she is in collusion with the three Moirai sisters."

"Hera is working with the Fates against you?"

"Against *us*. What Clotho has spun cannot be changed. But Lachesis who measures the thread, and Atropos who cuts it, might have already been persuaded by Hera."

Antinous began feeling sick to his stomach. "This cannot be happening."

"No, my beloved, listen to me: Only last night did I send a letter to Rome notifying the Senate that I intend to adopt you as my son upon our return—which means that as of today we will terminate the public aspect of our relationship."

Antinous felt his heart thumping against his chest. "And in private?"

"I have been considering this for some time." Hadrian's eyes glimmered. "Did you not see the plans for my new villa with its retractable bridges?"

Antinous laughed, throwing his arms around Hadrian's neck. "Why did I ever doubt you? Does anyone else know of your intention? Sabina? Pompeia?"

"Only Lucius. I entrusted him with the letter last night."

"It would be foolish to entrust Lucius with the safekeeping of a dog."

"He assured me this morning that the letter is already on its way, and I believe him."

"Why?"

Hadrian hesitated. "Because the letter states I will also adopt Lucius upon our return."

"*Lucius will be my brother?*"

"If anything should happen to me, or to you, there must be a line of succession—and I don't believe you have any prospects for heirs—or did you fall into bed with that pretty Egyptian princess who was eyeing you with such longing last night, while you reclined on your chaise? I see these things, you know."

Antinous shook his head. "I only desire you."

"Now Antinous, I know you and Lucius have love—and lust—for each other. But like beautiful sisters you eye each other with catlike jealousy. Can you learn to be kind to one another? Enjoy each other's thighs if you will—it would please me greatly."

"I . . . will consider it," Antinous glumly replied.

:::::::::

Over the course of the next few days everything appeared to smooth out: Hadrian claimed to be feeling better and Lucius warmed up to

Antinous considerably; Antinous even noticed an uncharacteristic playfulness to him that he'd seldom witnessed before.

On the third night in Alexandria, after an evening of wine and dancing and bawdy jokes, Hadrian retired early with his most trusted guards standing watch. The Egyptian sun and heat, as well as the frenetic day and the fine ale he'd consumed, had transformed the usually stalwart emperor into a drooping, yawning, middle-aged man.

Antinous had determined that he wasn't yet tired and had left the party to stroll through the palace, telling himself he wasn't looking for company but finding himself aroused as he eyed the glorious assortment of reclining, chatting, glossy-skinned men and women.

Eventually he came to a stone-floored room with a high, open ceiling through which to watch the stars inch across the sky. This chamber was furnished with artfully constructed chaises and chairs sheathed in gold leaf and jeweled mosaics, while in the center of the room clusters of papyrus swayed in the gentle breeze from the surface of a flat, trickling pool teeming with wriggling, vermillion fish.

Antinous was at last feeling fatigued, so he shed his clothing, stretched out onto a chaise, and sank into his dreams.

Sometime later he was stirred from his slumber first by the thud of heavy of footsteps, and then by a soft breath in his ear and a warm hand massaging his chest.

"They say he is even more beautiful dreaming than awake," the deep voice murmured, "and now I know this to be true."

CHAPTER

forty-six

Antinous opened his eyes and saw Lucius crouching next to him—a bit unsteadily for the ale he, too, had consumed. "It seems you've discovered my hiding place," Antinous said, lifting an eyebrow. "Now go away."

"Dreaming of the emperor, I see." Lucius glanced down and eyed Antinous's aroused state. "Or was it that angry stable boy who was brought in to be disciplined? With a rope and some tallow he could provide a week of fun."

"I have more genteel taste than you," Antinous replied, grasping himself and waving his cock in the air. "I only seek the company of men."

"And here is such a man," Lucius chuckled. "I have often looked forward to the day when I could take pleasure with you." He peeled off his tunic. "Might tonight be that day?"

Antinous reached out and fondled Lucius between his legs. "Better tonight than next month—"

"When we are brothers," Lucius finished. "And since you will one day be emperor, I am hoping you will take your pleasure with me tonight the way the emperor takes it with you."

Antinous palmed the twin brown planes of Lucius's hard pectorals. "Since I now have my emperor's permission," he pinched the twin brown nipples, "I will be delighted to accommodate you."

Lucius leaned in and kissed Antinous.

:::::::::

They slept in each other's arms that night, and were awakened at dawn by the cool breezes skimming off the Nile, and the first rays of sunlight streaking the sky pink and tangerine over the atrium.

"I have a secret to reveal," Lucius said, yawning. "But you must not tell anyone."

"I'm sure your secrets are nothing but weeks-old gossip."

"I've had a visit yesterday with one of the high priestesses here in Alexandria. She told me of an old temple far up the Nile where Isis gathered the dismembered body of Osiris. If we drink the sacred herb she gave me, the priestess assured me we will see Isis arise from the waters to walk the banks once again. Even Osiris sometimes accompanies her."

"Do his legs walk behind, or in front of, his hands and his head?"

"Antinous, did you not see how fatigued the emperor was last evening? He only tells you he is recovering, but anyone can see how much discomfort he feels. So when we see Isis, you can ask her to grant Hadrian a cure. And in the meantime we can play in the water like brothers."

Antinous was enticed by his proposal. "I must first check with the emperor to see if he desires my company today."

:::::::::

After consulting with Hadrian—who once again was experiencing his tiring numbness, yet was visibly pleased by their plans—the young men rented a wooden skiff and headed up the Nile, where they spent the morning watching the shoreline drift slowly past.

With the Egyptian sun not quite at its zenith, they enjoyed refreshments of grapes and cheeses and roasted goat and figs, and not a little Egyptian wine kept cold in a sack that bobbed along in the water behind them.

After their midday meal, Lucius invited Antinous to share the magical herb with him; he estimated that they were approaching the sacred cove and the drug would take little time once ingested to reach its desired effect. He prepared two vessels and handed Antinous the first. They looked into each other's eyes and drank the honey-sweetened potion and then began scanning the coastline for the cove, marked—as the priestess had advised Lucius—by a grove of tall, ancient palm trees leaning before a ruined, sand-colored temple.

As promised, the temple drew into view and Lucius jumped into the water.

"My skin is burning," Antinous complained from where he sat inside the tiny wooden boat, after noticing the crimson singe on his shoulders, biceps, and tops of his thighs. "Is it not the inundation season? Where are the cooling clouds?"

"You should join me." Lucius continued treading the Nile's green waters, droplets glinting on his cheeks and chin.

"But I am watching for the gods, for Isis and Osiris."

"Perhaps the gods will also desire a swim."

Antinous stood up in the boat and then dove into the river to join his companion.

The blissful wetness closed in over his head as he sliced into the current; then, just as quickly as he'd descended, he began rushing upward. "It's beautiful!" he shouted, shaking the water from his curls. "When will the herb begin taking effect?"

"Soon."

Only moments later, Antinous detected numbness prickling his toes and feet and creeping up his calves toward his knees. "I feel it!" he called out, treading water with wide sweeps of his arms while scanning the riverbank. "Yet I see no Osiris yet, no Isis." He turned to Lucius. "When did the priestess promise we would see the gods?"

"Very soon." Twin onyx eyes scrutinized him. "Very, very soon."

"Is the herb also affecting your legs?"

"It is not," Lucius answered coolly, his bronzed arms swirling the water with ease.

Antinous began struggling to stay afloat. "Why is it affecting me this way?"

"Because I only pretended to take the herb."

"Why?" Antinous now sensed only dead weight below his knees, and his fingertips had grown cold—and then, just that quickly, he ceased feeling his fingers at all, as if they had turned to marble. He looked around for their barque but saw it had drifted away, its unused anchor listing the craft slightly to one side. The riverbank now seemed as far away as the few clouds pressing the sky. "I feel great weakness, Lucius. Help me!"

"Do not fight the will of the Fates, whom you should see at any moment."

"The . . . *Fates?* You said we should see Isis and Osiris, not the Fates; Atropos only appears when one is dying!"

"You should not fear death, Antinous. You will awaken with the gods, and your beloved will receive the gift of your sacrifice. A life for a life. Your remaining thread tied to Hadrian's."

"No—"

"—Yes."

Antinous's breaths now came in ragged spasms. "You are—doing this because you know of—Hadrian's plan for me . . . but the letter has—been sent to Rome." The numbness had now traveled from his arms to his shoulders, and his breaths were increasingly labored, as if leather belts were cinching tighter around his torso. "My . . . beloved, this . . . will—kill him!"

"Henceforth it shall be written," Lucius said, "Antinous died so the emperor might live longer. This is what you must want for him: to be rid of his maladies, once and for all—"

"You cannot . . . know this! His healing . . . must come . . . from Hera herself!"

Lucius smiled. "Could it be that Hadrian has been suffering from what you suffer now? Numbness in the extremities? Faintness of breath?"

"*You've been . . . poisoning the . . . emperor?*"

"Thus your sacrifice will rid him of his maladies for now—although someday he will join you, and for him you must wait in the underworld. Together you will be like Alexander and Hephaestion or Castor and Pollux, bright constellations crossing the heavens; all of Rome will pray to you for protection and make sacrifices in your names."

Antinous sank suddenly below the surface of the water, but the other young man quickly swam to him and hefted him up so his head broke the surface.

Antinous gasped, coughing water.

"I—must—hear it—from your lips," Lucius panted, trying his best to keep them both afloat, "so I may—truthfully tell the emperor you said this: *I sacrifice myself—so the emperor might live a—longer life.* These are the only—words that will carry him through—his mourning: *I sacrifice myself so the emperor—might live a longer life.* Tell this to me!"

Now realizing he had no choice and his strength was no more, Antinous whispered, "I sacrifice myself . . . so the Emperor . . . might live a longer life."

"May I kiss you my brother, immortal Antinous, beloved of the Emperor Hadrian, savior of Rome? I want the gods to know your lips touched mine last, so we might also be joined for eternity."

With tears in his eyes Lucius pressed his lips to the lax mouth.

Antinous felt the tenderness of his assassin's kiss, at once recalling last evening's carnal pleasures—the frenzied drums and haunting music, the flickering firelight, the sinuous, sweat-lacquered bodies, the ecstasy of their simultaneous release.

Instinctively, Antinous drew his arms around Lucius's neck.

Stronger arms broke his grip and pushed him down. *Hard.*

Water garbled his protests.

Antinous forced open his eyes and saw before him the exquisite nakedness of his murderer flailing slowly and dreamlike amidst the shafts of sunlight spearing the emerald water.

He struggled against the hands.

Ten breaths were bursting in his throat.

Those hands were like iron.

His body erupted in one final spasm as his lungs surrendered.

The sacred Nile flooded him.

:::::::::

Peace.

:::::::::

"Ahhh!" Jeremy cried out and then lay silent, his eyes closed and chest heaving.

"What's wrong, Jeremy? What's happening?" Dr. Studski asked, leaning forward in his chair. "Have you changed your mind about allowing this regression to go forward?"

Jeremy let out a long sigh between pursed lips, like a punctured tire. "I've already lived through it again."

"But I only put you under a moment ago—*seconds* ago."

"I have lived it all."

Dr. Studski considered this. "Jeremy, sometimes time bends, or compacts, when we're in our deepest state of consciousness; what was actually a few seconds in this world might be days or weeks in a past life. Could this be what you experienced?"

"I've seen what I needed to see," Jeremy said and began to weep.

"Can you talk about it?"

Jeremy shook his head.

"Are you ready to come back?"

Jeremy nodded.

"I'll bring you forward to the present and you'll awaken totally relaxed. Would you prefer to remember or to forget what you've learned?"

"I will never forget this," Jeremy mumbled. "It's good that I remember it."

"Then I'm going to count forward from zero to ten, and when I reach ten and snap my fingers you will awaken. One . . . two . . . three . . . four . . . totally relaxed, completely at ease and feeling safe . . . five . . . six . . . seven . . . retaining all that you learned . . . eight . . . nine . . . ten.

Snap!

Jeremy opened his eyes, staring straight ahead.

"Are you OK?" Dr. Studski asked.

Tears continued trailing down Jeremy's face. "*No.*"

"I might be able to help you make sense of this, Jeremy. Nothing you tell me will leave this room."

After a moment Jeremy looked over at him. "I . . . Antinous . . . was causing a scandal for the emperor, for Hadrian . . . so he decided to put me in line for the throne by adopting me." He brushed the tears from his eyes. "Lucius had been poisoning Hadrian a little at a time so he'd hurry up and name his successors—me and Lucius—but then Lucius drugged me and drowned me so he could take my place. That's it."

The doctor mulled this over. "And how does that make you feel now, knowing this?"

Jeremy began sobbing. "It . . . it makes me feel so sad for Arthur, for Hadrian, for us. We loved each other . . . we laughed and loved each other so much!" Spasms shook Jeremy's body as he cried. "All I could think of as I fought for breath was that I had to fight for *him*, for my beloved. That Hadrian would never recover from my death."

Dr. Studski watched the renewed stream of tears streak down Jeremy's face, and he found himself struggling to contain his own emotions; the young man's unexpressed grief was as fresh today as it had been two thousand years ago.

"But it all makes sense now," Jeremy babbled, snot trailing from his nostrils.

"How do you think this affects what's happening today?"

"Don't you see?" Jeremy asked, turning to him. "In my lifetime in Thebes, Arthur held me as I died; then he mourned for me after I drowned in the Nile; and finally, during the Civil War, he grieved for me again. Arthur's carried me through so many lives, and he's taught me things and fought for me and loved me unconditionally . . . but I've never been there for him at the end. He's had to die without me by his side after having mourned me in each lifetime, but now it's finally happening . . . *Arthur's going to die!*"

"It's all right to cry," he told Jeremy, his own emotions swelling. "You cry, and maybe I'll cry. It's the worst part of life. I understand."

"I'm just so fucking sad."

"I'm just so fucking sad for you too—for both of you." Dr. Studski paused. "But now that you've figured out your karmic relationship with the Emperor Hadrian and Arthur and why he's battling this illness, how does this change how you look at Lucius, the one who was poisoning Hadrian and who drowned you?"

Jeremy looked up and wiped his eyes. "Yeah," he said, after smearing his nose on his sleeve. "I've given a lot of thought to Lazzaro, but . . . I never realized until now that he's been stealing what's rightfully mine for nearly two thousand years."

CHAPTER

forty-seven

Carmella stood in line at the bank, while Lazzaro and Tristan waited for her inside the Mercedes limousine idling at the curb out front.

"Miss Montes," the teller, a young woman, said. "What a pleasure to meet you! I'm such a fan of your work. How are you today? That hat suits you beautifully."

Carmella lifted her huge Hermès purse onto the counter and began filling out a deposit slip. "I'm very well, thank you."

"What may I do for you?"

"One of the studios in another country paid me in cash, and I need to have it transferred into a cashier's check." She opened the purse and began sliding the stacks of purple-inked euros, along with a sealed white envelope addressed to the bank manager, under the slot of the bulletproof partition. The teller retrieved each of the tightly wrapped bundles. Then she picked up one stack, pinched out a bill, and began examining it: She rubbed her fingers over the type, held it up to the light to see the watermark, and tilted it to check the dimensionality of its hologram.

"Didn't you see the envelope?" Carmella asked, an impatient lilt edging her voice higher. "It is addressed to your bank manager. Perhaps you should give it to him. I have very little time"—she made an exaggerated glance at her wristwatch—"and we only have moments to spare."

"*Please*, Miss Montes. I'm required to thoroughly examine any large denominations. I'm *so sorry* for the delay and will get you out of here as soon as I possibly can." The teller held the paper euro under an ultraviolet light, squinted at it, and smiled at her customer. She went through the same process with a second and a third bill, and finally dug out a fourth from the bottom of the stack and examined it in the same way. Then she smiled up at Carmella, her eyes glazed. "Thank you for your patience."

"The letter for your manager?" Carmella pointed to the envelope sitting next to Jeremy's cash, all stacked safely behind the thick bulletproof glass. "It is of *utmost* importance."

The teller continued carefully counting and logging the thick bundles. "If I stop counting now I will need to begin over again. Thank you for your patience, Miss Montes."

"Call your manager over and give him that envelope *now*," Carmella snapped, "*if you please*."

The woman looked up at her with bulging eyes. Carefully, she placed the stacks of bills below the counter, stepped to the back of the restricted area, and handed the sealed envelope to a well-dressed, tawny-skinned man sitting behind a stately mahogany desk.

Carmella began drumming her perfect fingernails atop the counter.

A few moments later, the teller and the gentleman buzzed their way out from behind the security partition to approach her.

"Miss Montes, I am Mr. Garcia, the bank manager," the man said. "Would you mind coming with me?"

"Did you read the letter?" she pressed. Then she glanced around and saw that many of the bank's customers had stopped their interactions and were shooting her furtive looks; one young man near the exit was even holding up his cell phone to film the event.

"Of course." Mr. Garcia grinned thinly. "Will you please step into my office?"

"*If you do not attend to this matter immediately*—" she hissed, glaring at him.

"—the matter you speak of has already been addressed," Mr. Garcia assured her, placing a gentle hand on her elbow. "Please, come this way."

Carmella began walking alongside Mr. Garcia as an armed guard followed behind her. Another guard made his way toward the door, released his gun from its holster, pushed the door open, and crouched down.

::::::::

Outside the bank, upon seeing the crouching guard, Lazzaro slowly opened the rear door of the limo, got out, and began casually strolling down the street—just in time to face three police cars, lights twirling but no sirens wailing—skidding around the corner.

The cars careened to a stop and six police officers burst from the doors and kneeled upon the cobbled street, their pistols aimed at Lazzaro. "Βρίσκονται στο δρόμο, μίας! χέρια πίσω από το αντίγραφο ασφαλείας σας! Τώρα!" the closest one shouted.

Lazzaro whipped his head around and saw the bank's armed guard was likewise pointing his gun at him, elbows locked and poised.

He turned back to the police officers.

Then back toward to the armed guard.

"Τώρα! Τώρα! χέρια πίσω από το αντίγραφο ασφαλείας σας!" the officer warned once more.

A loud, cackling laugh high in the sky caused Lazzaro to look up.

There he saw the winged figure circling hawk-like on an updraft, her outstretched wings sweeping the air in a lazy circle above the trees.

Lazzaro did as he was told and lay down in the street with his hands behind his back, his mind whirling with questions and regrets.

At that moment Tristan got out from the driver's side of the limousine and strolled over to where the police officers were standing.

"Tristan!" Lazzaro shouted, eyes wide. "Do something! *Help me!*"

"Oh, Sasha, no," Tristan replied. "I have been waiting a long time for this."

:::::::::

Back in Ballena Beach, Jeremy and Arthur had just sat down to their meal of chicken parmesan and broccoli when Arthur's phone began buzzing atop the kitchen counter.

"I'll let it go to voice mail," Arthur told Jeremy, his fork poised above the steaming plate.

"But what if it's the doctor's office calling about your MRI tomorrow?"

Arthur groaned, put down his fork, got up from the table, snatched the contraption from the kitchen counter, and checked the caller ID. "Hey, Agent Singer!"

Arthur paused.

"No trouble, and yes I'm fine and so's Jeremy. Do you have any news?"

Jeremy studied Arthur as he tried to ascertain what was being discussed.

"Uh huh?"

Silence.

"Yes."

More silence.

"Really? Within the hour?"

A long drawn-out pause.

"Outstanding job," Arthur laughed into the phone. "Thanks so much for calling—and yes, of course Jeremy will be here too. We'll both be anxious to speak with them when they arrive."

At last Arthur ended the call and shot Jeremy a grin.

"It worked."

CHAPTER

forty-eight

"You'd better talk fast because I'm dying to know what happened," Jeremy yammered.

Arthur affected a bored expression. "I'm afraid this is all confidential. Top secret."

"*Arthuuuur?*"

"I can't say another word until they get here. Twenty minutes. OK?"

"Tell me!"

Arthur chuckled. "Just wait—and trust me. Please?"

"I guess I don't have a choice." Jeremy grumbled, shoulders slumped. "Let's eat."

:::::::::

Jeremy had just returned from taking the dogs outside and was refilling their water bowl when he heard a car roll to a stop in the driveway.

Two doors chunked.

Then the doorbell rang and Jeremy sprinted for it, arriving at the foyer even before Bingham or Skipper.

He pulled open the door and jerked backward.

Marilyn Monroe!?

Laughing, the woman peeled back the blonde wig with her left hand as she extended her right. "Please excuse my overly dramatic entrance, Mr. Tyler," she announced in her exotic contralto, shaking his hand, "but I could not resist. I am Carmella Montes. May we come in?"

"Of . . . um . . . c-course," Jeremy stammered, stepping aside while noticing for the first time the muscular, brown-haired and mustachioed man standing in back of her.

"Agent Singer," the man told Jeremy as he shook his hand and then followed Carmella inside. "Nice place."

"For a zombie apocalypse," Jeremy muttered as he shut the door, "which I suddenly feel ripe for . . ."

"Singer!" Arthur called out, marching toward their visitors.

"Blauefee, good to see you." The men met and clapped each other on the back. "Does Jeremy know anything?"

"The Pledge of Allegiance and how to make turkey wraps," Arthur shot Jeremy a wink, "but as to that other situation, I've kept my word."

Singer laughed. "*By the Book Blauefee*, that's what they used to call you."

"I'd almost forgotten." Arthur motioned to the leather sofa. "Have a seat. Can I get you anything?"

Bingham drew up to Carmella, sniffed her legs, and began whipping his tail back and forth as if reunited with a long, lost friend; Skipper, in the meantime, settled calmly on the floor at Singer's feet.

"Thank you, but we cannot stay long," Carmella replied, vigorously rubbing Bingham's head. "We are only in Los Angeles for a few-hours stopover, and then I have another flight to Mexico for a novella I am working on—and we are expecting another associate any minute; he arrived with us, but needed to stay back to rent a car."

Jeremy looked from Arthur to Carmella to Agent Singer and back to Arthur. "Will someone please tell me what the hell is going on?"

Carmella held up her hand. "I need to clear up something with Jeremy before another moment passes."

Jeremy squared a look at her. "Please do."

"When we were in the Plaka together," Carmella began, "Lazzaro forced me to tell you something so cruel that I nearly betrayed my mission. About your partner's health. Please know that I had no choice."

"I remember thinking afterward that you seemed kind of hesitant . . . that you were kind of, uh, stumbling on your words," Jeremy replied. "But what do you mean by *your mission*?"

"Before I tell you, do you accept my apology?"

"Sure. And your mission?"

Carmella and Agent Singer glanced at each other, and she nodded to him.

"Miss Montes," Agent Singer explained, leaning forward, "is not only an actress. She is also doing her best to abolish human trafficking—but stopping this involves the dangerous task of unmasking and putting away the criminals who profit from it."

Jeremy leaned against the doorway. "What does this have to do with Lazzaro?"

"In addition to distributing dangerous hallucinogens," Singer continued, "Lazzaro Sforza also directed a sex tourism ring operating in Eastern Europe—a ring developed and headed by his father, Francesco."

"Sex tourism?" Jeremy asked. "You mean where tourists pay for sex with . . . you know . . . ?"

"*Children*," Carmella finished indignantly, "who are taken from the orphanages and streets to make money for their pimps. I survived such an operation, so after I grew too old for their trade I became an actress, vowing to catch those who victimize these children. This is my mission."

"So the whole time you were talking to me in the Plaka, you were trying to catch Lazzaro?" Jeremy paused. "But you knew where he was already. Why didn't you just have him arrested?"

"Lazzaro was in fact living with me," Carmella replied. "But even more important than capturing him was gaining access to his worldwide contacts. He held this information very close until the morning I turned him over to Interpol."

"But he probably figured there would be surveillance at the Plaka," Arthur broke in. "How did you explain to him why you weren't taken into custody as an accomplice by the police who were there looking for him?"

"Fortunately for us, a riot broke out at a fascist squat close to the Plaka, so he believed all the police were engaged there; I even made up a story about Tristan inciting the riot to draw resources away from our meeting."

"How would you have explained it if the riot hadn't happened?" Jeremy asked.

"I was formulating ideas when I saw the flames," Carmella replied, smiling. "Sometimes an actress gets lucky and the theater burns down before she can confuse her lines."

Arthur settled himself upon a nearby barstool. "Tell us about Lazzaro's arrest."

Carmella reflexively reached for her cigarette case, caught herself, and then withdrew her hand from her purse. "I was afraid Lazzaro would vanish with the cash—with Jeremy's money—the first chance he had, before disclosing his associates to me. So I convinced him to put the euros toward a property we could buy specifically to keep him well out of sight, for years if need be."

The doorbell rang, and Arthur went to answer the door. "Go on," he said. "I can hear you."

"On the morning of this real estate transaction," Carmela continued, "I threatened him again with exposure if he did not disclose his contacts for me to conduct business with, and then once I had his contacts and my clandestine sources had verified them, we drove to the bank to deposit your cash, at which time I provided the bank manager with a note explaining our situation. He rang the silent alarm, the police arrived, and Lazzaro was arrested."

"You did all of this in one morning?" Jeremy asked.

"I had help," Carmella replied, "and I believe he just arrived."

They all turned to watch a handsome young man enter the foyer, an uneasy grin fixed upon his features.

"Gentlemen," Carmella said, "this is Tristan Lorca."

Tristan held up a hand and waved. "Hello."

At once Jeremy recognized Tristan's turquoise eyes. "You were driving that motorcycle!"

"As I told you on that day and I will say once again—"

"*I am sorry to do this to you*," Jeremy finished.

"So you remember."

"How could I forget?"

"Do you have his check?" Carmella asked.

Tristan slipped his hand into his jacket's pocket and pulled out an envelope, which he handed over to Jeremy. "I hope the exchange rate is favorable for you."

Jeremy took the envelope, unsealed it, examined the amount, and turned to Arthur. "My money!"

Arthur relaxed back into his barstool. "I've been holding my breath for weeks."

Jeremy turned to Tristan. "But I remember Lazzaro talking about you from when you were together years ago. Are you an agent too?"

"No," Tristan replied. "Lazzaro used me like he used you—but I had no idea until the police came to my home one day and seized my computer. After he moved to the United States, Lazzaro gained access to my files and applications by sending me an e-mail with a link that allowed him backdoor access once I clicked on it, and he was using my machine as a mule to run his sex trade and drug trafficking. He refused to text me, because only e-mails gave him the opportunity to invade my computer with fresh viruses.

"So once the police investigators verified that I was not part of his operations," Tristan continued, "Interpol offered to me the chance to trap Lazzaro. After waiting some time for him to contact me, which Interpol believed he was quite likely to do, I offered him a place to hide while pretending to love him and keep him safe; and Carmella was brought in to pose as my greedy mother who wanted a share in his filthy operations."

"You must be incredible actors to pull all of this off," Jeremy told them.

Tristan and Carmella gave each other knowing glances, and then turned back to the men. "The assignment was not without its challenges," Carmella said. "For us both."

"But what about your real mother?" Arthur asked Tristan. "Didn't Lazzaro ever meet her?"

"Sadly, she passed away from a very aggressive cancer after Lazzaro traveled here to the United States . . . but fortunately for us, he never had the chance to meet with her."

"I'm sorry to hear that," Jeremy told Tristan. "My friend Carlo lost his mother to cancer, too." Jeremy cocked his head. "You know, I hope you guys get the chance to meet each other; something tells me you'd hit it off."

"Oh yes?" Tristan replied, smiling.

"Speaking of using computers as mules," Agent Singer cut in, "I need to mention something to you, Jeremy—and to you, Arthur."

The men looked over at him.

"Lazzaro's digital fingerprints were found all through your computer, Jeremy, so he was utilizing yours during the entire time you lived together and even when he was hiding in Europe."

Jeremy considered this. "He used to send me links all the time . . . like to hotels in the Maldives and watches he thought I'd like."

"Those were probably the ones carrying the virus," Agent Singer confirmed, "and Arthur, it looks as if he gained access to yours as well."

"But my laptop's running perfectly."

"Unfortunately, we confirmed that your security was compromised," Singer assured him.

"That e-mail!" Jeremy exclaimed. "Over in Greece! *Remember?* You asked me about an e-mail and I said I never sent it to you! I've been trying to put that together ever since."

Arthur looked at him. "The one . . . about some seaside café?"

"He must've sent you the link, you clicked on it, seeing it was sent from my computer, and that gave him access to all your files!"

"Which is probably how . . . he knew *about my brain tumor* and even what I looked like. Son-of-a-bitch!"

"Son-of-a-bitch is right," Jeremy said. "And what pure evil! I mean, what kind of human being kills his father so he can get a bigger piece of the man's child molesting empire?"

"It can take a lot less than that to drive people to commit murder," Arthur noted quietly.

Carmella pushed herself up from the sofa. "I cannot say how wonderful it feels to close this chapter. But Agent Singer and I must be on our way; I am lucky to have had the layover to meet with you, if only for this short time. My mission is my passion, but my novellas pay my bills."

Jeremy turned to Tristan. "What about you? I heard you rented a car."

"My part in this is finished," Tristan replied, "so after I meet with your FBI tomorrow, I will be exploring Los Angeles for a few days. This is a much-needed holiday for me."

"By yourself?" Jeremy asked.

Tristan shrugged. "I know no one here, but that is fine. I am happy to explore on my own."

"Well, I don't know if *we're* happy about it," Jeremy said. "We happen to know someone who could show you the sights, like, the day after tomorrow—that is, if everything goes the way we hope."

Tristan smiled again. "This is your friend Carlo, I imagine?"

"It is indeed," Arthur said. "And you can stay here tonight if you'd like and meet him in the morning; he's coming by with another good friend to take me to the hospital. For tests."

"I would never wish to intrude," Tristan replied. "In any case I already have a hotel room reserved. The London in West Hollywood. But I will definitely look forward to meeting Carlo after tomorrow, when we do not have such important events to contend with."

Arthur took Jeremy's hand in his and laced their fingers together. "For a moment there I'd almost forgotten."

CHAPTER

forty-nine

At just before ten, Margo pulled into the parking lot of the Cedars-Sinai Cancer Center and surrendered her car to the valet.

The foursome marched through the sliding glass doors and stopped inside the reception area, where an elderly man fingered a Mozart sonata on the gleaming grand piano at the room's center, its crystalline notes filling the lobby's dizzying atrium like prayers rising to heaven.

"If only these dispensed vodka," Jeremy said, taking his turn at the automatic hand sanitizer dispenser mounted inside the doorway.

"Reminds me of the holy water receptacles in church." Carlo rubbed his slickened palms together before making the sign of the cross. "In the name of the Father, the Son—"

"*Mi Shebeirach avotienu v'imoteinu,*" Margo recited. "*Avraham Yitzchak v'Yaakov, Sarah, Rivkah, Rachel v'Lei-ah, huy'vareich et Arthur.* It goes on, but that's all I can remember."

"The Jewish Prayer for Healing," Arthur said, smiling. "I'm honored."

"We'll come get you both as soon as we can." Jeremy's hand reached for Arthur's. "Let's get this over with."

"We'll be here," Carlo said as Jeremy and Arthur began strolling toward the elevators.

Margo pointed to a pair of empty loveseats. "There."

:::::::::

On the next floor up, Jeremy and Arthur checked in at the radiology station—where a dozen scrubs-wearing nurses studied their computers or leaned, gabbing, against the tidy Formica desks—and then found a place to huddle together on a sofa, where they heard the PA system blast doctors' names amidst room numbers and mysterious codes.

Eventually a kind-faced attendant in pastel blue scrubs asked them, in his elegant Nigerian accent, to follow him down the hall.

:::::::::

After Arthur was led inside the room occupied by the time-machine-looking MRI, Jeremy wended his way back through the hallway—past patients rolling on gurneys and rooms beeping with lifesaving contraptions—to hunker down inside the waiting area.

He'd scanned, from back to front, one *Autoweek*, a *People*, and an ancient *Disney Adventures* children's magazine when a slim woman in her seventies or eighties, wearing a black crepe dress, red-velvet cape, and matching beret, leaned her head inside the room.

She smiled at Jeremy, displaying tulip-red lips. "May I join you?"

Jeremy scanned her outfit again, wondering why she was dressed so outlandishly this early in the day. *Probably some old actress.* "Sure."

She entered the room—her black stilettos stepping noiselessly—and made her way to the opposing loveseat. "I was passing by and couldn't help but notice you; you're the very image of someone I once knew." Her eyes appraised him. "Family?"

"Partner."

She placed the oversized alligator-skin bag she was carrying on the seat cushion next to her. "Nothing tries the spirit as much as cancer. How fitting that it's represented in the zodiac by a crab."

"Why is that?"

"The Latin word for *crab* is *cancer*, pronounced *kahnker*, and I suppose there are justifiable parallels between the tenacious nature of the disease and the animal's dangerous pincers and seemingly impenetrable shell—not to mention its ability to crawl in directions one can never anticipate: forward, sideways, back, and in circles."

"I never thought of that."

The woman held out her hand. "Friends call me Audrey."

"Jeremy." He reached over and shook it. "I've always loved the name Audrey. Is it French? It's beautiful."

"Actually, my birth name is unpronounceable to most Americans, hence the simpler *Audrey*. My mother was from the Greek countryside; peasant stock with unrealized theatrical ambitions."

"That's a coincidence," Jeremy said. "We were just in Greece last month."

Audrey settled back into her seat and opened her purse. "I presume you saw Mykonos."

"Just Athens; that's all we had time for. Unfortunately, Arthur—my partner—got sick and we had to come back early for tests."

"I'm sorry you didn't have time to explore the islands, or even the countryside. Athens can be such an unappealing city these days—the riots and the traffic and the congestion and the graffiti—not at all like when I was young." Audrey withdrew several skeins of fine, rainbow-hued threads from her purse and placed them in her lap, along with a small tapestry.

"Is that embroidery?" Jeremy asked. "Those colors are so pretty."

"Thank you. My sister makes these especially for me."

"What are you embroidering?"

She began threading a golden needle. "A gift for a friend. And this one's nearly finished."

"Can I see it?"

"Oh, no one ever sees these until the last knot is tied." Audrey chuckled. "Did you at least visit the museum near the Acropolis? Their statuary is *astounding*; their collection from the fourth century BC is particularly sublime."

"No, we only got to see the Parthenon, the Plaka, and Hadrian's Gate. Oh, and the Gate of Athena."

"That's a good start. How long have you and your partner been together?"

"Not long enough," Jeremy replied, thinking, *in this lifetime*. "Are you visiting someone?"

"Actually, I'm a volunteer making my morning rounds."

"I can't imagine ever volunteering in a place like this. Too depressing."

She made a broad gesture with her hands. "Hence, my outlandish couture."

"I think you look fantastic; I thought you were a movie star."

"And I took you for a kind-hearted young man, which means one of us is a good judge of character."

"How long've you been doing this work?"

"Seems like forever." She fiddled with her threads. "I'm quite well-known in these halls—and I say this with all humility."

"Are you supposed to be seeing someone right now, cheering them up?"

"That's exactly what I'm attempting to do."

Jeremy laughed. "You don't have to do that for me. I'm sure there's someone else here who's a lot more depressed." Then he suddenly remembered the session yesterday with Dr. Studski and the karmic implications of the recollections brought to light. *It's my turn to mourn.*

"Your face . . . you looked so sad just now," she said. "Would you like to talk about it? I always keep everything in strictest confidence." Audrey leaned toward him. "Actually," she whispered, "now that I'm so old, I can't seem to remember even the most scandalous stories."

Jeremy looked down at his watch, and his hands began working at nothing. "I'm OK."

"May I ask what is ailing your partner?"

He glanced up at her. "Brain tumor."

"Prognosis?"

"Too soon to tell, but this is his second one, so things don't look great."

Audrey shook her head. "I've often wondered why such things exist."

"Me too."

He watched as Audrey began working the pattern, her deft fingers alternately poking the needle through the fabric and pulling the vivid purple thread taut. "I believe I'm just about finished with this color," she muttered while withdrawing a pair of rusty iron shears from her bag, then looked up at him with a smile. "Do you imagine he's ready?"

"Arthur's too strong and stubborn to let this disease kill him," Jeremy said. "And I'll be damned if I'll sit around feeling sorry—oh, I'm not sure . . . what you mean."

Audrey looked aghast. "I was referring to his being finished with the MRI. But now that you mention it, how are you dealing with all this?"

Jeremy sat up straighter. "I just need him to get better—but if it doesn't go the way we hope, I'll handle everything right up to the end. It's my turn this time."

Audrey looked surprised. "You know about this?"

Jeremy scrutinized her, eyebrows furrowed. "What do you mean, *do I know about this?* How would you know what I'm talking about?"

A flustered expression flickered across her face. "I was merely asking . . . if you've had . . . training in nursing or rehabilitation or palliative care. You seem so young, but then, everyone seems so young these days."

Jeremy relaxed. "What I mean is it's my turn to care for him, at least in the best way I can, because I *don't* have any training. Arthur's done it for me before—cared for me over and over when I've needed it, and now it's my turn. I owe him."

"So you are ready and willing to repay your debt to him?"

"I'm *more* than ready and willing. Actually, I can't wait to do whatever he needs me to."

Audrey carefully placed her tapestry and shears and skeins back inside her bag. "One would think I'd be better at this; I've been doing it so long—perhaps too long. Jeremy, I've just remembered another visit I was scheduled to make." She stood up quickly, gracefully, grasping her bag. "I do hope all goes well with your Arthur. I'll be thinking of you both." She stepped noiselessly to the doorway and turned, giving her cape a tiny furl. "And remember, even if your fate seems carved in stone, if you search hard enough you can usually find a chisel."

"I'd be happier with a nutcracker."

"A nutcracker?"

"Isn't that what they use on crabs?"

She smiled. "Clever boy."

Then she was gone.

Jeremy sat for the next few minutes replaying their conversation in his mind, when a young Filipino woman in mint green scrubs rounded the corner. "Mr. Tyler?"

"Yes."

"They're ready for you now."

CHAPTER

fifty

Jeremy was ushered through the doorway, where he found Arthur wearing his paper robe and sitting in a chair, his shoulders slumped and his head down. Dr. MacTavish was standing next to him, a comforting hand on his shoulder.

Arthur slowly lifted his head and their eyes met.

Immediately Jeremy felt the air go out of him. *God, no. God, no. God, NO!* He gulped, his mind racing to find the right words to say. "Arthur?" he croaked.

"We've got some talking to do, old buddy."

Jeremy glanced from Arthur to Dr. MacTavish and back to Arthur. "It's still there?"

"Yep." Arthur nodded as his mouth bent into a half-smile. "And it's bigger now."

"What . . . what are the options?"

"That's what we need to talk about." Arthur held out his hand. "Please, baby, sit down."

Jeremy stumbled to a nearby chair and sat, looking expectantly at Dr. MacTavish.

"The chemo and radiation haven't stabilized the tumor," she explained. "It's only grown slightly, but this shows that our current course of treatment isn't aggressive enough. And to make matters worse, its proximity to and pressure upon the optic nerve explains Arthur's problems with his vision."

"The broken vase," Arthur clarified.

"Won't stronger chemo and radiation work?"

"It might. But I'm afraid that if we don't opt for surgery now we might be facing another tumor or two down the road. The good news is that right now we are only dealing with one, but the difficulty lies in its location—it's a tough place to reach. If you decide on surgery there's a chance we could get it all, but there's also the chance that Arthur could 'stroke out' on the table, meaning he could suffer paralysis or blindness or memory loss, or worse."

"She means I could die," Arthur stated flatly.

"And what if he doesn't have the surgery?"

Dr. MacTavish began fiddling with the stethoscope around her neck. "One never knows, but in cases like these we usually see some significant deterioration after other tumors begin appearing. Most likely he will have about three to six months before his cognitive and motor functions are significantly affected, and then after that another three to four months until we begin exploring options for palliative care."

"Less than a year, old buddy," Arthur said.

Jeremy squeezed his eyes shut, swallowing hard. "I . . . uh . . ." He dropped his face into his hands and rubbed his eyes. But then the experience with Dr. Studski came back to him. *It's my turn to mourn.* He looked up. "Arthur and I need to talk about this. Will you give us some time?"

Dr. MacTavish nodded. "All the time you need. You can go home and think about it overnight and let me know in the morning. If you decide to go forward with surgery it'll take me a day or two to assemble the surgical team."

Jeremy and Arthur looked into each other's eyes and they both knew.

"When's the soonest I can have the surgery?" Arthur asked.

Dr. MacTavish looked from one to the other. "Let me make some calls, but I may even be able to arrange it for tomorrow. You'd have to stay here overnight though; prep is pretty extensive."

"Could we go out for a couple of hours and come back?" Jeremy asked, standing up.

"I don't see why not."

"Let's get you dressed," Jeremy said to Arthur as he helped him up from the chair. "We've got no time to waste."

:::::::::

Margo made a fast right out of the parking lot, and only because she floored the powerful Bentley did they make the left-turn arrow at La Cienega. Then the foursome sped north to Santa Monica Boulevard and made a left toward the Beverly Hills Civic Center and the courthouse.

After about fifteen minutes, a beaming Arthur and Jeremy were issued what they needed.

An hour later the foursome, along with Bingham and Skipper, Aunt Katharine, Reed and Sebastian—who'd arrived bearing several bottles of champagne and sparkling cider, and a dozen white-frosting-with-sprinkles-atop-red-velvet cupcakes from Vons—gathered in the gazebo at the Tyler Compound, where Jeremy's parents Tiffany and Jonathan had been married twenty-five years earlier.

And as the sun peaked over the sparkling Pacific, the ceremony started.

"Dear family," Sebastian began, "I'll keep this short, because these men have someplace important to be. But there are a couple of points I want to make before we see these two wed.

"There are forces in the universe we probably won't ever understand. Because we can't. We're too dumb, because God made us that way. Some of us are smart about certain things—building jets and skyscrapers and atomic weapons—but when it comes to creation and mysterious forces, we need to rely on intuition and faith.

"We think science is amazing because of how far technology has advanced our lives, but can even our most advanced technology create an eyeball? An insect? A tree? A sunset? How about a planet teeming with life?

"Through the ages, so much has stupefied man. Up until recently, we attributed the change of seasons to the kidnapping of Persephone by Hades, and the sorrow of her mother Ceres, goddess of the harvest. But for some time now we've understood that the earth wobbles as it travels around the sun. Likewise, some years from now we'll have a better understanding of other things that dumbfound and confuse even the brightest, most educated minds of our time.

"What I'm saying is sometimes we need to trust the universe instead of coming up with the wrong answer for something we're incapable of understanding. Like love . . . and how two people who are so perfectly matched wind up finding each other amongst the billions of humans inhabiting our mysterious planet.

"Two such people are Jeremy and Arthur. Lovers who are friends. And like the sturdy stem of a flower that supports its fragrant petals, their friendship enables their love to bloom.

"Arthur, you are about to embark on a walk along an unlighted road, but Jeremy—as well as each of us—will be walking behind you. We will be hoping and praying, watching each minute pass until we know you've reached safe shelter.

"Today I ask who gives away this man, Jeremy Jonathan Tyler, for marriage."

Carlo raised his hand. "I hate to, but I will."

"And who gives away this man, Arthur Francis Blauefee, for marriage?"

Margo dabbed a Kleenex to her nose. "It is my joy to do so."

"And now I'd like to give you the opportunity to express your feelings toward each other. Jeremy?"

Jeremy took Arthur's hands. "Arthur, I have loved you since the moment I saw you." He cleared his throat, gathering himself. He would *not* break down. "You are everything that embodies a noble man; and I know you see me as my better self—even on my worst days. I will love you, comfort you and support you, and I'll never take you for granted." He beamed at Arthur. "Your turn."

"Jeremy—" Arthur cleared his throat, too, and the two of them laughed. "Jeremy, I have loved you since the moment I laid eyes on you. And there hasn't been a day when I haven't been steadfast in my love, whether we were together or not. If I die tomorrow I will do so as a happy man, knowing I've managed to make right the greatest wrong of my life by bringing us back together. You are my one true love, Jeremy Tyler, and my spirit will ache to be with you until we are united again, whether it's in heaven or in some other lifetime. And wherever I am when I look into your eyes again—tomorrow when I awaken or two thousand years from now—it'll take me only half a heartbeat to recognize you. You have been my lover and my very best friend, and it is my duty and my joy to walk through life by your side."

The men turned to face Sebastian.

"May we have the rings?" Sebastian asked.

Margo handed over one gold ring to Arthur, and Carlo gave the other to Jeremy (and Aunt Katharine passed her handkerchief to Reed).

Arthur slid the ring onto Jeremy's finger. "I take you, Jeremy, as my husband."

Jeremy pushed the other ring onto Arthur's finger. "I take you, Arthur, as my husband."

Sebastian faced the gathering. "Jeremy and Arthur are now married."

Amidst a small chorus of tearful cheers the men came together and held their embrace—held it for so long, with Jeremy's face pressed into Arthur's shoulder—before becoming enveloped by the loving, protective arms of their family and friends.

CHAPTER

fifty-one

It's called *Intraoperative brain mapping,*" Dr. MacTavish told Arthur, after they had returned to the hospital and checked in late that same afternoon, "which means you'll be semiconscious during the surgery. The anesthesiologists will be carefully monitoring your level of sedation and will bring you out of it as we proceed to test how your cognitive and motor functions are being affected by the procedure."

"Sounds gruesome," Arthur said. "So this will be at what time tomorrow?"

"You'll go into prep at about five in the morning, and then we'll begin the procedure sometime after eight. How long it takes is anyone's guess, but by this time tomorrow you should be in recovery."

"Can I sleep here in his room?" Jeremy asked. "It's our honeymoon night."

Dr. MacTavish beamed. "*Congratulations.* Of course we can make sure you'll have a bed—but I can't guarantee you'll be comfortable."

"Couldn't care less," Jeremy told her.

"Is there anything I can get you in the meantime?"

Jeremy and Arthur looked at each other.

"We already threw everything in a bag we thought we might be needing," Jeremy replied.

"Then just buzz the nurse if something comes up. I'll be leaving after I finish my rounds, but I'll see you both first thing tomorrow."

Jeremy and Arthur thanked the doctor, and then spent the rest of the day and evening talking about everything that came to mind, eating their surprisingly delicious dinners, all the while watching the hands on the clock slowly inch toward bedtime.

Then just after nine Jeremy climbed into Arthur's hospital bed.

"Where should we take our real honeymoon?" Jeremy murmured.

"Where would you like to go?"

"No. You pick."

Arthur considered Jeremy's question. "Fresno."

"Oh, come on."

"No, I mean it. I'd like to see that apartment where you grew up and maybe even meet Mrs. Jackson, then we could drive over to your old high school; there's this whole part of your life I've heard of but have never seen."

"OK then." Jeremy rested his left hand atop Arthur's chest, admiring the way his simple gold band caught the light. "When we get back from somewhere really cool, we can stop off in Fresno. But where have you always wanted to go?"

"Honestly?" Arthur paused. "I'd really like to go back to Greece."

"No."

"Yeah."

"Why?"

"I know it's probably the very last place on your list," Arthur guessed, "but I still have this vision of the two of us standing on a cliff's edge looking out over the Aegean. I have this . . . *craving* to stand on that cliff, holding you in my arms and contemplating our lives and the joys of being together and what's happened in the past and what might come our way in the future. It's something that's gnawed at me for a while, and there's this picture I can't get out of my head."

"Then Greece it is—and I never thought I'd say that. But I'm curious: Why not Italy? Wouldn't you like to go see Hadrian's Villa?"

"I wouldn't mind stopping there on the way back, just to see if I 'feel' anything—*which most likely I won't*—but there's something that fires me up when I think of Greece."

"Then Greece it is," he said again. "Anywhere in particular?"

"Mykonos is supposed to be fantastic."

"That's funny." Jeremy peered into Arthur's eyes. "This strange woman in the waiting room today asked if we'd seen Mykonos on our trip to Greece."

"That's no surprise: Mykonos is gayer than a Kylie Minogue concert."

Jeremy laughed. "OK then. We could stay there and then maybe go to Turkey afterward. I love those Turkish wrestlers . . . all muscular and oily, grappling and straining against each other. What's not to like?"

"I thought we were talking about Mykonos." Arthur kissed Jeremy's cheek. "So why was this woman so strange?"

"She was old, and she wore drag queen makeup and was dressed like she'd spent the night at the opera—a black dress and a red cape and a beret—and as soon as she sat down next to me she started embroidering a tapestry."

"Was she also waiting for someone?"

"Said she was volunteering, making her rounds and cheering up people, and she grew up in Athens."

"Seems like all roads lead there lately," Arthur told him, stifling a yawn.

Jeremy turned onto his back, nestling into the crook of Arthur's arm. "I'll start researching flights and cruises as soon as we get home."

"That sounds *so* nice." Arthur was silent for a while as he rewound his thoughts. Finally he gently elbowed Jeremy. "Hey."

"Hay is for horses," Jeremy whispered.

"Are you going to be OK?"

"Don't worry about me. Just get yourself better. OK?"

Arthur yawned again. "OK."

Jeremy rested his head on Arthur's chest. "And you know what else I'd like to do when this is over?"

Arthur didn't answer.

Jeremy looked up and saw Arthur was sleeping, his eyes closed and a smile fixed upon his lips.

"I love you, old buddy," Jeremy whispered, and then lay awake for the next few hours memorizing the steady music of Arthur's heartbeat and breathing.

CHAPTER

fifty-two

The anesthesiologist's face hovered over Arthur.

"Mr. Blauefee, we're going to administer the anesthetic in your IV, and while we do this I want you to count backward from ten."

"OK. And call me Arthur." *Thank God for drugs.* "Ten . . . nine . . . eight . . . hey, this feels like two martinis . . . six . . . . five . . . ." A great sigh escaped him.

Peace.

His eyes rolled up in his head.

Flying. Flying over water. Or something blue. Blue air. Shimmering. I'm flying with the wind on blue air.

Haphazard images began flashing before him in a random slide show: A familiar house he'd never seen before—stairway—young woman's stern face—old man—paneled study with rain pouring outside the windows.

Arthur felt himself spinning and falling and flying, but he didn't feel frightened.

This is all a part of it.

Then he began trying to examine the details of the images as they flashed: he caught sight of a hairstyle and a shoe and a car from the 1940s . . . then some little boy kicking a ball across a yard. And a dog that looked just like Bingham that wasn't Bingham.

He fell further and further and the light faded and suddenly he couldn't see anything.

For some reason I'm not afraid.

Then it all stopped.

:::::::::

The sound of running feet atop the barque's wooden deck startled him from his writing. He looked up to see the young man standing in the doorway of his quarter, his naked chest heaving and his face streaked with tears. *What now?*

"My emperor!" Corydon shouted. "Something's happened! Please, please come with me!"

Hadrian could see that the young man was terrified. "What is it?"

"Please, I . . . can't say. *Something terrible.*"

Corydon turned and sprinted away, so Hadrian got up from his chair and began hurrying toward the door.

The Egyptian sun blinded him momentarily as he squinted out from within the boat's cabin. Then he could see a group of men standing in a circle around something on the deck. One of the men turned and, upon seeing him, barked an order to the other men, who gathered more closely around whatever they were guarding.

Instinctively Hadrian looked around. *Where is my Antinous?*

One of the men broke free from the huddle and began walking toward him, head down.

"What has happened?" Hadrian demanded.

The man looked up at him. "I regret to be the one to tell you this, my emperor, but there appears to have been an unforeseeable tragedy."

"Has one of my court taken ill?"

"I only wish it were so," the man replied, his eyes showing both panic and anguish.

Antinous? Hadrian's patience evaporated. "Clear away!" he shouted, and began marching heavy-footed toward the prow of the barque.

What met his eyes stopped his heart.

Naked and sobbing, Lucius crouched over Antinous.

Antinous. Unmoving.

"Get away from him!" Hadrian shouted as he sprinted for the young man. "Where are my physicians?! *Where are my physicians?!*"

Hadrian pushed Lucius away from his beloved and fell to his side, shaking his limp body and cradling his head.

"Antinous? *Antinous?!*"

He lifted the limp form into a sitting position, but the beautiful corpse only slumped over. Hadrian sat behind him, his arms hugging his torso, his head on his shoulder. "You cannot leave me! Don't do this! What has happened? *Come back to me!*"

Then the reality of his loss slugged him in the stomach.

"Who did this?!" Hadrian bellowed, looking around at the silent faces. *"Whoever did this will pay with his life!"*

There was no sound but the lapping of water upon the sides of the boat, and the soft sobs of Corydon.

"He . . . he drowned himself in the Nile, my emperor," Lucius whispered at last. "He did this for you."

"You speak nonsense!" Hadrian shouted.

Lucius looked at Hadrian, his sobs beginning again. "The words . . . that came from his lips . . . he said this to me: *I sacrifice myself so the emperor might live a longer life.*"

Hadrian looked around, wild-eyed, his breathing unsteady. "What did you say?"

Lucius sat back on his haunches, his arms hugging his knees. Then he drew a forearm across his face. "It just happened, my emperor."

"Tell me . . ." Hadrian looked down, trying to regain some semblance of composure. "Tell me from the beginning."

"Antinous told me . . . he desired a swim to escape the heat. We were only in the water a short time when he said the words, *I sacrifice myself so the emperor might live a longer life.* I heard the words from his own lips, I swear it! And I did my best, after he sank under the water I lifted him up and kissed him so relieved was I to see him, but then he said the words once more and sank himself like a bag of stones."

Hadrian eyed Lucius suspiciously. "What were the words again?"

Lucius breathed deeply. "Antinous said—and may Isis and Osiris and Zeus and Hades himself take the breath from my body at this moment if I am lying—Antinous said, *I sacrifice myself so the emperor might live a longer life.*"

Hadrian's head dropped onto his chest. "He did this . . . to save me?"

"The string spun by Clotho and allotted to Antinous by Lachesis is now knotted to your own. Atropos with her shears will not come for you yet. His remaining years are yours."

Hadrian fell back onto the wet, wooden planks of the deck and then slowly pushed himself up. Then he bent down and lifted the lifeless body of his beloved by the arms and hefted him over his shoulder, a soldier carrying his comrade off the battlefield.

Slowly Hadrian trudged to their royal quarters—his retinue following at a distance—and lay the body of Antinous of Bithynia, the emperor's favorite intimate companion, soon to have been his adopted son and one day Emperor of Rome, atop their bed.

Gently, Hadrian covered the young man's nakedness with his royal purple cloak.

He looked up and saw the faces of his court at the door.

"Leave us be," Hadrian groaned.

The heavy cloth was drawn closed over the door.

Hadrian stumbled over to the side of the bed and sat upon a stool—the same stool where Antinous had sat that very morning, lacing his sandals.

The world will never forget you, my beloved. I promise this.

And as he stroked the cold cheek that had only this morning been so warm and beckoning, he began to wail.

He prayed they could hear him atop Olympus.

:::::::::

As the sky dimmed that evening Hadrian prepared his scrolls and inks, and then stared at the blank white papyrus for what seemed an eternity.

Finally, as night fell and Corydon brought him a candle and some wine, Hadrian dipped the quill into the ink and began to write: *Today Antinous fell into the Nile.*

Those were the only words he could scratch before he felt himself rushing through the wind again.

It's happening.

Arthur detected light beyond his closed eyelids, and he heard some machines clicking and beeping and hissing.

"Mr. Blaufee?"

At once he realized where he was: *Operating room.*

"If you can you hear me, Mr. Blauefee, please say something."

Arthur tried, but found he couldn't speak.

"Mr. Blauefee, if you can hear me, please say something. Can you open your eyes?"

Arthur did his best but could do neither. His mind felt wide-awake, yet his body slept on. *I'm wide-asleep.*

He heard more voices, and some rustling in the room.

"His brain waves indicate he's awake," another voice said.

"Something's gone wrong."

"Mr. Blauefee, Arthur," the first voice asked, "can you move your hands or your feet?"

Arthur discovered he could not.

He drifted into blackness. *Perfect blackness.*

Moments later he heard someone calling his name.

:::::::::

"Captain Finnegan?"

CHAPTER

fifty-three

"Captain Finnegan? Sorry to disturb you, sir."

He looked up from his field desk inside the tent, his eyes burning and his head aching from the smoke curling up from the lantern in front of him. Winter was waning and the sun was rising behind the eastern mountain ridge a little earlier each day. *Dear Lord, let this war end before another summer comes.* "Yes, Private Montgomery?"

The black-haired man saluted him, and Arthur saluted him back.

"Hatcher's Run has fallen to the Union forces."

He closed his eyes, nodding. "As we expected."

"When do you imagine we will move on?"

"Whenever we receive our orders, if there is anyone left to issue them."

"Sir, have you had your supper?"

"Supper?" He laughed. "Last I was told, we have no more supplies. And there can't be a squirrel or even a rat stupid enough to come within ten miles of us."

"I am happy to tell you that the men discovered a farmhouse with provisions in the cellar. As famished as they are, they saved some for you."

"Tell the men they should fill their bellies first, and I'll eat whatever is left—if there is anything."

"As you wish, sir."

"Any sign of our missing soldiers?"

"Not yet, sir. But we will alert you as soon as we hear anything." Private Montgomery paused for a moment. "And there's been no word of Private Murray."

He only nodded, as though Jeremiah Murray were no more important than any other soldier to the Confederate Army. Though young Jeremiah was, of course, of utmost importance *to him*.

"Thank you, Private."

"Of course, sir. I'll let you know when the men have finished their meal."

As the man ducked out from under the tent flap and then trudged away in the mud, Finnegan removed his spectacles, lowered his head, and massaged his temples.

Where could he be?

Jeremiah had vanished four days ago, clearly deserting his post and leaving no indication of his destination. And ever since, the captain had been scrutinizing casualty reports for anyone who matched his description . . . unconsciously holding his breath while reading the names of the dead from the papers presented to him each morning as the first birds of the day chirped and warbled.

Finnegan refocused on the report he was completing, dipped his quill into the inkpot, and resumed the sentence he'd been writing before the interruption.

He heard some footsteps approaching his tent, and a few moments later looked up to see half a dozen of his men standing at the opening, with Private Montgomery in their center.

One stepped out from behind Montgomery and handed over a plate heaped with salt pork, apple preserves, and roasted turnips. "If ya' don't eat it, we're throwin' it over the wall to the Yankee prisoners," the gaunt man told him. "Please, Cap'n, your wife won't recognize ya' when ya' get home."

He smiled and nodded. "All right. Thank you, men."

"Our pleasure, Cap'n," they replied in unison.

He reached out and took the plate. The food was warm and artfully arranged, and the plate itself was translucent bone china with filigreed gold edges. Clearly, his men had gone to some trouble to present him with this meal.

"Oh," another said, stepping forward. "Almost forgot." He placed a large linen napkin and a sterling silver place setting before him. "People must've left in a hurry; silver's worth nearly much as gold these days, but not worth more'n a loaf of stale bread." He laughed.

He looked up and swallowed hard, touched not only by his men's kindness but how homesick the delicate meal made him feel for his wife and children. "Thank you, gentlemen," he managed to say. "When this is all over, I hope you will join me and my family in Charleston."

The men looked at each other, nodding.

"Oh, we'd enjoy that, Cap'n."

"Yes we would, Cap'n"

"Now enjoy your supper, Cap'n."

The men backed out of the tent's entrance to leave him alone.

As he ate, his mind went back to Jeremiah: The young man was bright, mischievous, and angry, with furtive dark eyes and a lightning-quick smile. He'd stood out from the other recruits like a young thoroughbred amidst a corral of mules, and Finnegan found himself seeking out Jeremiah's company and taking pleasure in watching him go about his daily tasks.

There was something about the way Jeremiah moved that struck a chord deep within him. His frame was well-proportioned and amply muscled for a young man of eighteen years, and his hands were constantly attempting to tie a knot or whittle a length of pine or polish this or pick at that. He could tell Jeremiah had a fine mind and was in need of something—*anything*—to break the monotony of this goddamn war.

So Finnegan had taken him under his wing: teaching Jeremiah how to tie a bowline and a square knot and a sheet bend and a clove hitch, all of which he'd mastered with remarkable alacrity; the only knot that consistently flummoxed him was the blasted taut-line. He'd also taken Jeremiah out squirrel hunting one day and found the young man could shoot like a trained sniper. And after bagging themselves half a dozen, they headed back to camp.

Then one day Jeremiah came trotting into camp with a spaniel mix he'd found wandering in the woods. He'd fashioned a lead out of some discarded rope, and he paraded that skinny, black-furred mongrel around as if it were a King Charles. Over the next two weeks Jeremiah saved part of each scant meal for the beast, and within a day or two discarded the rope lead because there was no need to use it anymore; that dog—he named him General Lee—followed Jeremiah around as if he were the only man in camp.

"Why'd you name him General Lee?" one man asked him.

"'Cause he's *general-ly* better company than y'all," Jeremiah answered, laughing.

"Sure is a funny sight, seein' General Lee wandering around camp naked as a jaybird," another yelled out. "What you do with his uniform, now?"

"Traveler got jealous and stole it," Jeremiah shot back. "But the pants are too small, so we're expecting to get 'em back soon." He tipped his hat. "We thank y'all for your concern."

Then one day, Jeremiah sought out his captain, his brow darkened, with General Lee panting happily by his side.

"Excuse me, Cap'n."

He felt himself warm at the sight of the young man. "Yes, Private?"

"May I speak with you, sir?"

"What's troubling you?"

"Sir, it's that dandy, Private Sousa. He keeps jokin' about eatin' my dog, sir, that it's a treat up at Andersonville and where can he get some mint jelly. But now I hear he's more than jokin'. I believe I'll kill him if he tries it, sir."

"Corporal Sousa is infamous for making idle threats. I'd pay him no mind."

Jeremiah reached down and patted the dog's side. "Yes sir, but Private Montgomery says Sousa found himself a rope a few days back. Says it's already looped and knotted at the end to throw over the General's neck."

"I hate to remind you, but having this dog as your pet is a violation of this army's rules. What if he contracted rabies or bit one of the men?"

"Everyone knows General Lee don't got rabies," Jeremiah answered sullenly. "And he don't got a mean bone in his body. The only one I ever seen him come at was Sousa; he was barkin' at him the other day like a hound dog treein' a grizzly."

"Look." He placed a hand on Jeremiah's shoulder. "What you're doing here with your dog is understandable, but you've got to know you're asking for trouble. What do you plan to do with him? You can't keep him here forever."

"Ain't got no plans," Jeremiah grumbled. "Might as well be dead, him and me. Then they can feed us both to them Yanks—mint jelly an' all."

He stifled the impulse to pull Jeremiah into a comforting embrace, and instead gave his strong shoulder a fatherly squeeze. "Young man, I don't know what to tell you. You just do your best to keep this hound safe"—he reached down and scratched the dog behind his ears—"and let me know should you hear anything else."

"Thank you, sir," Jeremiah said. "Sorry to bother you." He turned and marched away, with General Lee trotting happily at his heels.

:::::::::

The next morning Jeremiah and General Lee were gone.

"The night watch shot at someone last night," Montgomery quietly advised him. "Don't know if it was a Union spy or Private Murray, but we know he was hit. Found ants crawlin' in some fresh blood in the dirt. Happened plenty after midnight; dead a' night, in fact."

Finnegan's chest tightened as he recalled being awakened by the rifle crack. "Thank you."

Four days later he was worrying, once again, over their scant rations when he spotted a trio approaching—a pair carrying a stretcher with a blanket-covered heap atop it, and Private Montgomery, leading General Lee on a rope.

No! No, no no!

The men placed the stretcher on the ground as General Lee bounded toward him.

He kneeled down and massaged the dog's head and snout. Then he looked up. "Private Murray?" he asked, his voice somber.

Montgomery nodded solemnly. "Found him underneath an oak. Looked like he took a ball in the leg a few days back and then died trying to cut off—"

Finnegan squeezed his eyes shut and held up his hand. "Where was this dog?"

"Guardin' him, sir, growlin' at us like a mama lion guardin' her cubs. We had to crawl toward the private's body, whistlin' and callin' the General's name for better'n an hour."

"Good boy," Arthur praised the happy, panting creature, patting his side. "The other General Lee would be proud of you."

:::::::::

At once Arthur felt his consciousness rising, as if he'd been deep underwater for too long and needed to surface for a heavy gulp of air.

:::::::::

"Mr. Tyler?"

Jeremy startled up from checking his iPhone. "Yes? Is . . . he OK?"

"The doctor would like to speak with you. Will you please follow me?"

Jeremy's heart thumped in his chest. "*Is he OK?*"

"He's in recovery; Dr. MacTavish will fill you in."

Jeremy looked over at Margo and Carlo, dozing on the couches, then got up to follow the nurse. After hurrying down the hall, he was buzzed through two consecutive pairs of doors and then entered a private room.

Arthur was propped up in bed, his head wrapped in gauze and his eyes closed.

Jeremy's breath caught. *He looks so pale!*

Dr. MacTavish stood next to Arthur while examining an assortment of monitors that looked as if they'd been taken from the space shuttle.

She turned to him as he entered. "So far so good."

"Did . . . you get it all?"

"We did everything possible, but only time will tell. He gave us a scare, but Arthur proved that he's still a Marine."

"What do you mean?"

"He's still a warrior. At one point we couldn't get him to wake during the procedure, but it could have been his body's reaction to the anesthesia—or something we're not aware of . . . *yet.* But his vital signs are good."

"OK." Jeremy tapped his foot. "When will you know something?"

"After he awakens we'll conduct a series of neurological tests."

"Can I stay here with him?"

"Of course."

Jeremy went to the chair and sat. "Could you send word to my friends that everything's OK so far? They're outside on the sofas; a pretty blonde lady napping next to a good-looking shorter guy."

"I'll do that myself, right now. Is there anything I can get you?"

Jeremy looked at her. "I can't think of anything."

"Please buzz the nurse's station if there's any change."

Jeremy gave her a nod, and went back to staring at Arthur.

Then after the doctor left the room, Jeremy began stroking his chest. "I don't care if you were Hadrian or some broken-down farmer from Alabama," he whispered. "And I don't care if we've had a thousand lives together or will have a thousand more; all I care about is this lifetime here and now, and having you by my side."

Eventually, Jeremy's legs got tired of standing and his feet hurt, so he went over to the chair and sat.

His eyelids drooped and he fell asleep.

:::::::::

"Jeremiah?"

Jeremy jolted awake. "Arthur?" *Jeremiah?* Jeremy got up from his chair and went to his side. "I'm right here. What's happening?"

Arthur paused, blinking, looking up at him as if he didn't know who he was. "Tired," he said. "So tired." Then he appeared to recognize Jeremy, and smiled weakly. "I just had . . ." He faded off.

"*What?*" Jeremy asked. "Are you hurting? Is there some new pain?"

"No, baby. I just had this . . . weird dream. But now I . . . can't remember . . . any of it."

Jeremy relaxed. "That's understandable, considering you're on morphine, and half-a-dozen people just finished digging inside your head with forks and screwdrivers." He squeezed his hand. "I'm so glad to see you talking! I've got to go get the doctor to let her know you're awake."

"OK, old buddy."

"Oh—God it's so good to see you, Arthur. I missed you, even if you were right here, I missed you so much."

Arthur smiled. "Go get the doctor and we can talk later."

As he watched Jeremy scamper out of the room, an object on the sheets next to him caught his attention.

What's that . . . purple thread doing there?

Arthur closed his eyes, thinking how wonderful it felt to breathe.

CHAPTER

fifty-four

How are you feeling this week?" Dr. Studski asked.

Jeremy grinned. "Much better. A *lot* better. Arthur's been out of the hospital and back home now for weeks, and he's doing really well with his physical and occupational therapy. John and Greg bought half of Arthur's business so he's got less to worry about and some cash to play with; I've got my trust money back in the bank, and we just had the floors redone in our house; I'm celebrating my second month of sobriety; and I'm back to work at Tyler, Inc."

"Did you ever discuss with Carlo the information you uncovered from your regressions?"

"Yeah, Carlo and I talked about some of it—like the stuff that included him with Arthur and me back in Thebes. But nothing about Hadrian and Antinous. It's all a little too close to us having been Cleopatra or Napoleon"—he chuckled—"so I'm waiting for him to bring it up first."

"I completely understand." Dr. Studski smiled. "You look happy."

"I am."

"So," Dr. Studski said after the two of them had smiled at each other for a long moment, "have you reached any conclusions about all that's happened?"

"There's *so much* that's happened." Jeremy peered at him. "What specifically?"

"I'm referring mostly to what was revealed in your regressions, and how your past is affecting your present. Because now that we have the 'foundation' thoroughly inspected and approved, we can start to remodel your metaphorical house."

Jeremy laughed. "You're asking me to state the obvious."

"Sometimes that's helpful—especially because we're really starting to move forward now." He gave Jeremy an encouraging smile and a nod.

"Well," Jeremy glanced around the room as his mind tried to assemble his thoughts into sentences. "This is the part I can't explain away, no matter how much I try: We just found out that Lazzaro killed his father by overdosing him with Sueño Gris in much the same way that Lucius was slowly poisoning Hadrian and actually caused Antinous to drown: in all three cases a drug was administered that was pretty much harmless in small doses but could kill you if the dose was big enough—"

"And each man carried out his crime in order to take over another man's empire," Dr. Studski interrupted, "whether it was the Roman Empire or that sickening sex tourism ring Lazzaro's father was leading."

"And there's something else I should mention. Something we just found out. We got a call from that actress I told you about."

"Carmella?"

"Right. Get this: Francesco Sforza *wasn't* Lazzaro's biological father—and he overdosed him only after finding out that Francesco intended to make *someone else* his successor! So Lazzaro was playing out the same scenario—almost point by point!—of Hadrian and his adopted successors once again, *two thousand years later!*"

"And you knew nothing of this at the time of your regressions."

"No!" Jeremy nearly shouted. Then he calmed himself as he began looking around the room. "I feel like I'm in some kind of movie here, Doc. There's been too many coincidences here for me to brush this all off as random. It's . . . *creepy*."

"No . . . it's reality. You're just lucky enough that the original conflict between Hadrian and Lucius and Antinous was at least hinted at in the historical documents, as you discovered recently. Most people never have access to their past-life mistakes, so learning from them becomes difficult, if not impossible."

Jeremy grimaced. "So I guess we really do repeat our mistakes until we learn what we need to learn, huh?"

"It would appear this way."

"But why? I mean, if God or some force is out there arranging all this, how does He—or She, or It—benefit from our souls getting smarter?"

The older man's face opened into a satisfied smile. "I have some ideas about that, which I'll get to in a moment. But first, tell me what else you've learned."

Jeremy scratched the side of his face. "Well . . . aside from the fact that Arthur's and my relationship has picked up where it left off in two or three different lifetimes and we've finally resolved the big issues from each one . . . I guess the part that gives me satisfaction is knowing that even though Lucius cheated me out of my 'inheritance' in my lifetime as Antinous and almost did the same thing a second time, it was only with Arthur's FBI background and connections that Lazzaro was outsmarted."

"What does that mean to you?"

"I think . . . it means that even though I was the one who was the victim—the drowning and the swindling and the blackmail and the betrayals—Arthur was also heavily affected in each lifetime, and he was the one to resolve my situation."

"As you did for him."

Jeremy furrowed his brow. "What do you mean?"

Clickety-click-click—click. "How would you describe Arthur's soul?"

"His soul?"

"Some of us have nurturing souls: father and mother souls, whether or not we even procreate. Others are artists. Some are inventors and scientists or healer-shamans, and others are followers who seem to contribute very little to society—these are what we think of as 'young souls.' And of course there are those whose task, it seems, is to create strife for others through their purely narcissistic actions."

"Evil souls."

"You could say that. So which do you believe Arthur possesses?"

Jeremy began studying the water-stained ceiling tiles once more. "I guess I'd describe Arthur as having . . . *a warrior's soul.*"

"Why?"

"Because he's been in the Marines and the FBI, where he was a bodyguard for my family. He helped save my life in Brazil and now he owns a bodyguard business. He's always been a soldier of some kind—even when he was in Thebes and then Rome, and even in South Carolina."

"I was thinking the same thing. How do you think this has affected his health?"

Jeremy shrugged. "I don't have a clue."

"Would you . . . care to hear my theory?"

"Sure."

"I believe," Dr. Studski began, "with Arthur's 'warrior soul,' he has an intrinsic need to fight for and to protect those he loves, or whom he has been assigned to protect. His psyche has an exceptional sense of duty, and if he fails—or even perceives himself as failing at his soul's mission—it begins destroying his very being. Sort of like a border collie who does its very best, but still inadvertently herds a flock of sheep over a cliff, or into the jaws of a lurking pack of wolves."

"So his psyche took his inability to protect me as 'failures'?"

"Exactly. His self-perceived 'failures'—on that battlefield in Thebes, then in Egypt, and finally during the Civil War—hyper-prepared him for protecting you in this lifetime. But when his very understandable terror of losing you once again began gnawing at him and he sent you away, and then you proceeded to self-destruct, a part of *himself* also began to self-destruct—hence, *and this is only my theory*, his cancer."

"But my self-destructing was my fault, not his," Jeremy argued, leaning forward in his chair. "It doesn't make sense for Arthur to somehow punish himself like that. And he didn't even know about my tailspin until he ran into Katharine that day, which was well after his first tumor treatment!"

"I'm hypothesizing that it's even more complicated. Being able to save you in this lifetime healed a very deep gash in Arthur's psyche, and I'm suggesting that it somehow contributed to his surviving that highly difficult and risky surgery and being able to enjoy such a positive prognosis today. But there's . . . *something else* at play here that I'd like you to consider: I believe it's possible that Arthur's cancer was his body priming itself for death, so he would be ready to reincarnate with you again and to finally *do it right.* His soul—on some plane of existence that we're only now beginning to acknowledge—was *made aware* of your destructive spiral and was readying itself—"

"For *my* death?" Jeremy asked, wide-eyed.

Dr. Studski paused, allowing this idea to steep. "You've heard of elderly married couples where one partner dies within weeks or months of the other, yes?"

"Yeah?"

"I personally know of one couple where something even more amazing occurred. Fran and Jack had been married for over sixty years, and even though dear Fran had been incapacitated with Alzheimer's for nearly five years, had completely lost her cognitive functioning, and was institutionalized, when her husband Jack died from prostate cancer, Fran—with no knowledge whatsoever of the event—passed away barely two weeks after he did."

Jeremy folded his arms over his chest. "So you're saying that somehow his soul found hers . . . and let her know it was time for her to go?"

"It would appear that way."

Jeremy smiled, fighting sudden tears. "That's a beautiful thought."

"There are forces at work in our lives that we are ill-equipped to understand, Jeremy. But we see evidence of these forces every day."

"Like . . . seeing the vapor trail of a jet in the sky without seeing the actual airplane, because it's too far away?"

"Exactly."

"But you never gave me your theory about what God gets out of all this."

"Jeremy, what do you know about evolution?"

Jeremy shrugged. "That all living things adapt over time in order to survive changing environments?"

"Would you agree that consciousness is part of being alive, whether you are a dog or an apple tree?"

"Trees are *conscious*?"

"They obey the seasons and grow toward the sun, and their roots seek out water . . . all the while doing their best to thrive and emit oxygen and take our carbon dioxide to produce fruit which other animals eat. I'd call that consciousness of some sort. They aren't static."

"Then I guess plants have consciousness."

"And doesn't it stand to reason that this consciousness might evolve the way our physical genes do? I believe it does. Hence our consciousness continues returning to new bodies after we die in response to the laws of evolution. Quantum mechanics even goes so far as to theorize that consciousness is the 'gravity' that attracts our physical bodies in each lifetime, in much the same way that gravity attracts the gases in space that compress and explode to become stars—which contain exactly the same elements that comprise you and me and all carbon-based life forms."

Jeremy blinked at him, working to absorb it all. "But what does God get out of it?"

"Why have life even exist at all on this huge rock hurtling through space, Jeremy? Some things are simply beyond our comprehension—at least for now."

"So then—" Jeremy paused, crossing his legs, "—thinking back to what you said about Arthur's warrior soul: What sort of soul do you think I have, since I'm certainly not a warrior or a scientist or an artist? Or am I just a follower with a young soul?"

Dr. Studski only looked at Jeremy, waiting.

"So I'll never do anything important?"

"That entirely depends upon what you define as 'important,' Jeremy. But here's a thought: Do you know who Yoko Ono is?"

"Of course. She's the lady who broke up the Beatles."

"Actually, I think of her more as John Lennon's inspiration . . . the same way that Gala Dali was Salvador's inspiration and Edie Sedgwick was Andy Warhol's. In the art and fashion world, people like these—and there were many—are called 'muses,' after the daughters of Zeus, who inspired men to create."

"Please, not another Greek idea."

Dr. Studski smiled and went on. "The Greeks believed when someone was loved by a muse, their worries simply vanished, freeing the artist to create sculpture or music or theater. But today we understand a muse as one who helps another accomplish his or her work—be it amazing or everyday—simply by virtue of how inspiring and intrinsically wonderful and supportive they are."

"You're saying Antinous was this to Hadrian, and I'm like this to Arthur?"

"Your role, then and now, as I see it, has always been to inspire, to comfort, to soothe, to listen, and to excite. You are a muse, Jeremy.

And as long as you understand your role, you'll do it wonderfully . . . especially now that Arthur's amazing task before him is to regain his health."

"You may be right." Jeremy paused. "Because if being Arthur's muse means being his confidant, his cook, his trainer . . . his maid, his personal shopper, his accountant, his dog walker—*and* his lover, then there's nothing I could do that would make either of us happier or more fulfilled."

EPILOGUE

Finally—our first day in Mykonos," Arthur said, as they strolled side-by-side along the promenade with its crowded cafés and junked-up souvenir and T-shirt shops. "And look at this sky!" He threw his arms up into the air. "I've never seen a blue this blue . . . it's like what we saw in Brazil: *Doris Day blue*! Did you ever think we'd make it here?"

Jeremy stopped to examine a table piled high with counterfeit designer sunglasses. "You mean because we had to change planes nineteen times, or because we've been traveling nonstop for thirty-six hours?"

"I meant back when we were going through all those crises, did you ever think we'd get here?"

Jeremy grinned at him and resumed walking. "I knew what you meant—and yes, I always believed we'd get here," he lied. "Are you as exhausted as I am?"

"I'm too excited." Arthur noticed the sun inching down closer to the horizon, while the buildings' shadows were now stretched wide across the ground. He checked his wristwatch. "It's just about time for happy hour. Is there someplace you'd like to go before we have dinner with Carlo and Tristan? Have you even talked to them yet?"

"Yeah, they're coming over on the six o'clock ferry, and we're meeting at the restaurant at eight, so we've got some time to enjoy ourselves."

"Have you ever seen a couple more in love than they are?"

Jeremy laughed. "I see one each morning in the bathroom mirror; one of the guys is getting plenty of gray hair and the other guy just sprouted his first few."

"And I can't wait to give you lots more."

"Hey, I wanted to give you something back in the hotel room before we see them. Do you mind if we stop there first, and then we can find a place to ogle hot men and eat divine appetizers?"

"Hay is for horses, and anything you want to give me in a hotel room is fine with me." Arthur leered at him, and then looked around to check their bearings. "I think we should head back this way." He pointed to the right. "Didn't we walk past those four strange windmills when we came down the hill?"

"Yeah, we came down that little street straight ahead."

The men turned up the road and retraced their steps up a series of narrow, winding alleys, past jammed-together whitewashed buildings, each with matching doors and windows and balconies and shutters painted either all green, all red, all blue, or all black.

"Mykonos is even more romantic than I'd imagined," Arthur sighed as they marched uphill together. "And I know it sounds silly, but it already feels like home."

"I know what you mean." Jeremy shot Arthur a wary glance. "How do you feel?"

"Not winded in the least. I think I'm finally back up to speed."

"Want to rent some scooters tomorrow?"

"I'd love that."

"We can head out to that gay beach," Jeremy suggested. "To Ilia."

"I think it's Elia," Arthur said.

After the pair hiked up the last, steep rise, lined with dusty subcompact cars parked nose-to-tail like a dented metal wagon train, they arrived back at their hotel—a rambling white stucco compound with an expansive flagstone deck on a high cliff overlooking the Aegean Sea.

The men climbed the tiled stairs to their room, fitted the key into the lock, and opened the door. Jeremy trotted over to his suitcase, unzipped it, and pulled out a sloppily gift-wrapped package. "Happy anniversary," he said, handing it over.

"It's big." Arthur hefted it, looking at Jeremy quizzically. "And heavy."

"It's those cuff links you wanted," Jeremy joked. "Why don't we head outside so you can open it there? I don't want to miss the sunset."

Arthur extended his arm. "After you."

The men descended the tiled stairs and then strolled out through the lobby to the sunlit deck, where couples and groups of people already dressed for cocktail hour reclined on white cotton sofas or chaises, sipping drinks while gazing out at the glimmering, twilit vista.

"Over there." Jeremy pointed to an empty sectional at the edge of the cliff, and they hurried over to it before anyone else could claim it.

"The sun'll be down soon," Arthur told Jeremy as they approached the furniture. "Will you humor me?" He reached down and placed the heavy package atop the glass-topped, wicker table in front of the sectional and then stood tall, arms wide.

Jeremy went to him and nestled within his embrace, his back to Arthur's chest and Arthur's chin resting on his shoulder. "Am I doing it right?"

"You couldn't possibly do it wrong," Arthur murmured as the setting sun cast a coral glow onto their faces, and the cooling sea breeze ruffled their shirts.

"Look at all those jagged, rocky little islands," Jeremy said, "and that fantastic white tall ship down there—it's so James Bond. Wouldn't you love to be on that right now?"

"There's no place I'd rather be than right here with you." Arthur squeezed Jeremy tighter, his crotch tight against his buttocks. "I want to remember this moment. *Forever.*"

Jeremy giggled knowingly. "Something tells me we will."

They stood in silence for some time until Jeremy could no longer take the suspense. "Will you open your cuff links now?"

Arthur kissed the crook of his neck. "Only if it'll stop your nagging."

Hand in hand they stepped over to the sectional and sat.

Jeremy once again handed over the package to Arthur.

Arthur leaned forward, considered the package for another moment, and then tore off the paper.

He held up his new acquisition. "*The War Between the States*?"

"It took me a long time to find it," Jeremy said, eyes shining. "It's got pictures of battlefields and slaves and soldiers and plantations and everything; I think Ken Burns used a lot of these same photos in his amazing documentary—which I also watched—so it's one of the most complete out there. I must have gone through a hundred books like this before Margo and I found this one in that little old bookstore in Santa Barbara. Remember the last time we were there?"

"I thought you two were acting particularly sneaky that day," Arthur told him, giving him the side-eye. "I just hope there aren't too many pictures of bloated corpses—all those poor boys." He cracked open the spine. "So why's this book so special that you'd go through hundreds before giving me this exact one?" He began flipping through the pages. "Oh, I like this photo of Lincoln—he's always been one of my heroes."

"There's a bookmark," Jeremy told him, wagging his finger. "Check it out."

Hesitatingly, Arthur opened the glossy tome to its marked page, where he found a sepia-toned photograph of a stately bearded officer in his Confederate uniform, and a proud-looking, grinning dog by his side.

"Look at the man's face," Jeremy whispered.

Arthur gulped hard, his throat at once tight with emotion. "Jeremy, I . . . I can't believe . . . It's almost like I'm looking at a photo of myself dressed up for some crazy Civil War re-enactment costume party. That man could be my brother!"

Jeremy tapped the page. "Read the caption."

Arthur looked up at Jeremy and then back down at the page. Then with some effort he cleared his throat. "*Captain James W. Finnegan - Retired, C. S. A. with his war dog General Lee. Charleston, South Carolina 1867.*"

Jeremy placed a hand on Arthur's shoulder. "Look closely at the dog, baby. Do you see what I see?"

Arthur held the book closer to his face and his breath caught. That face, the long black fur and pale eyes. Even the white blaze on his chest and his expression were the same. "It can't be," he whispered, tears spilling from his eyes. "But somehow it is."

"I know," Jeremy murmured, leaning in. "That's Bingham."

ACKNOWLEDGMENTS

Thanks to my longtime partner—and new husband—Jaime for listening to me, challenging me, and shoring up my confidence. This story about timeless love is as much about us as it is about Jeremy and Arthur. I cannot imagine my lifetimes without you.

Cheers to my best friend Margo and our dear friends Art and Claudine for their interest and support. Margo, I will forever look forward to our dinners (and martinis) at Stanley's.

I will always owe so much to my sister Kathy for her steady ear and her unwavering faith in me. You were the first to listen without judgment. And to my dear cousin Debbie, whose husband Bobby wasn't as lucky as Arthur, thank you for sharing your anguishing and very personal war stories with me.

How can I ever thank Dr. Walter Semkiw, whose schema for investigating and confirming past life personae provided the gravitas for this tale? Walter, I feel very fortunate to call you my friend. Your research and passion are changing the world.

To my comrade and guide, Dr. Edward Reed: I feel honored and lucky to have had your keen insight during this transformative time (but we both know "luck" is something else altogether).

Huge thanks go to David Downing, my story editor. Your unerring eye caught blunders I was blind to, and your humor, enthusiasm, and expertise made this story sparkle. You taught me so much.

Thank you copy editor Scott Calamar for your surgical expertise. Your precision and input is so appreciated.

Finally, to Senior Acquisitions Editor at Amazon Publishing, Mr. Terry Goodman. These books would be shadows of themselves without your vision and support. I've told you this so many times and I'll say it again here, "I owe you, Terry."

ABOUT THE AUTHOR

Photo by Jaime Flores 2011

Nick Nolan wrote his first mystery in the fifth grade, then for many years afterward put his dream of being a published writer on hold. A graduate of California State University, Northridge, Nolan has worked with homeless teens, rescued dogs, and traveled extensively through Mexico. After self-publishing his novels *Strings Attached* and *Double Bound*, he won *ForeWord* Magazine's Book of the Year Award for Gay and Lesbian Fiction in both 2006 and 2008. His third novel, *Black as Snow*, hit No. 1 on the Amazon UK Kindle list. He lives with his husband, Jaime, in the hills of Los Angeles, California.

Made in the USA
Charleston, SC
19 December 2013